FROM
AWAY

LONA RUBENSTEIN

© 1997 Lona Rubenstein
All rights reserved
Library of Congress Catalog Card Number: 97-074606
First Edition ISBN 0-9659552-0-6

Book design by Mary Grey
Cover Illustration by Ty Stroudsburg
Production by Ciccariello Graphics, Inc., East Hampton, New York
Printed by Montauk Printing in the United States of America

Published in the United States by
Areté Press, 19 Railroad Avenue, Suite 430
East Hampton, New York/11937

FROM AWAY

LONA RUBENSTEIN

ARETÉ  PRESS

Acknowledgments

To my editor Rick Murphy for his exceptional skills, for his patience and for his understanding of the material;

To Mary Cummings, editor and proofreader, for her professional know-how and help;

To Marijane Meaker, for her tough encouragement and willingness to share secrets of the trade;

To Mary Grey and Ty Stroudsburg for the look;

To May Okon and Maureen Murphy for reviewing the manuscript in many stages and for their encouragement;

To Detective Lieutenant Ed Ecker, Jr., East Hampton Town Police, and to Linda Riley, Esq. for explaining police work and the law;

To Jim and Nancy McCaffrey for sharing their knowledge of the past with someone from away;

To John Donohue of the Southampton Zoning Department, and to Marguerite Wolffsohn of the East Hampton Planning Department for their invaluable information;

To Amy, Scott and David for their help with dates, music, baseball games and for sharing growing up in East Hampton with their mother;

Lastly, to my husband, Martin Rubenstein, for listening no matter what the hour, for knowing the score and for keeping the author on the right track.

Dedicated to
Cadie Frankel
1875 — 1966

and for
Barbara Bologna
and
Lynda Bostrom

"I have to protect myself. From my own son—"

"Are you going to be able to handle this?"

"I'm trying to keep it together."

"Suppose he comes back? Like before? There's been a pattern you know."

She hesitated, as if searching for the answer.

"Yes, well, I'll probably kill him," she said.

Prologue

The first time Sally Lamb saw Sing Sing she was in her mother's arms on her way to visit her father.

In her mother's worn leather purse, folded neatly, was the chaplain's letter, frayed from many readings. *Her father wants to see his baby . . . a blessing if you could visit . . . only an hour from the city . . . money for fare . . . a loan.* It was dated Dec. 16, 1935.

Her mother had hired an old yellow taxicab at the bus terminal to take them to the prison. It cranked along the icy road, past thick junipers, august pines, and naked, shivering oaks cloaked by an ashen sky. All at once trees vanished, replaced by a stone forest of staple box buildings. Sing Sing. Bullet-shaped outcroppings, towers of the guards, dotted the penitentiary's perimeter. Stitched together by tracks of The New York Central that cut across the prison were two recreation yards. The Death House, flat roofed and windowless, overlooked the Hudson.

Among the captive guests of this riverside resort was Sally's father, Mike Lamb — grand larceny, fraud, forgery, terms concurrent, five years in all, not counting good behavior.

"Mrs. Lamb?" a young priest asked, the name traveling on a puff of vapor as he opened the car door. He paid the cab driver, whose expression was sullen. It had been that way even before their delay at the guarded gates. "I hope you haven't been waiting long," he said. Reaching inside, he lifted 10-month-old Sally. He murmured a prayer, then made the sign of the cross over the sleeping child.

"We are of the Jewish faith," said Beatrice Lamb. "You must know that, sir."

"Ah yes, Mrs. Lamb, but a prayer to the good Lord never harmed anyone's soul, I suspect. There was no offense intended."

Beatrice gave a sorry sigh. "Bad times can make one tactless," she apologized. "You were so kind to send money," she added.

Extending his arm, he offered to help Beatrice Lamb out of the battered DeSoto. She accepted the young priest's outstretched hand in a graceful way, the way of women who accept the attentiveness of men as their due.

"You'll get your money back. I promise. I never did intend to visit, you know."

"I'm glad you changed your mind," he said. "It's especially hard for the men with no visitors, Mrs. Lamb."

Her slim body was held straight, regal, crowned by velvet black hair. "I haven't been *Mrs. Lamb* for . . . some time," she said, as if having to make things understood.

It was hard to tell if he'd heard her confession. He kept on walking.

"This way," said the young priest. Carrying Sally, he went through gates and up stairways to the visiting room. He nodded at a guard. Moments later, there was the grinding of a steel door. Sally stirred as her father was brought into the room.

"Such Irish good looks on a Jewish boy," said the priest. "Your lovely wife came after all, Mike, me lad. Didn't I tell you so? Never underestimate the power of the clergy." He pronounced it *clairgy* as he held the child for the prisoner to see.

Mike Lamb placed his hands on the steel mesh barrier. They were gentlemen's hands, slim tapered fingers, accustomed to dealing cards, tossing dice, caressing women. Somehow it was easy to see how things could slip through them.

"Hello Beatrice," Mike said, looking past Sally.

"Hello Mike. There's Sallylamb," she said, as if to remind him of the purpose of the visit. "There's your daughter."

"Budna," said Sally, smiling, her sleepy eyes drifting open.

"It's her only word," explained Beatrice.

"Mommy?" the priest guessed.

Beatrice shook her head.

"What then?" the fathers asked in unison.

"Bread and butter. It means bread and butter."

The baby, now wide awake, gurgled and laughed, safe and happy in this special place of maximum security.

"Budna," Sally repeated. "Budna."

PART ONE

Who are these people, anyway?

1

1965-Decisions and Opportunities

The large, yellow Checker taxicab coughed and belched into the Hawley driveway in East Hampton at 4:30 a.m. on the Friday after Labor Day. Most East Hamptoners were sleeping easy that Friday morning. Their town repatriated, those locals who let out to summer people — living with relatives in tight quarters — were safely home, with money in their pockets, and September, the best month of all, theirs.

But a few were not yet home safe, having relented to a new demand, extending the summer season an extra week after Labor Day. The longer season was one of the reasons the taxicab was in the Hawley driveway. Another was that Sally had pulled a classmate through a graduate course in decision theory that summer, and was offered the use of the grateful woman's East Hampton rental for this last bonus weekend. There was no catch, just no mess, no pets, no children.

Overjoyed at this opportunity to get away, she had to convince Joe to take the time off, had to persuade him that it was worth the drive from Manhattan in the middle of the night to this place they knew nothing about.

East Hampton, surrounded by ocean and bay on Long Island's eastern tip, was only a 100 miles from New York City, but there was no direct route. Zigzagging north and south, it took them more than five hours to reach the sleepy villages and rural hamlets on the South Fork.

"We probably woke up half the town with that tail pipe, Joe," she whispered in the darkness.

"It's the muffler, Sally."

"Whatever! It sure was a long trip. A trip and a half, Grandma would call it." She slid across the seat. Careful to avoid the miles-into-money taxi meter, the constant reminder that this car worked for a living, Sally kissed him beneath his ear.

"What's that for?"

"For leaving Thursday night so we could squeeze in the extra day," she answered, toying absentmindedly with her wedding ring. "We sure made a racket," she added, smiling, not because she wasn't concerned about the noise, but because she was so happy to be in the country.

She climbed out of the car. Stretching on the blacktop, Sally sighed as she uncoiled her lean, long-legged body, grown stiff from the journey. The yellow glow from the porch light fell short of the driveway.

"Click on the brights, Joe, won't you?"

Crouched before the headlights' beams, she studied a crumpled piece of paper. Glancing back and forth, she matched the two-story shingled house, its blue shutters and a large front porch, with the written description.

"This is it. Definitely," she sighed with relief. "Isn't it wonderful, Joe? Admit it; you're glad we came."

"I'll let you know when it's over," he said, still firmly seated, his muscular arms twitching slightly on the steering wheel.

But Sally was ecstatic, straining her neck toward the sky, raking her hands through her long dark hair. She stretched herself with pleasure. "It's so peaceful, so quiet, and the air's so clear and fresh. You can smell the ocean, too. And look at the stars, Joe. Come out and see. You can actually see the stars, not like New York. And it's all free. This holiday is free! Oh how I'd like to shout *East Hampton! East Hampton! The Singers are here!*"

"Nothing's free," Joe said quietly. "Nothing's for nothing." Like all street-smart New Yorkers, he expected little from the world and its people.

When it came to human nature, Joe Singer knew the score.

Sally often relied on Joe's street savvy. Just out of high school when they married, she was more at ease with ideas than things. "Give me a triangle, I can handle it," she told Joe early on. "But tents? That's a problem."

That's why Sally paid attention now.

"Nothing's for nothing?" she echoed, giving it some thought. "Maybe so! But this sure is close enough," she sang out cheerfully, spinning around in a touchdown dance on the blacktop. Joe's view of the world depressed her. This night, she refused to linger on his mine-field landscape, refused to contain her unbridled joy. "Look, Joe, the Milky Way," Sally went on, tilting her head and squinting at the sky. "Galaxy after galaxy up there, I think that's God's trick, teaching us a lesson for eating the apple. Whenever we look we find more, so faraway distance is measured in time, not miles. Do you suppose He uses mirrors?"

"Thinking about those things makes me uncomfortable, Sally."

"You may be right, you know. Increasing knowledge increases sorrows. That's what *Proverbs* says." She hesitated, then shook her head. "No, *Ecclesiastes,*" Sally corrected herself. "On the other hand, Pope said a little knowledge is a dangerous thing. Drink deep, or--"

"Sally, it's late. I'm bushed."

" . . . taste not from the Pierian spring."

"We're in the middle of nowhere. We've been driving for hours. What does the pope have to do with it, for Chrissake? What the hell're you talking about?"

"Not *the* pope, Joe—"

"Are we here yet?" a child's voice interrupted.

No mess, no pets, no children! But anyone who knew Sally knew she'd never go away without her children.

"Your timing's perfect, Michael, and so are you," she said warmly to her oldest son. "We're finally here."

"Unless it's the wrong house! I'd give even money on that." Joe's voice had a slight edge. It made Sally wonder if he was still upset over giving up his Thursday night poker game.

Poker meant a lot to Joe. He had fumed for a week after she managed to get them both kicked out of an easy game with neighbors. She had laughingly called her winning hand, "Two pair . . . of nines."

"We were winners in that game. You treat losers with respect, not laugh in their faces," he'd said.

"Being barred from a poker game is not the end of the world," she'd said.

When he started to play Thursday nights with the other cabbies, Sally was glad. But gaining an extra day in the country had to be worth giving up one Thursday night card game, she reasoned. That decided, she climbed into the back of the taxi to reach 8-year-old Andy, who frowned even when he was sleeping, and Ben, 7, who wore a smile though he'd had to curl his legs awkwardly over the large pot of goulash, part of a food supply she'd prepared at home to keep costs down. After all, Joe was giving up two days' work for this trip.

She was whispering instructions to Michael when Joe gave them a look. "What are you two up to now? Should I be worried?"

"It's nothing, Dad," said the 10-year-old. "Mom asked me to bring in the coffee pot."

While the boys helped carry the supplies out of the taxi, Sally found the house key above the door frame where her classmate's note said it would be. Then she sat down under the yellow porch light and untied her sneakers.

"Why are you taking your shoes off?" asked Joe.

"I'd like to leave the house spotless."

"Hah! You?"

"Yes, well, I think we all should take our shoes off, Joe, and leave them on the porch, despite your unsolicited opinion about my house-keeping skills. Watch out for splinters," she warned, good naturedly.

Once inside, after a quick review of the premises, Sally stored the goulash, the meat loaf, the tuna and egg salads, the coffee, the milk, the packets of sugar, the bananas, the large loaf of Wonder Bread and the butter in the roomy country kitchen.

"I feel so welcome here. Look, Joe," she pointed at a shiny electric coffee maker on the white-tiled counter. "We didn't need to bring ours, after all."

"That makes you feel welcome?" It was the kind of question that expected no answer.

"Michael, take your brothers upstairs and help them make the beds," she said. "Go right to sleep. We're getting up in a few hours to go to the beach." She kissed each boy. Andy, as usual, tried unsuccessfully to dodge it.

"We should shut down, too. You must be tired, Joe." She brushed his cheek with her lips. "Hold me," she whispered, resting her head on his shoulder. "I feel so happy."

After a moment, he pulled away and lifted her in his arms.

"You do that so easily," Sally murmured. "I love you so, Joe. Let's not fight this weekend."

"Stop talking so much," he said, carrying her past the polished oak stairway to the pink and white calico downstairs bedroom.

Afterward, when Joe was sleeping soundly, Sally hugged herself under the plump, flowered eiderdown. She wasn't tired at all. A few hours sleep would be plenty. Her heart sang. Three days in the country. Three days in the country! Sally was as happy as a girl, though she would be 30 that year.

2

Who Are These People Anyway?

When she stepped out of the shower, Sally heard angry voices and didn't know why. Everything had been going so well.

"For the last time, what's that damn New York City taxi doing in my driveway, Mister? Who are you people?"

Sally wrapped herself in a bath towel, her long hair dripping on the white carpet. "Is something wrong?" she called out.

"There's a guy here, Sally, says he's Charles Hawley. Says he owns this place," Joe shouted back.

"*Says*, dammit! It is my house, Mister. I'm the landlord and you're not my tenants."

"I'll be right there, Joe," she said, dropping the towel on the white carpeted floor. She grabbed for something, anything, and found Joe's yesterday T-shirt hanging on the doorknob. Pulling on her faded blue jeans, zipping them up halfway, Sally rushed out of the room.

Joe, shirtless, in khaki trunks, brown hair mussed, shoulders tensed in readiness, was standing in the vestibule dangerously close to the man who was shouting. Charles Hawley, in a blue suit and red paisley tie, his back ramrod straight, was set for serious business, too. He looked older than Joe, but he was taller and broader. Joe could take him like a shot, Sally knew. There was hidden strength in his wiry 40-year-old body.

She quickly placed herself between the two men.

There was another man, leaning against the open door, holding a clipboard, wearing a windbreaker, shirt collar unbuttoned. Ruddy faced, he vaguely resembled Charles Hawley, the thick, dark blond hair, the chunkiness, but he had a more interesting face, an imperfect nose tilting slightly toward the left. Beyond him, on the porch, Sally could see their array of abandoned shoes.

"You've met my husband, I see. I'm Mrs. Singer. Is there a problem?" She offered her hand to Charles Hawley. There was none to meet it.

"Yeah, I'll say there's a problem," Hawley snapped. "Whoever you are, you people don't belong here."

"I see," Sally said as if she saw. "There must be a misunderstanding. You see, we're weekend guests of—"

Stopping short, she tracked Hawley's gaze to the stairwell behind her. Standing there, barefooted, in swimsuits, with identical shocks of black hair and pale, frightened faces were Michael, Andy, and Ben. For a brief moment, her attention was stuck on a certain bemused expression Andy wore, but Hawley's loud voice pulled it away.

"Didn't I tell you?" he bellowed at the clipboard man. Then to Sally, "You're not guests of anybody, lady. Not in my house. Not with those kids."

Sally looked shaken. "Yes, well, the children . . . ." There was nothing more she could say.

"What about kids?" Joe demanded, body still tensed.

The clipboard man intervened. "I'm Jack Bennet, real estate broker. Mrs. Singer, you're in violation of the tenants' lease. It specifically states no children. We'll have to notify them." Forehead furrowed, he looked at Charles Hawley, clearly asking if this was enough.

"I want them out, Jack!" Hawley instructed, then spun around, slamming the door as he left the house.

"I'm waiting," Joe said to Sally, a cloud on his face.

"I wanted the kids to have a family weekend in the country, Joe. We've never been away. We'd have kept the house clean. It didn't hurt anybody."

"We weren't supposed to bring children. Is that it? I knew there was something. Shoes off! Hah! And you didn't say nothing to me?"

Sally looked defeated. The clock said 11:30. Only seven hours after they arrived, they were asked to leave. "If I told you, you wouldn't have let us come."

"You're way out of line, Sally. Way out of line." His mouth working angrily, he tossed a look at Bennet, then walked out of the room.

She knew she was wrong. *Justifiable wrongness,* she thought, a fresh air holiday for the children her defense. There had to be a lighter sentence for justifiably wrong. Why didn't Joe know that? Stick up for her? Weren't they his kids, too? "I'll do anything I have to for my children," she said defiantly, tossing the words at Joe's retreating back.

"Your children?" he said, without turning around, motioning to the boys, still frozen on the stairwell.

Sally gave a deep sigh. Nothing was going the way she'd planned.

3

If You Want to Make God Laugh,
Tell Him Your Plans

"Well," Jack Bennet said, a patch of sun-bleached hair falling across his forehead, his arms folded across his chest.

"I've created quite a mess," said Sally.

They were alone.

"You know you'll have to leave."

"The sun, the beach, we came so far . . . ." She brushed her eyes with her hand. He held the door as they walked out to the porch. "We're not unreasonable, Mrs. Singer. A deal's a deal. Put yourself in Charles Hawley's place."

"I've already done that," she said.

Bennet chuckled. "Look, you can have the rest of the day, leave by evening," he offered. "It's the best I can do. But there's a catch. No beach. The sand," he explained. "You might enjoy Montauk. Things to see, places to go." It was clear he'd seen her face collapse, because he added, "There's no nice way to do this, Mrs. Singer, I'm sorry." Pulling it from his clipboard, he gave Sally a Chamber of Commerce booklet.

"The real tenant didn't know about the children, by the way. It wasn't her fault," said Sally, head shaking from side to side. *Justifiable* was fading quickly. Looking up, seeing Bennet's focused gaze, Sally realized Joe's T-shirt was clinging to her wet body. She blushed.

"You do take a lot on yourself, don't you?" he said, without looking away. "Well, no need to call the tenant. The lease expires this weekend, anyway."

She sat down on a slatted wooden rocker, bracing her bare feet on the porch rail, rocking herself in a steady creaking motion. "I'm sorry for the trouble I've caused."

"This must have been pretty important to you," said Bennet. "Splinters," he added, pointing to her bare feet.

"Yes, I know."

Flashing an impersonal broker's grin, he gestured at the porch. "This part's all extra, you know. Came later. Saltbox, settlers from Kent called these houses. Emigrated here from England via Plymouth Rock over 300 years ago. Folks with the same last names still living in town."

"Are you one of them?" asked Sally, feeling he wanted to tell her that he was.

"You bet," he said, his agent's smile dissolved to one of pride.

She liked this man. He'd stretched out their departure. She credited him with reluctance in turning them out. He tried not to offend. "Do you mind if I ask you a question, Mr. Bennet?"

"Not at all. Can't promise you'll get an answer."

"Was it the taxi?"

He gave a laugh. "Oh, that one's easy. Of course it was the taxi. At first. A simple case of the wrong car in the driveway. There are no secrets in a small town, Mrs. Singer." He looked away for a second, seeming to remind himself of that fact as well. "Folks told Charlie you'd come in the middle of the night, lights glaring, noisy as hell, woke them up, you did. Then all those shoes, little shoes for little feet, right out there on the porch. Well . . . ." Bennet shook his head. "I guess you did everything but put out a sign."

Sally rocked harder, the wooden chair creaking underneath her. "That's not what I mean."

What she did mean bothered her. The question was always there.

The taxi. An emblem of the changes she'd caused in Joe's life, not delicate, airy changes but shifts of molten lava. Joe was where he was because she'd started so soon with her baby strategy. Before the children, he lived by his wits, a smart money hustler, tending toward secrecy, juggling a charmed life on the edge, not passively chauffeuring people around all day, hoping they'd give him a tip. But Sally wanted a family, to make up for never having much of one. So they had Michael. And she discovered that wasn't enough, that she had to protect herself, so profound were her feelings for him.

Her father, spinning in and out of her life through a revolving door, taught her plenty about feelings. Mike Lamb's disappearances, without warning, slashed Sally's soul, leaving a wound as wide as a football field. She came to fear the showing up more than the disappearing, expecting hurt and abandonment, the unexplainable rejection, that would follow. The logic was there. If Mike Lamb never walked in, he could never walk out. At first, Sally ran from his *return* embraces, her father chasing her down hallways, she, hiding in one closet or another, screaming when they pulled her out. There were terrible rows afterward when he accused Sally's mother of saying bad things about him, followed by Beatrice's harsh glare blaming Sally for the inauspicious start. Then the litany. "I almost died when I gave birth to you, the afterbirth wouldn't come out." Since Sally thought she was the afterbirth, the turbulence of these conjugal visits ended right there.

When Michael was born, the depth of her attachment frightened her. Solution: her baby strategy: safety in numbers. She decided to diversify — not to put all her eggs in one basket, so to speak. She would have several children close together, to avoid getting too attached to one. Sally'd reasoned that given a finite amount of love, she'd parcel it out, so when the children would leave, as she knew they would, her pain would come in bits and pieces.

For this plan, Joe needed a more reliable income. Enter the taxi.

It bothered Sally that people could tell what Joe did without asking. It was like being fat; people knew things about you whether you cared to tell them or not. Things that cubby-holed you. Some people went straight as an arrow from what you did to who you were. Lately, the kids' friends on Manhattan's Upper West Side were teasing them about their father's job. Joe knew it. Though he didn't act it, Sally thought it hurt him. And she felt guilty for thinking the boys might feel ashamed, and for thinking she had to defend her husband's job.

"A cabdriver and a Ph.D.?" Sally heard that often from some of the women in school, their noses pinched as if the very notion were acrid. Even the woman who'd let them use her East Hampton rental had said something like that. They could understand driving a taxi while trying to become something else like an actor, a writer, a lawyer, but for cabdriver to be the last stop, that was unthinkable. Sally repeated to Joe only the part about their thinking him sexy. And they did once they met him. After that, what he did didn't matter at all.

"I know exactly what you mean, about that taxi, Mrs. Singer," Bennet said, firmly. "We're not that way. Can't fault a man for working for a living. It boiled down to the children. The lease said no children. You shouldn't have brought them, seems to me."

"I took a chance."

"That was some gamble," Bennet chided. "Trouble finds us

soon enough, without making it, wouldn't you say? You should do something about the muffler," he added, with a glance at the taxi.

"You heard it?"

"I live down the street," he pointed with a nod. "Yep, I called the Hawleys, if you're wondering. I'm not just Charlie's broker, you know; we're related. Most of the town is if you go back far enough."

Sally looked up, stopped her rocking. An only child, notions of one huge family interested her.

Bennet went on. "Charlie never liked the idea of giving the extra week. That's something new, you know." He scratched his head, as if confused. "Used to be everyone left right after Labor Day and didn't come out before July when the club opened, our *summer colony*, that is, the people who own those cottages with servants' quarters on the ocean."

Sally caught a certain appreciation in Bennet's voice when he said *summer colony*, savoring the words as if they tasted good.

"But now, local folks are rattling on about the new element coming out, wanting more, wanting June and practically October. Renters, *city people* they call you, not too friendly either. I guess local folks would distrust anyone who'd *pay* to stay in *their* homes."

Deciding to back off from something that might be disagreeable, Sally said, "You do have a beautiful town, Mr. Bennet. I bet it's a wonderful place to live, to raise a family. There's something about East Hampton that makes me feel I've come home."

"You haven't seen much of it. And we haven't been very hospitable at all," said Bennet. "That's a strange way to feel at home."

"Yes, well, I was conceived in Patchogue," Sally said, as if that explained everything.

"Patchogue is 60 miles upIsland, ma'am."

Bennet laughed. So did Sally.

She glanced down the tree-shaded lane, seeing gingerbread houses with porches, rubber tire swings attached to broad maples, dogs lying lazily on front lawns. "I bet this is where *Dick and Jane* grew up."

"Sometimes it's more like *Dick and Nicole,* especially in the summer when you city people are out," he said.

Dick and Nicole. Diver. Sally knew he was alluding to Fitzgerald's *Tender Is the Night.* It happened to be one of her favorite books. Why did she think he wanted her to know he was literate? Was it how city people made local people feel? Like they might not know anything?

Bennet shifted his feet. "You'll be on your way later, Mrs. Singer, right? No need for me to come back to see you out." He handed her his business card.

You'll be on your way. See you people out. She started to speak, but her voice caught. Reality was back. Swallowing hard, Sally had to wait a moment longer before saying good-bye.

Back inside, Sally heard Michael in the kitchen. "Because she brought us to a place where we weren't wanted," he was saying. "We were favorites to get kicked out. We're lucky they didn't call the police."

"But if we're favorites," said Ben, "that means they like us?"

"Not that kind of favorites," said Michael, quickly putting a newspaper he held aside when Sally walked into the room.

Seeing the sour look of disappointment and hurt on the children's faces broke her heart. Then Sally remembered that other look, the faraway one on Andy's face as he stood with his brothers on the stairwell. She turned and rushed upstairs to the bedroom, calling Andy after her. All three boys followed.

"Oh Lord, Andy. How could you miss the rubber sheets?" Sally said in dismay, thinking of what Jack Bennet said about trouble finding you. "I brought two rubber sheets to be extra safe!"

Andy, grim faced, said nothing.

"They looked uncomfortable for Andy," said Ben, matter-of-factly, "I took them off. They're under the bed."

"I guess it's okay to wear shoes in the house now," observed Michael, holding the newspaper, looking down at the wet mattress.

In spite of everything, Sally couldn't help smiling. She loved Michael's sense of humor, loved that he could make her laugh. He was the one she felt closest to, not a choice, but a feeling, an accidental kindred spirit. So much for wanting to be fair. Had there been something else in his voice besides humor? A dash of disdain, perhaps? No. Michael was too young for disdain. He was too young for a lot of things — following the daily sports lines, knowing odds as well as he did, and, particularly, for reading *The Racing Form*, the newspaper he was now holding.

"Where did you get that?" she asked, knowing the answer.

"In Daddy's taxi," he said.

"Didn't I tell you not to look at tout sheets? What do you care about horses? My God, you're only 10!" For relaxation Joe liked to study the racing forms, pick winners, said it made his brain work. What could Sally say to that?

"Dad's showing me how to handicap. It's fun. You should try it. Looking for value, Dad says. You look at past performance, competition, rate the jockey, the trainer, the stable." His face was animated.

"I don't want to hear it, Michael. You're only 10," she repeated, this time hearing the implicit suggestion that it might be all right when he was 11. *"The Racing Form! Read The Wall Street Journal* if you want to see how gambling really works, damn it!"

"If you do it right, it's not gambling," Michael replied.

"Mister big shot," said Andy.

She didn't have time for this. "We've got work to do," said Sally, staring at the wet bed. Michael disappeared from the room . . . with his paper.

"Can I help, Ma?" asked Ben.

"You've helped enough," she said tiredly. Then seeing his crest-fallen expression, she added, "You can do the pillowcases, Ben."

Sally and Andy stripped the bed, taking the sheets and mattress pad downstairs to the washer. Then she scrubbed the Simmons Beauty Rest, trying to rub out the stain and succeeding in making a bigger one. They carried the mattress downstairs, through the kitchen past Joe who watched silently, and went out the back door laying it to dry in the sun on the redwood picnic table. A stain would remain, Sally knew that, but there was nothing she could do about it. They couldn't afford to replace the mattress.

They couldn't afford a lot of things. That was the reason Sally went back to school, five years ago, so they'd have more money.

Joe planned it. He found her looking through the want ads under "Secretary" one Sunday when she was fed up with his constant complaints about her housekeeping. He sounded so much like her mother. She told him so, too. "Always criticizing. I'll get a job and find someone else to clean the house, if you're not satisfied." She didn't want to care more about the house than her children and didn't seem to be one of those women who could do both.

"A secretary? You'd never make it. You don't type, you don't take shorthand, and you'd never last," he told her. "You could be a moneymaker, I'm not sure how, but I know you're no nine to fiver," he added.

"Moneymaker? I don't know what you mean. I just want to make enough so we can live without quarreling. Business schools have crash courses for typing and shorthand."

"Yeah, right! If you want to work, get a teacher's license."

So he pointed her in the direction of school, setting the academic course Sally had abandoned when she married him. He sent her to City College. No tuition, if you were smart enough. And Joe thought she was smart enough. "In those things anyway," he said. What he didn't expect, he told her later, was not having to wait for graduation for school to pay off. Sally caught on quickly to the educational money machine.

"This is easy," she said. "The kids at school think awards are bestowed from above. All you really have to do is chase them down, then sell yourself." Sally ferreted out grants, stipends, fellowships, loans — filling out every appropriate application the financial aid office had.

But, two and a half years later, in her senior year, instead of going for the teacher's license Joe had in mind for her, Sally decided to go for a doctorate in philosophy. She loved that subject. All she had to do was think, think about questions, not answers, about wonderful things that affected nothing. Anyway, she tried to explain to a dazed Joe, she would rather be a college professor than a schoolteacher. It was easier.

"You have to teach people something when they know nothing in elementary school. Do you know how hard that must be? And this way I not only skip student teaching," she told Joe, "I don't have to take any ed courses, either." Joe, on her turf, was easily defeated.

"I'm done packing, Sally." Joe's voice interrupted her thoughts. He'd changed from his khaki trunks into chinos and a white oxford shirt, sleeves rolled up beyond his elbows. He was still angry. He didn't say so, but he was moving his mouth and biting the side of his lower lip again.

Sally called to the boys, who were getting their clothes together. "Get out of your bathing suits. And Michael, please make sure Ben doesn't lift anything." Turning back to Joe, she said, "Look, Joe, we can go to Montauk for the afternoon. It should be—"

"I heard," he interrupted. "Things to see, places to go. . . no sand."

"I know we have a lemon. Why not make lemonade. Splurge! Let's have supper out. Then we can come back here, do what we have to and leave. We'll eat the stuff we brought at home. So what! Why not have some fun?" She really meant it. Setting aside Hawley's anger, Bennet's frankness, and her disappointment, Sally reasoned that she'd never been to this Montauk place. Why not see it? "It's an opportunity," she told Joe.

"You and your opportunities. I don't know why you helped that woman in the first place. As if three kids and a husband aren't enough. You said you were thinking about the kids when you pulled this stunt. They don't look too happy to me. And what about me? Do you ever think about me?"

"You must know I think about you. When you're working so hard, so many days, such long hours. I miss you. I wish we could be together all the time, like before. Don't be angry with me about the children. They're so young, so vulnerable. We want them to see things, have experiences. After all, they're our future."

"Our what?" he exclaimed incredulously.

"They're our future."

"Them? Those three? You're depending on them?" He laughed, clearing his angry face.

"And why not?" Sally argued, standing up, as always battle ready for her children's defense. "They're our future family. Two shots. The one you're born with, the one you make. It's like a second chance."

"My God, Sally, it's hard enough to get through one family. To survive. You have an only-child blindness, Sally. You and your Dick and Jane." Surprised, Sally looked up. "Yeah, I heard that part, too," Joe said. "It's simple. We shouldn't have brought them. And if we had no one to watch them, we shouldn't have come."

There were tears in her eyes. "Well, I didn't think we'd get caught, Joe. I thought no one would know the difference. And I never thought people would actually ask us to leave."

"Never thought? It was an out bet we'd get caught, Sally," Joe said, once again the instructor. "It's not like the city. Everyone's related — yeah, I heard that, too. Everyone knows everybody's business. I bet it's a pastime. Honestly, Sally, I don't understand how you can be so naive. Never thought!"

"I was wrong. What more can I say?" She shrugged her shoulders and sat down at the kitchen table. No one had eaten. And there was so much. She'd give out bananas in the car. No point in making more of a mess at the Hawley house.

"Will you tell me something else? Without crying?" Joe asked, all the anger gone from his voice. "If you were trying to hide the kids, why on earth would you put their shoes on the front porch? I mean a New York City taxicab sitting in the driveway attracts enough attention. But their shoes, too? Jeezuz!"

"I never thought of it."

"Yeah, well," he rolled his eyes. Then he said, "Are we going or not?"

"Going?" Sally echoed, not sure what Joe meant.

"To Montauk. Lemonade out of a lemon. Isn't that what you want? But you have to put something on. You'll get arrested in that T-shirt." He winked then shook his head, smiling, "Two shots! Two families! I still can't believe that one."

There was no question about it. Sally loved the way he looked when he wasn't criticizing her, when they connected — so lean and wiry, his no nonsense body — a body that not only gave her pleasure, but had run interference for her in those parts of life she was fuzzy about. Even his face was sexy, uneven features put together in a manner that made him attractive in a Marlon Brando kind of way. A face that told people nothing about himself, relaxed yet in control. She was tall, but Joe was taller. They *did* fit. She didn't care what anyone said.

"We'll wait in the car," he said, his hand skimming across her T-shirt draped breasts with an easy motion, as if he'd read her feelings.

"Take the bananas for the kids," she called out. "And a paper bag for the peels."

Upstairs, Sally splashed her face with cold water, gathered her damp hair in a pony tail, and tucked the denim work shirt in her blue jeans. Catching herself in the mirror, she stopped and bloused out the shirt. Joe preferred she wear her clothes loose. And today he was her master. Like old times. She would go out of her way. A promise. She went downstairs, locked the front door, put on her sneakers and ran toward the waiting yellow taxicab.

The Checker's engine rumbled and thundered as they drove down Dayton Lane in the heart of East Hampton Village, trying to make the best of it.

4

People and Places

Riding east toward Montauk on Route 27, they passed gas stations and body shops, a tiny deli across from a liquor store, a plaque that said Entering Amagansett Fire District.

"Amagansett, Montauk, and Springs are hamlets in the Town of East Hampton," Sally read from the Chamber of Commerce brochure Jack Bennet had given her. "East Hampton Village and Sag Harbor are the only incorporated villages in the Town of East Hampton, and only half of Sag Harbor at that. The other half can be found in Southampton." I should hope so, she thought, smiling to herself. She looked out the open window; a salt breeze washed over her face.

A restaurant sporting a Closed Till Next Season sign rushed by. Clothing shops bannered Ready for School, two white clapboard churches, a red brick grade school, a firehouse, and a railroad station lined up pleasingly, as in a Hopper painting. Main Street, U.S.A. New England style. After the car dealership and some shingled houses advertising Scallops For Sale, they were out of Amagansett on to a fragile strip of Montauk Highway separating ocean from bay and forest.

There were double dunes, tired-looking beachfront motels, and stretches of undisturbed, glimmering sand. The sea and bay sparkled emerald green in the September sun. Everything was still, except the yellow taxicab — the lone car cranking along the narrow road. Everything was still except Sally, unavoidable second thoughts stirring, delayed reactions — so characteristic of Sally — now close at hand.

A free holiday! It was so small a thing. Three days away. But there was no free holiday. Joe was right. Nothing's free. They'd all paid a price. She was angry at Charles Hawley and his button-down suit, at Jack Bennet with his precious *the summer colony always left after Labor Day, new element, city people* — but most of all, angry at herself. She never should have taken that chance. She didn't do the right thing. Some people got away with wrong things. She never got away with anything. Sally recalled her worst night-mare: killing herself and getting caught.

There was forest on both sides of the road now. Through the trees, you could glimpse slivers of white-crested ocean, highlighted by a waning midday sun. It was beautiful yet indifferent, like Merseault's heavens. She wondered what that felt like. Probably like nothing. She caught herself. This was not going to be fun un-less she cleared her head, dispelled the shadows.

"Okay, Joe," she said, trying an old standard. "What if a man were to fall off a roof and— "

"Sally, I'm not in the mood," Joe stopped her. "I'm never in the mood for that one."

She shrugged. "Did it ever occur to you how many times you don't want to listen to what I want to say? How many times you say, 'I'm not in the mood' or 'Sally, don't start?' "

"Don't start, Sally," he said, pausing. "Is that what you mean?" He threw her a wink, gave her that charming half-smile.

Sally relaxed, moving her legs closer to his. "You know, Joe, that theory I have about faulty *premises* in life, as in logic, yielding bad conclusions. Well, we were on the wrong *premises* in East

Hampton. Therefore, the bad conclusion." Smiling, she underscored the pun.

"What's so funny about being asked to leave town, Sally? Am I missing something?"

"No. But given the option, I'd rather laugh than cry."

"We were the wrong people," said Joe, finally. No smile.

"And what's more, that Hawley guy wasn't really against children in his home, Joe," she said, as if he she hadn't heard him. "He was against *damage* to his home and connected that to children. But adults can cause damage, too. His thinking wasn't straight."

"And it was your job to straighten it?" he asked. The taxi picked up speed.

"I was going to see that *we* conformed to *his* real intention. Caring for his home. Which I did . . . except I went too far, with the shoes, that is."

"Forget the shoes," Joe replied. "I don't want to even think about that. What about the mattress, Sally, the one on the picnic table in his backyard? What about the wet towels you left on the bedroom rug? When did you become housekeeper of the year?"

Joe had a point. He wasn't being mean. Although before she went back to school, Sally was very sensitive on this subject. She tried to picture their apartment with impartial eyes, knowing that soon, when she worked, it would no longer be a mess. It was, indeed, perpetually disheveled. And not because of the children. No way she could blame it on them. She had a tendency to spread her presence throughout. Summer school had not yet been cleared away and here it was the fall semester. She saw textbooks piled on the dining room table; an overdue term paper with research notes across her desk, index cards stacked alongside; overdue books from the

college library next to the living room lamps; her backpack hanging from the door of the hall closet; philosophy journals stacked on
the bathroom clothes hamper; house bills collected on the kitchen
counter; yellow legal pads throughout, and the ever-present Sources
of Financial Aid in Higher Education on the night table, within
Sally's reach when money went low. Powdered over everything,
peppering the carpetless parquet floors, the puffs of dust balls, the
curves and crevices of decorative *prewar* moldings, was a mari-
nated mixture of exhaust fumes and petro filth that wafted across
the Hudson on prevailing westerly winds from New Jersey refiner-
ies directly into the Singers' West Side apartment. Soot and sprawl,
that was it.

Joe was saying, "We don't belong in this place, Sally."

"Is that what you meant by wrong people? Why don't we belong?" She straightened up in her seat. "What do you mean we
don't belong?"

"You know exactly what I mean. It's not for us."

"No one can tell us to sit in the back of the bus, Joe. No one.
We belong anywhere we want to be. You have to take chances with
life."

"This place is not for us. Bet on it!"

"I don't believe that, Joe, not for a second. It's just different.
That's all. People seem to live in an earlier age. A simpler one.
Their roots run deep. Did you see the sign that said Founded 1646?
It reminds me of something . . . that cocoon-like feeling . . . encap-
sulated . . . shielded . . . preserved . . . *Brigadoon!* That's it!" she
exclaimed. "We've strayed into a place from a different time. A
better place. It's a space/time conundrum—"

"Don't start that stuff, Sally," he warned.

"Well, I've found my *Brigadoon,* Joe, only this one doesn't disappear." Sally took a breath. "We have to rent a house here some summer. "

"They throw us out of town and you want to rent?" He looked at her as if she were crazy.

"I refuse to let them make us feel that way," Sally said, hearing Jack Bennet's *summer colony* echo in her mind.

They were passing rickety-looking motels on her right, the ocean side, the kind she'd seen in certain movies, inexpensive motels with neon hearts selling love cheap. Then she saw the Welcome to Montauk sign. Joe swerved to the left. For a moment Sally thought he was reacting to her rental idea, but they pulled into a gas station, whitewashed and flat-roofed. Joe asked a leathery-faced man in overalls and a blue-visored cap to fill her up.

"Muffler needs fixing. Out of your turf, aren't you? Some far," the attendant mumbled as he squeegeed their windshield.

"Sally," Joe turned to face her, his arm resting on the back of the seat. "What do you think a summer costs here? I don't pay through the nose to prove something to people I don't care about in a place that takes five hours to get to just to go for a swim and that's if they let you." He glanced at her hands. "You're going to lose that ring, pulling it on and off all the time, like you haven't decided if you're married."

"Why, Joe! That's unfair. You don't even wear a ring. Nobody knows you're *taken*. How do you think that makes me feel?" Sally said. "The way girls fall over you."

"Don't flirt with me," he said, paying the man in the overalls.

"Joe, I know what the Hawley house cost for July through Labor Day. Bennet told me."

"Expensive, right?"

"$2,200."

"What? And you're talking about renting? You're dangerous," he said. Joe barely looked east or west before re-entering the road, but there was no traffic at all. "You would spend over two grand for two months out here when that pays two years' rent at home? You got no respect for money. Rent out here? No way. Not in a million years."

Not in a million years? She decided not to answer and studied the brochure. "Let's keep going east," she said. "There's a landmark we should see."

An over-ripe banana fragrance floated to the front of the taxi. Turning, Sally traced the too-sweet scent to the brown paper bag on the floor near popcorn droppings from the trip out. A box of opened Uneeda Biscuits for Andy's car sickness sat on the rear window ledge with the bottle of Coke syrup on its side. Three baseball mitts were under the jump seats, plus a bat and hard ball that kept bumping into Ben's blue Frisbee. A ragged copy of *The Racing Form* was sticking out from under the driver's seat.

Her attention was drawn to Andy's face. It was turning blue — a quarrel with Michael, something to do with money.

"It can't be Ben," Andy gasped at Michael. "Ben never takes anything he can use."

"Mommy says I'm her artistic child," Ben piped up in the way a child repeats something he's overheard. "In my jeans." He pointed to his worn denims, making no sense at all.

"Stop holding your breath, Andy," ordered Michael. He was looking out the window.

"I write poems," said Ben.

"Ma, Michael always takes my stuff," cried Andy.

"Do you want me to shoot him?" asked Sally, calling up her standard reply. She was told by the pediatrician to ignore Andy's breath-holding.

"Stop taking my money, Michael. I'm not Mommy."

"Now what does that mean?" Sally asked.

"You know damn well!" This from Joe.

Michael told Andy, "Your money's on the dresser at the Hawley house, okay?"

"Why couldn't you say that to him in the first place, Michael?" Sally chided.

"Because he asked if I took his money, not where it was. He asked the wrong question." Michael was still looking out the window.

Sally thought his chiseled profile particularly handsome at that moment. His voice seemed detached. Is that how 10-year-olds were supposed to sound? And how did he know Andy was holding his breath, when he was looking out of the window? It made Sally wonder if, like the forest, ocean, and sky, there wasn't something beautiful and indifferent about Michael.

"You knew the right answer, Michael," Joe said sharply. "You're being a wise guy."

Michael said nothing.

Sally sighed. Joe was harder on Michael than Sally was. Saw more things that could be improved. Sometimes Sally thought Joe was against their oldest son. Defending Andy. Babying Ben. Attacking Michael. It wasn't fair. Michael had less of a childhood than his brothers. Like a ball team's designated hitter, Michael was called to stand in for his parents from time to time.

Joe depended on Michael when she wasn't around for things Joe found difficult — talking to teachers, writing notes, dealing with friends' parents — conventional things he was uncomfortable with, where he felt he was at a disadvantage. "I can't play their game, Sally, not when they have the edge," Joe said.

Meanwhile, Sally swore *never* to depend on *any* of her children, let alone Michael. She knew children were on loan, that she had to prepare carefully to let them go, that love prorated in 10 or 11-month intervals would avoid the trap of excessive attachment to that which *had* to be detached. There'd be a natural inclination to overdo. But she'd persevere. That's what she'd planned. After Michael, it was 26 months before Andy arrived.

Not that she didn't try. But things had gone wrong. German Measles. Lifting a playpen. Stretching to hang drapes. Two beguiling years alone with Michael. And in those two years she didn't know she'd forgotten children were on loan, she came to adore Michael so. Then when Ben came a year after Andy, Sally was advised by the doctors not to have any more.

"Three aren't enough. I need insurance." Sally wailed to her grandmother. "It's not what I planned."

Grandma, kneading dough for the Friday night *rugalech*, pastries stuffed with cinnamon and raisins, didn't bother to look up. "You want to make God laugh, Sally? Tell him your plans."

As it turned out, three children were too much for Sally. So she made Michael a designated parent before Joe did. She needed Michael's help raising just a *few*. Needed his company, too. Joe was starting with the cab; he was never home. And Michael made her laugh. Laughing made things seem less serious, altered her perspective.

"Did you hear what I said, Michael? You're being a wise guy."

"You could have handled it better, Michael," said Sally, putting an end to it.

They were east of Montauk's Main Street, but the din continued from the back of the taxi. Andy was complaining about the

new methadone clinic in the lobby of their apartment house. He
was afraid of the junkies. Michael said he was afraid of everything,
that Ben was braver, standing up to the guys that wanted to steal
his bike. Andy said he didn't hand over his money like Michael.
Michael said only some money. He kept the rest in his shoe for
himself, that way keeping everybody happy.

"Stop!" Sally cut in. "It kills me that you know so much about
ugly things."

"If they understand, they know what to keep away from," Joe
advised. "That's how you get by in this world. There's always something to trip you up."

"Oh, Joe. What's the point," she cried. "Vacation is an act of
vacating, emptying your mind of one place to fill it with another."

She didn't want visions of Manhattan's meanness in the midst
of East Hampton's *Brigadoon.* Sally believed there was a mystery
about time and space and the incompatibility of certain events, a
first-order truth waiting to be discovered. There had to be for the
world to make sense.

It started with war movies she'd see every Saturday afternoon
in the children's section of the RKO Coliseum, overseen by the
white-coated matron. Movies showing old men dragged by their
beards through cobblestoned streets, movies showing children, with
unblinking eyes, their hands raised in surrender. Movies showing
fair-haired men in black-booted uniforms shooting babies with one
unwasted bullet, as their mothers keened inhuman howls, tearing
at their hair. Movies about Auschwitz. She turned to Joe. He was
driving with one hand on the wheel, a cigarette in the other.

"You know, Joe, during the war, the Nazis, I wonder what everyday things everyday people were doing while those unspeak-
able acts occurred nearby? Gassing and cooking? Carnage and

potatoes? How was it possible?"

"How was what possible?" Joe said, impatiently. "We've been through this. People next door might be killing each other and we're eating French toast. What's the goddamn problem?"

"You don't know how to deal with the big picture, Joe," she said, annoyed that he sounded right. "Those events can't be compatible."

Joe tossed his cigarette out the window.

"That's dangerous," said Sally.

The car picked up speed.

There was something else about those Saturday afternoon war movies besides time and space. Her own vulnerable Jewishness. It would make Sally squirm in her seat. Watching atrocities committed on youngsters with Stars of David sewn on their sleeves, atrocities inflicted by doctors and nurses in white coats. Her eyes would play tricks on her.

The white sign with black block printing saying children's section changed to Jewish section. The matron's white dress had a swastika, a club replacing the flashlight in her right hand, a menacing hypodermic needle in her left, filled with thick blue-eyed dye. Sally had to swallow hard over the rock in her throat to stop from screaming. Then, wait a minute, *I have blue eyes*, she remembered! The magic words! Everything went back to what it was.

When she talked to Joe about these old feelings, he asked if she ever listened to herself.

Now, she squeezed her blue eyes shut, pushing away images of the war zone that was Manhattan's Upper West Side, dispelling thoughts of her street-smart family — Michael so shrewd, Andy distrusting, and Ben dangerously unafraid.

"Watch the scenery, guys. We're coming to the easternmost point in New York State." Sally was quoting Bennet's brochure while looking for the promised landmark. "See! There's the lighthouse, a beacon for boats."

"What's a beacon?" asked Ben.

"Something that can't be lifted," said Andy.

Sally laughed. Her world righted. It was funny. Andy was funny! Michael was grinning, too. She wouldn't have to shoot him, after all. Andy gave Ben a playful punch. And Joe's low opinion about future families notwithstanding, she saw sweetness and caring, saw good things and a second chance through her boys, as they drove slowly around the point, then headed back west.

The yellow taxicab was on Montauk's Main Street. Joe, at Sally's direction, went north at the Circle toward the remains of the old fishing village — destroyed in the Hurricane of '38, Sally informed everyone — and found Gosman's, a waterfront restaurant, "prices surprisingly reasonable," said the brochure. Only a few people were there and service was quick.

Somehow the children always finished first. They were playing outside, feeding sea gulls leftover biscuits. Sally could hear their laughter each time a gull swooped close. Here, outside was quieter than inside, so different from the city with its cars honking, engines clanging, sirens screeching, ambulances wailing.

She walked out on the dock, watched her happy children playing safely against the aquas and sky pinks of the horizon. The air was a bouquet of sea and salt and lingering summer fragrances. It was from this place, this still and beautiful place, they were banished by Hawley and Bennet and her own misdoings. Motionless, tears streaming, she watched fishing boats cruising through the channel from Long Island Sound to Lake Montauk, a *ping* signaling their return to safe harbor. Standing on Gosman's Dock at sunset, her chin jutted into the summer/fall breeze, Sally Singer swore she, too, would return to this refuge hidden on the eastern tip of Long Island. "We'll *come back, and we'll come back right*," she vowed, leaving half her seafood platter uneaten.

The damp mattress was back on its bed. The pot of goulash, the foil-wrapped meat loaf, the tuna salad and egg salad, the Wonder Bread, the butter, the coffee and coffee pot were back in the large Yellow Checker taxicab. Fifteen hours after they'd arrived, the taxi was trumpeting its way west on the Montauk Highway, Route 27, the Hamptons' connection to the rest of the world. They passed a diner, farmhouses. They sped by acres of farmland that once stretched from sea to uplands, but now, like a torn seam, were ripped apart by the tarred two-lane road. The sequined sky was midnight blue by the time they crossed the Shinnecock Canal.

Come back here? *Not in a million years,* Joe'd said.

Sally stopped fiddling with her ring, took two slices of bread and buttered them with the knife Ben lifted from Gosman's.

5

1966-A Cause and a Promise

Uncle Milty's Colossal Tornadoes, an eatery in a banged-up trailer with a closed-up look on Montauk Highway, was easy to miss unless you had children. It had the air of a place that would not be there tomorrow. The Colossal Tornadoes were roast beef heros piled with stringy, shredded lettuce, hints of tomato, and globs of mayonnaise. The Singer children, eating in the taxicab, claimed they were the best heros in New York State.

Watching the boys chomp away through his rearview mirror, Joe Singer did not feel like a hero. *Not in a million years,* he'd said 10 months earlier about renting in East Hampton. And here he was the very next summer, en route to that same East Hampton, to settle his family in a rental house, June 17th through Labor Day. They didn't even get the extra week at the end.

Sally had won, after all.

During the months that followed last year's fiasco, East Hampton was never far from Sally's thoughts. Always comparing East Hampton to the city, she was relentless in pointing out the dangers of Manhattan's Upper West Side, the streetwalking addicts, their hypodermic needles in gutters, roaming gangs of disadvantaged youngsters (overwhelmingly Black and Puerto Rican) looking for prey, the mushrooming "transient" welfare hotels, old, overcrowded buildings where drug dealers conducted business daily among terrified families sentenced there. She could sell you anything, if you weren't careful; she was so convincing, so sincere, so logical.

"The boys are learning fear and deceit," she would say, "hiding money in their socks, not taking bikes and mitts and basketballs to parks. They're learning that all Black and Hispanic people are threats. They have to see there's another way people live."

Sally could paint a picture of the West Side all right. But that's why they could live there in their large prewar apartment, because rents were lower, supply greater than demand, reflecting all the flaws of a neighborhood in flux.

"I wish we could take them back to East Hampton," she'd say about the kids again and again.

Then a visiting Oxford professor wrote a glowing letter of recommendation. Unexpectedly, she was offered two courses to teach in the spring. She told Joe in January she wanted to use the extra money for East Hampton, describing it as "an opportunity for the boys to see there are other ways people live. You can take long weekends, Joe. And some time in August. You deserve it. It's good for everybody. I've called Jack Bennet. I promised we'd go back right."

To convince him further, she played the albums from *Brigadoon* and *West Side Story*, making the point in her Sally kind of way — *Brigadoon* versus *West Side Story*, the boys surviving or succumbing to gang wars and worse.

She was a pain in the ass.

He remembered sitting down, opening a newspaper, saying no more. He remembered believing anything he said wouldn't make a difference. Anyway, Sally could be pushed just so far.

For no reason at all, he recalled the first summer they were married.

Sally'd landed them jobs as carnies in an aging, blue-collar amusement park at the seashore called Rockaway's Playland. Hawking suckers to play against the odds was a hustle so Joe didn't mind the work. He did Pokerino, where people bought tokens, but Sally's booth worked on cash. When he told her to skim money, that everyone did it, she'd been firm.

"It's not mine. How can I take it?"

"They're paying you peanuts for seven days a week, 12 hours a day, Sally," he said. "And you're good. You're busy when the rest of us are standing there."

"If I didn't like the pay, I shouldn't have agreed to it. But I did. And I won't."

Two weeks later, she handed over seven dollars she'd taken from the concession that day.

Why the change? A lesson, it seemed. The concession's owner had called her aside and accused her of skimming money even though she wasn't, because he knew everyone did. He said he'd give her a second chance because she was a good worker.

"That was so unfair," she told Joe, teary eyed. "So unjust. As long as he won't trust me, I'll do what he thinks I'm doing. That'll teach him," she sobbed in her dedicated way, and averaged between five and eight dollars a day for the rest of the summer.

You could never tell what Sally would do when pushed too far. Now East Hampton. A cause *and* a promise. Nothing he said would make a difference.

On a February Sunday, they leased Hawley Bennet's new beach house — Charles Hawley, Jack Bennet, Hawley Bennet — all cousins! Did these guys use each other's names to confuse people? It was at a spot called Barnes Landing. The house was near the bay and walking distance to a small grocery. It didn't matter that she'd be without a car, she said.

"It'll be perfect, Joe. It can't g t better than this."

He could hear that determined voice, brimming with optimism, as he pulled the large, yellow Checker taxicab into the Hawley Bennet driveway.

"This is great, Sal," said Doug Slavka. "I can see the water."

Another of Sally's bright ideas. Doug Slavka and his leggy date — an auburn-haired James Bond girl designed for brief bikinis — were seated in the back. Doug Slavka was a smooth, short-cut kind of guy, good-looking and into pretty women. He treated Sally as if she partially belonged to him because they'd known each other since they were 12.

"Great spot, Sally," Doug repeated.

The con was on. Joe almost gagged. He was sorry he used Doug Slavka's bookmaker, placing bets through Doug. Sloppy! It wasn't just that he knew Doug made money off him, though that pissed him, too. But, more important, it let Slavka know too much about his business. You don't give edges away. And knowing about his business was an edge.

"Remind me to ask you something later, Slavka," Joe said. He wanted that phone number.

"Sure thing, Singer," said Doug. He helped Joe carry boxes from the taxi. "So what's the price tag, Sal?" he asked.

"Seventeen hundred for the season."

"A bargain!" said Doug.

"Easy for you to say," said Joe. "I wish I had a rich uncle supporting me, then I could be a sport, too."

"Those are the breaks," said Doug, smiling.

"Jack Bennet said the rental was below market value, Joe," Sally said.

"Yeah, the broker. Right! You didn't even bargain, Sally. Bennet had a field day."

Joe held the screen door open for Doug's date. Her name was Susannah, as in *Oh Susannah,* she'd sung and laughed, holding onto Joe's eyes a moment too long when they were introduced. A *comfortable* kind of girl. Joe had known comfortable girls from the coast, from Vegas. Wholesome cheerleaders off the farm who zeroed out in L.A. and left for Nevada, a tightness around their lips that hadn't been there before.

Joe looked around, glanced at the water down the road, then at the beach house. He shook his head. "I still don't know how I got here," he said.

"You married piss and vinegar," Doug said, laughing. "I could've told you that."

Sally cringed. First Doug's cavalier attitude toward money and now the kind of proprietary remark that could set Joe off. She wanted them to get along. She wanted this weekend to work. Doug was more like a brother to her than anything else — a brother Sally never had. That's how it started between them and that's how it was now. There was, of course, a part in the middle.

They had been rising stars together in the fragile firmament of a minor sport, table tennis. The midtown Broadway club where they played was a dark and dingy place, "no better than a pool hall," said Sally's mother. Doug's parents felt the same way, "For bums," they would say, favoring his older brother, Max, an attorney. "He's preparing himself for the probate battle," Doug said often, laughing, confident his uncle wouldn't disappoint.

Parents can be so blind, Sally thought. Just because Max was a lawyer, they didn't see his flaws. They complained about Doug's life style, his not working, his gambling, never seeing that Max was a gambler, too, a wheeler-dealer.

Sally remembered the Nationals in South Bend. She was 14

and Doug was three years older. They got to the finals of the mixed doubles, an upset. They were up against a better team. Right before the match, Doug told her their opponents were going to dump. Max had arranged it. Max was betting big for himself with a small piece of the action for Doug. Doug offered to share his winnings with her. "It's only mixed doubles, Sally. You know what a joke everyone thinks that event is."

"It's not a joke to me," Sally said. 'The one thing I do that's pure is sports. Table tennis isn't like the rest of my life where I have to make myself up half the time to please people just to survive. There's no holding back. I hit hard. I fight for every point."

They lost the match. Sally dumped it to the dumpers.

"But you did the same thing you were criticizing. You didn't fight at all," Doug reasoned, as they toweled off afterwards.

"Yes, well, it was a different fight, that's all."

"Max will be pissed."

"Too bad," Sally said. *Too bad* was what she was thinking now, too bad how parents can be blinded by their children.

She watched Doug's good-looking date survey the inside of the beach house. Sally had seen the beach house only once, that time four months ago. She had worried that it wouldn't look as good. But it did. Wood and glass, with whitewashed planked flooring, the cedar-paneled living room where sliders framed the outdoor green that hugged the cedar siding, an army of oak emerging among spruce and juniper. Since February, the landlord had added a rocker, ottomans for the club chairs and yellow throw pillows on the tan Naugahyde couch.

"It's better than I remembered," Sally said. "It will be a good change."

Susannah followed Sally into the large country kitchen. She

took a quart of Glenfiddich out of her shopping bag and placed it on the counter. "If you fix me a tall drink with short ice, darlin', I'd be happy to do dinner tonight," she offered, her voice dripping with Southern comfort.

Sure enough, an hour later there was a steaming platter of steak and french fries with a tossed salad pretty enough to frame on the kitchen table. The children ate quickly, asking to be excused before dessert.

"Too much Uncle Milty's," Sally observed, steering the boys to an upstairs bedroom. Two bunk beds were lined up catty-cornered against the wall. Sally helped make their beds with the linens they'd brought from home. There were no more rubber sheets.

She returned to the kitchen in time to hear Joe say to Doug. "I've meant to ask you this for a long time. I need the—"

When he saw her, Joe stopped talking. He's always so secretive, Sally thought as she poured herself some coffee.

"I do feel a headache coming on," Susannah said.

Too much Scotch, Sally thought.

"Too much Scotch, I think," she said, giving a happy Tinker Belle laugh.

"I brought aspirin," said Sally, reaching for her dark green tote bag on the kitchen counter.

"Thank you, darlin'." Susannah pushed aside a half-eaten plate of blueberry pie and ice cream. "But I have my own antidote." The way she said *antidote* made it sound like a relative. "I came prepared for the weekend." Fumbling through her handbag, she came up with a white, round, plastic case. Flashing a superb smile, Susannah held the case up for display.

Sally thought it was a compact. It took a moment for her to realize that the container carried the girl's diaphragm.

"You need another drink," suggested Joe, in his sexy, quiet way. "You look like you're feeling good. Like the fun's just beginning."

"I'm beyond that, darlin'," said Susannah, with a special smile for him. "I regret I'm going to have to leave you folks." She walked unsteadily toward the back bedroom.

"I'm going to bed, too," Sally announced abruptly.

6
Screams in the Night

Did he think she was blind not to see the special attention he was paying Doug's date, that lingering look, or that she was deaf not to hear that suggestive tone? It was meant to hurt her. She could feel it. She knew flirting came naturally to him, but Joe wasn't stupid. He shouldn't do that in front of her. It was disrespectful.

Should he do it behind your back? asked a voice in her head.

Sally shook that question off, switching on the pink ceramic lamp that sat on the wicker night table. But the voice went on talking, anyway, as Sally untied her sneakers. Went right to the Talmud. To that question that drove Joe crazy.

"A man falls off a roof. He lands on a married woman and enters her. Have they committed adultery?"

Why did she think of that now. Why did those men who studied the Talmud have to think of questions like that? Was that really religious? She wasn't even sure it would count as ethical. But the question remained. Maybe its importance was in the thinking, the other questions it raised.

She went through the drill. Is it adultery? Does intent count or result? Or do both? Are there two kinds of adultery, accidental and intentional? Did the man fall by accident? Did he jump? Did it make a difference? If intent, then is just thinking *adultery* adultery? If result, then there it is — a married woman entered by a man not her husband. Would the woman be stoned? Was *she* stoned? Was there any place in the middle to hide?

She shrugged her shoulders and yawned. Is that adultery? Doug's brother, Max, had said "forget adultery. It's actionable. There's a lawsuit there." What you get for asking a lawyer!

Sally looked around. This bedroom was a comforting room, all chintz and pale blue, a scent of lilacs from sachets discovered in her chest of drawers, a personal touch from Hawley Bennet. How thoughtful, especially for a bachelor. She'd have to send a note. But first, it occurred to her, that it would be a good time to shower, to be alone, the bathroom to herself, a private place. A private, private place. Where she'd whisper *I have blue eyes,* make this a happy night, the one she'd thought about since last September, about coming back *right* to East Hampton. She wouldn't let Joe spoil it for her. She'd have her shower, then she'd bury herself under the red and blue Early American quilt.

Barefooted, she padded across the shiny, wide-planked floor into the bathroom. It was windowless. Sally turned on the exhaust and found the soft hum soothing. Pulling the band from her ponytail, she felt a torrent of thick, straight, black hair caress her bare shoulders. She stepped over the shaggy pink cotton mat, feet testing the cool, blue tile floor. She placed the mat closer to the glass shower door.

The privacy of the large stall shower, the soothing warmth of water on her skin, welcomed her to East Hampton. Sally blocked out the rest of the world. Joe's flirting was an annoyance, an inconsiderate annoyance. Particularly at this time. He knew how sensitive she was. Her loss six months earlier was a deep and open wound, of grief for Grandma and anger at her mother.

When Grandma lay dying, only Sally was watching at her bedside, tears cascading down her face. *"Mein zeesah kindt, veint nischt!* People shouldn't cry when they die. They should cry when they're born," Grandma whispered. Then, breath rustling, lips twitching, she passed away.

After Grandma's death, Sally was overwhelmed by an avalanche of doubts: about intimacy, about career, about the paths she was taking, seemingly away from Joe Singer. Her death made Sally extra vulnerable to Joe's criticisms about the children, about her housekeeping, about her sporadic sexuality — she thought that was why he was doing the Susannah thing — made her feel as if she weren't up to grade.

She often wondered if men married only for a steady lay and regular meals, neither of which she provided. So often she felt like the cow in Grandma's depressing tale about women's expectations, the cow who believed the farmer loved her because he squeezed her tits every day.

Joe Singer wanted to squeeze her tits every day. What else did Joe want from her? Really want from her. To stay the same? To stay 18? When did love become want? Was she a bad wife? A good mother? She had qualms about her roles in life. Family was virgin territory.

I know how hard it is for you to be a mother, Ben once said. How could he know that every step was a major decision? She recalled Michael's accusatory question, too, when Ben had those crying spells. When Michael had to step in. *What kind of mother doesn't know how to help her baby?* And Andy. Forget Andy! He judged her all the time, blaming her for his not being born first, wanting attention already paid, coveting an ordinary-everyday-conventional-type family where adults knew what to do, were sure of what was right. He had her number. The best she could do for Andy was shoot Michael, get rid of him, to make Andy number one.

"You can't depend on men," Grandma said, warning her to keep

a secret bank account when she married. That advice never interested Sally, who wanted to believe she could depend on everybody.

She had problems with the everyday things married life en-
tailed. Mashed potatoes. Joe, from the beginning, demanded fresh
mashed potatoes every night — every night — spotting the instant
ones no matter how she doctored them. Eggs! She never guessed
they were something to scream about. He demanded his eggs this
way and that way — she never got them right, too soft, too hard,
and *Hydrox, Sally, not Oreos, how many times do I have to tell you?*
And the intimacy. Every day? Anywhere?

It was too much for her.

That was it, she decided, turning her face up to the warm spray
of water, loving the privacy, the moments for herself. Loving that
she'd figured it out. That was it. Like that woman from school she
helped last summer who didn't have the prerequisites for decision
theory — the one whose friend hadn't shown up for the course —
so Sally had no training at all for this *wifemother* position, no experience in how *real* families worked. How husbands and fathers
worked. They should have checked her background. She was an
only child with transient parents whose concept of family came
from Louisa May Alcott. Marmee. Father March.

They should fire her. She should resign.

Joe Singer trudged up the stairs to the bedroom, listening to
the creaky bed sounds, to Susannah's groans of encouragement,
coming from Doug Slavka's room.

He'd paid a little more attention to Susannah than he had to. So
what! At least that one knew the score. Did Sally really think he
married her for her company? Telling him, with that annoying
laugh, that quality counted more than quantity. As if she'd said

something funny. The direction she was going in made him feel left out. Her casual attitude about money made him look cheap, the way she trusted everyone made him seem paranoid and Sally seem like a sucker.

Trusting everyone she liked, that is. He took off his shirt, hanging it from the back of a wooden rocker. Liking was different from trusting. Shit, you're better off not liking someone, if trust is the kicker. People you don't like don't get close enough to hurt you. He tossed his pants on the chair. He'd married a kid who trusted him, a kid he could tell anything and she'd buy it. Once that made him feel good. Now it pissed him off. That and all her new ideas.

The bathroom door was shut, but he could hear the shower. Joe went in quietly. There was a humming. Through the frosted shower door, he could make out Sally's lean body with its surprising curves. Her arms were raised, hair thrown over her face. She was attractive. Dropping his shorts to the tile floor, he opened the shower door and stepped quietly inside behind her. Reaching around, he touched her, cupping her breasts, squeezing her tits.

Sally screamed. She turned, saw him and screamed again.

"I'm sorry you feel this way," he said, stepping out of the shower, water dripping on the pink, shaggy cotton mat placed close to the shower door.

Once in bed, Joe refused to listen to her defense of privacy, of knocking, of the unexpected, of how she couldn't help herself, of how she didn't know why.

7

Is Something the Matter?

Sally surrendered herself to darkness that cool June night in East Hampton.

She dreamt about *Catholic Jackie,* her Sally Lamb Protection Program, an alternate identity invented for those times when life suggested that *Sallylamb* was less a maternal endearment, more a disclaimer, a Sally *Lamb;* when life with father was hide and seek and Sallylamb was always *it.*

She was in a room. It was dark. Catholic Jackie, a Sally Lamb clone, was there. Then Catholic Jackie was gone. Someone who talked like Marlon Brando and looked like Joe Singer was gone, too. Sally Lamb was left alone, making signs of the cross.

It woke her. Feeling sad and too tired to sleep, Sally left the bed, careful not to awaken Joe. A sliver of dawn sifted through the screens painting a whitish belt below her waist. Sally pulled on her jeans, grabbed a sweatshirt, slipping it over her head. Her long, dark hair was unruly from last night's shampoo. She combed her fingers through it and quietly went downstairs.

"I didn't expect you," she whispered, entering the kitchen.

Barechested, Doug was sitting at the table drinking something. She couldn't tell what.

"You can't sleep either?" she asked, walking over to the refrigerator. She saw the open bottle of Glenfiddich on the counter. "How's Susannah's headache?"

"It vanished in the bedroom," he said, grinning. "She can really put it away, can't she? I found myself a drinking partner."

"Are you really drinking that stuff at this hour, Doug? That can't be good."

"That's when it's best, kiddo. What was that scream? Susannah thought you'd seen a bat."

"Joe surprised me in the shower." Her voice shook.

"Who'd you think it was?"

"It's no joke. I feel awful."

"Let's see what we can do about that," said Doug, lighting a joint. "Are you game for sunrise at the beach?" He offered her a drag. She shook her head, no.

"You're a frigging candy store. I don't believe you. You smoke this early in the day?"

"How do you think I get through it?"

"That's depressing."

"Yeah, depressing. Come on, Sal. Let's see the sunrise."

"Joe wouldn't like that even without the shower scene."

"Joe'll survive. C'mon, Sally. It'll do you good. " He grabbed a windbreaker from the hook near the door. "Leave loverboy a note."

She got up from the table, searching unsuccessfully for a pencil. A walk would do her good. Her trained body missed physical exertion. Maybe that's part of my problem, Sally decided, her shadowy mood shifting.

"Have you talked to your brother lately? I was thinking about him before."

"Max? That cocksucker? That mutant piece of shit? I'd like to see him in hell. That—"

"Doug! My God!" Sally exclaimed, startled. His face was transformed, becoming dark and ugly, like a summer squall. His voice was harsh, humorless. She didn't know this Doug at all.

He must have sensed it, because he put his arm around her and said, as if it didn't matter, "C'mon Sal, you know I haven't seen the Mouthpiece. He makes me sick, that's all, just thinking about the son of a bitch." He sounded like himself again.

Had she imagined someone different? "You scared me."

"My girl afraid of me?" He bent over and kissed her cheek, at the same time giving her a reassuring hug. "Doesn't my sister-in-law talk to you anymore?"

"I'm afraid she's abandoned me, bit by bit since they got married," said Sally. "It was easy for her to set aside high school friendship, I guess. I introduce her to Max. Liz gets a husband. I lose a friend. Haven't talked to her for a while. I don't know exactly how long. She was always the numbers person. Anyhow, you know what they say about good deeds," Sally said.

"Good deed? Come on, Sal, you're talking to the Doug. Your pal Liz was runner-up. She knew that. My brother had the hots for you. He couldn't believe you married Singer."

She was surprised at the girlish pleasure she felt as Doug recited history. "Okay, forget Liz Slavka! And Max, too. Pay attention! I have that question for you again, Doug. I'm giving you another chance," she teased, skipping along the sand, feeling suddenly like a teenager and not a failed wife/mother. "A man falls off a roof and he lands on a married woman and enters her. Have they committed adultery?"

"Same answer," he said.

"Yes, but if it's technically adultery, say, have they done anything wrong?"

Doug patted her on the head. "Who the fuck cares, Sal? There is no right and wrong, anyway. Only situations."

Walking along the beach, her hand in Doug's, Sally thought of

another beach, an earlier Sally. Her thoughts traveled 6,000 miles
west and 12 years back to the beach at Inchon, the Korean Riviera,
to Inchon by the Sea and the swaggering, homesick, American troops
they entertained there, Doug Slavka, Sally Lamb, and the rest of
the United States Table Tennis team.

Inchon, Korea, has the second highest tides on planet Earth,
second only to Nova Scotia. It was here that the Americans launched
a successful surprise counterattack during a war named a conflict.
Floating in on landing craft at high tide, the G.I.s took this remote,
but key, seaside village. Inchon. On this faraway Asian beach, Doug
Slavka did not take Sally Lamb.

The American Army on red alert halted their lovemaking, sur-
rounding the two athletes, guns cocked, in the high grass near shore.
The beach was off limits, those same record-book tides an invitation for gook infiltrators who were winning the peace by *slickying*,
stealing everything in sight and underground, even siphoning U.S.
oil from pipelines that stretched to the 38th parallel. Sally thought
the G.I.s waited before flooding them in lights. "Voyeurs, eaves-
droppers, listening to us pant in the dark. They had a platoon there,
for God's sake," she told Doug afterward. In any case, Doug with-
drew.

It hadn't mattered. Sally had always known Doug Slavka wasn't
for her. Not for marriage. Too romantic, too charming, too unstable.
What did Joe call him? A shortcut kind of guy? Her mother took
those chances, not Sally. Despite his appeal, despite his broad shoulders, she sensed she couldn't count on Doug.

When she returned from the Far East to New York, still a 17-
year-old high school senior, Sally binged on *Guys and Dolls*, a re-
run of the Brando movie at the Harris Theater on Times Square, a

half-mile from the Ping-Pong club on Broadway. She needed a transition to help her settle into real life after her trip abroad. Watching the movie five consecutive afternoons after school, she had an epiphany: the *Guys and Dolls* world of Broadway grifters and gamblers, of Benny Southstreet, Society Max, and Big Julie was one and the same as the world of her father, Mike Lamb, and one and the same as the world of a sexy hustler, an older guy, from the Ping-Pong club who'd been nice to her. His name was Joe Singer.

Mike Lamb, by that time, had graduated to a heavenly floating crap game in the sky. Once a mover and shaker in that Hollywood Industry of make-believe, he'd died on the skids in an overcrowded Bellevue ward with 60 other lost souls, his heart succumbing to a lifetime of lost bets, a 14-year-old daughter he barely knew his only visitor.

Her *Guys and Dolls* vision told her this was where Mike Lamb was when he hadn't been with her while she was growing up, with his own kind of people, Harry the Horse, Nicely Nicely, Nathan Detroit — all compatriots of her father, all singing *Fugue For a Tin Horn* in gamblers' heaven. By watching the film each day, she was visiting her father, getting to know him, loving this Sky Masterson/ Marlon Brando version of him. *Guys and Dolls* showed her what Mike Lamb and his world were really like.

And *Guys and Dolls* made her feel that, maybe, she, also, belonged in Damon Runyon's unconventional, romantic world, the good girl in the Damon Runyon universe: Sister Sarah/ Sister Sally Salvation. (Wasn't Sarah Brown the daughter of a gambler, too?)

Now, Sally'd first noticed Joe Singer on film, too, old movies of the Table Tennis Nationals where she and Doug danced their *Barefoot Contessa* routine at the tournament party. There were a few frames of Joe Singer exhaling smoke rings at Sally's hips. Sexy, she thought. They played Ping-Pong. Close games that made her feel she'd win if she played him forever.

Joe Singer was a *Guys and Dolls* character; he came from that same Mike Lamb world, she decided, sexy Sky Masterson/Joe Singer who looked out for Sarah Brown's interests in Havana, who saved her mission by providing sinners. And sexy Mike Lamb whose escapades were reported to Sally by her mother. It was starting to make sense.

In Vegas before Joe returned to New York, he lived by his wits like Sky. Joe was sexy and comfortable like Sky and Mike; Joe didn't work, like Sky; Joe seemed in control, like Sky. And like Sky, Joe was respected by his peers, that underclass of people who populate Ping-Pong parlors and other havens for marginals, misfits, and men of vision. Joe was street tough like Sky and card smart like Mike. He even looked a bit like Brando.

So there it was. With tenuous mental wizardry, more intuitive than rational, Sally reached a grand conclusion. Joe Singer was her trinity incarnate — her father was Joe and Sky Masterson, Sky Masterson was her father and Joe. Therefore, Joe was Sky Masterson and her father! Six weeks after her return stateside, right after graduation, Sally, loving her idea of him, married Joe Singer at Manhattan's City Hall. She had it all — a choice her father would be proud of plus a road map to get her through that minefield called life.

There had been no colorful sunrise to welcome Sally and Doug to Barnes Landing beach that morning, only a smear of steamy light embracing the bay. But now the haze was dissolving. The sun had won the battle over mist. The damp was almost gone. Sally had no idea how long they had been walking when they arrived at a jetty, bay water separating one part of the beach from the other, high pilings guarding the breach. There was nowhere to go, except back.

Doug bent over, letting sand skim through his fingers. The sky was the palest of blue. The bay looked black. White foam rimmed gentle waves. "I'm still chilly. You must be cold without a jacket," he said, hunkered down on the warm sand. "Come on into mine," he invited her, holding the windbreaker open. Sally declined, but sat down beside him. He put his arm around her.

"Do you know how disgusting the smell of liquor is in the morning?" Sally asked, turning her face away.

"That's terrific, Sal. Very romantic," he said, still sheltering her with his arm.

Sally was sliding her ring back and forth on her finger.

"You're going to lose your wedding band doing that."

"Pretty girl," she said.

"What?" said Doug.

"Susannah," said Sally. "A pretty girl."

"Oh, that one, my Southern comfort?" He jerked his head westward toward the house. "Yeah. Very pretty. Dynamite. You jealous?"

"No. Happy for you." She gave a laugh, twisting her hair in a whirl on top of her head. "What time is it?"

"Almost 11."

"Not that late! Oh God, Joe will wonder where we are."

"I told you to leave a note."

"I couldn't find a pencil. I had no idea it was so late. Come on. Race you," she challenged, getting up in her easy, leg-crossed way. She started to run, kicking the sand high with her long-legged stride as Doug easily sped by.

The children were at the beach. Ben, 8, in his trusty artistic jeans, and Andy, a year older, were roughhousing in the sand, Ben on the bottom laughing loudly as Andy tickle-tortured him. They were too busy to notice Sally and Doug. Sally called out and waved. Michael interrupted construction on what appeared to be an intricate sand castle, protected by two moats with seashell bridges. He glanced at them, giving them a nod.

When they returned to the beach house, Joe was sitting at the salt and pepper Formica topped kitchen table. There was a container of orange juice on the matching Formica counter and two almost empty glasses in front of him on the table. He was drumming his nails on the tabletop.

Doug scanned the room, quickly noting a half-filled glass of orange juice next to the whiskey bottle. "Where's my girl?" he asked.

"She went back to bed," answered Joe, eyes glaring at Sally.

"I didn't realize the time, Joe. It's after 11! I'm sorry." She poured herself juice in one of the rinsed glasses from the previous evening. Susannah must have done these this morning, she thought. The washed dishes were lined up in a mustard-colored rubber drain over a matching rubber mat. "We saw the boys at the beach," she said to Joe, without facing him.

Joe sat there, tapping harder.

Doug left the room without a word.

Sally noticed how clean the rubber mat was, yellow throughout, none of those familiar, shadowy stains that lingered on hers no matter how she scoured. She turned around. She could ignore it no longer — the angry tapping, quicker and louder, like drums at an execution. "Is something the matter?" she asked.

"Fish is the matter."

"Fish?" said Sally.

Fish was the bookmaker.

8
Concept of Fish

"You bet with the bookmaker," Joe said, his voice charged with anger.

"Yes and I lost! So what's the problem? I don't understand why you're so upset. I was bored and I bet. You do that for interest when you're watching a game." It was her own money. After all, it wasn't as if she were a hard-core gambler.

"Did Michael have anything to do with this?"

"Well, I asked his opinion. It's better than decision theory and Boolean algebra making the mistake for you," she said, going off on one of her tangents. "How can they quantify choices? Choices are supposed to be subjective."

"Don't start with that bullshit, Sally. You asked Michael's opinion."

"What's wrong with that. You always do."

"How did you get the bookie's number?" The veins in his neck were taut.

"Doug gave me the number, of course."

"Doug gave you the number," he said, the echo louder than its source. He moved his chair away from the table roughly and got up. "He never told me, never asked my permission."

"Asked your permission?" Sally bounced back. "What permission was needed? He's my friend. It's my money."

"What happened to money being something that's ours?"

"Yes, well, ours is fine, Joe. Except you never have to ask for anyone's consent, but you always want me to. That's your concept. What's mine is yours and what's yours is yours. Where's the our? It's an attitude—"

"For chrissake! I don't want to hear that stuff again."

"I wouldn't think so. Lower your voice, please. After all, *I* lost, not you."

"I had money riding on the same game, Sally, with the same bookmaker." He hadn't lowered his voice one bit.

"Ours or yours?" she said, but then backed off. She gave a shrug. What did he want from her? "Yes, well. I'm sorry you lost, too."

"I didn't lose. *I won.* I won," he shouted. "Don't you understand? We were betting against each other with a bookie. You gave him a gift. The vigorish! He made the vig either way."

"Well, I wouldn't have bet against you if I knew that, Joe. But I didn't and it wasn't a bad bet. I almost won."

"How much?" he asked.

"Don't you know?" Sally said. "You spoke to Fish."

"You think I was going to ask him. Look like a real fool? What did you bet?"

"Thirty times," she said, looking away, instinctively knowing she'd bet more than he had.

"A-hun-dred-and-fif-ty-dol-lars?" Joe hurled each syllable. "I won $50 and you lost a $165! Jesus, I feel like a fool." He slapped his hand hard on the counter, making an explosive sound. "Supporting a bookmaker! You and your buddy, Doug Slavka. That fuck. Giving you a bookie's number. I'd like to see how he'd feel if I did the same to his wife."

"Doug doesn't have a wife."

"Don't get smart with me, Sally."

"I thought I'd interject some levity. It's not the end of the world."

"Levity? Levity you said? Does that mean funny? You're making jokes. Losing money isn't a joke. Doug Slavka isn't a joke. He was out of line. Way out of line." He slapped the table now, crashing one of the glasses to the floor. He seemed not to notice, at least not to care. "Don't you know Slavka gets some of the bookmaker's action? He sends him business. They're having a good time laughing at us . . . at me!"

Sally got up, carefully avoiding broken glass. "Watch out," she said, looking for a broom in a small closet next to the pantry. "Get me some bread, Joe."

Seeing his startled look, she said, "Not to eat. To clean up. White bread will pick up the slivers."

"Fuck the slivers, Sally," Joe cried. "The bookie calls himself *Fish*, does that mean anything to you, Sally? Does that tell you something? Only fish support bookmakers. Only suckers. I'm no fish and I don't want to feel like I'm married to one, either."

"Jesus, Joe. Help me with the glass."

"Have you done this before? Huh? Have you?"

Sally was about to answer, but changed her mind. She would not be treated like a child. Instead she said, "Fish, sucker, what does it all mean? You know what the Stoics say. It's how you take it, an insult's not an—"

"Fuck your goddamn stoics and Doug Slavka, too, for Chrissake," he said, storming out of the room. He muttered "Schmuck," at her as he crushed glass fragments beneath his shoe.

"Mrs. Schmuck," she hurled back, getting two slices of soft white bread for the floor, then adding two more for herself. "I'm only a schmuck by marriage."

9
Falling Off Roofs

J oe Singer walked the empty, narrow beach at Barnes Landing. A white smear of sun worked the early mist over Gardiner's Bay. He needed to get a handle on things after last week — the shower, the bookmaker, his fight with Doug Slavka on the way back to the city. (He'd straightened out Doug and, later, Fish. There'd be no percentage to Slavka anymore, not with his money.)

Everything was getting worse. Especially this place. This place was a series of disasters. Angrily kicking sand as he walked, he noticed a gull swoop down, do that funny cake walk on the water surface, bury its head and come up a winner. Joe had to laugh. That's what life was all about, wasn't it? Survival. Letting out a deep breath, he pulled off his sneakers, knotted the laces together and slung them around his neck. Then he began to jog.

You have to take care of yourself, Joe thought. He'd learned that early. A late and accidental arrival to his family, he'd raised himself with children of other immigrants on teeming city streets. Working people all their lives and suspicious of their new surroundings, Ben and Anna Singer left their hopes in Eastern Europe, uniquely unconscious of the American dream. Growing up in the absence of expectations other than imminent misfortune, Joe forfeited any great plans for himself other than survival.

And he did survive, he thought, picking up his pace into an easy run.

Hustling. Small-time maybe, but it got him through. People

liked letting Joe Singer take their money. In fact, they begged him
at times, making bets they couldn't win, bets Joe told them they
couldn't win. But they loved it, loved him, always came back for
more, because Joe Singer —a magnet for fish and those sick cats
who had to gamble — knew his suckers, treated them kindly, never
taking more money than they could afford to lose. He never lost
more than he could afford either, never going beyond his stake. He
made his hit at night, hustling at Phil's Bowling Alley, hustling at
the Ping-Pong club (which was a step up, a better clientele). He
slept all day. His family called him a bum. Early on they severed
all ties.

Breathing easily, Joe increased his speed, selecting a firmer
surface on the wet sand left by the ebb tide. From time to time he'd
lose his concentration, drifting too close to the water's edge, the
cold on his ankles giving him a start. The sandy stretch got nar-
rower and rockier, but Joe kept his course. The alternative was
prickly, high-grassed dunes rimming the upland side of the beach.

Sally. He didn't really notice Sally at the Ping-Pong club. It
was at a tournament. But when she was putting on a dance show
with Doug Slavka, he'd taken a hard look. Moving with the fluid
grace of a fine-tuned athlete, every muscle going with the music,
she'd attracted him. Sally Lamb had the kind of body that was a
well-kept secret. Joe appreciated that right off. But that stuff was
always available to him, if he bothered to look. To tell the truth,
most of the time he could take it or leave it, until of course, he was
married and supposed to get it automatically. But when Joe was
single, it had to come to him. There were more important things.
Sally seemed to notice him after she came back from the trip. She
flirted, even though he'd expected she'd come back belonging to
Doug Slavka.

So, as was his manner, he'd handicapped Sally carefully and seriously, from every angle. Maybe she was smart, but probably not as smart as she thought. She had a tendency to trust too much, an easy mark for someone who was nice to her. She was good looking enough to worry you. On the other hand, she did have a certain kind of respectability, the kind that resisted someone like him — could even be a moneymaker if handled right — and she didn't seem to mind the gambling scene, either. He was going up in class, always a risk. But he figured he could guide Sally along, be her trainer and her jockey, steering her through life's muddy tracks, in directions where he felt safe, which meant where he felt in control. All in all, Joe touted her as a winner in a world from which he'd been scratched.

However, it hadn't worked out that way.

He'd gone along with the baby thing, though it put him out of action and forced him to get a job. There was nothing much a guy who hadn't finished high school could do. There was no percentage in his job pushing dollies through the garment center, even though he got to bring home samples, which he sold to the women in the neighborhood. Which he got Sally to sell, that is. Nevertheless, there was no percentage.

He'd gotten Sally to borrow money from her mother so he could buy himself a cab, be a taxidriver. A good decision! He was in action, meeting people, hustling deals. He was very astute at pushing long hauls and doubling and tripling up on the short ones. He'd paid off the guy at the airport to look the other way when he broke into the line. He made his own hours, could stop at the flats in the afternoon, even the trotters at night if he had a reliable tip. He could come and go as he pleased. He never had to explain 12- and 14-hour days. It was decent money, too.

Despite all that, Joe never had enough to cover his way of life and the overhead of a family. When he had the shorts, the family suffered.

He had to admit Sally's Ph.D. thing was actually a better deal in the long run, more money for less work. These college professors really had it made. Sally got along well with them. They treated her like an equal. She liked what she was doing. It bothered him more and more because he wasn't part of it and she talked a lot about things that made no sense at all.

Up ahead, Joe could make out a jetty. It appeared the beach ended there. He slowed down gradually. The sun was out in full now, the beach warming up. Joe bent over, finding a flat rock, and hurled it at the bay to skim the water. It didn't work. He was more than a little surprised.

This place, he thought, shaking his head. He never missed at the lake in Central Park. He'd been doing it since he was a kid. Nothing fucking works here! He felt like a foreigner with the locals, like the Hawleys and the Bennets.

And, the *city people*, they were something else again. If the locals were unfamiliar to him, he damn well knew the *city people*, the people who came here for the summer. He had them in his cab all year. Men in suits, men who'd never make it in his neighborhood, couldn't play ball for shit, couldn't protect themselves either. Guys who now had the upper hand in life talked down to him, treated him like he was nothing. People like me peak too early, he thought. The stickball champs, the sandlot heroes who — if they didn't end up in jail or on the hustle — turn out to be bus drivers or mailmen.

Broads from the city, they were a piece of work. Spoiled, dissatisfied women, looking for kicks, who spent their husbands' money, expected extra service, and were an out bet to stiff you on the tip. They didn't give a shit about no one.

Stepping over the washed-up seaweed, Joe found another rock. He tried again. It didn't skim the second time either. Strike two. This place was not for him. Joe gave a deep sigh. All in all, he'd gone to sleep with a young athlete in a second-rate sport who didn't know the score, and had awakened 12 years later next to a stranger, an independent minded intellectual who worried about time and space and men who fell off roofs.

"Shit," he said aloud.

"Hi," said a woman's voice from behind. "Great day, isn't it?"

Joe looked back, taken by surprise.

"Finally a clear day. A great day to get out early, isn't it?"

"If that's what you like," Joe replied, automatically. He thought the woman would pass, and waited to let it happen. But she stopped near him as if she expected a conversation. He glanced down the stretch of beach. She was alone. His age, he thought, maybe younger. He'd make her about 37, 38, in decent shape. "That's a nice tan you have." He had no idea why he said it.

"I work hard at it. You're Sally's guy aren't you?"

Now he was confused.

"Jack Bennet's my broker, too," she explained.

"Am I supposed to know you?" Joe asked.

"Of me," she said. "I'm the gal who paid for the mattress."

That got his attention.

"Last year at the Hawley house. I'm the tenant who lent you the house. Remember that little episode? Everyone else does. At least everyone that counts. The scandal of the off-season. Tells you how boring *our* lives are." She hooked her two fingers together in that kids' time-out gesture. "*Finns*," she said. "Okay? Forgotten.

Not another word. Actually you guys provided a story that lasted through an otherwise very dull winter in New York. I'm Nancy Ryner. Without your wife I never would have passed that course."

"Joe Singer," he said. "You're the classmate? The one that gave us the rental house?" he asked, still off balance, buying time.

"That's me. But I had no idea how many 'us' turned out to mean. What was your wife thinking of? A stunt like that."

"You don't know Sally."

"Well, I know she helped me. I was in the throes of a joint venture, a kind of partnership for investments --"

"I know what a joint venture is," cut in Joe.

"Of course you do," said Nancy Ryner, smoothly. "But my partner, the numbers person, my so-called friend didn't show up for the course. I was stuck," she explained. "Tough to be stuck, don't you think?"

"I have no idea," Joe said. "I wish you'd given up. It would have saved us all a lot of trouble," said Joe. "A lot of trouble," he said almost inaudibly.

"I don't give up that easily. And I love new experiences. I don't have an inkling as to why your wife agreed to help. You know, with the children . . . with you . . . a husband, that is." She was shaking her head, as if perplexed at something that didn't make sense to her. "I'm not sure I would have done the same."

There's a tip-off. Joe smiled, deciding he'd just gotten a real glimpse of this woman. Stingy with gratitude. He'd expected more from someone in distress rescued by a stranger.

Nancy went on. "But she must have her reasons. Everyone does."

"Sally? She made herself a promise. And she takes promises seriously. A friend once helped her out and paid a price for it. So this is like a . . ." Joe fought for the word, "like a penance. That's what she calls it. My wife is very Catholic, you see. She believes in sin."

"Well, whatever. I benefited." She gave a little skip. "Actually I'm a sculptress. Don't be impressed," she held up her right hand as if taking an oath. "My husband still supports me. He was against this joint venture bit. It's too independent for him, but don't feel sorry for him, because he can afford me."

Joe gave a laugh. "At least you're honest."

"Sometimes," she smiled, even teeth glowing in her bronzed face. "Don't count on it."

"Count on it? Are you kidding?" he said, finally feeling comfortable. Count on it. Hah!"

"Lot of seaweed this morning . . . and jellyfish," she said, walking apace with him, stepping over tangled green strands strewn haphazardly on the shoreline. "Much cleaner at the ocean. It's supposed to be very calm today." She pulled in front of him, with a small skip, turning to face him, walking backward, smiling.

She was wearing cutoffs slung low on her hips. He noticed her muscular thighs. He couldn't help it. There was nothing subtle about her. Her shorts were so high, so tight around her crotch, she was either on the make or a tease. Her tan was spectacular, the kind you worked for.

"How do you like the Bennet house, the bay?" she asked looking directly at him. She didn't wait for him to answer. "I saw you at asparagus beach yesterday afternoon, after the shower, without your wife. I knew you were Sally's husband."

"Asparagus what?"

"That's what locals call the beach in Amagansett where the singles go. It's really the Coast Guard beach. They had a station there during the war."

"Singles, huh? What were you doing there, then?" Joe asked, looking straight at her platinum wedding band.

"You're not the only one who likes to watch and who doesn't need permission," Nancy said, emphasizing her independence. Joe liked that. He decided not to ask about the name *asparagus*.

"How did you know who I was?"

"The taxicab. Hard to be a mystery in East Hampton," she said, smiling. "We're renting nearer the ocean this year. You should try the ocean today, too. No jellyfish there. Occasionally, sharks . . . man-eaters, but that's only if you're lucky!" She gave a laugh and picked up a smooth pebble, skimming the water perfectly. "It would be too bad if you missed the ocean today. You have to grab calm ocean days when you can." Playfully, she did an about-face once more, and walked astride, matching Joe's footsteps. Her arm brushed his as they walked. She said, "You're awfully quiet."

"I'm listening," Joe said. "You seem to know a lot about oceans."

They walked silently together for several minutes in the sun's warmth as it dissolved the last of the white gray mist, their arms brushing in that accidental way.

"Well, do you want me to show you, Mr. Joe Singer?" said Nancy Ryner, in a soft, husky voice. She said his name easily, as if they understood each other.

"Show me what?" Joe said, looking straight at her. She didn't look away. He thought she was working very hard at this game. A little too hard.

"The ocean," she said. "Dick sleeps in on Sundays. We could go to the ocean in my car."

"Dick?"

"My husband. He couldn't care less," she smiled a secret smile before finishing her sentence, ". . . about the ocean, that is. However, he hated paying for the mattress."

Joe put his hand up like a traffic cop.

"Oops," she exclaimed. "I promised not to mention it. But, I warned you not to trust me."

Joe paused. He stopped walking, bent down to take a handful of pebbles. Crouching low, he held them, rubbing them between his fingers. Then he picked up a flat rock. "Three strikes you're out, Singer."

"I beg your pardon," she said.

"Nothing," Joe replied, hurling the stone. It skimmed four times before disappearing. "Well?" asked Nancy Ryner, shrugging, lips pursed, half smiling, her hips thrust out, a challenge. "There's a certain symmetry of use, of exchange here, yes? A weekend husband. A weekend house. You are a weekend husband, aren't you?"

He turned to face her, sizing her up for the second time. A capable bitch in heat. "Is this how you thank people who help you?" he asked, his gaze steady.

"I gave the house for that," she said easily. "It was only a three-credit course, after all," she added, giving a laugh. "Well, are you game?"

He shrugged, blowing staccato sounds of air out of his mouth. Brushing sand from his hands, he made his decision. Right here in Sally's paradise.

He said, "Why not? Why fucking not!"

In the shelter of the moving car, Joe's skillful fingers found her wetness in seconds. She was driving and pulling at his zipper to free the bulge beneath it. Off Amagansett-Springs Road onto Town Lane, parking in the woods at Stony Hill, they came together in the back of the red Volvo less than an hour after they'd met.

It crossed his mind, before he went down on her, that this was adultery.

It was only the beginning.

10
Beach Reports

"This summer will be some wet," predicted Mrs. MacMullin, handing Sally a brown paper bag at the Country Store. "No relief till August's end, I'll wager. It's like this every few years."

"Are you local, too? Like the Bennets, I mean? Jack Bennet's our broker."

"Not like the Bennets my dear. Next to them we're strangers," said the elderly woman. "We came out of Nova Scotia we did, some 50 years ago, all fishermen and their families. Bunker fishing at Promised Land and trap fishing in Montauk offered an easier life."

"Bunker fishing?"

"That would be menhaden to you folks."

Sally decided to let it alone. She understood milk, Wonder Bread, Yodels, Scotch Tape — things that were in the brown paper bag. Leaving the neighborhood grocery, Sally felt the thin drizzle. She was glad she'd taken Michael's bike rather than walk.

It was only June, but everything was overgrown, wet and green with thick foliage, bushes and trees pushing and shoving each other, competing for the sun's sparse attention, guzzling moisture without restraint. Wet and green meant more mosquitoes, gnats, silverfish, and a particularly annoying screen-proof bug. She didn't like insects, anything that crawled or scampered, in the house with her. They didn't belong there. Wet meant high grass, too. High grass meant ticks.

Last week Ben discovered one tick feeding on another, both

residing in Andy's scalp. Dr. Rowe of the East Hampton Medical Group advised Sally by phone to remove the primary parasite with tweezers, weakening its grip by smothering the blood bloated insect in Vaseline. But it hadn't budged, so she called Schaefer Taxi for a ride to the Medical Group, a one-story building on the Montauk Highway. The doctor put Andy on the gurney, doused ether on the bloodsucker and removed the host and its friend from Andy's head. When Andy screamed, Michael vomited in the hallway. Ben, however, watched the procedure with interest through the half-open door. Sally learned some ticks carried Rocky Mountain Spotted Fever, a fatal disease if not attended.

Damp not only accompanied wet, it survived it. A creeping, felt-like cover of gray-green mildew was growing indoors. She used Clorox, turned the heat up to eighty twice to dry the house out, and flooded herself with 6-12 insect repellent.

To defend against the bug attack, Sally was busy putting Scotch Tape over tears in the screens when she saw them. She didn't know exactly what they were, until she looked closer. That's when she let out a scream, making the bats expand their membraned wings — now they were huge — and leave their perch on an exposed rafter to dive-bomb past her head. She screamed again. The boys ran in as Sally ran out of the house.

"Call the police, Michael. I'm not going back inside till they're gone."

"I don't know the number, Ma."

"Get the operator."

When Michael came out of the house with Andy — Ben wanted to observe the flying mammals, Michael said — he told Sally the police had first laughed, and then, when they heard where they were staying, said they'd call the fire chief.

"They can call the National Guard," Sally declared. "But I'm not going back in till they're gone and I'm sure they don't have relatives with them, too."

The fire chief showed up 20 minutes later. It was Hawley Bennet. A short slender man, at most 30, with boyish Mel Ferrer kind of looks. "That's why they called me, Mrs. Singer," he laughed. "The guys knew the house was mine. Some unwanted guests, I understand."

"Two that I could see. They flew at me. My son Ben is inside, by the way. Is he in danger? He wanted to watch them, if you can believe that. They must have switched babies at the hospital."

"My kind of guy," said Hawley. "You know they *are* harmless."

"Hah! Easy for you to say."

'They devour bugs. That's why I built a bat house in the back yard."

"A what in the back yard?"

"A bat house."

"I'm going to kill Jack Bennet," she said. "Do you know how scared I am?"

"Come in with me, I'll show you how nice these creatures are."

"Are you crazy?"

"Yes, well," Hawley Bennet gave a crooked smile. "Seems you have more to fear from two-legged upright mammals than these fellows, Mrs. Sing—"

"Call me, Sally. And please get them out. And check for more. I beg you." As Hawley Bennet went inside, Sally called out. "Don't mind the house. I know it's a mess. I haven't cleaned up after the weekend." If it weren't for the bats, she would have lain down across railroad tracks before allowing anyone in to see the cluttered jumble, let alone the landlord.

Hawley came out of the house 15 minutes later with the two uninvited guests in his gloved hand. He released them in the woods. Ben was with him.

"Mom, I touched them. Mr. Bennet let me touch the bats," Ben cried.

"I didn't see any others, Sally," Hawley reported. "And I couldn't find any bat droppings in the house. My guess is they came down through the chimney. I shut the damper. Keep it shut. I'll put a screen on the chimney for you." When he saw her face he added, "today."

"Thank you so much. Can I make you some coffee? Lunch? Breakfast? I am so grateful."

"That would be nice," he said.

Over coffee and grilled cheese sandwiches, Sally learned that he hadn't returned home to Bonac — what the locals called East Hampton — after college. He'd gone to New York, lived in the Village, and worked in the theater, stage design. Missing home, he returned somewhat richer and was now a pricey furniture maker for people from away, that is, for non-Bonackers. He built several rental houses, too. "I build them; Jack rents them." He asked Sally if she liked his town.

"I love it here," she said. "I haven't seen too much. Except for Montauk, last September."

"Yes, I heard," he winked and gave a friendly smile. "Who christened the—"

"I can't tell," said Sally. "Family secret."

"Fair enough! I'm going to have Josephine call you, by the way."

"Josephine?"

"She cleans my rental houses."

"Yes, but I don't think—"

"It's included in the rental price, Miss Sally."

"Jack never mentioned it," she said. "Then again he didn't mention the bat house either."

"She'll give you a call. Come when you're not around, so as not to intrude."

"You're not impressed with my housekeeping, are you?"

"To tell you the truth, it scares the heck out of me."

Sally laughed. The pizza boxes from the weekend were still on the counter, with the leftover crusts, and some smattering of cheese and tomatoes. Newspapers were everywhere. Dishes were in the sink with coffee grounds. The boys' toy soldiers were strewn around the living room floor. Clothing of various sizes hung from the door-knobs. Sand was underfoot, as were rainwear, thongs, and sneakers. It was a mess. And he hadn't seen the bedrooms. She'd had two restless nights that weekend. She and Joe fought on Saturday. And he behaved strangely, leaving early on Sunday. The house was a reflection of her state of mind. Confused and uneasy.

"I never did thank you for the sachet. My grandmother used lilac."

"My pleasure, Miss Sally."

"May I ask why you're calling me Miss Sally?"

"Because, I like you," he said, sheepishly.

"Well, you've been very kind, the bats, the house cleaning. I'll give you high marks as a landlord." She noticed the day had cleared since the morning drizzle.

"I can give you a rundown on the beach scenes, if you'd like, so you'll know your way around."

"Sure, but I'd love to go down to the bay. Get some sun before it rains again. With it raining all the time, you have to grab opportunities when you can. Like to join us?"

"Please do, Mr. Bennet," said Ben, who had evidently found a hero — a bat man, and a fire chief. He hadn't left Hawley Bennet's side.

"I'd like to show Ben the bat house first."

At the beach, Sally parked them off to the side, away from the handful of women and children vacationers. "I treasure my privacy," she explained to Bennet.

"I can relate to that," he said. He helped Sally spread the beach towel, then hunkered down on the warm sand. "Okay, now the tour. Barnes Landing you can see for yourself. During the week, women are carefree girls at Barnes Landing. The harem without the sultan. No responsibilities, hired nannies, and absentee husbands. That changes on Friday when the Long Island Railroad delivers the husbands to them, by express, a little juiced from the Club Car. Scene changes to ocean beaches for the weekend. First of all, most wives draw the line at asparagus beach. A singles' beach, mostly. Too much competition there."

"Asparagus beach?"

"The old Coast Guard beach in 'Gansett, Amagansett to you, my dear. A U-boat dropped off spies in 'Gansett one night during World War II, you know."

"A Nazi submarine? Here?" Sally's security blanket was shredding.

"A Coast Guardsman name of Cullen spotted the spies who claimed they were beached fishermen. Wrong! He knew there was no night fishing in wartime. They gave him $300 to forget their faces. Unarmed, Cullen took the money and reported the incident. Meanwhile, Ira Baker at the railroad station was suspicious. He stopped the men trying to board a train, then he let them go. Our defense was very civil, you see. Two weeks later, their capture was announced by the F.B.I. Suitcases of explosives and cash were found buried on the 'Gansett beach."

"Did Cullen return the $300?"

"I don't know, actually. Never thought about it."

The story was unsettling. "Nazis in Amagansett! Is it safe anywhere?"

"Not at asparagus beach," Hawley said, with a broad grin. "Hunting grounds for upscale city folks approaching middle age, all of them rutting, uhh, in season. They share large rental houses for the summer. I let out one down in the cranberry dunes, a simple A-frame. I'm not sure anyone gets sleep in that house. Though the beach has enough room for a high school, they stand together in bunches, like asparagus.

"There's a gay beach, too, closer to the village, Two Mile Hollow. You'll find successful, accomplished, well-kept men of all ages, pun intended. They're in season as well. Always are. They stay off to the side, their own private enclave. They have their own clubs, too."

"Clubs?"

"The gays don't want to be with straights any more than heterosexuals want to be with them. They open their club doors to straights in the interest of not being raided by our tight-assed cops — their terminology. One of the clubs, the Millstone, legitimizes itself every summer Saturday night by welcoming straights. Great dancing. Do you dance?"

"As if my life depended on it."

"Me too," he confided. "We should go to the Millstone this summer. I'd love to take you and Joe. I ran into him at the IGA last weekend. He wanted to know who handled the local action. There's bingo at St. Andrews in the Harbor on Tuesday nights if you want action," I told him. "That's such a New York kind of question. I felt I was back in Greenwich Village."

"What beach do local people go to?" Sally asked, wanting to shift the conversation. She couldn't understand why Joe would ever ask that question in this town.

"Most local folks don't get the chance to see the beach during the season. They're too busy making the summer colony happy. On the bay, they favor Maidstone Beach off Three Mile Harbor, not to be confused with the exclusive Maidstone Club on the ocean. For the ocean, they go to Main Beach in the village because they have their own lockers and there's refreshments."

"Is it mined for Jews?"

"I beg your pardon?"

"The club. Is it restricted, Hawley? I got the impression it was."

"The old summer colony beaches and plays there. I caddied there when I was in high school. My grandmother did laundry for the members. They're invisible in a way, traveling between the club and their sprawling summer cottages, food delivered by Dreesen's, booze by Kelly's, everything prepared by servants. That's why they have old kitchens, from the twenties and thirties. They never use them; the help has to manage."

"Is it restricted?" She noticed the same kind of tone Jack Bennet had when talking about these people. Locals seemed to hold them in awe.

"The club's bylaws are preferential to Daughters of the American Revolution families and to children of present members. Hard for any ethnics to beat those criteria. It doesn't mean they're anti-Semites. The members like to be with their own kind."

"That's how it starts," Sally said, wandering back to those scenes of young blonde soldiers in helmets dragging aged dark-haired men in yarmulkes by their beards along cobblestone streets.

"I'm your guide, not the judge. I try not to judge."

"That's an easy out. At least you didn't write the bylaws, did you?"

"Let's forget the club. The ocean beach of choice for city people, *the renters,* is Indian Wells in Amagansett. The city shrinks keep to themselves off to a side of the beach, like the gays at Two Mile Hollow. They're not friendly at all, never smile at you. Bad for business, I guess."

Sally had to laugh. She was toying with her ring, sliding it up and down her finger. The sky had turned sharp blue. The salt air, rinsed from the morning shower, had that fresh after-rain fragrance. Sally breathed deeply, loving the air's taste. The bay was too cold for swimming. The boys were off playing Frisbee.

"Your turn. Do you need to talk to someone? You seem down."

"Why do you say that?"

"You're easy to read."

"Well, I'll have to do something about that, won't I?" She gave a small smile. Was he presumptuous? It was easy to forget he was only her landlord, after all.

It was as if Hawley Bennet read her mind. "Summer connections are like shipboard romances. Anyway, we locals are so used to knowing everything about everybody in town, nothing is taken seriously. Can't help knowing when everyone's related one way or another. "

"Jack Bennet said something like that. He said there were no secrets in a small town."

"There certainly aren't," Hawley agreed, with that Mel Ferrer vulnerability washing across his face. "Jack wants to write a book about it all. He writes well."

"Then why is he selling real estate?"

"People have to eat, put bread on the table, Sally. Anyway, folks say I'm a great listener."

Sally sighed. "Yes, well, I'm having a hard time dealing with my grandmother's death."

"So it's mourning you're into, coping with the emptiness," he commiserated. "With a big family, we see a lot of death. You, too? Big family?"

"Nope. Not your concept of family, I'm afraid."

Grandma was her family, she thought, making her recall her mother's long ago long-distance conversations. *"Mike's on the lam, again, Mama, please come. I have no money. I've got to work."* Her mother would plead from wherever they were at the time. She recalled her own confusion. *Lamb on the lam? What did it mean?* Grandma always came to the rescue, arriving on a Greyhound bus with her bag of food for the trip because she was kosher.

"I come from a very different place than you, Hawley."

"Don't let beautiful country fool you, Miss Sally. We have our share." He sounded dead serious for the first time that afternoon. "Your grandmother was all?"

"My friend Doug, he's like a brother, I suppose. My mother's in Florida. When we were asked to leave last year, Grandma was asked to leave, too. Mother was hoping to remarry and wanted to put Grandma in a home." She got up, straightening the beach towel to hide her tears.

"You're going to bury a thong," he pointed out, as Sally was about to cover a blue rubber heel surfacing from the sand with the blanket. "So what happened?"

"I told my mother no way. Grandma, all 57 inches, 86 pounds of her, was shipped North to us."

"I see. Your grandmother died with *you* then."

"My mother never came up," said Sally, voice quivering, face tight with anger. "Grandma did so much for her, she raised me for her, and my mother never showed."

"All of us disappoint our families or are disappointed by them one way or another."

"I wasn't prepared. It was so good to have her with us. Graduate school was lenient. I wangled permission for an honors tutorial with a visiting professor from Oxford. I worked at home so she was never alone. She died at 92 and I still wasn't prepared."

"Well," said Hawley. "I guess—"

"What is that awful smell?" Sally asked, sniffing. The air had suddenly turned rotten.

"Oh that! A southwest wind," Hawley Bennet answered, "from our fish factory in Promised Land. Just east of us on the bay. My tour didn't cover that."

"I didn't hear about it when I rented the house, either," she joked, because it was gone as quickly as it came. "Just like my father," she mumbled.

"What's that?"

"Noth—"

"My God," Bennet exclaimed, looking up the beach away from Promised Land. He jumped to his feet. "Take a look at that, Miss Sally! Hurry! You'll miss it."

Down the beach, a woman was paddling a dinghy toward shore. There was a small yacht, seaward. A uniformed nanny and a boy met her at the water's edge. She embraced the boy as if she had returned from a long journey. Then she paddled back to the waiting boat. It was done in a way to attract attention.

"You'd think she sailed from Portugal, when she really last saw him an hour ago after lunch," he quipped. "How's that for a show?"

"Is that the mother?" asked Sally.

"They rent everything. That *ship*, too," informed a woman's voice from behind. "She almost drowned last summer with this stunt. Conspicuous consumption if I ever saw it."

Sally thought the voice she heard sounded familiar, but Hawley Bennet had her attention.

"A tough act to follow," he said, smiling. Brushing sand from his jeans, it was clear the visit was over. "Remember the Millstone. I'll screen the chimney. Watch the outdoor lights. Bugs go to light. Bats go to bugs." With that, he glided down the beach toward the parking lot.

"Is this your ring?" asked the voice from behind. "Wouldn't want to lose it, would you?"

Sally turned. No wonder the voice sounded familiar. It belonged to the woman who couldn't deal with mathematical logic in the decision theory course, the same woman whose East Hampton rental they used for a few hours last September. It belonged to Nancy Ryner.

11
A Sunny Day Friend

"**I** know nothing about raising kids, Sally," said Nancy Ryner in the car driving to the beach. "but when I came to pick you up, I swear he was reading *The Racing Form.*"

"Probably an old one," said Sally. "I'm sure they don't sell it at MacMullins."

"Old or new, what's the difference? He's a kid, not a jockey."

"I'm not sure jocks read that. Gamblers and touts do. My father did," she whispered so the boys wouldn't hear. "Michael picks it up from Joe. On weekends they handicap together."

"Quality time," said Nancy, sarcastically. "He's the one who should take decision theory if he's going to spend his life betting on horses."

Sally wasn't sure if Ryner meant Michael or Joe. "They don't bet. They pick horses. Then see what happens. It's a game."

"Why don't they pick stocks?" asked Nancy.

"I said that, too," she sighed, seeing Michael as Sky Masterson and Sister Sarah's child. "Look, I'm not happy with it. Let's forget it. What beach are we going to today?"

Since they had met at Barnes Landing, Sally and Nancy saw each other often, though Nancy traveled to the city regularly. That first day they met at the beach, learning that Nancy was going into New York, Sally suggested she call Joe. "My husband drives out Friday evenings. You could hook up with him." It was her penance for the mattress.

Sally spoke to Joe that same night. "We're getting someone to clean the house," she said, not mentioning the bats. "Free! Included in the rental price. That should make you happy. I bet you can't guess who I met at the beach today?"

"Jack Bennet."

"No, not Jack Bennet, my decision theory classmate, the woman that lent us the Hawley house last September, Nancy Ryner. She was very friendly, considering. Anyway, she's going into the city; expect a phone call from her for a lift this weekend."

"How did that come about?"

"They're renting here again, Joe. She didn't make a big deal about last year. I know she had to pay for the mattress, so I suggested the ride. Think of it as company on a long trip."

"It's not smart to offer your husband's services to another woman."

"It depends on the husband and it depends on the woman." Her mind detoured. It occurred to Sally that *character* might be another variable. Was that relevant to her adultery problem? Intent, purpose, accident, result and character — all/some/none of the above?

Joe did bring Nancy Ryner out that weekend and others when their schedules coincided.

The rest of the time, Nancy sought Sally out. Like today, Nancy said they were going to Louse Point, a fragile sand spit dividing Accabonac Harbor and Gardiner's Bay, with high beach grass, weaving gulls and horizon views of water, Hawley Bennet told her. He also said that a long time ago, East Hampton schoolchildren were deloused there. Now, summer people, especially artists, writers, and minor and major celebrities, had their cocktail hour there as the sun went down.

Nancy Ryner said it was her favorite bay beach.

It was flattering, being singled out by Nancy Ryner, though unsettling. Ryner seemed to know everybody, but chose her. There seemed to be something irregular Sally couldn't put her finger on. Nevertheless, Nancy was smart, attentive, polite to the boys, and would laugh at Sally's jokes. She taught her backgammon, which they played on a miniature magnetic board on the large Ryner beach blanket. The sculptress spoke a great deal about social wrongs and summer gossip while tanning herself, sun reflector resting on the planes of her chest like a tinfoil shelf. She mentioned, in a disinterested way, that her husband was a woman chaser with lots of money.

"Everyone's coming out soon. The important people," she told Sally, once they were settled on the harbor side of Louse Point. "Only a few more weeks to August. "

"August?" asked Sally.

"August is big. The shrinks are on holiday. And everyone follows their shrink to the Hamptons."

"So watch out for neurotics in August?" Sally quipped.

"Only celebrated ones," Ryner shot back.

The sun was approaching its noonday high. Nancy lazily shifted her body toward it, the zipper of her denim cutoffs open, letting the rays drift below her navel. "Did you get the cleaning woman for me, Sally?"

"Would you believe I've never met her? Her name's Josephine. We call her the phantom. We talk on the phone, all business. She cleans when I'm not there. Makes sense."

"Did you ask her when you spoke to her, then?"

"No. Hawley said I was the last house she'd take on, that she was a very busy lady."

"They're so unreliable out here." Nancy shifted her body again.
"And expensive."

"Not Josephine. Hawley says she's reasonable, fair."

"Blacks are always exploited."

"I don't think she's Black."

"How do you know? You've never seen her." Nancy's tone
changed to argument.

"She doesn't sound Black," Sally sallied.

"What's 'sound black' supposed to mean?" said Nancy, in her
most social conscious way.

"Oh, God, don't start that. Black was your assumption in the
first place. Because she cleaned houses. Remember? Talk about
suppressed premises."

"I'd rather talk about repressed women," Nancy bantered, end-
ing social consciousness for the moment.

Sally was relieved. She pulled out the thermos of lemonade
and poured herself some in a paper cup. "I have a secret, Nancy.
You're the first to know. Do you want to know?"

"You're going to tell me. What's the difference?"

"I've been invited to Oxford, Nancy. Invited to Oxford to complete my doctorate there."

"Are you kidding? To Oxford? How did that happen?" Nancy
asked, as if she couldn't imagine it. There was a stingy tightness to
her voice.

"I did a tutorial last year with a visiting professor. He has a
chair at All Souls and he invited me." Sally, still all smiles, hugged
her knees, though she'd expected more from the telling.

"You'd leave Joe and the children?" Nancy asked, her voice
carrying a frown.

"Oh no! They'd come, too. I've been lining up grants, funding. We could sublet our apartment to Columbia students. With the direction the humanities are going in higher education, I'll need that kind of cachet to get a post. Definitely a buyers' market for philosophy professors. And it would be the closest thing to being presented at court for the boys, spending a few months at school in England."

"But what will Joe say about all this?"

"I think I have to sell it to him. Like I sold him East Hampton. Look how happy he is now! Imagine me at Oxford. Working on Aristotle's concept of *Akrasia.*"

"His what?"

"*Akrasia.* Moral weakness," Sally explained. "Why people know what's right and do what's wrong. Socrates and Plato thought it impossible — that everyone aims at the good, but they are mistaken about what *is* good. Aristotle has a more practical view of human nature. There's remorse, there's guilt, but they do it anyway. It fascinates me and it's a wide open topic."

"No wonder! Hits too close to home for most people. Moral weakness, remorse, guilt, " scoffed Nancy, as if she didn't want any part of that or Oxford for that matter. "You haven't been buying grapes, have you?"

"I buy grapes. I love them."

"I knew it! How could you?" Nancy said indignantly, telling Sally about the grape boycott in California, the rights of migrant workers and a hero named Chavez. "We have to support them."

"I had no idea they were so meaningful."

"You must have read about it, Sally. I mean everyone knows about the grape boycott."

"Yes, well, I try not to read the papers. It's mostly bad news I can't do anything about."

"Irresponsible, the worst kind of denial," Nancy said sharply.

"Thoreau never read the papers, called them gossip sheets," Sally pointed out.

"Paine."

"What?"

"It was Paine, Sally, not Thoreau."

"Do you want to bet?"

"I don't bet, I invest," said Nancy smartly. "Anyway, you may be right. Look, for Chrissake, do me a favor. Give up grapes. And read *The Times*."

"The grapes I can do," Sally conceded, gesturing to Michael to swim closer to shore.

"I know how *I* would run this town if I lived here," Ryner said, having buried Oxford and finished with grapes. "Have you thought about what women make in this town, Sally? Or laborers for that matter?

"Nope. That's another thing I can't do anything about. Now, it's my turn, Nancy," Sally said, packing sand around her ankles. "Think about this. When terrifyingly evil events occur side by side with everyday events, don't you find it scary? When you really think about it, don't you find it unthinkable — that they can be going on in the same world at the same time?"

"That *what* can be going on?" Nancy shifted again, repositioning the reflector.

"These two kinds of events. Don't they seem mutually exclusive? Like Auschwitz and some Polish kid nearby doing homework and the coffee boiling over. Yet we say they're happening at the same time."

Nancy sat straight up, upsetting the tinfoil shield. "What on earth are you talking about, Sally? That kind of nonsense makes me dizzy."

"Joe says that." Disappointed, Sally could see there'd be no provocative conversation.

"Sally, it's simple. You make it complicated. I can be sitting here telling you about real grievances, about the sweat and blood of workers. And on the blanket over there women can be discussing what they're wearing this weekend to Chez Labbat's. The same time. Different place. What's the problem?"

"But that's not the same," Sally objected.

"Yes it is," Nancy insisted. "It's just a question of degree that seems to whack you out." With that she dismissed Sally's topic, continuing her own. "What do women make in this town? Well, I can tell you they're exploited, 100 miles from New York and they aren't even organized. Employees here don't have unions. Can you believe it?"

Sally shrugged her shoulders. "What would you do if you knew tomorrow was the end of the world ?" she tried again.

"For God sakes, Sally."

"I know what I'd do. I'd kill myself."

"You're definitely weird." Ryner shook her head. "And that adultery nonsense, for God sake!"

"Did you think about it? Remember — intent, results, accident, purpose, guilt, character?"

"I thought about it. Did they come?" Nancy burst out laughing.

Sally joined in. She felt giddy. Maybe this woman was okay after all.

Gasping for breath, Sally signaled the boys to come to shore. She made a note in her head to get the boys new swimsuits, particularly Ben, his cutoff jeans were torn and threadbare.

12
The Natural

"Tell Nancy to mind her own goddamn business. Why are you so close with her anyway?" asked Joe.

"Anyone would wonder why an 11-year-old reads the racing form," said Sally.

"He's almost 12."

"Joe, I'm serious. I don't feel right about this. I've told Michael several times. You said you liked Nancy when you met her. I had the reservations."

"Michael's not her affair," he said grimly. "Handicapping's a game and he's good at it. He's got a natural feel for odds. A bit too cocky, but I swear he knows more than I do sometimes. I've bet some of his picks. And," he added, "I don't care what these people think out here."

"Is that why you asked Hawley Bennet for a bookmaker? To let people know you didn't care?"

"I don't come out here weekends to argue with you." He got up from the table. "I'm going for a ride."

It was like her father all over again. Joe was doing the dreaded "walking out."

One more word about the money, Beatrice, and I'm walking right out. Sallylamb knew Grandma would be coming soon.

Except now, Grandma was dead.

There was something else. Something hidden. Though she expressed dismay to Michael about his inappropriate interest, there was a secret place in her that was proud. *Yes, proud.* It made him so familiar in a special way. And she was drawn to him because of it.

Did Michael discern that when she said no, there was some yes in it?

13

Sit for Me

Sally launched the boat with Nancy in it, then easily lifted herself aboard. When they began to row together, Sally's side was stronger. They spun around.

"Adjust, adjust," cried Nancy. "I'm getting dizzy."

They returned to Louse Point the following week because Nancy arranged to use a renovated fisherman's cottage on Accabonac Harbor, a friend's summer rental for which he paid a pricey four grand. It was too small for more than one person, but it worked fine as a comfort station. The refrigerator was a convenience, too, allowing them to spend the day. They were in the tenant's rowboat, spinning around, Sally consumed with laughter.

"You're rowing too hard, adjust," said Nancy, starting to laugh, too.

"We're going and staying at the same time. An anomaly," she said, maintaining the imbalance despite Nancy's pleas.

Fishermen in a boat farther out stopped to watch. "Need some help?"

Nancy laughed harder, holding her head against her oar.

As the boat pulled closer, Sally realized they weren't fishermen at all. They were men fishing. Jack Bennet and Hawley. She was aware the top of her white handkerchief bikini was traveling up with each stroke and that Jack Bennet was following its journey.

"Oh shit, Joe would kill me if he were here," she said, pulling it down over the whiteness.

"Forget, Joe. I wet my pants," said Nancy, still laughing. "Send them away, please. I don't want them to see me. And stop the spinning. I'm going to vomit, Sally."

Sally stood up in the boat, arms akimbo, seeking balance. Bennet's smile broadened. She checked the bottom of the bikini. It was in place. "Good fishing?" she said, inanely.

"Want some eels or snappers?" he asked, pointing to the catch in a wooden fish box.

"Join us tonight. Sally," invited Hawley. "We're jacklighting. Bring your flashlight. We'll supply the crab net."

"Thanks, but we have to go," said Sally, waving them off, picking up the oars and turning the boat landward.

"Nice seeing you," said Bennet. The smile remained on his face.

Nancy slid out of her cutoffs, rinsing them in the salt water.

"You'll never get them back on."

"Watch me," Nancy said, rolling over the top of the boat. "If we're both wet it's easy."

"Have you done this before?" asked Sally, as Nancy, fully clothed, lifted herself back into the boat.

When they reached shallow waters, Sally pulled the oars into their locks, settling them crisscross on the boat's bottom. Climbing out, Sally said, "Did you know that was Jack Bennet?"

"Of course not. Did you see him sizing you up? Mr. Cool, looking on as if he were assessing a property. I have an idea. Let's stop by my studio before I take you back to Barnes Landing. I'll show you my work."

"Your work, Nancy?"

"I'd like to convince you to sit for me."

Sally was surprised. "I don't think so. Where would I find the

time? Besides, why not sculpt Joe? He's muscular, good defini-
tion—"

"I'm asking you."

"I'll think about it," Sally said vaguely, bending over to brush
off the seaweed.

"Will you get my things, Sally? I'll tidy up inside."

Walking toward the point, she hailed the boys, one by one. As
they were toweling off, Andy said. "Ben, put back that shell you
lifted from the man's house. There's a million of them on the beach.
Why do you do have to take that one?"

Michael laughed. "Leave him alone. It's just a shell."

"Don't encourage him, Michael," droned Sally, as if she'd said
it a thousand times. "One day he'll lift something that has value
and it won't be funny."

"It's not funny now," said Andy.

Back at the fisherman's cottage, Sally took the key from the
nail on the side of the house and returned the seashell which had
traces of ash along the inside.

"Let's go," Nancy said, impatiently. "I want you to see the studio."

They drove south toward the ocean with scarcely a word. When
they reached Spring Close Highway, Nancy pulled the red Volvo
into a narrow driveway.

The Ryner rental was larger and more fashionable than the
Hawley house they had rented a year earlier. Dick Ryner, a writer
with a reputation for chasing women, had hit it big, selling a screenplay to a major film studio on the coast. The rear boundaries of the
four-acre property fanned out, belying its narrow frontage on the
road. A guest house at the back served as the homeowners' residence — a Town Trustee and his wife who worked in Town Hall,

the source of Nancy's union grievances. Their children stayed with grandparents at the family's summer camp on Three Mile Harbor.

Hawley had explained to Sally that many old families had these minimal but comfortable unheated cabins on the water in town. "No need to leave Bonac," he said.

There was an old barn on the property, too. Nancy used it as a studio. The main house, a large, clapboard Victorian with a wide wraparound porch, was too big for two people, so many nooks, crannies, and unexpected rooms, but the Ryners did a lot of entertaining. Like the ocean's tides, guests flowed in and out all summer. Nancy told Sally it had been on the market briefly for $65,000, but was no longer for sale. They drove past the house to the small shingled barn.

"Wait here," said Sally to the boys. "I'll be right out."

Ben nagged, saying he should be allowed to see the studio because he was the artistic child, as usual without much conviction, but Sally was firm. She had the impression Nancy was not keen on their traipsing around sculptures. Once inside, Sally was glad she'd left the boys in the car. Lined up on shelves and pedestals were more than a dozen nude and headless sculptures of women, uncast, featuring breasts. All kinds.

"Busts of busts, I call them," bragged Nancy. "Like fingerprints, aren't they? Each one so different."

Sally's attention was caught by one particular work, a sculpture whose budding breasts on the narrowest of frames looked pre-pubescent. She recognized those breasts, remembered teasing the girl who owned them at high school, remembered trying to soothe her by saying, without conviction, "Less can be more . . . at times."

"That's a friend of mine," informed Nancy. "As a matter of fact, my joint venture lady, the one that missed the class we took.

We were going to make millions together."

"Liz Slavka."

Nancy's mouth fell open. Gaping, she said, "How could you know?"

"We graduated from high school together. I introduced her to her husband."

"To Max? You should be ashamed of yourself. I'm amazed."

"I don't think she's ever forgiven me," said Sally, eyeing the bust. "I haven't seen her for years."

"Yes, you have," Nancy contradicted. "That day at Barnes Landing. Remember that garish scene? That was Liz in the dinghy. Max in the boat."

"Those people calling attention to themselves? Can't be. The Liz I knew was a private person. Her mother named her for the Queen of England — the only Jewish girl I knew who was named Elizabeth — and she was expected to behave accordingly."

"Yes, well, stunts like that are good for Max's business. And if you know her, you know Liz likes money. What a head for figures! I suppose I have one too," Nancy said, grinning at her own pun. She liked to laugh at her own cleverness. "That stunt brings attention to Max, his success, their money, and, as important, the fact that he's capable of doing anything. That's what people want in an attorney."

"I thought they wanted good judgment," Sally argued.

"Trust me. They want an animal."

Sally was still staring at Liz's breasts. "I can't believe you know her. That she would pose for this. She was so embarrassed about her *condition,* as we called it, ruthless girls that we were. How did you get her to do this?"

"Never mind now," said Nancy. "I'd really like to do you, Sally. You must sit for me," she coaxed, casually letting her sculptor's hand graze over Sally's breasts. "They are beautiful, you know."

Was the touching an accident? Or a professional move? Sally didn't care. She had to get out of there. "How long have you known Liz?" Sally asked, moving toward the wooden barn door.

"Did I scare you?" Nancy asked, laughing lightly. "No offense." Then she said, "I've known Liz four, five years, maybe more."

"How's your joint investment business? Did the course help you with risk taking?"

"The investment business is history," Nancy declared, as they walked back to the waiting red Volvo. "Liz is history, too, for me," she mumbled.

On the way to Barnes Landing, Nancy invited Sally and Joe to her birthday bash the first weekend in August. "Liz will be there with the animal. And most of those busts that you saw in the studio. Fun to mix and match? I do want to sculpt you. Think about it."

"Liz," Sally echoed. Liz who was thankful she hadn't been named Margaret Rose. Liz and Max here in the Hamptons. Wait until Doug hears all this.

"Can't you stop them, Sally?" Nancy said, turning toward the children.

The boys, howling with laughter, were practicing farts in the back of the car.

"Stop," said Sally, mechanically. She was tired. It had been quite a day.

"Regrets only on the party," Nancy Ryner reminded her as Sally walked toward the Hawley Bennet beach house. "It's the midsummer special event, you know. My birthday party. I really want you and Joe to come."

14

Happy Birthday

Sounds of Ray Charles crying *Georgia* floated from the ste-
reo, speakers resonating inside the house and out. *Georgia.* It called
to mind that long-ago time in high school when Sally told her friends
Joe Singer made love the way Ray Charles sang. That memory felt
good. Yes, she would have fun tonight, she decided, when Joe turned
into the Ryner driveway, then dropped her off to find a place to
park. She'd have fun even though they'd quarreled earlier.

Sally knew she shouldn't have brought Oxford up before the
party, but she was feeling so elated about financial aid's commitment of funds for Oxford that she blurted it out. She hoped Joe
would be happy. The trip included him. A Singer adventure.

"Do you think I'm a fool? What will I do there?" Joe'd said,
without even acting surprised about Sally's Oxford invitation. "*Your*
feelings, *your* plans — what about me?"

They *were* her feelings. She thought he shared them.

But tonight would be uncluttered with the present. They would
dance, put everything aside, remember old times, old ways of being together. She'd see Liz again, as well. Tolerate Max. Jack Bennet
was expected, too, "without his wife," Nancy emphasized.

Just breathing gave her pleasure tonight. Party time! The full
moon, beaming through broad maple trees, painted shadows on
this unique land formed from detritus of age-old glaciers — rich
farm soil and ocean sand side by side. Whiffs of steaming hors
d'oeuvres, charcoal embers, sweet tobacco, and whiskey seasoned

the crisp salt air. The August night was wonderful. It held a trace of turning, of change, and an eerie sadness for summer fading. There was a *last-night-at-summer-camp* feeling, a promise of September. Hawley Bennet had described the wonderful freshness of September to Sally, "Bonac breathes again, people from away gone until next year."

There was a lack of restraint in that night air. It made Sally feel joyfully reckless. It made her feel like a girl. Where was Joe? She wanted to dance. Dance. Dance. Dance. She walked to one of the standing bars asking for straight Scotch from the man in black slacks and white shirt. Lingering over her drink, feeling friendly to the world, Sally chatted with the bartender.

"I teach history at the high school," he told her, "'just picking up extra bucks for the summer." He must have sensed some surprise in Sally because he added with a grin, pointing to an aproned man bent over the barbecue, "That fellow over there is a member of the school board."

She mused over that kind of egalitarianism as Louis Armstrong chanted *Blueberry Hill*, then scanned the crowd for Joe.

Short-short skirts were in, but Sally felt fine in her jeans and chambray work shirt. The men were strangely of a kind — beards, sideburns, mustaches, deck shoes, white pants, blue blazers, patterned silk handkerchiefs accenting breast pockets. How did wives ever locate their husbands? They all looked alike. So why was Joe so hard to find in his Chinos and black cotton shirt? She didn't see him anywhere.

But she did see Liz Slavka, walking toward her, in black leather tights with a metallic black top that emphasized her extreme thinness. The gaunt frame was familiar. She had changed her hair, her face. Gone were the chestnut curls, replaced by sheared hair skull close. Her powder was lighter than her tan, giving her face an eerie quality.

"Liz?" Sally said tentatively, then hugged her as if she knew it was. "I wasn't sure, your hair, so different. I think you're thinner, if that's possible. I'm so glad to see you. Can you believe we're all in the Hamptons together?"

The woman pulled away. "You look exactly the same, Sally. Good protoplasm, I suppose. I certainly was surprised to learn you were in the Hamptons."

"Why's that?" asked Sally, putting aside her drink, falling into long established patterns with her friend, as if they'd seen each other yesterday.

"Don't be oversensitive. I simply never expected you and Joe to know the Hamptons."

"As a matter of fact we were here briefly last summer. After Labor Day."

Liz hesitated, then said, "Don't tell me you were the people at the Ryner rental? The mattress? The ones who were thrown—"

"Does everybody know?" Sally sighed. "We're heading in the wrong direction, Liz."

"My God, it was you. That story kept Nancy going all winter."

"My grandmother died this year, Liz."

"Oh, Sally. I am sorry. I know how much she meant to you," said Liz, the first hint of their old friendship breaking through.

"How's Adam? Max? We should get Adam and Michael together."

"Max is flourishing. Adam's at Pathfinder."

"But Nancy said he was here with you."

"Pathfinder's a day camp in Montauk," said Liz, as if Sally

ought to know. "I expected you to call once you knew I was here. We have a summer listing." Her angular face was taut, flat, a lean and hungry look that had won her the role of Cassius in their senior show.

"I thought about it, but, we're listed, too. It was you who pulled away, Liz. Anyway, Doug was out here in June."

"I have no interest in Doug."

"Oh, Liz, you're not still nursing Max's grudge."

"He has no regard for Max, vacuuming up Uncle's money—"

"Uncle's not *your* uncle," Sally pointed out, as usual coming to Doug Slavka's defense.

"Nothing's changed, I see. You think you know him, Sally." A deep frown lined her forehead. "He's a bum and a gambler. And he's mean."

"Finns!" Sally said, curling one finger over the other. "Will you listen to us? We're old friends on holiday meeting again. We shouldn't be arguing. I was looking forward to seeing you tonight. Though I'd kind of seen you in Nancy's studio." Sally couldn't resist that one. Liz paled beneath her light tan, giving her powdered skin a grayish pallor. "Where is Nancy, by the way? I haven't seen her all night."

"The last time I saw her she was kissing your husband in the bathroom, as a matter of fact. Very, very kissing."

It occurred to Sally at that moment that her old friend was an unhappy woman. "That won't work, Liz. I trust Joe."

A hand latched on to Sally's elbow. "You don't mind, Liz, if I capture your lovely companion. Let's dance!" said a mustachioed man with sideburns who didn't wait for an answer. "I'm Dick Ryner. The man who's footing the bill."

Before Sally knew it, they were moving to Bunny Berrigan's *I*

Can't Get Started, inching steadily toward one of the buffets and
the woods beyond. Ryner was a smooth dancer, but he leaned into
her a little too much.

"What's your name? You're a new face."

"Sally Singer's her name, darling. My good-looking friend I told
you about," Nancy replied. She and Joe were dancing right behind
them. Nancy was wearing the briefest of low slung mini-skirts sporting a tanned walnut navel and dark, strong thighs.

"I wondered where you were. Happy Birthday," Sally congratu-
lated her, pulling out a folded pennant from her back pocket. *World's
Greatest Tan* was emblazoned across it. She had picked it up at
Marley's Stationery Store on Main Street.

"Thanks," Nancy said, dismissing the token while hanging on
to Joe. With her free hand she tucked the felt cloth into her skirt
like a belly dancer's reward.

"I was looking for you, Joe. We missed *Blueberry Hill* and *Georgia.*" Sally moved away from Dick Ryner.

The four had stopped in front of the buffet. There were wines,
cheese, and large platters of grapes, small seedless greens, large
deep purples, darker greens, plump and juicy black ones the size
of small plums.

"You're serving this?" Sally waved her hand over the spread.
"After all your sermons about grapes and boycotts and inequities.
I haven't had grapes for weeks. Neither have the kids. What hap-
pened to your friend Chavez?"

"You have to learn to separate, Sally."

"Hah!" said Dick Ryner. He invited Joe for a tour of the property.

"Separate?" Sally exclaimed, as the men departed. She plucked
one purple fruit and stuffed it in her mouth. "You must be kidding.

Separate what?"

"Distinguish one thing from another. When you separate, my dear, your beliefs don't bump into each other and cause problems. Like space and time dilemmas."

Sally shook her head, reaching for another grape, the pale green kind with seeds. "You were so convincing! You're dangerous, Nancy. Separating sounds like mere convenience to me." She held back the word *hypocrisy.*

"Whatever, Sally. Have it your way. Thank you for the gift." She took Sally by surprise, kissing her on the mouth. "Look at you, you're blushing."

"Did you kiss my husband like that?" asked Sally. Seeing Nancy's raised eyebrow, Sally explained, "Liz Slavka."

Nancy shrugged. "That woman'll say anything to make trouble. I have to take care of that."

"Did you kiss him?"

"Don't be a child. It's my birthday party! Look around you. It's Liberty Hall here tonight."

Sally saw couples wrapped up in each other, swaying in the shadows to The Mamas and the Papas' *Dedicated to the One I Love.*

"Who are all these people?" Sally asked, moving away from her unanswered question.

"People who count in the Hamptons," bragged Nancy.

"People who count? Count to whom? And what are Joe and I doing here?"

"C'mon, Sally, relax. It's my birthday. Have fun tonight." She kissed Sally again, this time on the cheek, and walked toward the house.

Left to herself, Sally strolled through the crowd picking up pieces of conversation — *An extended expressway would cut our drive time in half — Moses is planning one, I understand — We'd shut down for the winter. Can't miss the season in New York — You'd have equity and it's a potential growth area. — Don't forget the write-offs! Aren't we committed to the Hamptons anyway?* It appeared that renters, *the city people,* were interested in buying second homes. Even the Ryners. Nancy told her last week that she was about to make a deal on a house in Amagansett, using Max Slavka as her attorney. "He'll get me the best situation," she'd said.

Jack Bennet's on a roll, Sally thought, returning his wave. Guests were crowding around the real estate broker. Sally caught a glimpse of Joe, leaning on the rail, alone, on the large back porch. She hurried over.

"Finally," she said. "Are we going to dance?" She started to sway to the rhythms of *Creeque Alley.* Joe picked up the movement, joining her. Arms akimbo, they danced close, without touching, lithe bodies in harmony with the primitive cadence of the music. Sally's eyes were shut tight. In that intimate and casual way they shared, she said, "Liz tried to blindside me, told me you and Nancy were seriously kissing in the *bathroom.* In the bathroom?"

"Liz always liked to pull your chain. Some friend!" Joe said with an abruptness that was piercing. "It's Nancy's birthday. She's kissing everybody. I know how to handle myself with these people, if that's what worries you." He spun around, leaving Sally dancing alone to *Sol 'n Denny working for a penny, tryin' to get a fish on the line.*

Sally's high spirits vaporized. What happened? What was the matter with everybody? A flood of emotions, old and familiar, overwhelmed her.

When she was little her mother and Aunt would be talking in hushed tones, when, at Sally's entrance to a room, the murmuring would stop, replaced by a stern silence and harsh eyes directed at her. She'd guess they'd been talking about her, secrets about her father, about things that connected her to him. A Sallylamb feeling! Everyone talked about her father in whispers and looked away.

Right now, she felt like that little girl — confused, defenseless, alone. Lightheaded, she sat herself down carefully on the deck stairs as Nillson crooned *Maybe.* This expectant August night was a broken promise, the reckless joy twisted into rejection. After a while, she went into the Ryner house.

Joe was in the kitchen with Dick Ryner, Max Slavka and Nancy. There were a group of men arguing Viet Nam. One of the help, a striking woman with Mediterranean features and a chef's apron, was loading the dishwasher. Jack Bennet stood in the doorway, talking real estate.

Sally barely acknowledged Max as she approached the group, an unnecessary liberty for which, somewhere down the line, she knew she'd pay. He was so unlike Doug — taller, shared features, but charmless and vindictive.

"It's been a long time, Sally. So you made it to the Hamptons. Still playing Ping-Pong like my brother?" Max said, volume up, making the sport sound silly and childish.

Sally wanted to say *fuck off*, instead she turned to Joe. "Let's go home. I'm fading." She had to talk louder than she wished over the churning dishwasher.

"I'd like to stay," said Joe, pouring himself a shot from the bottle of Jack Daniels on the counter. "I'm having a great time. Dick was showing me around."

"I want to go home now, Joe," Sally said, wondering if Dick included the studio.

Joe tossed the shot down. Max and Dick seemed to be enjoying the encounter by the smirks on their faces.

"I suppose I can call Schaefer Taxi," Sally said, expecting Joe to object. She could have taken their taxi, but that would have made a scene, abandoning Joe without a car.

Nancy, carrying her drink with her, walked abruptly away from the group. Liz had come into the kitchen and was standing near Jack Bennet. Nancy joined them.

Liz let out a shriek.

Nancy said, holding her now empty glass, "I don't know how that happened! Forgive me, Liz. I'll get a sponge."

"That was no accident," Liz howled, attracting more people into the kitchen, her black metallic top dripping bourbon.

"I said I don't know how that happened. But don't ever upset my guests again." Liz began to cry. "Oh for Christ's sake," said Nancy, as if they were alone in the room. "The only damage is to your ego. Come on, Lizzie. Let me clean you up."

Liz whimpered, but seemed calmer, as Nancy gently sponged down the front of Liz's shiny leather bodice, then used paper towels to dry it off. Then, as if remembering her guests, she quipped, "Forget it folks. It's a personal thing. We do this every year."

"This is a zoo," muttered the woman in the chef's apron, shaking her head as she left the kitchen with a tray of baked clams.

Sally said to Joe. "Do I have to call a taxi? Let's get out of here."

But Joe, a passive smile on his face, was watching Nancy and Liz. There was no objection.

Mustering whatever dignity she had, Sally turned away and walked toward the phone. Dick Ryner, of the fashionable sideburns and reputation for philandering, followed behind her.

"I can take you home, honey."

Joe said, "Okay with me."

Nancy put her arm around Sally's waist. "Do you want me to take you home?"

"I'd love to take Sally home, but I came with my wife," Max said, as if the scene between Nancy and Liz hadn't occurred.

"I'm taking her, Nancy," said Dick, a predatory leer in place. "I insist."

"Sally, I could take Joe later," Nancy suggested. "You can have the car."

"I don't understand what's going on here," Sally burst out.

"Why isn't her husband taking her? He's the driver by trade," chimed in Max Slavka.

"Let it go, Max," Liz said, tersely, staring hard at Nancy.

"Sally's riding with me," Jack Bennet stepped in. There was a momentary hush. "I planned to leave early. Mrs. Bennet's waiting patiently. I'd be happy to take her, Joe."

"I bet you would," said Joe, his tone surly, reaching once more for the Jack Daniels.

Sally thought there'd be trouble. Bennet's muscles tensed, shoulders lifted inside his blue blazer. Sally had seen linebackers make that move. She put her hand lightly on his shoulder. Bennet relaxed. Composing his face, he brushed a patch of dark blond hair from his forehead.

"I'm leaving, Joe."

"Do whatever you want," he muttered, without facing her.

Bennet took Sally by the arm and steered her out of the house. She heard Max chuckle, "Trouble in paradise, it seems."

She was about to turn around and engage the man who once wanted her to dump a match at the Nationals when Bennet held her more firmly, whispering, "Let it go, Sally. He's an asshole."

15
Accidents

They walked together to Jack's blue Ford station wagon parked in the back near Nancy's studio.

That studio! Sally remembered the uneasiness she felt in there. She found it hard to believe she'd posed for Nancy. She was ashamed to admit she didn't know how to say no to Nancy's persistent requests. The woman had certainly extended herself for Sally, the trips to the beach, getting Ben to the doctor's when he'd fallen off his bike, shopping for the boys' swimsuits. It wasn't her nakedness that had made Sally feel uncomfortable, but watching Nancy as she molded the wet clay, watching the pleasure of her lingering hands, a caress that didn't want to let go.

"Watch your hands," Bennet warned.

"Hands?" she repeated, confused, as if something were left over from another scene. But he was only holding the car door open for her.

He brushed aside the dark blond patch of wayward hair that slipped onto his forehead, uncovering a deep frown. "That was some scene inside."

Sally nodded in agreement, but she needed to get away from what happened in Nancy Ryner's kitchen. "I'm sorry Mrs. Bennet wasn't here tonight. I would have liked to meet her. You never talk about your wife, Jack. Is Mrs. Bennet a secret?"

"I told you once before, Sally. There are no secrets in a small town."

"So you did," she replied, sighing. "Joe usually doesn't drink so much."

"No need for the safety net. I didn't say he did," Bennet pointed out. "Don't you ever get angry?" he asked. It must have been on his mind because the frown disappeared.

His question took Sally by surprise. She leaned back and thought about it. "How angry?"

"Appropriately angry," he replied, switching on the ignition. He began to weave his way through the herd of cars on the Ryner property.

"I got real angry, when I was seven—"

"When you were what?"

Sally had to smile at her clumsy shift from events of the party to her childhood. "A big kid at school said something bad, went too far. Next thing I was sitting on her, banging her head on the concrete ground of the school yard. I didn't know how I got there. It took five teachers to pull me off that girl."

"What could she have said?"

"She said my dress — my grandmother had just bought it for me with her last two dollars — didn't look right. She said they weren't going to let me sing with the Glee Club that afternoon."

"For that you almost killed her?"

"It was important to me," Sally replied, matter of factly. "My mother had this beautiful voice. I didn't. I was so proud to make the glee club. I never did get to sing. I sat in an empty classroom as punishment. Funny, I didn't feel like crying at all. I felt quiet inside and good. So, to answer your question, I do get angry. Appropriate? That may be a relative term."

"Perhaps you should practice that feeling more often. The getting angry," Bennet suggested, with a grin. "Then you won't have to lean toward murder."

Sally smiled, too. It crossed her mind why anyone so intelligent would ever sell real estate. It was an opinion she didn't know she held. She hugged herself feeling a chill. The disappointing and unwholesome evening returned.

Liz's typical troublemaking. Nancy's childish revenge that seemed to confirm what Liz had told Sally. Most of all, Joe's strange behavior. She felt huge splinters in her chest. She felt humiliated. And that infuriated her. Why should she feel disgraced when it was Joe who behaved badly? It wasn't until they passed Abraham's Path that she was able to speak. She needed something to put aside the turbulent emotions pulling at her. Something of the mind.

"I have a question, Jack. It may not be the kind you're used to, but bear with me."

"Shoot," said Bennet, his charming broker face back on.

She realized who he looked like in her movie star world. It was George Peppard. George Peppard, Rafe, in *Home From the Hill*. Rough good looks with an unruly patch of dark blonde hair. Rafe who'd married a girl carrying a child not his own, but wouldn't consummate the union until *she* asked. A man in control.

He slowed down at the Stony Hill turn off. "Want to ride some? I can take the long way?"

Sally nodded. He seemed to understand she needed time.

He veered to the left where the paved road became country marl. "Stony Hill, one of our lover's lanes a long time ago when most of the weddings in town were shotgun." Bennet laughed as they passed through the Amagansett forest. He dimmed the lights, using the moon to silhouette the tall trees.

"A shooting star," exclaimed Sally. "Did you see it?" She rolled the window down, peering at the dark end of a boundless country sky.

"Better at the end of August," he said. "That's when the stars put on a show for us."

"I love the stars. I think it's God teaching us a lesson. His sense of humor. Our wanting knowledge so bad. As soon as we think we have it all, we find more stars, more galaxies."

"God getting even," Bennet said.

"Why, yes! Exactly. You surprise me, Jack."

"So what was your question you thought you had to warn me about?"

"Yes, well, you see, a man falls off a roof and lands on a married woman and enters her. Is that adultery?"

"Come again?"

"A man falls off a roof. He lands on a married woman. He enters her. Is that adultery?"

"Are you kidding me, Sally? Making fun of this poor country boy?"

"You know I wouldn't do that, Jack. But think about it. Is that adultery?"

They came off the dirt road on Accabonac. Turning up his headlights, Bennet took a right to Old Stone Highway, passing Louse Point Road. When they reached Barnes Hole Road, he hung a left to Windward to the Hawley Bennet beach house and the sleeping Singer children, under Michael's care.

"Sounds like adverse possession to me," he said, pulling into the driveway. Leaving the motor running, he turned to face her, eyes twinkling, an arm thrown comfortably around the back of the seat.

It took Sally a second to realize he was addressing her adultery question. "Adverse possession?"

"Real estate way of taking something without it being given."
He laughed.

"The point of the question is, is it adultery?" She persisted.

"How about an accident?"

"Someone said there are no accidents. But I think that's wrong.
Aristotle believed in accidents. But he meant something without
purpose, that couldn't be explained."

"I know what I mean by accident, Sally. Something that was
never intended." He was treating the question more seriously. "If
the man entered her by accident, it's an accident. Adultery is
serious, has to do with trust. It's something you do, not something
that happens to you."

"Are you saying it's an act not an event?"

"I'm saying adultery's not a technicality. Unless, of course,
the man and the married woman planned it that way," he said,
grinning again. "You know, uhh, a flying whatever. Then it was
adultery."

Sally considered Jack Bennet. Had he passed some Sally Lamb
test? But her attention was wearing thin. Arriving home without
Joe reminded her that Joe hadn't taken her there. Why? All kinds
of doubts surfaced. She wondered how Joe knew the turn into the
Ryner driveway. Confused, she didn't remember directing him.
Was it her imagination? On the other hand, there was the music!
Clearly that announced a party. Tears started. Words spilled. She
got out of the car.

Leaning in the open window, she whispered, "You were right,
Jack. The summer's more like *Dick and Nicole* than *Dick and
Jane.*"

From an upstairs bedroom window, a dark-haired, sleepy-eyed

boy, awakened by the running motor, watched his mother until she finally left Jack Bennet's blue station wagon.

16
Works in Progress

J oe walked down to the studio, knowing Nancy would follow. The din of the party was lessening. It was after two. On the house tour earlier, Dick Ryner had not taken him to the studio. Joe wondered why. He'd been there before.

"Sally finally told me about Oxford," he said to Nancy, when she caught up to him.

"Are you going?"

"How can you ask me that? You know what I'm going to do. Are you going to be a pain in the ass, too?"

"People change their minds."

He didn't answer. The barn was dark, as usual, except for the dim spotlight focused on Nancy's work-in-progress.

"What the fuck is that?" Joe exploded, looking at the spotlighted work.

"Exactly what you think it is," Nancy shot back, standing behind him, rubbing against him as they both gazed at Sally's smooth clay breasts.

"You didn't tell me about this, Nancy. What are you doing fooling around with Sally?"

"I'm not fooling around with your wife."

"Why are you so goddamn friendly with her? How could it get so far?"

"You're asking that!" She gave a dry laugh. "Look, the whole friendship thing started because I was trying to make it easier for us during the summer and afterward. Anyway, now I'm sculpting her."

"Don't bullshit me, Nancy. I know you."

"Good. Then we have an understanding. As it worked out, I'm only sculpting her," she said defiantly, hips thrust forward, challenging.

For some reason, that turned Joe Singer on, in fact, aroused them both. They had their best sex ever, into the night, under Nancy's version of Sally's grape-like nipples.

17
August Showers

Sally could hear the shower running through the closed door. She had tried to wait up for him, overcome by a profound abandonment that was childlike in its pervasive purity. The splinters stuck inside her had turned to steel. Covered only by the light summer quilt, she was lying naked in bed.

Slowly, as if sleepwalking, she went into the bathroom. For a few seconds she stood outside the shower door watching him wash, wondering what kind of episode Joe was sponging away? Only the shower light was on. He was whistling softly. She had to brace herself on the towel bar against a churning heave.

She opened the shower door and slid in behind him, pellets of warm water sprayed her, diluting her hot tears. Before Joe could say anything, she embraced him, her legs matching his, her stomach grinding against his buttocks, her hands searching, grabbing, stroking. She turned him around, then knelt in the shower, engulfing him in her mouth, her hands pressing him close, closer.

When he responded, he lifted her from her knees. Stepping out the shower door, he guided her body down to the cool blue tiles.

Sally made desperate love with Joe that night, a willing slave trying to please, trying to fill her emptiness, trying to fight back. When he slept, snoring lightly as this night of darkness turned into day, Sally, sleepless, stood in front of the dresser mirror. The bedroom smelled like that westerly wind from Promised Land.

"Who are you?" she asked the drawn, frightened face in the glass, the reflection of a woman she didn't quite know. "What have you become? Who are you waiting for to help you? What are you waiting for? You can't send for Grandma. Catholic Jackie's a myth."

Sally felt sick. Sick of herself. She rushed into the bathroom. On her knees, once again, she vomited into the cool porcelain commode. Rinsing her mouth, she saw her tortured reflection in the cabinet mirror. She began to gag again. Dry heaves. There was only emptiness, and one certainty.

"Sally Lamb Singer," she said aloud. "No matter what, you will never act like this again, never."

She looked for a gesture to seal her oath. All that came to mind was basketball players crossing themselves before a free throw. She crawled into bed and fell asleep dreaming that someone had joined forces with Catholic Jackie to help her survive.

Nancy called as Sally was making breakfast.

"Did you let Liz get to you last night?"

"Liz is a very unhappy woman," said Sally. She was soaking the last of the white bread in the bowl of eggs and milk. "A very unhappy woman."

"Max Slavka is running around. Their nanny! Can you imagine? A nanny! He's too old for a nanny?"

"Who? Adam or Max? I thought Adam went to camp in Montauk."

"The kid gets home early. They have so much money it doesn't matter."

"How come you know so much about Liz Slavka's life?"

"Max's my attorney," said Nancy, as if that explained everything. "Look, I know you're upset about last night. If anything I did or said caused you distress, I apologize."

"What happened is between Joe and me, Nancy."

"I thought we were going to be friends, after the summer, back in the city—"

"Why are we talking about the fall?" Sally cut in, irritably. The butter was splattering. She flipped over the browned egg-drenched bread, added cinnamon, and lowered the flame.

Nancy hesitated. "There's, uhh, something you should know, Sally. Joe was in the studio."

"What was he doing in your studio?"

"I don't know. I suppose Dick brought him."

"That's right," she remembered. "The grand tour! Everything's so complicated. God, how did it get this way?"

"What's more important, Joe wanted to know what *you* were doing there. He was pissed."

She sounded conspiratorial, chummy, like schoolgirls with a secret.

"I have to hang up, Nancy. I have no time for this."

Sally dumped the grease from the skillet, grabbed two slices of french toast for herself in a napkin and dashed out of the house. She needed to walk on the beach alone.

That afternoon, Joe and Michael stayed at the house watching TV, settling for the Red Sox game, because East Hampton received only New England stations. Sally went to the bay with Andy and Ben. Afterward, all of the Singers drove to Sammy's Beach in the Northwest part of town to see the sunset over the bay. They had promised the boys to go there before Joe returned to the city that night. (Sammy's Beach was a sand spit. It separated Gardiner's Bay from Three Mile Harbor.)

Andy and Michael in their new red swimsuits, Ben wearing

new cut-offs, were down toward Old House Landing, gathering mussels along the shore. Sally didn't know why, because they must know she wasn't going to cook them.

"You were hot stuff last night," Joe said, leaning against the hood of the taxi.

"Stop smirking! It was for all the wrong reasons. I learned a lesson though, being alone is better than being disgusted. Why was taking me home an issue, Joe?"

"You went with Jack Bennet, remember?"

"I came with you. It's not like you to let these things happen."

"I'm not the one who wanted to come to this place. This was your thing, Sally."

"But we did come. That's not the point. Why are things so different?"

"So I kissed her," Joe conceded in exasperation. "So what! We were all feeling good. Maybe it was bad judgment, knowing you."

"A kiss? Is that what you think this is about?"

"I don't know what this is about. If you're pissed at Liz Slavka, don't take it out on me. And how the fuck could you pose naked for a stranger? You don't know what she's all about."

"It's you that I can't figure anymore, Joe. . . us," she whispered. The fire-red sun was sinking slowly in Gardiner's Bay. It occurred to her that it was taking her marriage with it. "Something's wrong with us. Something's happened."

"Look, Sally, we're best when we work toward a goal together. Maybe we should buy a house out here like everyone else if we're going to come every summer. Renting's a waste of money. Even you understand that."

Sally was dumbfounded. "Buy a house? You didn't even want to come here in the first place. Buy a house?" she cried. "I've heard of save-the-marriage babies, but a save-the-marriage-house?"

When he didn't laugh, didn't smile, Sally understood he was dead serious. At that moment, she didn't want to know why.

"Well, we don't have that kind of money," she pointed out, picking something familiar. "Why do you say we're going to come here every summer, Joe?"

"You like it here. *Brigadoon?* Remember? Look, you have that Oxford money. Maybe your mother could help again."

"The Oxford money is for Oxford, if we go. We haven't ruled out that possibility. The work permit's a problem, Joe. But there might be something unofficial for you to do."

"For a New York cab driver? Give me a break, Sally."

Joe opened the car door as the boys approached with buckets holding their catch. The mussel odor made Sally queasy.

"Why don't all of you put those black things back where they belong," Sally suggested. "You'll make some mother very happy."

"It's up to you, Sally. You'll have to decide what's important."

Driving back to the house Joe's outrageous idea did ring a Sallybell. He had a point! The reason they were here in the first place. Wasn't that the point?

If they had a house out here, the boys would be guaranteed summers away from the city, away from filthy West Side streets, the hypodermic needles, away from roaming gangs that preyed on them, away from dangerous misfits who camped in transient west side hotels, away from drug dealers looking for new customers — away from the nightmare New York City neighborhoods had become except for the rich.

Rich? Rich brought Sally to a reality she could deal with. How could they afford to buy a summer house?

18
The Deal

"You're being foolish," advised Max Slavka. "You don't sign a deal for a non-contingent contract when you're looking for financing unless you're a fool or desperate. Are you desperate, Sally? I know you're not a fool."

Sitting with Max in Jack Bennet's real estate office on Newtown Lane, they were reviewing the broker's deal sheet which served as a memorandum of agreement. It recited the elements of the contract.

The office was a tiny storefront sandwiched in-between an insurance agency and Eddie's luncheonette. It was furnished plainly, three desks, a ceiling fan, fresh cut flowers in coffee can vases, roll-up bamboo shades with patterned curtains but no windows, four dark wood captain chairs for customers. It had the smell of fried eggs, bacon, and burgers. Sally was thinking bacon, lettuce, and tomato on rye toast as Max Slavka was counseling.

"I'm your lawyer. I advise against it. Why the hell do you need that pressure? And that's the least of it!"

"Do it, Jack! Get it over with," Sally said, despite Max's advice.

Bennet was sitting behind his oversized oak desk that looked more like a library table. It was almost mid-August; the summer was slipping by.

Once she made the decision to buy a home in East Hampton, Sally wanted to walk through the process. She hated shopping, unlike her mother, who spent hours looking for something even after she'd found it. And Sally wanted to get the transaction over with before the fall semester, before going back to the city. She was using Max for convenience. He was there in East Hampton. He was about to close for the Ryners on a vintage Amagansett house. Max wasn't all bad. For example, because of what Max called Joe's *exposure* on the taxi, the house would be in her name. That point bothered Joe.

"He likes to stick it to me," Joe said. "He's not so different from his brother." Yet, he let the dispute go quicker than usual, Sally noticed. Probably because none of the money was his anyhow, she decided.

Trusting Jack Bennet, Sally didn't have to see every single thing on the market, either. The Foster home on Dayton Lane had a lot of pluses. Though not a beach house, it made good sense with her car-less state. It was less than a mile from both the ocean and shopping in East Hampton Village. There was vacant property, quarter-acre lots, on each side of the four-bedroom one-story ranch. The fourth bedroom was more than they needed, but it was an important feature to her mother. The house was down the street from the Bennets, across the road from the Hawley home, the one they were asked to leave. Taking Bennet's concerns seriously regarding other Realtors' bids in this exceptionally active market, Sally made the full price offer to the local family — $18,000, furnished.

"Why do you have to always be the kind of person who pays 100% on the dollar?" Joe had argued unsuccessfully. This whole thing was his strange idea, but Sally was going to do it her way. Fast, simple, painless.

She asked her mother for another loan.

"You haven't finished paying me back for the taxi yet, young lady," Beatrice said on the phone from Florida. Yet she agreed to come up with $3,600 for closing the deal.

Sally notified financial aid she was withdrawing any pending requests tied into Oxford, and she had picked up another class — she'd be teaching three courses this fall.

It was Bennet who suggested offering the bank the larger than usual down payment — 30 percent — because it wasn't easy for a woman to get bank loans whether secured by property or not. The university grants for Oxford already received provided the 10 percent contract fee, $1,800; that, with her mother's money, left a few hundred for closing costs. Her teaching salary, without Joe's earnings, could cover the $80 and change a month carrying charge. The bank was offering six percent financing.

The Fosters wanted to close quickly so their children could start school in the house they were buying up west in Wading River, closer to Grumman, where Mr. Foster worked. The week after Labor Day was their goal, less than four weeks away. She had arranged with Hawley Bennet to extend the lease for a couple of more weeks so that she could move things in from the Barnes Landing house, instead of taking them back to Manhattan.

"No one signs a non-contingent contract, even when they have money, Sally. No one pays full price either, without negotiating." Max was rustling the memorandum of sale in the air.

"There wasn't room to move, Max," Bennet explained. "People were interested in this property. Besides, local sellers usually ask for what they want. It's not like New York."

"What do you know about New York? This man represents the seller, Sally. Do you understand?"

"I want a sandwich," said Sally, getting up.

"I'll get it," Bennet offered.

"Bacon and tomato on rye toast, light on the mayonnaise."

"Can we get back to business, here?" Max asked. "I advise against these terms."

"It's what I want to do, Max," Sally insisted. "Okay, Jack, I'll sign the agreement."

"Make copies," Max ordered with a sigh of disgust.

"It'll take a bit," Jack Bennet said pleasantly. He was patting the portable copier on the stand against the wainscoted wall. "Has to warm up. Have to make it hum before we use it."

"Like a woman," mumbled Sally.

"For God's sake, Sally," Max snapped. "This is serious."

"Serious? I don't even know why I'm doing it." She was trying hard to forget that her attorney was the same guy who had set up a dump match at the Nationals.

"I'm going next door to feed this woman." Bennet smiled at Sally. "Anything to drink?"

"A glass of milk. Remember rye toasted and light on the mayonnaise. That's important."

"That's important! It's the first time all day you've shown some interest. Jesus, Sally! Grow up! Look at this deal! I'm on record against this," Max repeated himself. "Remember what happens if you can't close. Your money goes down the toilet."

"You're on record, Max," Sally said, casually, though she knew he had a point.

She would have to sweat out the mortgage approval. The idea of $13,000 in personal debt didn't thrill her. And that was not counting what she owed her mother. It was typical of Sally to rush full steam ahead on something she didn't really want to do.

She told herself it would be good for her boys. It would be good for them to get away from the city every summer, even winter holidays. It would expose them to another life, a better world. Yet they might have seen that at Oxford, too, no matter how briefly. She didn't really know why she was doing this.

Oxford was what she truly wanted for herself. That wonderful life of the mind, the challenge of ideas — they were her passion. Giving up Oxford for the Foster home, Sally suspected she'd cut a part of herself off, an essential part of her nature. On the day she'd made that decision, she'd had the same nightmare again, about killing herself and getting caught.

But this time there was an accomplice. Joe Singer. Together they carried her unconscious body to the railroad tracks and left it there to meet the train.

19
Foster Homes

"**B**etter look out the window, Ma, a surprise is about to happen," said Michael, shaking her awake.

Sally dragged herself out of bed, drawing the chintz curtain aside. Since she'd signed the contract and was waiting for the bank to act on her application, she was sleeping more than usual. Giving an exhausted yawn, Sally peeked outside.

"Oh my God," she whispered.

A black limo was pulling away. Three matching bags of luggage were sitting next to the mailbox. Beatrice Lamb was parading up the driveway.

She looked nothing less than regal. At 65, Beatrice was still beautiful in a simple ivory knit dress, ebony summer jewelry, an elegant streak of white parting her cap of black hair. Sally'd bet the dress was lined so as not to wrinkle from traveling. Her mother knew about those things.

Sally gave a shudder, then made herself go downstairs.

Her mother was there before she was. She kissed Sally saying, "Why are you so thin? Aren't you taking care of yourself? You look like a mannequin. And the way you dress." Beatrice was critically eyeing Joe's baggy cotton tee shirt.

"These are my night clothes, Ma," Sally defended herself, kissing her on the air above her cheek. "What are you doing here? Why didn't you call? The house is a mess. Why do you do these surprises? I should be used to them." She meant *by now*, after 30 years experience.

Surprises? Why once, long ago, when Sally, was four, she barely survived a Beatrice surprise. It was on their Sunday stroll, the day dedicated to Sally since her mother worked the other six, the day she was without the protection of Grandma who needed time off.

A sign — CHILDREN BOARDED/ FOSTER CARE — in a ground floor apartment window caught her mother's eye, had beckoned to her, Beatrice would say later. Avoiding the grimy, aluminum pails on the sidewalk where anyone could drop their garbage, they climbed the steps of the shabby Riverside Drive brownstone. They were welcomed into the dark apartment behind the sign by a painfully colorless woman in a stained housedress. Beyond her, in the large front room that smelled of sour milk and dirty diapers, children, too old, were housed in wall to wall cribs with metal slats. Some wailed; others were sitting stonefaced, rocking, passively serving their sentence behind bars. Sally thought she was in a place for bad children like the one she'd seen in Pinocchio.

"How'd you like to stay here, Sallylamb?" asked Beatrice, the 'here' in a lilting voice, so inviting, as if she were offering Cinderella her palace.

"It's wonderful, Mommy," Sally dutifully replied, smothering her panic, waiting for the moment to pass. She clung inside herself to a standby savior, Catholic Jackie. "My name is Jackie and I'm Catholic," she introduced herself to the pasty bland woman.

That must have jarred her mother, because Beatrice didn't leave her in the foster home that day, choosing instead, to martyr herself, chained to this strange child, as she often referred to her daughter.

Foster home. That's it! That's why she's here. The Foster house.

"I want to see the house we're buying. You might have said no. And isn't it always?" said Beatrice, answering the three questions that Sally had already forgotten. They always spoke to each other this way.

"You could come for the house, but not for Grandma," Sally blurted.

"Still judging? That'll catch up with you one day, young lady," warned Beatrice.

"I can't believe you're here," Sally backed off from that sensitive subject in a sudden childlike fear of omniscient mothers.

Beatrice was rubbing her hands together. "My, it's chilly here."

"You left hot in Florida, Mother. August is crisper out on the eastern tip of Long Island. It's almost September. Next week's Labor Day."

"The town is packed. The roads were clearer on the way out."

"East Hampton's occupied for the rest of the season. The neurotics from the west."

"West?"

"From New York. They follow their analysts."

"Don't talk nonsense, Sally," Beatrice said, as she wandered through the downstairs rooms. "Why aren't you dressed?"

"I am, Mother," said Sally, but Beatrice had floated out of the living room into the kitchen.

"It's almost lunch-time. Ben, you've gotten so tall. Go write Grandma Bea one of your poems. Michael, you need a haircut . . . before your bar mitzvah next year. You are taking care of that, aren't you Sally?"

"The haircut or the bar mitzvah?" Sally asked tiredly.

"You look more like your grandfather every day, Michael. Come over and give Grandma Bea a kiss," she galloped on, no replies necessary. "Look at you Andy, you're perfect, what a handsome fellow you are. Sally, have these children eaten?"

"Not since you last saw them," sighed Sally, waving off any more criticism.

"When will you grow up?" Beatrice asked, granting a smile. "Where's your husband?"

"Joe comes out Friday night. I'm sure he'll be delighted to see you."

"Sarcasm is a weapon for the weak," proclaimed Beatrice.

"I wasn't being sarcastic. He knows you lent us money again."

"Yes, well, I really must have a bedroom with a private bath." She announced this as if it were a doctor's prescription.

"Get your grandmother's luggage, Michael," Sally said. "Take it upstairs."

"Don't scratch it, darling. It's Vuitton, after all," Beatrice said.

"I'll take the downstairs bedroom," Sally said, surrendering.

"It was awfully nice of that landlord of yours to let you stay longer than the lease. And *gratis!* When I heard that Sally, I knew I should come visit, that it was meant to be."

"He's the broker's cousin, Ma. I told you that. He's helping things along, so we can get our summer things installed in the new house instead of taking them back to Manhattan. There's no mystery."

"Yes, well, I want to see this house I'm buying."

"You're lending money for it, Ma, not buying it," corrected Sally.

"With what you owe me, Sallylamb, it's the same thing."

Ben, the artistic child, seemed embarrassed, eyes hugging the floor, as he gave Sally his untitled on-the-spot creation. *Grandma Bea came. No one's to blame,* it read. Sally crushed it in her fist and gave him a hug.

The Steinway arrived before Joe did.

"This doesn't feel like a *visit*, Mom," Sally told her as Home Sweet Home movers, having removed the legs, angled the piano through doors and hallways.

"It's for the new house. I know just where it will go, from the floor plans you sent," said Beatrice, directing the movers at the same time.

"Why would your piano be for our new house?"

"Sometimes, Sally, you don't see the handwriting on the wall," Beatrice said impatiently, turning her attention to the movers.

When the Steinway was established in the upstairs master bed-room (dressers shifted to the boys' room, the vanity into the master bath, the bed shoved against the wall), and after the piano tuner from Patchogue had adjusted it for the moving, Beatrice sat down to play, singing in her dramatic way, *As Long As She Needs Me*. She was a mezzo-soprano with perfect pitch.

"Remember this, Sally?" Beatrice said, segueing to *The Maiden's Prayer* for a tear-jerker instrumental.

It was Friday, but Sally felt her mother had been there a year instead of five days. She was up to *Eli, Eli* — sung cantorial style in plaintive Yiddish wail — when Andy rushed in.

"He took the last Yodel, Ma."

"Who?" said Sally, knowing full well who *he* was.

"You know who. Michael! That was for me. He didn't even eat it. He's feeding it to the birds. And he's laughing."

"What do you want me to do? Shoot him? Tell me what you want me to do."

"You always say that but you never do it."

"I should hope not," sang out Beatrice to the *Eli, Eli* melody.

"You've lived with him nine years, Andy. Can't you work it out yet?" tried Sally.

"You've lived with him almost 12 years and you haven't worked it out," Andy shot back.

"Here, go to MacMullins and buy more Yodels," said Sally, about to hand him a dollar bill.

"I don't want Yodels. I want a normal family," he said, throwing a look at Beatrice, too, before he marched out of the room.

Beatrice stopped in the middle of *Chinatown, My Chinatown.* "What on earth did he mean by that, Sally? Me?"

"How could he possibly?" said Sally. She twirled her ring, sliding it up and down. Andy and Michael's squabbling always set her off.

She was letting the boys miss school next week, because of this house deal. The first week of school. She felt funny about that. She hadn't heard from the bank. They had said before Labor Day. Here it was Friday. True, the mail hadn't come yet. Yet, she was starting to get a nagging feeling about not listening to that disgusting Max.

And over it all she could hear Grandma, "If you want to make God laugh, Shifra, tell him your plans."

Sally wanted to ask her mother again if there was back-up money she might have, just in case the bank failed, but couldn't. Instead she said, "You know we're going out tomorrow night. It was planned before you arrived, Ma. I can't get out of it."

"You told me about it," said Beatrice picking up at, *"Hearts seem light, and lights seem bright in dreamy Chinatown."*

Joe called that evening. "I'm coming out Saturday. Less traffic. Anyway, you've got your mother there."

He'd pick up Nancy, too. She'd been away during the last days of her precious August. Dick was on the Coast. He made his own plans to get back to East Hampton for the weekend, guessed Sally.

They were going to celebrate the Ryner house closing at the Millstone, finally going to Hawley Bennet's gay place for dancing. And there was to be a Ryner surprise, too. Sally wondered if Nancy, who looked particularly radiant lately, was with child.

20
The Women

"Here's the story. I'm getting a divorce. Losing a Dick, gaining a house, thanks to my lawyer, whom we shall now toast," Nancy Ryner said, raising her glass with an extravagant gesture. "To Max Slavka, attorney par excellence, particularly when you need an animal."

"I'll drink to that last part," cracked Doug, who clearly had too many drinks already.

Max's face tightened, but he joined in the laughter.

"I knew inviting him was a mistake, Max," Liz said, crossing her thin legs nervously, her white linen slacks and navy striped shirt hanging loosely on her thin frame.

Susannah flashed her apple-pie smile, meant for everyone.

Susannah and Doug, still an item, were staying at Liz and Max's for the Labor Day weekend. Sally had no room for them with her mother visiting. It was not like Max to have Doug stay. Sally supposed as long as Susannah drawled *darlin'* and wore clothes that came off easily, like this evening's spaghetti string slip, the James Bond girl could get things Doug couldn't. Susannah had called this morning.

"I know you're disappointed darlin', but you do things to Doug I can't, so maybe it's for the best . . . until I'm a fixture," she'd said without rancor. "From what I can see going on here, sugar, we'll probably never get another chance to stay with his brother, at least

Dougie won't." She gave a short rippling laugh before hanging up.

Nancy continued with her surprise.

"So, Mr. Ryner is no longer in residence," she said glibly, sitting on the arm of a couch in the large living room where weeks earlier they'd celebrated her birthday with Mr. Ryner in residence. She was outfitted in black leather with a metallic top — similar to what Liz had worn at the birthday party — except there was a short, short, skirt.

"Would you believe, I thought she was pregnant," Sally murmured to Hawley Bennet.

"So it's getting rid of a dick celebration," Nancy repeated.

"That pun is wearing thin," Hawley Bennet whispered back to Sally. "You look great, sweetheart. You'll be a sensation at the Millstone."

Sally bought denim hip huggers for this end-of-summer occasion. With it she wore a loose denim vest, its v-neck stopping where it had to. Her bare arms were dark brown smooth from two months in the sun.

"So that's my surprise." Nancy finished, more than a little drunk as she waved at Joe.

Joe had left the room for the announcement. Sally didn't know how long he had been standing in the doorway. His face was serious, noncommittal.

Hawley lightly jabbed her with his elbow, rolling his eyes in a way that said "what will these people do next?"

"One more toast," Nancy called out, lifting her glass again. "To my friends . . in need."

"I may vomit," Liz Slavka snickered. "Are we going dancing or are we going to drink ourselves to death in your house?" she asked Nancy. "Let's move!"

They formed a caravan following Hawley Bennet's pickup west to Bridgehampton, then turning north passing miles of farmfields until they came to a narrow country road, winding through thick forest. After what seemed like an endless ride through pristine, desolate woods, Hawley Bennet's truck pulled over. There were a myriad of parked cars cramped along the road's shoulder.

Beyond, Sally saw a shanty-like cottage, green and orange string lights above the entrance. There in the remote woodlands of a glacial forest, in the sky black night, yellow light slipping through mullioned window panes, the isolated roadside tavern whispered a tempting invitation. It suggested a clandestine excitement in an untouchable place. The message was heightened by the tom-tom beat of disco music and the castanet chatter of a million crickets. In that seductive harmony she imagined a safety zone, a protective sound barrier shielding a wanton world. Before crossing the invisible line, Sally felt high breathing the cool, green night air.

She had never been to a gay club, but gay or not, the Millstone held no secrets. They walked in and there it was — woodsy, unpolished, lights party-dim, small tables along the wall, a confined, dance floor. The bar was off to the left. Shelves displayed Heinekens, Dewars, Gordons, Gilbeys, Jack Daniels; wooden racks were stacked high with sparkling tumblers. There was a heady aroma of alcohol, tobacco, and perspiration, doused with sexual tension. Sally thought the mix should be bottled for parties.

Mostly men were on the bar side, crowded three deep, shielding the bar stools. They were handsome men, beautiful men, men with style, their slim and wiry dancers' bodies dressed artfully casual in custom jeans, black chinos, fitted khakis, open shirts. There was a manner among the barside men that said they knew fun, they understood letting go. It was their place.

The few worn, wooden tables were for Saturday night straights, ordinary people, like herself. Both men and women sat at them.

The dancing was the best she'd ever seen. Whatever was kept imprisoned all week in their conventional life, was liberated at the Millstone. Sally studied the rhythmic, writhing bodies as they became one with the music, moving to the Supreme's *Come See About Me*.

"Okay, Sally Singer, let's see what you can do," said Hawley Bennet, grabbing her hand before she could sit down.

He danced like they did, these graceful men, with just the right balance between abandon and restraint. She was with him, every beat, feeling blessedly free. Someone cut in, a stranger from the bar-side. Hawley turned to dance with the man whose partner was now with Sally.

And that's how it went. For hours. Tireless. Sally danced. Forgetting about the people with whom she had come. Forgetting about dancing with Joe. Forgetting about the bank's letter she had received that morning. It was a night for forgetting.

Hawley taught her the *Madison*, the line dance the regulars broke into from time to time. She loved it, feeling so accomplished with the kicks, the turns, the body movements in unison. Dancing to Creedence Clearwater's *Bad Moon Rising*, Hawley explained that the *Madison's* birth was not as happy as its steps. It was designed to avoid same sex dancing, a criminal act in many places. That bit of news was sobering enough for Sally to take a break.

Sweat-drenched, she moved through the crowd to the bathroom at the end of the bar. Liz and Susannah were in the one-stall rest room.

"Is this place great or what?" Sally asked. "Liz, I saw you dancing with Doug. Good for you to let old grudges go!" Sally added, feeling joyful and generous, as if detoxified by the salty perspiration rolling down her body.

Susannah, remaking her face, was wiping smudges off the mirror with a paper towel.

Liz was watching Sally.

"What?" said Sally. "Is something wrong?"

Liz gave a shrug. "So now you know your landlord's gay," she said. "Does that matter?"

"What kind of a question is that, Liz? Of course it doesn't matter."

Liz stared at Sally.

"What now? I hate when you do that, Liz. You know that."

"Sally, you know Max is Nancy Ryner's lawyer?"

"Yes. So?"

"And you know he's handling the divorce for her?"

"I learned that tonight." Sally washed her face and was wiping it dry, standing near Susannah, who was still working at the mirror.

"Max would kill me if he knew I was talking to you about a client." Liz looked around as if she expected him to appear. "Sally, I know Nancy Ryner. She's no friend of yours."

"What?"

"Nancy Ryner's no friend of yours."

"What are you talking about, Liz?"

"Oh for God's sake, Sally, what's wrong with you? Open your eyes."

Susannah looked quickly away.

"Liz," Sally cried.

But both women were out the door.

Flashing through Sally's mind was a copper-tanned Nancy in cutoffs — strong legs, powerful thighs. Men could fantasize about

Nancy's thighs, see them wrapped tightly around them, their bodies imprisoned in the sexual act.

Did her husband know those thighs?

It was hard for Sally to breathe. Though Liz Slavka had talked about Nancy, Sally knew she meant more. She couldn't avoid it nor was she prepared to deal with it.

"Where Did Our Love Go" was blaring through the wooded slats of the tiny bathroom. Sally sat on the commode, her head bent low between her knees. She was dizzy. It was an effort to be blind.

There was ringing. Sally reached across the bed. Joe wasn't there. She reached for the phone, but it wasn't there, either. Then she remembered she was in the phoneless downstairs guest room, her mother was in the upstairs 'full service' master bedroom. Scrambling out of bed, she caught the call in the kitchen on the sixth ring.

"I have such a hangover. You must, too. Doug said he never saw you drink so much. Are you okay?" asked Susannah's voice.

"How can I be okay? You were there, Susannah. I know Liz was talking about Joe when she said that. . . that stuff. But I don't want to believe it. He's been a bastard lately. But that?" said Sally, wondering why she was telling this to another woman stranger. Balancing the phone with her shoulder, she grabbed some Wonder Bread and laced it with butter. "I don't know what to believe."

"There's an old saying where I come from, Sally, about dry babies, clean floors, faithful husbands," she paused as if deciding whether or not to continue. "Don't do anything too quickly. You need time to sort things, no matter what Liz said last night. Joe?" she paused, a question mark in her voice, "It's not what he expected, you know. You were so young when he found you in that ping pong club; so adoring. So much changed, Sally darlin'. I don't think Joe ever planned to parade like a shadow through your life."

Sally swallowed the bread. "Parade like a shadow? How come *you* know so much about Joe, Susannah?"

"Why on earth would you want to ask a question like that, honey? Look, I have to go," she whispered. "Liz's coming down as I speak."

Sally held the receiver at her side, feeling like a world in collision unable to get away. Was Joe running through *all* the women she knew? Perversely, the idea of two women was easier to face than one. Sally hung up the phone.

So did Beatrice.

21

Leaving Things Behind

Beatrice Lamb had heard enough.

Cradling the receiver, she chided herself for eavesdropping. But listening on telephone extensions was a Mike Lamb survival technique and she was an honors graduate of the Mike Lamb School of Deception. Beatrice knew there was trouble in paradise. As her own marriage had failed with Mike Lamb, as her mother's marriage had failed with "Louie the Four Flusher" whom Beatrice had adored, so Sally's marriage was failing with Joe Singer. Would Sally get through this? She knew what *this* was. The Mike Lamb memories came, though Beatrice never liked to recall those times.

Christmas Eve at Luchows. Scents of holly and pine, the sweet heavy aroma of orange glazed ducks. The fresh wreaths and satiny red ribbons made cheerful the deep brown paneled walls. People were milling around sipping spirits from ornate flasks that management refused to see. He'd asked to be introduced to her at the theater party.

"You're the best looking woman without makeup I've seen this year," Mike Lamb had said in 1927. "And there's only a week left!" (That night, worshipping her olive-skinned body, he told her she was more an exotic queen than a Jewish girl from Harlem.)

"I understand you're a publicity man just in from Los Angeles. Why did you leave, Mr. Lamb?"

"I didn't leave. Warner threw me out of town. And it's Mike."

"A delicate situation with Mrs. Warner, I was told."

"I wouldn't touch Mrs. Warner so she told her husband I had," he said, his gray eyes teasing. (It was not until months later that she would learn about the throw of the dice, the crapping out on a double six, that lost him his actor clients.)

They went to the Roseland Ballroom after Luchows where Flo Ziegfeld walked over to them, greeted Mike familiarly, then bowing from the waist kissed her hand. Ziegfeld had said, before moving on, that if she were two inches taller she'd be one of his girls.

They married nine days later at New York County City Hall. It wasn't nine months later she found him in a hotel bed, a chorus girl on each side.

"Men. Men. For what? They rip your *kishkas* into small pieces," Mama told her.

But she had endured.

Later, the fruit of their union, a syphilitic boy, died in infancy. Then a divorce. That failed, as well. Sally was the issue of their dissolution, conceived years later during one of Mike's pit stops. For this transgression, she had been duly sentenced to nine months and hard labor, a solitary confinement from which Mike was barred. It almost killed her.

"The afterbirth wouldn't come out," she had tried to explain to young Sallylamb. "I was poisoned."

Sallylamb replied that she thought *she* was the afterbirth.

Mike Lamb? A mistake repeatedly made.

Beatrice winced away from her past, absentmindedly stroking the hand that Flo Ziegfeld had once kissed.

Now Sally would go through the same troubles.

What was it Mama always said? *Ven es kompt tszevishen du und die veldt, vet auf die veldt.* When it comes between you and the world, bet on the world. Well, the world had won again. But she couldn't handle that world right now, handle Sally's messy life and the feelings it dredged.

"I can't stay," she told her daughter later that morning.

"I know," said Sally, seeing the waiting limo. "I'm not surprised."

Beatrice took everything but the Steinway.

22

Machiavelli in Multiples of Five

"Your mother left in a rush," observed Joe. They were at Barnes Landing beach. "I thought for sure she was staying until the house closed. What is it, another 10 days?"

The boys were nearby building castles and fortresses. There was a man listening to a news report on a blaring radio as he oiled a woman's back from a dark brown plastic squeeze bottle.

"That radio's too loud," she mumbled.

"Maybe he'll put a ball game on later," said Joe.

Sally's mind was on other things. Her marriage, for one. *You didn't have to fall off a roof to commit adultery.*

And there was the letter — yesterday's letter now hidden safely in her bikini top — the letter from the Sag Harbor Savings Bank, where Charles Hawley was vice-president. Good old Charlie! Back in the picture. Was it by chance that the coming Friday was the day they'd come and gone from East Hampton a year ago, the Friday after the Labor Day weekend?

The good news was the bank would take a mortgage. The bad news was they would not lend as much as Sally had asked. She could get 50 percent financing instead of the 70 percent for which she'd applied, read the letter signed by Hawley. Jack Bennet, disgusted at the news, told her it was the woman thing.

She needed more money to close the deal: $3,600 more, to make up the difference, needed it in one short week. It might as well have been $36,000. There was no place to go for money. She'd lose her deposit, too.

Sally had managed to pick up another $1,000 from a Machiavelli research grant. His 500th anniversary was the following year. As usual, she'd been quick on the draw. But that money was back-up, extra closing costs, lawyer's fees and for any surprises.

"When are you going to hear from the bank?" Joe asked. "You don't have much time. You should have gotten a break on the commission, too. From your friend Bennet."

She could tell he was still chafing at not being on the deed from his aggressive tone of voice. "It never occurred to me to ask about the commission, Joe. That's how Jack makes his living."

"What's commission?" piped up Ben, digging and pouring as if to rearrange the beach.

"A commission's like a tip. Like Dad gets for driving people around," said Andy.

"It's the broker's vigorish," said Michael. "Like the bookmaker's take."

The commission was like the bookmaker's take?

Sally stopped twisting the ring on her finger. She'd exhausted grants, fellowships, her mother's largesse. She thought about selling the Steinway, but she couldn't do it quick enough anyhow. *The commission was like the bookmaker's take. . . .* Everything was happening too fast.

Buying a House. Giving up Oxford. Susannah on the phone this morning. Her mother walking out. Liz's talk about Nancy last night. My God, she'd posed for that woman! That made her sick to her stomach. There was only one thing to do to save the house, the Foster home that suddenly had become so important to her.

"That radio's giving me a headache," she said, brushing off the sand as she slipped on her sneakers. "I'll bring back lunch, fresh coffee and lemonade." Grabbing the picnic basket, she turned to Michael. "I want you with me," she whispered.

She couldn't talk to anyone about this — except Michael. She knew people would think she was crazy. It didn't matter. Asking for advice was a masquerade for a decision already made. You ask someone who's going to tell you what you need to hear and you keep asking until you find that someone. It's your responsibility at the end. Always. Sartre knew that.

Once in the house, Sally went through the pile of newspapers in the living room. Handing one to Michael, she outlined the situation.

"But how're you going to pay Fish if you lose, Ma?"

"I'll worry about that, Michael. Find a game, the very best game, and hurry." She went into the kitchen.

"It's not like ordering in a restaurant, Ma," Michael called out.

Preparing food and munching on white bread, Sally figured the Machiavelli money would cover something if she lost; she could teach extra classes, give up next summer's holiday, and there was always the Steinway. She ate more bread to settle herself.

When she returned 15 minutes later, Michael gave her the game. She dialed the number.

"Fish?" There was a pause. "No, no, I haven't got time for sweet talk," she said to that faceless, silky voice.

He would answer the phone gruff, then when he heard her voice, he'd turn it on, slow it down, smooth it out, sound really good. *My Gal Sal?* he'd say, melting the words. Sally got a kick out of that, would laugh, play the game.

"Not today, Fish. Today I want to place a large bet on the Orioles game, on the—"

"Don't say who you like. First check the line, Ma," coached Michael.

"Even-six, Baltimore," she whispered, turning to her son. "That means we're laying six to five on Baltimore in Boston, right?"

"And you're getting even money, if you win, Ma. But with Palmer pitching — he's 14 and seven this season, a right-handed power pitcher to deal with the big monster in Fenway—"

"You're telling me too much, Michael. I don't know what you're talking about," Sally stopped him, still whispering, as Fish was holding on the open line. "Once more, is it a good bet?"

"Boston's in a three-way tie for last place and Baltimore is nine games in for first. Baltimore has a club batting average of .258 against Boston's .241. Ma, the top four hitters on Baltimore — Aparicio, Snyder, Blefry, Brooks Robinson — are hitting higher than any Boston player. And Boog Powell and Frank Robinson are battling for the RBI crown. They'll be trying even though the team's so far ahead. It's an underlay, Ma. Baltimore should win. You're getting value."

"Value?"

"An underlay. The odds are wrong in your favor. I think you should be laying eight or nine to five, not even-six."

"Sally, Sally are you there?" cried Fish's velvet voice over the receiver.

"I'm here. Give me a minute."

"Sal, honey, I'd give you the world, but I can't tie up the line like this. It's almost game time."

"Are you sure you want to do this, Ma? There's no such thing as a sure thing," he warned. "But if you're going to do it—"

"Michael, we don't have much time."

"If you're going to bet and you don't have money, why not go for the whole thing?"

"Are you crazy, Michael?" she whispered, the words catching in her throat. "Get me some water."

Sally took a deep breath and rolled her shoulders straight up as if preparing for battle.

"I want to bet $3,600 on Baltimore over Boston this afternoon."

"$3,600?" Fish echoed. "I don't mean to be out of line, but isn't that a little steep for you, Sal? I know you must have a good opinion on this game, but—"

"$3,600," she repeated. "Baltimore over Boston 720 times," she calculated quickly, saying the bet in multiples of five the way Fish was used to taking it.

"C'mon Sal, what kind of number is that? I know you've never stiffed me—"

"Is $12,600 better?" Sally cut in.

She felt giddy, 12,600, 3,600, what was the difference? Throwing numbers around on the phone was easy once you started.

"Hey, listen, I'm not tellin' you what to bet, honey," said Fish, his voice not quite as smooth.

"Okay, $12,600," Sally said, feeling exhilarated. "That's Baltimore over Boston, let's see . . ." she quickly did the math in her head " . . . 2,520 times."

Michael walked back in the room with her water.

She took the glass without thinking. She was betting with short money. So what! She wasn't planning to lose. She already lost Oxford. She wasn't going to let the house slip by, too. So what did a little more matter? She'd bet what she needed or not bet at all. Somewhere along the line the house had become an issue. She had to have it.

"Am I down or not?" Sally asked Fish.

"I guess you know what you're doing," Fish said.

"You don't have to worry," Sally said. "Especially if you play the piano," she mumbled, starting to giggle, not believing what she was doing. It was surreal.

"Ma—"

"Just a minute, Michael. Am I down or not, Fish?"

"But Ma—"

"Baltimore, even-six," the bookmaker confirmed. He hung up.

"I never believed you would do it, Ma. It was just an idea. You got down on the pitcher, right? That's what I was trying to ask you. The whole bet is Jim Palmer pitching against that monster wall in Fenway Park."

"I didn't specify a pitcher. Can you bet like that, Michael?"

"You can bet anyway you want."

"Yes, well, I'll call him back, but I want you to get the food down to the beach, then come back," she said, picking up the phone to re-dial Fish. In the picnic basket there were enough Tuna Fish sand-wiches for a high school and a thermos of instant coffee. "Tell your father I'll be spending the afternoon at the house." As he was about to leave she called out. "What station, Michael?"

"Channel 6, CBS out of New Bedford/Providence," Michael yelled back, walking out the screen door.

Her cavalier mood, that rush she'd felt moments earlier from living life on the edge, diminished as soon as the Boston Red Sox announcers appeared on the small black and white TV screen. What she was doing became all too real.

God must be laughing, without her telling him anything, Sally thought, as she rubbed a spot becoming tender at the base of her spine. Grandma would have been wagging her finger at her, too. Not so much because Sally was bad, but because she was a fool.

"A *nah*," Grandma would say. It rhymed with Hah!

23
The Game

"Phoebus? No, that's wrong. That has to be wrong, Michael. I didn't hear him say Palmer."

"He didn't," said Michael, staring at the screen. "You got back to Fish, right?"

"The line was busy."

"The line was busy?" he repeated. "Yes, well, you're not very lucky, Ma," he sighed, shaking his head with a peculiar smile, settling in to watch the game. "I guess there's nothing you can do about it now, except pray . . . uhh . . . a lot."

"Can this other guy pitch?"

"He's a rookie, only 19, a lefty they brought up from the minors. I think it's his first game." He gave a laugh as if there were something amusing about the turn of events. "It gets worse, Ma. I think he's a finesse pitcher — a lot of stuff, but no power. That's good for Boston. It plays into Boston's strength, the monster wall," he explained, giving a small laugh.

"Boston's strength? But I have the Orioles."

"That's why it's so important to bet on a pitcher, Ma, if that's what you're betting on in the first place. That underlay we had just became an overlay." Michael sounded as if he thought that might be funny, too. He must have read her face. "Don't panic! Boston still has the worst record of any team against the Orioles."

"Where's Jim Palmer," she insisted. "He must be somewhere."

"They're telling you right now."

The broadcaster was saying Palmer was pulled because his shoulder had tightened up from the unexpected chilly Boston weather.

Only a high of 66 degrees expected for today's game. Not like the humid late August heat Palmer's used to back home in Baltimore. It was 48 degrees, folks, early this morning here at Fenway Park.

He sounded amused, too. Sally hated the cheerfulness she heard in his voice. What's more, she learned, Frank Robinson, Boog Powell, and Dick Snyder, all three top hitters for Baltimore, were resting up for tomorrow's Labor Day double header. Their replacements, Blair, Reznovski, and Lau, had nowhere near the power, according to Michael.

Folks, we may have a ball game here, after all.

Sally knew this experience was going to be worse than having children. Something huge and jagged was pushing against her lower spine. She took a soft throw pillow and placed it behind her back and watched Boston score a run in each of the first three innings on two homers over the wall — Carl Yastrzemski and Tony Conigliaro — the third off a wild pitch from young Phoebus.

"Nerves," commented Michael. "First time out jitters."

Baltimore tied it up with a three-run inning in the fifth — Davey Johnson hit a homer with two men on. Sally knew that was good rather than bad, but felt no joy. Boston scored in the sixth and seventh, Scott and Petrocelli over the wall, to go ahead 5—3.

The Boston sportscasters were as good as cheering. Sally considered calling the F.C.C.

"See what I mean about Boston's strength, Ma?"

The spasmodic pains in her back were at shorter intervals. Her spine was dilating. She would deliver in the ninth. Sally wanted to call the whole thing off, but, like birthing, couldn't.

"They broke a record at the Bridgehampton racetrack, Ma. This guy from England, in a practice," said Michael, reading the newspaper during the seventh inning stretch.

"Where did you get *The Times?*"

"MacMullins. I like their sports coverage."

The eighth inning was uneventful. It was down to the wire. Sally could hardly bear it. Had she mistaken a nervous breakdown for euphoria? She stood up and paced the floor, but the back pain made her sit down again.

The Red Sox will use every edge to protect their two-run lead. They've gone to the bull pen in the top of the ninth. Who's coming in? Is that Shelton? Yes, Shelton, a left-handed pitcher is coming in to face the two left-handed hitters coming up for Baltimore. Listen to that hand for McMahon as he leaves the ballpark.

"Lower the volume," said Sally.

After getting the first two batters to pop out, Shelton walked the next two men.

Watch Baltimore now. Their pitcher is up with two men on base and two out. They're sure to bring in a pinch-hitter. Yes, there they go. Baltimore has called . . . let's see . . . yes, that's big Frank Robinson to pinch-hit for the pitcher, Tom Phoebus. What a trial by fire for the young rookie. He won't forget this one. They gave him plenty of time to show what he has. Shelton will face one of Baltimore's best, big Frank Robinson, trying to close out this game.

"Shelton needed more warm-up," said Michael, to explain the pitcher's predicament.

Frank Robinson, batting .310, has the chance to beat his team-

mate, Boog Powell, in their tight RBI race with this hitting opportu-
nity. So there's a lot riding on these pitches.

Sally ran to the bathroom to throw up. She had finished half a
loaf of Wonder Bread with nearly a pound of butter.

"Yesssss!" shouted Michael, standing up, right hand jabbing
at the air.

"What happened?" asked Sally, rushing back.

"Frank Robinson cleared the bases — a three-run homer. You're
winning by one run, going into the bottom of the ninth."

Baltimore has to go to the bullpen for a pitcher. Frank Robinson's
big three-run homer put Baltimore in front for the first time this
afternoon, ladies and gentlemen. And Robinson gave himself a two-
run lead in the hotly contested RBI rivalry with teammate Boog
Powell, who, for those of you who just tuned in, got the afternoon
off. That looks like right hander Mo Drabowsky walking out to the
mound, coming in to pitch for the Orioles. It is Drabowsky. A solid
relief pitcher, he'll pitch to the bottom of the Boston order, Jones,
Petrocelli, and Ryan, in the last of the ninth. It's Baltimore leading
the Orioles six to five in what's turned out to be a roller coaster day
here in sunny, but chilly Fenway Park.

"Arthur Ashe upset Roy Emerson in the Davis Cup exhibi-
tion," said Michael, glancing at the paper.

Dombrowski walked Jones.

Joe Singer walked into the living room.

Petrocelli hit a long ball to left field, toward the monster wall.
The ball was blown foul.

"What's going on?" Joe asked.

"I guess you're lucky, Ma. That could have been the game."

"Shit, you didn't bet on this game, did you, Sally? Not on Baltimore without Palmer. I was listening to the game at the beach. No

Robinson, no Powell—"

"They scored three runs in the top of ninth, Dad. Baltimore's got a one-run lead."

Joe ignored him. "This is what you had to do this afternoon, Sally?"

On the next pitch, Petrocelli hit a flyball to left center. Blair made the catch. Jones looked like he'd go for second on the throw to avoid a double play situation, but the coach held him back.

"Tough call," said Michael.

Ryan, batting eighth, one ball and one strike on him, went for a bad pitch and grounded into a double play.

Joe walked out of the room.

The game was over.

Baltimore won.

Sally won.

She should have been elated, but instead she felt awful, exhausted, 100-years-old.

Is this the life her father lived? What happened to *Guys and Dolls?* No Sky Masterson here. No Nathan Detroit getting into scrapes and bursting out *Sue Me.* No Nicely Nicely singing about handicappers who are real sincere. Nothing but pain. Where did Damon Runyon hide the pain in his story? She wasn't all her father's daughter, not altogether a Sallylamb. She didn't have the stomach for it. It was the worst experience in her life.

"I have a game for tomorrow, Ma," said Michael. "If you want to buy another house."

24
Bust ups

Sally waited a few minutes before going into the kitchen, waited to become a person again. Confronting Joe — lying, deceit, betrayal — couldn't be worse than the ball game.

"I heard from the bank," she said, exhaustion passing for calm.

Joe was seated, having a beer.

"When was that?"

"Yesterday"

"Yesterday?"

"I got the loan."

"Oh yeah? Well, lucky for you. You still shouldn't have signed a sucker contract. Even that asshole Max told you that. Did you get what you wanted?"

"I worked it out. "

"Worked what out?"

"It doesn't matter. It's none of your business, Joe."

"None of my business?" Joe was chewing his lip in that ugly way.

"I'm not going back to New York with you," Sally blurted.

Hearing herself, she knew it was true. Knew why the house figured so importantly, knew why she did the crazy thing she did.

"I'm staying in East Hampton. I know what you've been doing with Nancy. It's disgusting. You could have said you wanted a vacation, wanted time away from me. I wouldn't have liked it, but at least it was honest. I need time away from you, Joe. You're not who I thought you were."

"Wait a minute. You've got nothing—"

"I'm no fool, Joe. I'm no fool," she said, her voice getting shaky, talking louder. "Isn't what you've done enough? Are you going to lie, too?"

"You're out of line, Sally."

"For God's sake! You want Nancy Ryner? Take her. But not while you're living with me."

"I don't need you to tell me who to take, Sally."

"I want to stay here. And I want you to go."

"You think you can just throw me away? What about the boys?"

"Don't even think about it. The schools are better for them out here. The world is better, after the summer people take their garbage back west with them."

"You'll never make it without me, Sally."

"Yes, well, watch! I can go to school from here. Maybe my mother will come back for her piano. Maybe she'll help." She'd slipped into defending herself. It made her angry.

"You and your mother? Hah!" he said, sarcastically. "And your friendly broker? On the same street. Will he be here, too?"

"Joe, I want you to leave. You're not the person I thought I married."

"You're not the girl I married, either, Sally."

"Look, you can see the boys whenever you want—"

The ladder-back kitchen chair crashed to the floor as Andy stormed into the room, tripping over it.

"It's your fault," cried Andy, pointing at Sally. "I saw you. It's all your fault."

She tried to help Andy up. He pushed her away. The letter from the Sag Harbor Savings Bank fell out of her bikini top onto the tiled kitchen floor.

"I saw you that night in his car. I saw you!" gasped Andy, his face crimson.

"What's that?" asked Joe, pointing at the sweaty envelope.

"For God's sake, Andy. What did you see? What could you see? There was nothing to see!"

"You and Mr. Bennet—"

"What is that?" Joe repeated, reaching for the envelope.

"You and Mr. Bennet," Andy repeated. "The night of Mrs. Ryner's party . . . ."

Sally grabbed the Coppertone spotted message, tearing it to shreds.

"Was that from the bank? It was from the bank, wasn't it?" accused Joe.

"It's your fault. It's your fault. It's your fault," Andy was screaming over and over, hysterically.

"This is making it?" Joe snickered.

Sally started to sway. She held onto the table.

"You're no good for me. You never will be," she shouted, angry words hurled at Joe.

But, somehow those words were intercepted by Andy. The child turned gray, his face went blank.

"Not you, not you," Sally gasped, reaching toward him. "My God, Andy, not you."

Andy stood up, moving backward, eyes glued to Sally. Then his face shattered. He ran out of the room.

"Andy," Sally cried.

The front door slammed shut.

"Nice work," said Joe.

Sally couldn't breathe. She ran out of the kitchen. She had to get out, but she had to find Andy, too. She passed Michael, staring at the after-game talk show.

"Michael—"

"I'll do it, Ma."

"But—"

"I said I'll do it."

Sally tripped, scraping her leg, going out the door to the car. She scrambled up, having to get away from the house. To get away from this thing called family she wanted so much. Was this what she was counting on for her future? Her second chance?

The keys were in the taxi. Ben was huddled in the back, pale and withdrawn. Obviously, he'd heard, too. She said nothing as she got into the car, pulled out of the driveway, crushing a plastic Frisbee on her way. Sally grimaced. She knew, without looking, that it had to be Andy's blue one. Quickly, she made the turn on Barnes Hole Road, the turn that would take her toward the ocean. And toward Nancy Ryner's house.

Minutes later, finding herself on Spring Close Highway, Sally veered, wheels screeching into the Ryner driveway. She pulled the taxicab up short on the wide front lawn.

"Joe?" Nancy Ryner's voice called out from the shadows behind the screen door.

"Stay in the car," Sally told Ben.

Sally walked past the house — Ben trailing behind her despite her instructions — past the decks and guest cottage. Trance-like, she walked into the studio, deliberately, on a programmed mission like that brainwashed Lawrence Harvey in *The Manchurian Candidate*. She smashed the replica of part of herself on the concrete floor, wishing it were Nancy's head instead, wishing she could do it over and over again. Looking around, she smashed the bust of Liz Slavka, too. Before she got on a roll, Sally walked out of the studio.

Nancy Ryner was standing near the yellow taxi, parked on her rented front lawn. In the background, the stately, classic, Victorian East Hampton house threw a long shadow on the manicured greenery.

"Get out of my way," said Sally, her voice deadly calm, her face clear.

Riding back to Barnes Landing, Ben said, "I never saw you really angry, Ma."

That night, Sally sat alone in the darkened living room, her reliable bread and butter at her side. There was nothing on her mind. She was numb. The phone had to ring five times before she recognized it as a call. There is nothing he can say that would change anything, she prepared herself. She lifted the receiver.

"I thought we were going to a movie tonight, Sally," said Nancy Ryner.

"You what?" That was enough to wake her.

"C'mon, Sally. For Chrissake. This stuff goes on all the time. It doesn't mean anything."

"Are you crazy?"

The afternoon's feelings of wanting to bash this woman's head broke loose, churning through her bread and butter balm.

"I thought you knew, Sally. Everyone else did. I know you're not stupid. I thought it didn't matter to you after my birthday party. I took your silence to be your tacit permission. I mean that carnage in my studio. I'll try to forget that. I like you, Sally."

There was a long pause.

"C'mon, Sally. Don't pull this—"

"You don't understand," Sally cut in softly, straining to hear the sound of truth through the turbulence clouding her mind. When it came it was as tangible as hitting the ball right, when that exquisite tuning fork goes off inside your body.

"You don't understand, Nancy. I just don't like you."

Having said that, she hung up. Understanding that truth was a better cure-all than Wonder Bread, wasn't it? It was emancipating, wasn't it? Spinoza was right, after all. Like it or not, the truth shall make you free, she reasoned, as she climbed the stairs to her recaptured bedroom.

Avoiding the abandoned piano, she put herself to bed, too tired to change her clothes. She felt cracked, fragmented. Yet, she'd survived this terrible day, put things in neat little packages, figured things out.

So why were tears flooding her eyes, overflowing, cascading down her face?

PART TWO

There are no secrets in a small town.

25

There are no secrets in a small town.

It was turning dark by 7:30 nowadays, the sun hurrying, it seemed, to make the Vernal equinox, as if it could possibly miss it. On Dayton Lane, white and yellow shasta daisies, pink asters, red geraniums, blue monkshood, all kinds of mums — were flourishing in fall flower gardens, belying the coming of winter. The September weather, despite August's cool promise, had turned sticky, hot, more like July.

As Sally walked down the path from the Foster house, still dressed for summer in a black linen sheath and sandals, she wondered if the locals kept a separate summer, a secret season, for themselves to be used after the *invaders* left. Ocean temperatures were, after all, at their highest, close to 70 degrees.

She couldn't see the Hawley house from her driveway and was glad. It was only a little more than a year since the rental incident. Both Jack and Hawley Bennet had said their cousin Charles Hawley was not a forgiving man, that he'd changed after the birth of his son, Junior. The fact that Cora was gone, only made it worse.

"Cora?" she asked.

"His wife," said Hawley.

"She died in childbirth," concluded Sally. "How awful!"

"No," laughed Hawley. "She ran off with the plumber — Plumb Foster, a third cousin on her mother's side — a few years later. That's how you got the house in a way. Plumb's brother Amsy couldn't live across from Charles after that. Charlie's never been the same, definitely not a forgiving man."

Sally didn't want to hear more. She couldn't deal with unforgiving men.

Looking up and down Dayton Lane, she once again admired its charm. She wouldn't mind walking to the district offices over at the high school on a night like this. Of course she had a stick and some biscuits. The dogs she'd seen lying so lazily on Dayton Lane lawns a year ago, chased after you when you walked by. She left plenty of time to get there for the evening appointment with the guidance department. Now that the boys had been in school a few weeks, she thought it important to check up on them and to explain the pressures — new home, new town, no father . . . .

She stopped short and looked again. There was something in the middle of the road. Walking to the curbside, even at dusk, she could make out the body of a child. There was a child lying in the middle of Dayton Lane in front of her driveway.

About to scream, thinking the youngster might be dead, Sally checked first. And was glad she did. Moving closer, she saw that what she took to be a child, was a woman, a woman so frail, so wraith-like, she could easily be mistaken for a young girl. But the semblance ended there. Curled over, sleeping soundly, a harsh snore escaping the parted lips, the woman smelled like old alcohol. It was overpowering. She was, nevertheless, in jeopardy lying there in the street.

Dropping the stick, Sally went back in the house and called the village police, then returned outside with a flashlight to direct traffic, any that happened by. It seemed like only a moment later when Jack Bennet showed up. Sally was silenced by Bennet's grim bearing.

"This is my wife, Jean," he said tersely, lifting the woman from the road. "No need to call the station house next time. They'll only call me." Turning, he walked down the street to his home.

Sally said nothing. What could she say? She watched them disappear, flashlight at her side. Then remembering her appointment, she exchanged the flashlight for the stick on the lawn and hurried up Dayton Lane toward the high school followed by the snarls, barks and growls of the neighborhood dogs.

Once there, Sally climbed the two flights of stairs, rushed down the hall looking this way and that until she found the guidance office.

"My God, you look like hell."

"I beg your pardon," Sally countered, still shaken from the events of the evening. "Are you speaking to me?" she pointlessly asked the woman. There were only the two of them in the room.

"*Marrone!* Your voice! You sound like my grandmother's grandmother. You're not doing so well, eh?"

Sally looked at the woman closely. It hit her. The chef's apron! The woman in the kitchen! She was stockier than Sally remembered, but still darkly handsome with a mass of undisciplined curly hair.

"Did you work the Ryner party this summer . . . August on Spring Close Highway?"

"I was there. I saw you. You look terrible now."

"I'm Sally Singer. New in town. Do you have a child in school, too?"

"No, I don't. You're late for your appointment."

"Yes, well. Looks like the counselor's late, too. I walked over from Dayton Lane," Sally explained, no point in telling more.

"No car?"

"Not yet."

"Well, I can give you a lift home if you want. That's not a short walk."

Sally ignored the offer. After the summer experience, unsolicited friendships scared her.

"Damn," slipped from her mouth. "Am I trespassing on your appointment? I'm sure Mrs. Wolff said 7:15." She was referring to the assistant to the principal. Sally looked at the clock on the wall. It was about to hit 7:25.

"I'm the guidance counselor, Mrs. Singer, Mrs. Aquistapace. Ah-keesta-pachey! A bringer of peace with a degree in school psychology," she explained pointing to the *J. Aquistapace* nameplate on the door. "I cover the S's . . . N through Z actually. I'm the boys' guidance counselor," she added. "The J is for Josephine. I did your house this summer."

"Josephine? My house? You . . . Josephine the phantom cleaning lady?"

"That, too," said Josephine Aquistapace, "and you'll see me behind the counter at Rowe's drug store on Sunday mornings. We do whatever we can around here to make ends meet."

Sally could think only of one thing. "You saw my housekeeping?"

"Yes, well, I hope you're doing better around the Dayton Lane house than you did last summer. I know it was a vacation, but that house was like the Collier Brothers."

Sally laughed, letting go of some the night's tension. The Collier Brothers — two recluses discovered at home after death with everything living and growing in their messy house, including cash.

"Orderliness escapes me. I can't find anything when I put it away."

"You couldn't have come from a large family," Josephine reasoned. "My mother would throw anything out the window that wasn't put away. That was three stories down to the yard. But we were nine."

"Nine children?"

"Nine and poor, too," said Aquistapace, sounding proud. "But Corona was like East Hampton. Corona in Queens," she answered Sally's unasked question. "You could live there poor." She shifted toward a bookcase, taking a clip board from the shelf. "Enough about me. Listen, have you looked at yourself lately?"

"It's been difficult."

"But not unexpected, eh?"

Sally looked surprised.

"I put two and two together at that party. What a menage! *Marrone!* And then your staying out here the extra weeks. I closed Hawley's house after you left. He likes you, by the way." She eyed Sally carefully. "Mrs. Singer, you look like you're taking a slow beating."

"Something happened on the way over . . . ." she let it trail. "Okay, I admit, I've been feeling sorry for myself. Overwhelmed. We were together almost 13 years, Mrs. Aquistapace. Or is it Doctor Aquistapace?"

"No doctor, please. I don't use it. That's all I need is one more thing to stand between me and the students. It's Mrs. Aquistapace at school . . . 13 years, eh? Married young. Out of high school, right? Like me. What did we know?"

"It was hard to believe to tell you the truth. My husband and I were friends, too, I thought."

"Yes, right! Friends. But hard to believe, you say? Please!" She made two syllables out of it: puh-leeze. "You think you're immune, eh? You know what Italians say, faithful husbands, spotless floors, clean diapers—"

"I thought that was a southern expression," Sally interrupted.

"It's in every language that women speak," Josephine Aquistapace observed, in an all knowing way. "So how are the boys at home? Doing better than their mother, I hope." She sat down on one of two worn club chairs in the corner of the room in front of the metal desk.

Sally seated herself with a sigh. "Michael's quiet. Andy's angry with me. Something happened. I can't talk about that right now. Ben's confused."

"Who's *The Racing Form* reader?" She must have seen Sally's surprise. "They were always around the house, Mrs.Singer," Aquistapace explained, "under beds, behind the hamper."

The picture was sinking in. The woman knew all the secrets of her flawed housekeeping, knew the scene in the Ryner's kitchen the night of the party. She could draw some pretty private conclusions about Sally's life.

"Don't worry. Your secrets are safe." Aquistapace laughed again. "There are no secrets in a small town, you know."

"I'd heard," said Sally.

"There are friends, though. Support when you need it. That makes up for all the gossip. Let me show you the school. Your oldest will be here next year in the junior high." As they walked down the hall of the two story brick building, Josephine added, "I met your boys at registration. I meet all new students. Make it my business. Don't worry, we'll keep our eyes open. They've got good teachers. The one called Ben tells me he's your artistic child."

"He writes poetry," said Sally.

"He told me; said he does his best writing in his jeans, but he doesn't really feel artistic."

Sally looked away. "What about, Andy? We have a tough time together."

"Andy struck me as being made for this town. A regular guy. Athletic. A jock."

"He's a fine athlete. His father's absence might be toughest for him."

"You'd be surprised."

"About what?"

"About who reacts the most. You can't ever tell," said Josephine, showing her the well equipped gymnasium. "The quiet ones worry me."

Sally refused to worry about Michael. If Michael couldn't handle it, they'd all go down the drain.

"How do they feel about Jewish children in this town?"

"You don't have to worry."

"Do they give them a hard time?"

"You don't have to worry about that. Not in East Hampton."

"Why?" Sally asked.

"Not enough Jews!" said Aquistapace.

Later, on the drive home, after they had stopped for a drink in the cellar at the 1770 House, after she learned Josephine and her husband were childless by choice ("I was the eldest of nine; I had my children"), after she learned that six years earlier they came out to sleep on an East End beach to escape the sweltering city heat and ended up buying a building lot for five dollars down, after sharing her space/time dilemma, her interest in moral weakness and her confusion over chaos, after Josephine asked her why she held things in until nothing less than murder was appropriate, Sally put the adultery question to her.

"I have no time for that stuff," said Josephine. "You know, your Greek philosophers could sit around and think about these things, Sally, only because their slaves did all the work."

26
Not The Way I Planned

October 3, 1966

Dear Mom,

Don't stay angry about the house. I didn't mean to be abrupt, but I had to hang up when you said I reminded you of my father.

I didn't know why the house was so important to me, until I knew I would have it, Ma. It gave me independence. You know Joe's attitude, his money was his and so was mine. But I hope you understand now. Look at the upside. You got your money back.

Now that we're settled — thanks to Hawley Bennet and his pickup and the trip to New York, I can finally explain about the bar mitzvah. I suppose I should start with the Springs Community Chapel Annual Covered Dish Supper at Ashawagh Hall.

Jack Bennet, you remember the real estate broker and neighbor, invited us. (I ran into his wife, by the way, sort of.)

In any case, the Minister was showing us the Chapel, very simple, very stark, everything white even the pews. Michael said, "I think God lives here, Ma."

I was moved by his spirituality and told Michael that I had to pay more attention to his bar mitzvah, if we could afford it.

Anyway, the Presbyterian minister, obviously moved by

Michael's comment, said, "Mrs. Singer, if you can get a Rabbi, we'd be happy to have your son's bar mitzvah in our Chapel. No fee. You could have the reception in Ashawagh Hall, an old-fashioned Springs covered dish party."

A free bar mitzvah! In a church! What could be more right for East Hampton ? The town is so Christian. Where else have a bar mitzvah but in a church?

The other option was the new Jewish Center for the few Jewish families that are here. (I'm told it was donated by some very rich Jewish man, his revenge for being rejected at the local country club.) It's Reform! They talk about organs. The men don't wear prayer shawls. No one reads Hebrew. Imagine what Grandma would think? You know what orthodox think about Reform.

"We'll cover the cross," the minister offered, "in case it offends anybody."

"How could it offend anyone?" I said.

Well, it offended everyone. I searched from Long Island to New York to find a Rabbi that would do it. They all said no. I even tried the Lubavitcher Hasidim in Brooklyn. They said I should bring the boy to them after his 13th birthday. They'd keep him a few days, bar mitzvah him, but no service in the presence of a cross.

"But it would be covered, I told the Rabbi."

He said, "covered dish, yes, covered cross, no. It's an 18th Century edict."

I argued that the 18th Century was supposed to be the Age of Enlightenment.

"Jews never benefited from European enlightenment," he replied.

So I went to the Jewish Center. They had heard about the church. And a man named Wolff, who owns an accounting firm and who has a reputation for suing a lot — some mucky muck at the Jewish Center — asked about the kids getting free lunches at school. (It was there, Ma. We qualified. I took advantage of it.)

Needless to say, Mrs. Wolff is assistant to the principal. I told this guy Wolff how I felt good being in the Jewish Center even though it was reform and they didn't wear *Talisim*. He said, "What's the matter? Reform isn't good enough for you? With the children on free lunches you can be such a big shot?"

The next week, thinking it more discreet if I weren't there, I dropped the boys off and came back to pick them up. Wolff started with me again, "Why aren't you here? Why isn't the mother here? Why isn't the mother here to celebrate the Sabbath with us?"

"The mother isn't Jewish, that's why." It came out of my mouth before I realized it. I was so angry and hurt, everyone was looking at me like they knew everything about me. (I did not mention Catholic Jackie, I swear.)

Later I was told by Hawley Bennet who laughed — easy for him — that he'd heard it from someone who was told by somebody who heard from someone who was there, that Wolff said, "Just what we need, a poor Jewish family in East Hampton." Too bad, I told Hawley.

There isn't another Synagogue in a 60 mile radius. The one in Sag Harbor shut down. Not enough Jews. I'm sure I'll be struck by lightning. I hope G-d doesn't punish Michael, too. It's certainly not his (Michael's) fault if we can't make this thing happen. I really feel bad. I feel Grandma's looking over my shoulder, too.

Besides everything else my friend Doug Slavka split with his girl-friend. The nice one. You met her when you were in East Hampton. He's going to Florida to stay with his rich uncle. He said he'd call you and take you to dinner. Don't count on it. He's unreliable.

I know this might sound familiar, like an ambulance call —

Grandma, you and me all over again — but do you want to come for another visit? My schedule takes me into the city only once a week for my Machiavelli obligation. I gave up the courses I was supposed to teach. No way I could handle three times a week now — no car, too many hours. The boys stay alone only the one day. (The department's appointed a dissertation committee for my thesis on moral weakness.)

Yes, Joe sees the boys regularly. He comes out weekends with his girl friend. She has a home in Amagansett. Joe's moving into that house. He's giving up the taxi business, but he's not selling the medallion. Wants to wait till it's worth more, so says Michael. He's investing in a new car and leasing it out to two hackies, one day-shift, one night-shift. That was never for him. I suppose.

This from Michael, too, Joe's heard about poker games out here. He's going to take a shot at that. Tax-free, no overhead, no mainte-nance, he said. How about no income, I say. You'll be getting your monthly checks, Michael said. As for me, I'm not counting on any-thing.

On a more reliable note, I can teach two courses at Queens col-lege next semester if I get a car that can get me there. Stony Brook still a possibility for the following year.

Love,
Sally

P.S. The boys are excited their father is in East Hampton. How do I feel? Like a failure, sometimes. Things have turned out a mess. A broken family and three children. It was not the way I planned. Josephine Aquistapace, the school guidance counselor and a new friend — one who's happily married — says that feeling will pass, that it's a phase. Will it, Ma? Anyhow, about the living arrangements, Hawley Bennet says a lot of that goes on in town so I needn't be mortified that my husband is living nearby with another woman. Well, actually it's two women. Liz Slavka moved in, too. No telling what's going on there!

27
Homecoming

Ben jumped when a shrill, high-pitched alarm pierced the air during the first quarter of the football game. Assorted men, like jack-in-boxes, popped randomly out of the stands, members of the volunteer fire department scampering to answer the siren's call. Even though his father and brothers were at the varsity game, too, Ben was standing along the 50-yard line with Hawley Bennet. He had come to adore the young Fire Chief who, one afternoon, had taken him out on the big red truck.

Ben ran back to the stands. "There's a fire, Dad. Hawley's going to help put it out."

"Hawley's a brave guy," said Joe Singer, watching someone called Johnny Chain who was marking the downs on the side of the field.

"Dad's made a line on every game and been right," Michael said proudly. "Wouldn't it be great to make book on this?"

"You think you're such a bigshot, Michael," Andy said, feeling left out in these conversations and embarrassed, too. He wasn't sure that's how people spoke in East Hampton. "You don't have to talk so loud. Everybody can hear you, show off."

It was the Saturday of the Columbus Day weekend. Leaves had turned further west, yet East Hampton's trees remained dressed in green thanks to the temperate effects of the Gulf Stream. Farm stands blossomed along the highway, selling fall crops of cauliflower, cabbage, turnips, and broccoli.

The weather was still hot and sticky.

Earlier, the Village bustled. Young mothers, laughing girlishly with each other, pushed strollers on Main Street. Kids were hanging out in bunches at Herrick Playground across from the High School. People were coming in and out of the Five and Ten, its windows decorated with pumpkins and witches anticipating Halloween. John Wayne was starring in the *Sons of Katie Elder* at the East Hampton Cinema. Housewives, in short sleeves, slacks, and makeup, heads wrapped in colorful cotton bandannas guarding Saturday night coifs, were doing their week's shopping at Bohacks and the A&P. A storefront beauty salon buzzed with the bee-hive activity of bent-over dowagers, their blue-haired heads corking protective plastic capes.

A few folks were sitting lazily on the grass around Town Pond watching the swans, their dogs running back and forth to the water's edge. But there was an unmistakable, energetic hum throughout the Village in anticipation of the high school varsity football game at Herrick Park. The Bonackers were playing Southampton at home.

Like most of the town's people, Joe went to the varsity football game, played on the field behind the new A&P. The kids got a kick out of the school marching band, spiffy and polished in maroon and gray. It added to the excitement as adults of all ages crammed into packed bleachers. Between the stands, autumn yellow jackets, breaking formation to buzz the fans periodically, swarmed around the large trash cans filled with sticky sweet candy wrappers, pomegranates, Dixie Cups, and leftover sodas. When the first note trumpeted, the spectators rose as one to sing loud and proud: *East Hampton High is marching, come take the lead, firm friends and classmates, we will always be as one in word and deed. We love our alma mater and this will be our cry, to hold up the colors of East Hampton High.*

Joe thought it was a little corny, but the men in the stands talked football and Joe could talk football. So far the guys he'd bullshitted with showed no real understanding of the game. They'd talk pro ball, too, of course, about betting on winners, not even taking into account the lines. Neither *Newsday* nor *The Long Island Daily* showed betting lines in their papers, but it was hard for Joe to believe these guys didn't know about them. Nevertheless, he declined to make any small bets with the more aggressive guys when they'd gotten used to seeing him every week. Fish were always there to be hooked. No hurry. He wanted to set up a poker game, play and take the house cut, not win small bets. In fact, he was willing to lose a few bets to suck them in.

"Don't they teach these kids defense?" he criticized, as the visiting team's quarterback made another first down.

"The kid misread the block," said a voice in the rear. "He'll adjust. Watch him!" It was Jack Bennet sitting in the bleachers two rows back.

"I knew you were talking too loud, Dad," rebuked Andy, accustomed to his father yelling at the TV set, at players, coaches, and managers. "It's only a high school game."

Jack Bennet was right. The team went with the same play, but the Bonackers sacked the quarterback to the crowd's delighted cheers. Joe turned around, giving him a nod. So did Nancy Ryner, looking both bored and disgusted at the same time. She had an open copy of *The New Yorker* on her lap.

"Only men and Republicans could think something so primitive a sport," she commented, over chants of *Hit'em again! Hit'em again! Harder, Harder!*

"It's the homecoming game against Southampton," Bennet explained, nodding at Ryner. "The kids are pumped up, but a little nervous."

Next to him was a fragile looking woman, her face pasty-white. She moved her hands constantly, twisting pieces of tissue that weren't there. Though it was uncomfortably warm, she was wearing a hacking jacket that had seen better days.

"That's Mrs. Bennet," Andy told his father.

The firemen returned before the game was over. There were whispers behind them passing along the report on the alarm. "Waste of time, Bub. Only a grease fire in a kitchen oven. The Foster house."

"Isn't that us?" cried Ben, looking alarmed.

"Ma's cooking for our birthdays," Michael said. (Each of the boys was born in October so they celebrated on one day. They were 12, 10, and 9 this month. Michael traced their births backwards to his father's winning football bets on the last games of the season.)

Squirming in his seat as news of the Foster house fire spread through the crowd, Andy looked uncomfortable. "She'd have to do it during a football game," he said, red-faced.

Ben went down to the field to be with Hawley Bennet. "I want to hear it from the Chief," he said to Joe, who was shaking his head, as if he'd been there before.

The Bonackers whipped Southampton's Mariners 14 to 0 that afternoon. The exhilaration was tangible among the crowd. In the long shadows of the coming sunset, parents and fans, friends and families, saluted each other amidst the loud cheers and gaiety while moving on to their evening's plans.

"I bet it was like this at Nuremberg after a rally," said a handsome, dark-haired woman to her companion as she passed. "Hello, Michael . . . I understand your mother's trying to burn down half the town," she said before disappearing into the crowd.

"Who's that?" asked Joe.

"Mrs. Aquistapace. She's our guidance counselor at school," replied Michael. "She's pretty smart," he acknowledged, with a grin. "She cleaned our house last summer."

They walked some more. "I have an idea, Dad. Will you give me five dollars for every player I can get for you for a poker game?" Tawdry suggestions sounded less so in Michael's refined manner.

Joe Singer smiled. "You're not talking to your mother, now, Michael. No way," he said emphatically. "Never hustle a hustler," he added, more as instruction then reprimand.

They climbed into the red Volvo. They were eating a second birthday dinner at Nancy Ryner's house for the first time. Their mother's old friend Liz was doing the cooking.

"The deal isn't so bad," Michael told Ben, who was worried that going there might be disloyal to their mother. "No one's doing anything to Ma. That happened already, Ben. Look at it this way. Ma's cooking, too. So we get to celebrate twice. We get two meals instead of one. Which for us is pretty good. Like a parlay."

"I don't like Mrs. Ryner," said Ben.

"You don't have to. Dad does. Why do you worry about Ma so much?" asked Andy. "She's the one that asked Dad to leave. It's all her—"

"Stifle yourself, Andy," Michael commanded, his voice stern. "Are you going to upset Ben again? What for? It's over. That's that."

"Why isn't Adam living with his mother? whispered Ben, before Andy could respond.

"A life style issue," Andy recited, sharply, having overheard a conversation.

"What does that mean, a life style issue?" Ben asked.

"It means just shut-up," snapped Andy, who wished he could stay with his father the way Adam Slavka did. He missed not having Joe at home and hated having to take orders from both Sally and Michael. He didn't mind Nancy Ryner, as long as she left him alone.

"I don't want to shut-up," said Ben, sounding hurt. "I wrote a poem."

From the pocket in his blue jeans, Ben took out a nail clipper, a discarded advertisement for discounts on garden equipment, a pink sponge, a rusty key chain, and a small card-sized envelope, still sealed. The poem was scrawled on the envelope's back.

"Can I read it?"

"You have more junk in your dresser than the dump," said Andy.

"You shouldn't look through other people's things," Michael intervened.

"Only you should, right?" his brother shot back.

Ben cleared his throat.

Upsidedowness
by Ben Singer
Daddy's gone but he's here
Does it make sense to you?
When he was here, he was gone,
And five is two plus two.

"It's nice, Ben, but I don't know what to make of it," said Joe.

"It's normal," said Nancy, pulling the car into the driveway on Meeting House Lane.

"How would you know? You don't have children," Joe pointed out, sharply.

"Then what are *they* doing here?" she said, face tight, as she climbed out of the car.

Ben's attention was on the envelope. He'd opened it, finally, though it was addressed to his mother. He let out a small sigh, feeling better when he saw his name. The card read.

> You're Invited!
> What: *Annual Halloween Party!*
> Where: *PQ 6*
> When: *October 28th, 1966 1 P.M.*
> To: *Benjamin Singer*
> RSVP: *Miss Vogt 212 561 4141*

What's PQ 6? A code? Was he supposed to call someone? he wondered, slipping the envelope back in his pocket before getting out of the car.

While the red Volvo traveled the four miles to Amagansett, Jack and Jean Bennet stopped at the Foster home after the game.

"I'm Jack's wife, Mrs. Singer," Jean Bennet introduced herself in a wavering voice, as tentative as her fragile appearance. "But I suppose you know that." Eyes shrouded, her thin lips gave a nervous smile.

Once again it struck Sally how tiny and frail this woman was. And sickly. A ghostly pale washed her tiny face, made almost grotesque by the rouged cheeks, intended, Sally thought, to give a healthy impression.

"Jack's told me so much about you," Jean Bennet went on.

"Only the good things, Sally," Jack Bennet interjected, in his best broker fashion.

Jean laughed nervously, as if her husband had said something terribly funny or terribly wrong. "That night? Please forgive any inconvenience I might have—"

"We thought we should stop by after the fire. No damage, I hope," Jack Bennet cut in.

"Nothing a paint job won't heal," said Sally, not feeling altogether at ease. "By the time they came, I'd poured salt over everything and put it out. I felt awful for the fuss."

"Oh dear," said Jean, her hands moving over each other, as if to keep them in place.

"Mrs. Bennet, I've been looking forward to meeting you. I can't offer you anything. Kitchen's still a mess," Sally apologized, waving her arms toward the kitchen and rolling her eyes.

"We can't stay," mumbled Jean. "I told you we should have phoned first, Jack."

"Perhaps you can stop by again, Mrs. Bennet," Sally invited. "Tell me about circuit breakers and water mains. We apartment dwellers are truly helpless in a house."

"Grandfather Foster built this house, you know. It was right after the war. There was a whole rash of ranches," she said, her nose pinched.

"They had to quarantine the village," Jack said, caustically, glancing briefly at his wife.

"Things change, don't they, right in front of your eyes?" Jean Bennet added, dreamily. "Well, yes, Mrs. Singer," she said, as if pulling herself back, hands fidgeting again. "I hope I can stop by, pay a call."

Sally wanted to say, "Call me Sally," but held back. Something told her that prim and proper was the tone Jean Bennet needed at this, their second meeting.

When the boys returned home that night, Sally carefully avoided asking them anything specific about their day. They went to bed after watching Gunsmoke on TV.

Before turning in, Sally lit a low flame in the oven, cooking tomorrow's turkey overnight. She'd splurged. Well greased and seasoned, the 27 pounder came freshly killed, from the Ludlow farm in Bridgehampton. She was glad she'd impulsively invited Hawley Bennet to join them. He'd seemed so concerned when he marched into the house that afternoon in response to her call for help.

She was tired. It was exhausting, being extra careful about what you said to your own children. And awkward. I've got to learn how to play this broken family game, she thought, turning off the night table light. There ought to be a handbook.

Brooding on ways to handle children, parental visits, and other women, she finally fell asleep. Sally dreamt about her father that night. She dreamt that Mike Lamb came back, a visit from the grave. She was so happy. Joe was in the dream, standing there stiffly, a one-man lineup.

"I'm so glad you're here, Daddy! I want you to meet Joe Singer. I married him because I thought you'd have so much in common, because he was your kind of guy."

Mike Lamb, looking a lot like Michael in the dream, studied Joe Singer as if he'd watched him all along.

"My kind of guy? You must be crazy."

Despite her father's reaction, she would have stayed asleep, if it weren't for the smell of smoke coming from the kitchen. For the second time that day, Sally called the Volunteer Fire Department.

28

You're not and I'm not

November 23, 1966

Dear Joe,

I prefer not to have Thanksgiving together.

It's six months since the beach house and my blindness, but I have it straight in my head now. I've had a lot of time to think and grieve.

There's no doubt that something was lost, Joe. But the part I found the hardest to deal with was the deception. It hurt me and it made me angry. I probably always will be. That's why I'm writing, not talking to you.

But thinking things out, and, because of a dream I had last month — among other things — I see we did start out on shaky grounds with mistaken expectations. I think I was living with someone I made up and therefore couldn't really deal with you. For you that had to be a lonely situation. But you could have told me you'd found someone else! And that would have been that. I always felt you'd married me more in the hopes of what I'd be, rather than what I was. Two people making a serious error. I understand that — I understand a lot of things.

You're not what I thought you were, Joe. I'm not what you hoped I'd be.

So we shed a tear (maybe a few) and life continues.

I understand from the boys that you're living out here now. You may continue to see them at will as long as you let me know. No surprises, Joe. By the way, should you want a divorce, I suggest you file for it.

Finally, because it's better for me, I'd prefer that we continue any communicating in writing.

Sally

P.S. If Michael hasn't told you already, I don't think he'll be getting bar mitzvahed. There was some trouble at the Jewish Center.

29

February 1972-Thin Ice

A long time ago, he'd figured out brothers were more important than parents. Though parents endured, brothers ultimately lasted longer.

Still, this guard duty wasn't for him. It was too cold standing around doing nothing. Stamping his feet on the grass to stay warm, Michael Singer, now 17, watched his younger brothers ice skate on Town Pond.

Since his Mom broke her arm her first time out on the ice six years earlier, she insisted that the younger boys be watched, despite the fact they were 14 and 15 now. Grandma Bea was visiting back then, too. Michael recalled her reaction when his mother came home from Southampton Hospital.

"If you want to live like a gentile, then suffer like a gentile," she told Sally, without compassion.

No doubt Grandma Bea, who was visiting again, was angry because he hadn't been bar mitzvahed. Neither of his brothers were either.

"Once you don't do the right thing," his mother confided, "it's amazing how easy it is not to do it again. That's a lesson, Michael. Try to do the right thing."

Besides the lesson, Michael thought there was some peculiar sense of maternal fairness involved, too. Since he hadn't, they wouldn't.

He watched closely as Ben fell yet another time on the ice, even though the volunteer firemen hosed it down only last night to make it smooth. Every time Ben fell he'd lift himself up, look over at Michael, and call out, "It's all right. It's all right. Now I've got it. I've really got it."

There's a lesson here, too, thought Michael. People come back for more, even when they get hurt. They keep making the same mistakes over and over, as if once done the error was wired in for good. He'd read an article about fundraising. After the first mailing, the fund-raisers went back repeatedly to the people that had given, never to those who hadn't. Same with the fish his father hustled in poker.

There were other lessons.

While in high school, he worked each summer at the tennis club on Abraham's Path. He rolled the Har-tru courts, arranged games, and, a natural player himself, was a hitter if there weren't enough members. He met renters and second home owners. Nancy and Liz and his father played there. In fact, all the city people who couldn't get into Maidstone played there. He saw how people with money — new money, the locals called it — acted. He saw how they were treated with superficial respect by the staff. They weren't all that smart.

They weren't as smart as his father, but they had money.

Sure, some had talent. The celebrities. But they didn't get Michael's attention. It was the wheeler dealers that caught his eye, easy to read, easy to handle, always having to prove they'd made it. You acted as if they did . . . *most* of the time. The rest? Well, it was good to make them feel they had to show you. They, too, like Ben, always came back for more when challenged.

Yet, Michael craved that kind of treatment even though he knew how shallow it was. When he was in his whites at the club and someone mistook him for a rich man's son, for an operator, he liked the feeling. Money was the equalizer.

So he tried to have it. It didn't bother him that money seemed to slip through his fingers. He just tried to get more. Taking advantage of the local interest in sports, reading all the papers and going to every game as manager, he began to make lines for high school basketball, football, and baseball games. His sold his own tout sheets, mimeographed on school equipment, for the big races, too. All those years studying *The Racing Form* paid off.

At first only his classmates were involved. Then the upper classmen. Then the coaches and some of the teachers, too. He was a good handicapper and a better promoter. He was always in action.

That was why he was stuck at the Pond. He shivered as an icy gust of wind invaded his wool jacket. His mother was at the high school seeing Mrs. Aquistapace, his guidance counselor. Michael Singer had become the high school bookmaker.

"Do you think I care he's taking bets, Sally? That's breaking the rules, but it's not what worries me. Those dopes. If they didn't bet with him, there'd be no business. I'm worried about him and you."

Sally gazed at Josephine Aquistapace as she paced in the small room, wild dark hair, hands waving, intense eyes.

"The Rose Tattoo! Anna Magnani? That's who you're playing, Josie."

"Forget, Magnani. Do you ever see the money he's making? Does he have things? Does Andy? Ben? Maybe a girlfriend? Does he give you money? Offer to buy his own clothes? He's a caring boy. Does he help out?"

"You're going too fast. No to most of them. He buys his own clothes with the summer money. What's so important?"

Aquistapace thought for a moment. "Is he on drugs? Does he drink?"

"Michael won't even take an aspirin. Drink, drugs! We're Jewish, for Chrissake!"

"Hah! Your tribe isn't immune anymore, not in this country."

"Josephine, he's wrong to make book. But what are you getting at?"

"The money, Sally. Where's the money? It's been bothering me all weekend. I don't know. Has any problem ever occurred to you? There is such a thing as a gambling habit."

"You don't have to tell me, Josie. My father was afflicted."

"Do you think Michael may be gambling?"

"Come on, Josephine, where would a 17-year-old gamble?" Sally asked, at that moment recalling his composure that day long ago when they bet for the house. Sally corrected herself. When *she* bet for the house. It annoyed her remembering it as *their* venture. He had nothing at stake. "What makes you think of gambling, Josie?"

"It's a consideration. Where does his money go, Sally? Do you ever have money missing?"

"I really don't know."

For Sally there was either a sense of enough or too little. She never knew exactly since she didn't care about money too much, only about money too little.

"I'll have my mother talk to Michael. If Michael is working off people's weaknesses, it might be a good idea to talk to someone who's been harmed by it."

"It's his father who makes a living off people's weaknesses, who understands them. Everyone in town knows about the poker games. I think he'd recognize a potential client."

"Joe went back to his own life style, a hustler, that's all. My mother lived with a gambler."

"Michael's smooth, maybe too smooth for your mother. Do you know what he told me when I talked to him about this? Told me with that charming smile on his handsome face? He asked if I ever heard of a Walk-in Theory? Trying to tell me that his dead grandfather, one Michael Lamb, does walk into him from time to time. He says he's helpless. *Per favore!* He's too smart for his own good, that's what he is."

The kind of things Michael came up with. Sally had to smile. Walk-in theory! Her Father, no less! Her concern had been with Mike Lamb's *walking out.*

"Someone he owed complained, Sally. Then he was paid. Consider that, Sally. Do you check your bank statement?"

"Are you suggesting forgery? You are, aren't you? I can't believe that. I lent Michael some money, Josephine," said Sally. "Why are you against him?" she asked, getting up from the chair. "I have to go. It's getting dark. Michael's at the pond with his brothers."

"I'm not against Michael, Sally."

"He's so refined, you've said so yourself," Sally pointed out. "People in town call him a gentleman."

"So's the Prince of Darkness a gentleman, Sally. Read King Lear! Better still read this!" She pulled a book from the shelf. *"Dependencies and Family Behavior.* Addictions aren't a heavy duty subject for philosophers like yourself, but read it anyway."

"I appreciate your trying to be helpful, Josephine," Sally

said, unconvincingly.

"By the way, have you gotten a job yet?" Josephine asked as Sally was about to leave.

Her teaching at Queens ended last semester. Her car — she'd inherited the old Checker taxi from Joe — overheated in traffic. It was impossible for the 200 mile round trip drive to the city and back during rush hours.

"Don't ask," Sally answered. "My mother and Michael have some ideas. I'm going to be 37 and they're planning my future. If you haven't depressed me already, Jo, I'm sure their suggestions will."

30
Jobs

Sally parked the taxi at the pond on James Lane where Main Street forks down a bit from the Huntting Inn. Through a soft curtain of snow, she gazed at the white spires of the Presbyterian Church, elegant in its chalky clapboard simplicity. Then she scanned across St. Luke's Episcopal, a gray stone fortress against papal infallibility, to the shy 17th Century saltbox squatting on the Mulford Family Farm. They were all framed by Dutch elms, majestic in crystal and ermine finery, icy bracelets on their boughs. Amidst this frigid splendor, colorful, tasseled scarves and knitted wool hats, their pom-pommed tails in pursuit, glided across the ice, a Currier and Ives winter landscape. A sigh of pleasure steamed the wintry air as she rolled the window down.

"How much to Town Hall?"

"I beg your pardon?"

"Is five enough to get me to Town Hall?" a male voice asked, roughly, opening the Checker's back door. He seemed out of breath. Sally guessed he came from the Inn.

"Hop in front, if you don't mind doubling up," she said, thinking fast. "I have another fare."

Swinging a shiny black attaché case with brassy initials on it before him, he climbed in next to Sally.

When the boys reached the car she said, "I have another fare to Town Hall I have to drop first. I'm sure your mother won't mind."

It was the truth. Their mother *didn't* mind. Five dollars was five dollars. On the short ride, up Pantigo, Sally's thoughts returned to Josephine. Where was the money? She had no answer.

When she first talked to Michael about bookmaking, lending him the money to pay off his debt, he said he was unlucky. Stories about fumbles, shots at the buzzer, errors on ground balls. And the ponies? That was a mistake, he admitted. A couple of longshots could tap him out. He wouldn't book horse bets anymore.

"You're not going to book anything anymore, Michael," she'd ordered. "It's a small town. Reputation is everything."

"Whatever you say," he said. "But a lot worse goes on in town than my taking a few bets."

At Dayton Lane, Sally stopped Michael while his brothers hobbled into the house on their skates.

"Michael, have you been taking money from me? Have you had to take it when you couldn't pay off?"

"Why would I do that, Ma?" he asked.

She tried to scrutinize his face before he slammed the car door shut. He was as polite, as refined, as innocent looking as ever.

Sally climbed out of the car, walking into the kitchen through the garage door. She found her mother slicing the meat loaf, her sons seated at the round kitchen table with its fake maple top.

"Ma picked up a fare at the Pond," reported Ben, with a grin.

"F U, too," said Andy. It was clear he didn't approve from the scowl on his face.

"Just watch your language," Sally said sharply.

"It was on the guy's briefcase," Andy shot back. "F period. U period, II."

"Okay, I'm sorry. How do you notice everything?"

"I have to," he said, "in this family."

"I *knew* it wouldn't be long before you'd be driving the taxi," Beatrice intervened, borrowing Andy's scowl.

"He went to Town Hall. There's a Planning Board Meeting tonight," contributed Michael, to nobody's interest.

"An accidental five is hard to refuse for a four-minute ride," said Sally, with a smile, seating herself next to Beatrice. "You know, Ma, the job thing, it's all over a second-hand car. Don't you think you could lay out some money for a car? It would be less than a thousand. And I've already got five."

"We've been through this, Sally. I thought it was clear before I got here," Beatrice reminded her, passing around the mashed potatoes.

"I know, but I checked at DiSunno's," Sally continued. "They have one."

"Why don't you do the taxi, Mom?" suggested Ben.

"Me?" Sally asked, incredulously. "I'd need a navigator. You know I can't drive and look for signs at the same time."

"I thought the car was a dead issue," said Beatrice. "You already gave up those two classes for this semester."

"I did, Ma. But I can teach in the summer. There are openings in both sessions. And I could continue to teach next year. Moral weakness is almost finished, the research, that is. I just have to tie the Greek in with the English translations. I could be defending my dissertation within 18 months." Sally was animated. "Then I'd only need fill-in jobs 'til summer, not a new career."

"It amazes me, Sally, at your point in life you haven't been able to put together a thousand dollars. Your management of money leaves much to be desired. Well, that's your business. I gave what I could to you and Joe. You and the children will get whatever I have when I'm gone, but I come first while I'm breathing. Who would take care of me if I didn't? There aren't many eligible men around, for your information. In Florida they're either married or waiting to die."

Beatrice Lamb still attracted the attention of men. She was one of those women who, though aging, seemed to get stuck at fiftyish for a long time.

"There's always Mr. Hawley across the street, Gramma," piped up Ben. Andy began to choke. Michael smothered his laughter with a napkin. "A joke. A joke," Ben said. "Grandma Bea hates Mr. Hawley."

"Don't get me started on that man," she exclaimed. "All these years, living right across the way and never saying hello! What kind of person is he? You and the boys are so nice to his unfortunate son."

Beatrice was referring to Junior Hawley. The grown man, 36, had the mentality of a 10-year-old. He would visit with the Singers, stopping by for *hard* bread. Junior loved bread. Sally told him she did, too. However, Junior had to eat his bread stale because he had swallowing difficulties. Since childhood he'd wandered freely around town, dropping in at friendly homes that kept stale bread on hand in case Junior Hawley came by. But Charles Hawley continued to ignore them. That made Beatrice indignant.

"Mr. Charles Hawley's not important in the scheme of things," she said in her grand way. "Why waste time on him?" Yet, she always did when she visited, watching him from the window, staring him down if their paths crossed. "It's no wonder his wife ran off."

"Maybe I should see that guy Kingsley," Sally said, changing course.

Early on, Jack Bennet tried to get her into local politics. The

Town Republican Chairman nixed that. "How would a liberal professor from away, probably a New York City Democrat, at that, know
about our town, about our kind of people?" he reportedly said.

Back then, Bennet offered to take Sally to Jess Kingsley, the
State Assembly Leader from Montauk, who really ran the show —
they said he'd run for governor — but Sally declined. Not only was
she not a city liberal, she'd never voted. Raised in a one-party city,
what did it matter? Sally supposed she should re-think Jack's old
offer. Kingsley didn't look so bad from his pictures in the newspapers, right out of central casting with his cloud of white hair and
Lincolnesque features.

"I should see Kingsley. Times are different, more competitive,
since Nancy Ryner and Liz and that group of transplanted New
Yorkers took over the local Democrat party."

"A political coup," said Michael, who followed that sort of thing
in the local paper. "They ran their own candidates for the Democrat Committee last year while the local Democrats were snoring,"
Michael explained to his grandmother. *The East Hampton Star*
and *The Easthamptoner* seem to like the action. They keep writing
about next year's local elections."

Sally agreed. "The local Republicans do need help in the `73
election."

"Don't bother with Republicans," said her mother, sounding
like Nancy. "I bet that Charles Hawley's a Republican."

"As a matter of fact, he's the Town Leader," Sally said, dryly.

"Hah!" said Beatrice. "I could tell. There's only one thing you
should do about a job, Sallylamb. Michael and I agree."

"What's that?" she asked with resignation, picking at the bread
and butter, too tired to eat.

"Real Estate!" said Beatrice. "This is a growing place! A resort area. I saw what happened to Miami Beach. If your father had only invested in Coral Gables' miracle mile before the war, instead of the horses . . . . " Her voice trailed as she remembered a long time ago. "Ask that Jack Bennet for a job," she advised, shaking her head to the present. "I'm surprised you didn't do that in the first place, especially after that poor woman passed away. You need a regular job."

"Real estate!" Sally exclaimed. "I know nothing about real estate."

"That never stopped you before," Michael pointed out.

"Sell real estate," echoed Sally, resurrecting her low opinion of the profession she forged coming home from an East Hampton summer party long ago. She was trapped in a cliché, the lesser of two evils. "I'll try Kingsley."

31
November 1973-Power Brokers

"**I**'m telling you, I know Sally. To her it's about winning, not power," Joe Singer said, standing underneath the *Democrats in '73* banner. "You guys are on the wrong track. Pay attention to your campaign, not theirs."

"That's easy for you to say. Your neck's not on the line," Nancy said impatiently. "You said she never voted and she's acting like a goddamn Harry Treleaven."

"Who's that?"

"The guy who sold Nixon to the American public in '68," Liz answered. "Calm down, Nancy."

"Where did she learn to target districts? You can see that's what she's doing. Besides having no social conscience, she's a goddamn Republican."

"Michael has to be helping her. That's how his mind works." said Joe. "I'd bet on that."

"He is, Dad. He came home every weekend in October, but not just to watch me play. He studies those enrollment books like they were tout sheets. Besides the football games, he's made picks on the election: Nancy for an upset win and the Republicans to hold the Board," said Andy, 17. "Do you guys want me to give out more flyers? Coach wants me dressed by noon, but Dunny and I can walk the village before the game."

B. Duncan Slykes, known as Dunny and as a Maidstone brat,

had volunteered to help the Democrats' campaign. (The B stood for Bainbridge.) He was on holiday from St. Paul's Prep and hung around headquarters whenever he could. Liz thought he might be a Republican plant and watched him carefully.

"Dunny can do that. You hang around a little longer, if you don't mind," said Liz Slavka to Andy, now a tall, wiry, dark-haired boy who resembled his father more each day.

It was the weekend before Election Day. The radio was blasting in the small storefront on Main Street that served as Town Democratic Headquarters. They'd had a lot of breaks — Watergate and the GOP; the Saturday Night Massacre, Nixon's desperate attempt at a wholesale break-up of the Watergate Investigation, and, best of all, Jess Kingsley's indictment, railroaded by a governor of his own party to stop Kingsley's surge for higher office.

But Sally Singer had to stick her nose into all of this, right here in town, siding with the Republicans, running the most effective part of their campaign.

"She's a fucking traitor, that's what she is," growled Nancy.

"Who did she betray?" Liz asked, without looking up.

"The people, the workers, the women's movement . . . .." Nancy listed. "Promoting those guys, those good ol' boys that get drunk whenever there's more than two of them together — I mean did you hear Ben Hawley at Guild Hall? 'The wife and I really thank all of you'," she mimicked. "With their pot holders and ball point pens . . . Neanderthals!"

"Please, Nancy, spare me! You're talking to Liz, now. You're running well against a very reluctant Ben Hawley. That's what our numbers show. If Republicans sense his ambivalence about giving up his law practice, if they see their party with a jaundiced eye because of the scandals and don't come out to vote in protest, and, if we get our vote out, we could win."

Liz Slavka was poring over the numbers now, large broad sheets spread across the collapsible picnic table rented from the American Legion Post.

"I'm still pissed with her insider/outsider theme, the takeover of the town like the takeover of the Democratic Party—"

"It was you who convinced all those New York Democrats to vote out here, Nancy! To protect their tax dollar," interrupted Joe.

"Well, they should. They have every right. But those Republicans, led by your ex-wife, the one masquerading as an ivory tower lady, wrote that draft dodger letter. How can we be draft dodgers? We're running women!"

"What the letter said was that we could have been draft dodgers, because none of us supported the Viet Nam War. It may be a stretch, but it isn't a lie," Liz pointed out.

"She needed a job, they gave her one. It's that simple. She understands winning, for Chrissake. She competed all her life. It's not about politics," Joe insisted. "Sally hates politics. It has too much to do with the real world."

"Well I can see she has two apologists here. I don't need this. I'm sick of hearing about Sally Singer! Who are you rooting for anyway, Joe? You're supposed to be on my side, not hers." Nancy turned her face away from him. "Can't someone shut that fucking WLNG off. All they do is make a lot of goddamn noise. Swap and Shop, for crying out loud."

"I thought we were supposed to listen for . . . . "

"Wait, one is coming on," said Liz, cutting Andy off.

"What's that voice?"

"Nancy, shhh!"

"Yes, yes Bub, we folks been around here some long time. Now, we may look ignorant, but we ain't stupid. And that's what these newcomers, these people from away, are countin' on, seems to me. Listenin' to what they say, they think you and me can't tell the difference between a piss clam and an oyster; can't tell the difference between those bunch of guys raisin' hell down in Washington DC and our own local Republicans who've worked hard for us. Our Republican neighbors are askin' you and me to give them our vote on Tuesday. So they can keep workin' hard for us. Well, Bub, they got mine. Anyone from Bonac knows if it ain't broke don't fix it. We don't need fixin' by a bunch of strangers. So I'm votin' Row A all the way 'n I hope you are, too.

Paid for by The East Hampton Town Republican Committee."

"What the hell was that?" asked Nancy, in a steely voice that bordered on an explosion. Her face was darkening beneath its fading tan. "Was that fucking Will Rogers? What was that?" she screamed.

"Some guy who's lived here for a 100 years doing a radio spot for Ma," said Andy. "They were over the house all week. She was looking for a voice. Ma said she wanted a folksy Will Rogers with a Bubby accent."

"A what?"

"Bubby! As in yes, yes, Bub! A recognizable Bonacker. I think she found it," Andy said, torn as usual between maternal loyalty, disliking Nancy Ryner and his mother's searing words. *You'll never be any good* was a permanent scar in his memory. The Democrats were using a professional from New York for their commercials.

"That lady doesn't see what's coming out here, " growled Nancy. "She's sitting on the wrong side of the fence. She'll be sorry. I promise."

"What?" said Joe.

"Dayton Lane isn't always going to have Hawleys and Bennets and Fosters, that's what. And that prick Kingsley with his big ideas isn't going to be around for long either," she spoke as if hypnotized. "This place is too important, a gold mine for money and power. The mother lode!"

"What happened to the workers, the people, the women?" asked Liz, smiling.

"You've got some fuckin' mouth, Nancy," Joe said darkly.

"Do I?" She went to the phone. It rang three times before Sally picked up. "I heard that new spot. You think you're smart, don't you?" Ryner screamed. "You'll pay for this."

"Jesus, you sound like a shrew! I thought the spot was pretty good. Now I know it."

The following Tuesday, when the returns came in, Nancy Ryner was a gracious winner, barely, over Ben Hawley for Supervisor. She promised to serve all the people in town. The Republicans kept control of the board by a three to two margin. Jess Kingsley credited Sally. The Democrats registered over 900 New York City voters who had second homes in East Hampton. They were brought to the polls by buses from the city or they voted absentee.

Michael Singer, other people's money in his pockets from his winning bets on the election, stashed away his bus ticket, called Long Island Limousine and Allegheny Air and arranged to fly back to Albany State University out of Islip MacArthur.

He had to hand it to his Mom. She'd learned the politics game from scratch and played it well. She knew how to sell the candidates, understood the constituency. People trusted her, too. His father was right. She could be a moneymaker.

"Kingsley's your Rabbi and he's not going to be around much longer. He'll never make governor," he'd told her before he left. "Like it or not, Ma, you better steel yourself for real estate."

32

Closing Calls-Seven Years Later-1980

"We can't leave yet," Sally told her sons when they pulled up to the real estate office in the silver stretch limo. "The buyer's attorney called the seller's attorney early this morning. They're not comfortable with the language of the town's resolution on the waterfront lots. They want further protection before signing off."

"The deal's going south," said Andy Singer, 23, looking very New York in his dark pin stripe suit. "I told you it would never close."

"What aren't they comfortable with?" asked Michael.

He had put the package together, getting the listing from the Unger Brothers, New York investment bankers who loved their mother and each other, then finding the Filipino group to buy it.

"They want a tighter representation to make sure the building permits will be issued once improvements are in, according to Ben Hawley. Max Slavka just said get it done and hung up on me, but he'd want to close no matter what. He shouldn't have rushed this, but that's what happens when an attorney has a piece of his client's action."

Ben Hawley was Frederick and Franklin Unger's East Hampton attorney, their point man in the application process with the Town Board and Planning Board, both known for putting road blocks in developers' paths. Max Slavka represented the Ungers as their lead attorney in every other respect. He and his son, Adam — a

pear shaped, shorter version of his father who had become an attorney — were responsible for this time of the essence, do-or-die
closing in New York, scheduling it on the Friday morning of the
Fourth of July weekend.

"Pressure, pressure, pressure. Do you really want to hold a gun
to someone's head, Max, on a deal so complicated ?" Sally asked.
"You're inviting all kinds of surprises."

"You do your job, Sally. I'll take care of mine. Just remember
we represent the same client. Time of the essence accelerates, not
delays. This should have closed three months ago. They don't close,
they lose their money. That's it. Tell Michael to tell that to his Filipino group."

You lose your buyer, lunkhead, Sally thought. There aren't many
investors that would touch that property with its protected habitats
for marbled salamanders and rattlesnake plantains. It was riddled
with catch basins, kettle holes, and more pink and blue ribbons
defining wetlands, than a baby's layette. A guardian of the trophic
chain, East Hampton Planning was steeped in ecology. The tagged
shrubbery on the 900 acres resembled a christening. All had to be
scrupulously protected by the developer.

"I don't for the life of me understand these big deals, Sally, the
money you guys'll be making today!" Jim Foster, out of uniform,
spoke up. "Why in cash?" He was sitting in the front of the limo
with 22-year-old Ben Singer, who was driving them in to the city.
"Ask those guys again to pay the commission by check. Save me
the trip, you a paycheck. Cash! Is it drug money?" Foster asked,
his policeman's mind in gear.

"That's how the Unger brothers pay brokerage fees, Jim,"
Michael explained. "As far as the Filipinos, we know Marcos and
company are stashing money anywhere in the world there's a stable

government. They pay the price because return on investment is less important than security. Planning his getaway, I'd bet; 15 years of power is borrowed time in that country. Before this there were—"

"Who the fuck cares?" interrupted Andy. "You're not making points here, Michael."

"The world's gone mad," Foster went on, paying no attention to the fuss his young brother-in-law was trying to make. "This town's gone mad. Locals used that swampy land with its spindly oaks and thick underbrush as wood lots when I grew up."

"Yes, well, don't say that in front of the buyers," warned Sally.

"I'm going to Dreesen's. Can I get you guys coffee?" asked Ben, the black visored cap he'd lifted from a Long Island Railroad car, perched on his head. "I like to hear Michael explain things. He's always interesting."

"So are fairy tales," Andy snapped. Seeing the sudden cloud on Ben's face, he added. "For God sake, Ben, I meant fairy tales not *fairy* tales." When Ben's sober expression didn't change, Andy said in exasperation, "You can't say anything in this family without someone getting sensitive." Nevertheless he went over, hugged his brother and slipped some bills in the pocket of his shirt for Dreesen's.

They all wanted something. Ben made a list in the notebook he always carried with him to jot down phrases and thoughts he might use later in a poem or an essay.

Michael climbed out of the car walking toward the storefront office. Andy followed close behind, as if to make sure he wasn't left out. Still compact and lean, hair cut short framing her face, Sally, at 44, looked more like her sons' sister as the three walked inside.

The Sally Singer Inc. real estate office, founded as a family business that her sons wanted no part of, was designed for comfort and to impress — cash-green carpeting, pastel upholstered chairs, wainscoted walls with paintings and photographs depicting East Hampton and its people. The ambiance was meant to lull prospects into believing it was all right to discuss cash positions and discretionary capital, to negotiate plus or minus a few 100,000 or a few million in soft, well-modulated tones in what had once been a hardware store. Sally's approach was unique. She taught customers, articulating compelling arguments, bringing them to the point of inference that was inescapable. Buy it! *Quod Erat Demonstratum!*

It was in these confines that Sally learned of the existence of a personal magic number that made otherwise civilized people resort to savagery. It was all relative what someone would kill for, steal for, lie for. If you were broke it could be 20 bucks; if you were a millionaire, 20 million.

After Kingsley lost the gubernatorial, Sally backed into her last resort, East Hampton Real Estate, getting a job with Jack Bennet. She knew nothing about real estate and didn't think much of it either. So she treated it as an academic subject, learning everything about it, including the lingo. Sally became a professional in a business that attracted amateurs and dilettantes. She opened her own firm in '79 when Bennet decided to write a book about local genealogies, settlers and natives, before all the Indians and founding families disappeared from town.

"It's been done before, but I want to include the Indian Nations, too. The Montauketts, The Shinnecocks, they were here first. At least the Shinnecocks have the reservation. But us settlers? We're the endangered species, not those salamanders," he said, referring to the fashionable environmental zeal in fashionable East Hampton.

A real estate boom was on in the late 70's, the northeast excited about the Carter presidency and depressed about fuel oil shortages, long gas lines, terrorist bombings in Rome and Great Britain, hostage-taking in Iran. The Hamptons were hot. Americans were vacationing close to home.

In fact, Hawley Bennet's Barnes Landing beach house, the one they rented, was the first property she'd sold to some hotshot Georgetown attorneys.

There was a growing international market for prime resort real estate, too, Far Eastern billionaires looking for stable governments to safeguard their wealth, thriving West German investors, suitcases full of green stashed in the trunks of their Mercedes. In fact, a colleague of the Oxford professor Sally had studied with spent summer holidays in the Hamptons renting through her firm.

So much raw land opened up in East Hampton once the proposed highway extension from Water Mill to Amagansett went south. Defeating it had been an issue that helped Nancy Ryner get reelected Town Supervisor along with 24 year-old Dunny Slykes and Angus MacMullin, the son of the Barnes Landing store owner, a scion of those sturdy fisherman who'd come down from Nova Scotia a half century earlier. A mushrooming exile of urban emigrés seeking second homes and safety were changing the political scales in town. Spec houses altered the look — an invasion of angular white-coated contemporary abodes screaming architectural statements over the rooted 17th Century saltboxes. They were sold with foundations barely dry.

Nancy Ryner! In her fifties, she was hard looking now, but attractive in a Joan Crawford kind of way. Sally was still amazed everyone knew yet no one cared that Nancy lived with her husband and an extra woman, but it was, after all, an *East Hampton* type of arrangement.

Honking horns pulled Sally's attention to the silver stretch limo standing in the no parking zone. Angry cars and people were dodging each other. Well, Jim Foster would make sure they didn't get ticketed. It was a gray day; traffic was impossible. The invasion started the night before, because the normal two hour trip from New York on the Expressway (it extended to Riverhead, now) could take three and a half hours on a summer weekend, particularly a holiday summer weekend.

East Hamptoners had done their heavy food shopping by Wednesday afternoon. It was the early arrivals from the west jamming the parking lot and stores. Locals wouldn't see the Village again until after the holiday. If you'd asked they would tell you they wished they could do without seeing the Village until February. "You can't park." "Those new shops catering to summer people are too expensive for us." "Why if the A&P and Rowe's Pharmacy weren't there, we'd never go into the Village at all," they'd say.

"Now tell me again," said Michael quietly, standing in front of Cora Foster's desk.

Sally's office manager — the former Cora Hawley who'd run off with the plumber — was still the butt of local sniping, about leaving a husband and retarded son, about her instability, about her tendencies toward recklessness and melancholy. She had an attitude, perhaps because of her own stigma, a niggardly resentment toward people from away. *Arrivistes,* she would mutter, typing each made deal. But Sally found Cora Foster competent, and, she was, after all, Andy's mother-in-law.

Michael was waiting for the explanation. "Why aren't the buyers satisfied with the resolution?" he persisted.

This deal could make it for Michael, have heavy hitters seek him out for Hampton real estate investment opportunities, make people forget about last year's incident.

"The waterfront pieces bother them because of the coastal easement restriction," Sally said. "That's the bottom line. For $12 million, they have a right to want things clear, Michael. I told Franklin Unger that. That jerk FU2 was screaming about the buyers not being real, that he would sue, da-dah-da-dah, you know the song."

"Forget Frank Unger. Fred makes the final decisions," Michael said. "They have to close, Ma. Their limited partners are screaming."

"Yes, well, we have to get a letter from the Planning Board in the next half hour, if we want to close it. You know how the Planning Board feels about FU2. Fred Unger they could live with, but Franklin's alienated everyone."

"And you don't think that means there'll be no closing?" cut in Andy.

"That's a double negative—"

"You!" Michael intervened. "You're lucky you're getting a commission. Ma and I did all the work!" He turned to Sally. "You're going to have to call the Supervisor, Ma."

"Puhleeze! The two of you! Not now. We've got business to do." Sally said. With a resigned shrug, Sally went into her office to call Nancy Ryner.

Ryner was in and took her call. "I want this deal to close as much as you do. I don't need Ungers on my back, more lawsuits. But I have to track down the Planning Board Chairman."

"Nancy, Liz is the Planning Board Chairman. Stop the bullshit! She needs your say so!"

"This last minute stuff isn't very professional, Sally. Timing is everything, you know." Her voice became conversational. "I bet you never imagined you'd be such a wheeler dealer."

"Yeah right, professional! It's the July Fourth weekend, Nancy. We could lose this by a traffic jam. I don't have time to play games. I'm on my way to New York. I'll have Cora Foster stop by your office in a half hour." Sally gave a sigh, massaging the aching muscles of her neck.

Since trading concepts of reality for the practice of realty her family constellation had changed, some celestial shift, Joe more like a favorite relative to the children, a kindly aunt, an older brother, she, anything but the nurturing care-giver described in manuals. The very best she could give herself was *father,* the kind who, harumphing and clearing his throat, reviews family bills pierced on a spindle.

By 1977, she'd stopped crying on her way to work. She no longer parked along wooded roadsides with a container of coffee and tears. This was it. There'd be no rescue. Not with Ben at Purchase majoring in poetry, Andy dashing between New York and East Hampton, his lifestyle exceeding his income, and Michael's income supporting no life style at all, coaching girls' tennis at the Catholic High School until summer when the tennis club he managed re-opened. During her first 18 months working for Jack Bennet she'd earned $150,000.

She didn't need to depend on her sons to take care of her, after all. Realizing that, and troubled about the changes in her role with the boys, Sally came up with the family business brainstorm. A family business to leave to her sons, to make up for all those years she wasn't there for them as mother, to erase memories of bounced checks and worries about money. They could live their lives without depending on others for a job.

"It's not for me", Ben said. "I'd rather drive a car."

"Do what you want. You'll probably leave everything to Michael anyway," was Andy's response.

"Take your 50 percent and let someone else take the risks," suggested Michael. "I'm not interested in selling houses."

But things had changed for Michael in the past year, since the incident. Ten months earlier, Michael Singer had found himself in an impossible position. The owners of the tennis club weren't taking his calls. He'd run over budget. Members weren't paying their bills on time. He owed $25,000 to his mother, $33,000 to vendors, $20,000 in salaries, $3,700 to *The Easthamptoner*, $2,700 to *The Star* — and then there was Unger's bookmaker, Freddy the Finger, on his back, threatening him again. He'd even gotten to Andy.

His local staff left for college in August without paychecks. And his mother had no idea the money she'd lent him hadn't gone where it should have, lost, instead, on sure things that hadn't worked out. Checks were sent out without a penny to back them to stop the club phones from ringing, blasting away at his head, like a carpenter's drill.

So with his duffel bag slung over his shoulder, three Prince racquets, $400, a flashlight and a heavy heart, he walked the Long Island Railroad tracks in the middle of the night, the four miles to the East Hampton train station. The 24 year-old took the milk train to the Port of Authority and got on a bus to Las Vegas. (Only Doug Slavka had predicted that's where he was, that Michael was a compulsive gambler, and that's where gamblers ran.)

It was Andy who insisted his mother go to the police to report him missing, telling her tomorrow's headline could be FINGER SNUFFS SINGER.

After two weeks in downtown Vegas, his roach-infested hotel burned down. From the second floor, Michael broke a window,

jumped, and got his name on the hospital survivors' list. So when
Sergeant Jim Foster, on a hunch, called the Vegas police, they found
him.

He didn't want to go back to East Hampton.

After leaving the hospital, Michael stayed at the Salvation Army
Mission. They gave him money for clothes which he proceeded to
lose in the poker room at the Fremont. He gambled away money he
got from selling the Prince racquets and the money he earned from
the construction corner, where each morning at 6 a.m. builders
found loser labor cheap. Finally, he called home broke and desperate.

He was able to get two more weeks out of his mother, relying on
certain fundamental principles of fundraising. After selling the
second airline ticket Sally booked and losing the proceeds, Michael
returned home, knowing no one in town would give him a job. Not
after the story, picked up from the police report by *The
Easthamptoner* and run above a Sally Singer Inc. advertisement.

Ben drove him home from the airport. He slept for four straight
days, like a dead man, blankets over his face. When he got out
from under the covers, there was his mother's face, as he knew it
would be. She announced his second chance. It was always his
second chance. (It was Doug, too, who warned Sally about taking
Michael into the business, though, he said, he loved the kid like
his own son.)

He could work for her. Repay his debts. Stop gambling. Stop
lying.

Michael never wanted to sell *houses* in the Hamptons. From
his years working at the tennis club, he understood ambitious men
with deep pockets, understood people like the Unger Brothers. It
was always the operators that you could get back into, whose atten-

tion you could get with the intoxicating promise of money and action. He waited and learned, studied transfer reports, went to planning board meetings. He'd learned patience from his father. Between Nancy Ryner and his poker games his father was doing okay, had what he wanted.

Michael could, too, with the ultimate weapon. The deal!

When the silver stretch limo got to Bridgehampton, Michael called the office from the Candy Kitchen. He learned that Cora Foster had picked up the document from Ryner's office and faxed it to Slavka as instructed. The Winston Estates had to close. It had to close today.

33
The Joy of Closing

Walls of glass enclosed the large conference room at Chase Manhattan Plaza. Sally felt like she was in an observation tower overlooking downtown New York. The room could easily seat 50 people. They were about half as many around the circular table that hugged the perimeter of the oversized space — the banks' attorneys, the closer from the title company, the three Ungers (Hilda Unger, was seated between her two sons), their team of New York and East Hampton lawyers, the Filipinos and their attorneys, the three Singers, and off in a corner, Mrs. Unger's ever-present nurse, for emergencies, ready to administer oxygen due to her ailing heart.

"We deserve some kind of kicker. I don't know why I gave in. A mistake! It's hard to let go after all we went through with that town. Some of your action. Just a taste! You make. We make. My brother and I want a piece at the back end," Franklin Unger rambled on.

"I'm hungry," said Sally. There were trays with pitchers of water and hot coffee available, telephones scattered on the table, but no food. "We left the extra bagels in the car with Ben."

"What's that, Frank?" asked Fred, one hand covered by his mother, the other clutching a shabby attaché case. Along with his younger brother, Fred was a general partner of Winston Estates Limited, the entity selling the real estate. He looked as if he were surprised at Franklin's demand for more money.

"They're doing a last minute Mutt and Jeff," Michael whispered to Sally. "See that attaché case Fred's holding onto? Our commission's in that case. Watch Mrs. Unger, too. She's the coach of that team, giving hand signals to Fred."

"Let's not make this deal more complicated, Mr. Unger," Ben Hawley advised Franklin in his best Bonac twang, a harsh remnant of 17th Century English. "It's no secret the property has more lawsuits attached than barnacles on a schooner."

The huge Winston Estates parcel, 900 acres in East Hampton's Northwest, with 4,000 feet of water frontage, sporting sunsets, endangered species, wetlands, disputes over public trail jurisdiction, was a problem. The Town Trustees alone, created by an 18th century gift from England's King George to the settlers, were a major headache. The parcel was bought cheap by the Unger Brothers, the younger of whom, called himself FU 2 because he shared his older brother's initials and because his *fuck you* money was in the safe. He was a ruthless negotiator whose handshake was as good as Michael Singer's checks.

"Let's get on this, Mr. Unger," suggested Ben Hawley. He maintained a cool distance from his clients, staying close enough, only to collect his fee. "You know that point is non-negotiable. We made a deal. Let's abide by it. Buyers have no patience with those they can't trust, those who try to renegotiate at the last minute."

Sally smelled trouble. She'd seen million dollar deals collapse over who'd get the sconces, over whether they were furnishings or appurtenances. She kicked Michael's foot under the table.

"I'm not asking for anything out of pocket," argued Franklin. "I'm looking for a small percentage on the come. You guys can throw us a point. I don't have to do this deal, you know. My New York lawyers can find a way out."

"This is going to be a long day. My stomach is rumbling. I would die for a piece of bread."

Mrs. Unger hadn't changed her pleasant expression.

"They're bluffing," Michael whispered again. "But I'm not sure these Filipino guys will put up with it."

"We've got a contract, Frank," said Max Slavka, his son Adam seated next to him, busily shuffling through papers. "The time to fight was before you signed. As I advised you, by the way. Now, I think you're jeopardizing this closing."

"You must know that's a deal-breaker. You're raising an issue that is not in the interest of your partners," Michael reminded him.

"Stop leaning on me, Michael. I want a piece of the action," Franklin Unger screamed in an outburst of temper. "I was squeezed to make this deal."

The Filipinos and their crew started to put papers back in their briefcases.

"This is nonsense. A deal's a deal!" said Sally, pulling Franklin Unger over to a corner of the room. "You want to do more business in East Hampton? Everyone in town will hear you killed the deal. That you don't know how to close. Lawsuits are at risk. Your fiduciary relationship with your partners is at risk. It's a problem property with more covenants and restrictions than both Testaments. Sit down and sign off. I know you'll keep your word."

All eyes were on them.

"I'm dealing with a hungry broker, here. She's more interested in her fee than in her clients' best interest. Okay, Okay," he conceded. "Let's do the damn thing, get the paperwork over. But I want an apology!"

"An apology? From whom?"

"You'll do," he snapped at Sally.

Adam Slavka put down the phone and was whispering to his

father.

"Fred, we have a bigger problem," announced Max Slavka. "The funds are not yet in our bank. Adam just spoke to them. I won't let you walk out of here until the $8 million is safe and sound with the other four. "

"We put you in touch with our bank, sir. You know the funds were wired last night." said one of the Filipino's attorneys.

"Which last night?" shouted Franklin Unger. "Yours? Mine? You're jerking us around with that dateline business. It's not in your bank, not in our bank, where the hell is it?"

"I get in trouble for kiting checks, Ma, and they can't find $8 million floating around. Someone's enjoying the interest on those funds. The Federal Reserve's in on it, too. They're all crooks, legalized crooks. It's only the entrepreneur that can't get away with anything."

"Yes, well, you better stop talking like that, Michael. You know the Sally Singer Inc. motto — honesty before a deal."

"While you guys are whispering to each other, this deal's going down the drain. FU 2 gave them an ultimatum," informed Andy. "They have one hour to deliver the money or else Unger Brothers walk with their $4 million down and keep the property."

"Get stuck with it is more like it," said Michael,

"Yes well, that money ain't chopped liver."

"I'm hungry. Anything. Bread will do," said Sally.

"There's enough bread in that brief case for a high school," Michael pointed out.

Just then the call came in. The floating funds had docked. The attorneys let out a communal sigh. Legal documents traveled around the table again. Sally looked out at the World Trade Center and New York Harbor. Franklin Unger was standing up, about to talk.

Once more she kicked Michael.

Michael fixed his eyes on the man about to speak, as if his gaze could stop him from bungling things. A loose cannon, but he was the man who'd leave with a bundle. Franklin Unger, like the other bigshots he knew from the tennis clubs he'd worked at since he was a kid, wasn't special. They were all like children. Shrewd, energetic, greedy children trying to get away with things — to play out of turn or squeeze out extra time on the court, to bring guests in without registering, running up bills they delayed paying. All the while their Porsches were parked in the lot. They were kids at camp and he, their teenage counselor, had been in charge.

Now Michael was ready to play with these heavy hitters. When this deal closed, he'd have the money to get started. His life would change. It was in development, not brokering, where the real money was. Where the real operators were. Where the real action was. He was as smart as any of them. But it had to close today. Some people were impatient.

"For the last time," snarled Unger. "I want to remind you . . . ."

Andy Singer couldn't watch FU 2. He looked up at the ceiling. It was too important to him. How did Michael do it after last year's trouble at the tennis club? He bet his mother had something to do with cleaning that up. Once Michael'd brought the Unger listing in, he wanted to find a buyer, too. He was a broker! They'd been screaming at each other for weeks, he and Michael, over who would offer what to whom and who owned which contact. His mother finally said, "In the interest of peace, if any of us sells it we'll split the commission equally. Seller's end only! The office must see its 50 percent share. There are bills to pay." Andy shifted in his chair. Maybe he wasn't as bright as his brother. Or his mother. But they'd never beat him out of anything. He had his own family now. He and

Em were the team. He'd get closer to the Ungers. Anyone who could make that kind of money had to be special. Andy worshipped special. He loved his father, but he respected and admired the affluent men he met in East Hampton. Staring at the ceiling, he prayed Franklin Unger wouldn't say anything stupid.

" . . . . This is how we do business. You're not in the damn Philippines . . . ."

Sally was anticipating the commission, too. Inc.'s end. In her mind she was creating a crash advertising campaign to attract personnel as well as customers. And she thought of the bills she could pay. No matter how successful, she was always playing catch-up, staring at phantom money on paper, but not in the bank. People thought she owned the expensive properties she advertised, to boot. Every charitable cause in New York State had her name on its list. "Because you give," an exasperated Michael once told her! Well after today, she could satisfy the loan, build up her credit line. As to her selling agent share, her personal take, she'd pay down the mortgage, the money borrowed to go into this business. She could take her mother, Jack, and the Aquistapaces to The Palm to celebrate. Not over the holiday weekend, of course. Not in the summer either. Not for the Jewish Holidays in September. She would find some break before the Columbus Day surge. Yes, that was it, next October.

". . . . Therefore, it seems to me . . . . " Franklin was about to make some kind of demand. Unger's last stand, his hand poised to pounce on the remainder of the circulating paper work. She had to act. Sally got up quickly and shook that raised hand, "Congratulations," she said to Unger, before he could speak further.

"Ahh!" Unger gave a sound of disgust, "Never mind. You can't ever get a fair deal from bottom fishermen like you guys," he nodded at the Filipinos, knowing they'd paid top dollar, hadn't low-balled at all. "I'm not thanking you or shaking your hand," he snapped at Sally.

"Sally Singer Inc. found you a buyer willing to take on a problem piece. We negotiated the best deal we could on the Winston Estate's Partnership's behalf," Sally said to no one in particular, looking over the commission receipt document.

"I could have made a better deal. That's the trouble with hungry brokers and ignorant partners. *You can always tell a friend by his cover.*"

Don't argue with her, Frank," said Slavka. "It's a waste of time. Pay her off."

Gibberish mode! *You can always tell a friend by his cover. A man's word is as good as his promise,* he said that when they reached a meeting of the minds. *A bird in the hand gets the worm* — he said that at contract closing. Sally considered it a good sign. The closer he got to profits, the less lucid his chatter became.

She signaled Michael to get Jim Foster as Fred Unger gave his brother a slight nod, like the Godfather okaying a hit. "Bring the bagels, Michael," she added, noticing that Hilda Unger's hands were now clasped before her. After a brief introduction, no words had ever passed between the two women.

Franklin Unger scratched his signature on the deed after his brother.

The shabby attaché case was pushed towards her across the conference table. She was glad to get rid of the Unger Brothers, to get rid of Max Slavka, tired of playing real estate broker. To that extent there was joy.

Andy leaned over. "Count it before signing off, Ma."

Sally shook her head. She knew the Filipinos put up the cash.

They were honorable. Hadn't they just freed Aquino and those other National Leaders? Besides, where the hell was she going to count $500,000, anyway?

"Take your time, Ma," said Michael, walking back into the room with Jim Foster. "No bagels. Ben's not back yet. He ran down to Bellevue, again."

34
The Accidental Poet

Bellevue Hospital was founded in 1736 as an infirmary on top of an almshouse. Ben Singer had looked it up because his grandfather died there when his mother was a teenager. That's what he knew about Bellevue.

Until 1973.

In 1973, Ben Singer decided to call the RSVP number from his stack of PQ6 Party invitations. He discovered PQ6 was a ward number, Bellevue Children's Psychiatric. He found out he had been in Bellevue, too, had lived there for two years. There was a misunderstanding, he learned. It turned out his mother was saying *autistic* all along, not artistic, and, in his jeans meant in his *genes*.

Dr. Rosewell spoke with him. "We're so proud of you, Ben. Your mother keeps us informed." she said when he was ready he should come for a visit.

His mother spoke with him. "It seemed innocent enough, your misunderstanding. I don't know what else to tell you, Ben, except how much I love you and how very special you are."

Both the doctor and his mother agreed he was a miracle.

The misunderstanding left its mark. He was stuck in blue denim and bad poetry. Oddly, there was some relief. He never felt really creative. On the other hand, he had welcomed being something, fitting somewhere, always feeling a step behind or a step ahead or a step off to the side. Artistic had been an explanation for that.

Now where did he belong?

It wasn't until a year later, when Ben turned 16, tall and lanky with a thatch of straight black hair, that he was ready to visit the hospital. Things were troubling him. Ben had to know if complications in his life were part of this whole autism thing.

A late but lush bloomer, he found his nascent sexuality too much for his newly shattered self to bear alone. It was a kind of sexuality with strange, intense stirrings, both disturbing and unfamiliar to his passive, easy way. The feelings were unmistakable. He was desperately in love, too. Yet he felt his identity so brittle he couldn't share his sexual fears with anyone, not even his older brothers.

Dr. Rosewell told him to bring his poems. "Everyone wants to see the works of our accidental poet," she joked. Ben wasn't going there to discuss poetry. The past year had been the worst in his young life.

His mother offered to accompany him to the hospital. Michael did, too. Andy begged off, saying he would probably faint and make matters worse. It was Hawley Bennet who ended up driving Ben in his pickup to the facility on East River Drive.

"Ben, we didn't come to look at the architecture," Hawley had said, sitting in the blue truck, in front of the hospital's 29th Street entrance. "It's nothing to write home about, no *belle vue*. We can't just sit here. Let's go inside; just do it. No one's going to grab you with a net. Here, look at yourself," he added, turning the rear view mirror for Ben to see his reflection. "You're a wreck! They'll think all their work was for nothing."

Ben saw a bony face, taut and pale, looking back at him. His longish hair was unruly, going this way and that as if torn at a crossroads, ragged from being raked so many times with his nervous fingers.

"Take this," Hawley went on, handing him the Manila envelope with his poems. "It'll give you something to do with your hands. It's only a visit, Ben. I won't let them keep you."

They went into the aged stone building, took the old Otis elevator to the sixth floor and stepped out to a small windowless vestibule, its two-toned peeling walls painted mustard-yellow and orangy enamel, the sheen now dull. There was a large door, a steel door painted over, with a small wired glass window. There was no knob, no handle, only a big key hole.

Ben began to knock, palm flat, and at the very moment of his pounding to get in, he recalled he'd done the same thing before, as a child, a toddler, from the door's other side, pounding on it, screaming at it, to get out. That vivid memory assaulted him so, he almost collapsed into Hawley's arms.

Inside the locked ward, the younger children were off to the left in a separate wing. There were more boys than girls, which was typical, Ben learned. They were white, black, Asian and permutations of the three. Autism was an equal opportunity illness.

He and Hawley missed the scheduled part of the children's day, the music, the dancing, the painting, the playing in the yard, the so-called stimuli barrage. When they arrived, the children were starting their favorite free time activity, walking in circles in front of crib-lined walls. The staff called it 'the go around.'

"Was I like them?" Ben asked Dr. Rosewell, a plain lady with intelligent eyes. She wore a short white coat over her blue print dress.

One boy started the ritual, repetitive ambling around, gazing at invisible forms made with his own hands and fingers in the air, forms bracketed before his eyes. It was clear that the boy saw things no one else did. One by one, others joined the other-worldly dance. They were somewhere else, in orbit, all doing things, complicated, stylized, with nimble hands and fingers.

Ben had not heard one child speak or utter a sound that wasn't an alarm. Among those few who weren't on parade, some rocked, some bounced, some sat and stared, occasionally screaming for nothing. At least nothing that anyone in Ben's world could provide.

"Was I like them?" Ben repeated to Dr. Rosewell, sneaking a look at Hawley to see if he were overcome by it all. Hawley's face was composed.

"Oh, you were in there, Ben. You ate wood whenever you could get at it until you were three. You preferred pine, I think," chuckled the doctor, who would touch or talk to a child as he passed, not seeming to mind that her gestures were ignored. "You were two when we got you. The youngest child ever. Most parents wait until school time and then come for help. The prognosis is dismal when there's no speech by five years."

"When did I talk?"

"After two years here, when you were four. Though you were communicating, making language sounds earlier. We didn't leave you alone, you know, just bombarded you with stimuli until you decided to join us."

"These children are crazy," Ben said, matter-of-factly.

"We're all a little nuts, Ben. But lucky for us, *our* craziness is in the majority so they don't lock us up."

One child was putting on and taking off her sweater. She began to scream. An aide rushed over to help her.

"When her arm comes through the sleeve she doesn't recognize it as her own body," the doctor explained. "She thinks it's something foreign attacking her. Or at least that's what we think she thinks. Others panic when the arm goes into the sleeve. They think it's gone."

Ben walked over to the sweater girl who'd stopped screaming. He kneeled down close.

"Watch out," warned Dr. Rosewell. The little girl rammed Ben hard, their heads colliding. "Sorry about that! They don't know you're a person. They can't empathize, we think."

"So how did I get here?" he finally asked, rubbing his forehead.

"Your mother. She sat in the lobby downstairs and wouldn't leave until we saw you. She picked up your strangeness early, alerted the pediatrician before you were three months old. It wasn't just that you'd rejected her milk, but you were able to withdraw no matter what she tried. It's hard for us to discern between the placid, passive infant and an autistic one. It was 18 months later that a diagnosis was confirmed. Your mom called Creedmoor first. Dr. Bender told her what we were doing here. Working with children. Research on chemical imbalances in the genes."

At the word genes, Ben gave a small smile.

"Why did I get better, Doctor?"

"Well, you certainly had a mind of your own. We let you know we'd prefer you to use it in our world. Young was the key, Ben. I'm convinced. Duration of treatment, too, and, as important, you brought ego strength. Your mother let us keep you as long as we needed."

"And my father?"

"He visited you often."

"Did it cost my folks a lot of money?"

"Everything was free for those who qualified. This is Bellevue, a city hospital!"

"My father says nothing's free."

"Yes, well, talk to your mother. She looked through all financial criteria. Took care of it. You qualified."

His thoughts slid to free school lunches. "There were no more
children after me, Doctor."

"I suppose I should let your mother tell you, Ben. We strongly
advised no more children. You were a handful. Your brothers were
so close to you in age."

"Why wasn't my mother more honest with me?"

"We suggested she shouldn't, Ben. What would be the purpose?" she asked. "Now tell me who is this friend of yours, that's
been standing so quietly. A favorite teacher? Is that what Mr. Bennet
is? And what's this about being in love, you mentioned on the
phone?"

His eyes darted to Hawley, a strange expression on his face.
He said to the doctor, "Thank you, for everything," emptying his
poems out of the manila envelope, presenting them to her.

"Thank you," she said. "But tell me! Why is love a problem?"

"It's Mr. Bennet I'm in love with," he blurted.

"My God, Ben," Hawley said, turning pale and teetering as if
punched in the stomach. "My God!" He grabbed a crib rail for
support. "Doctor, I had no idea," he said to Rosewell. Turning to
Ben, he added. "You could have told *me* first, at least. Forget the
net! They'll have me on a moral's charge, for goodness sake."

"Is it wrong? Healthy? Real? A by-product from another world?"

Ben went on, words spilling out over his amazement at finding
courage. Were ego strength the magic words? The doctor said he
had plenty. He wasn't fragile and brittle, needn't rupture on matters of identity, needn't collapse over difference.

"Are these feelings from the autism? I have to know."

Dr. Rosewell looked grim. "It doesn't make life any easier, Ben, but love is love in any place. The rest you'll have to work out with Mr. Bennet."

By the time he was 18, he had.

Now 22, driving up the East River Drive from Chase Manhattan Plaza, Ben remembered the things that happened six years earlier. He'd had a lot more visits under his belt since then.

He double parked the stretch limo on the red bricked dead-end street and hopped the boxcar to the sixth floor. Six for PQ6. The ancient elevator grunted all the way as a thin-haired, pot-bellied man steered it on its slow motion ascent.

Ben thought it strange that a hospital should smell so sickly, like boiled cabbage and asparagus cooked in scrubbed bodily fluids. He breathed the recycled air through his mouth. It was no wonder Andy got sick in hospitals.

Exiting the elevator he felt a chill in front of the oversized steel door, now painted green since administrators learned that color had therapeutic effects. Ben took his deep breath — he always had to — and thumped on the door.

Once inside, he quickly put himself into the swing of things. Different patients, same go around. In slow-motion-under-water-time, Ben walked his own circle along with the wraith-like children, their gestures spectral remnants of other worlds. For no reason at all, he recalled everyone's reaction to his *it's Mr. Bennet I'm in love with.*

Michael and his dad didn't blink. They liked Hawley. Andy had taken the news the hardest, worried about how it looked. "At least I'm out of high school," he said. "Everyone knows I'm okay," he reassured himself with his jock record and his athletic ability with girls. Then, a week later, he apologized, looking so ashamed of himself. "If you have any trouble with anyone, Ben, let me know," he said.

After the initial stir, their liaison was treated as unremarkable. It was a very East Hampton kind of arrangement. The town's large gay population was establishing year-round roots.

His mother acted disappointed because she wanted grandchildren. She was working on her third family theory, the second having washed out. Secretly, he thought she was pleased and relieved to get him off her worry list.

Grandma Bea thought the story nonsense and refused to acknowledge it, flirting with Hawley whenever she visited. But when his grandmother came up for Andy's wedding and stayed extra long because of Junior Hawley's funeral and that trouble with Michael, she'd mercifully backed off. Instead, she took to consoling Charles Hawley, because, she said, she, too, had lost a son, no matter she'd known the damaged infant only three months.

Walking the go around with the children, Ben gave a sigh. People were really weird.

The aimless orbiting, with a gratuitous spin here and there, made him feel good as always, but he had to go back. The Winston closing ought to be near done. He dropped away from the dreamlike loop, where no one cared less, and gathered his things. The manila envelope he brought each visit to share his work with Dr. Rosewell held yet another **PQ6** emblazoned pillowcase he'd lifted from one of the cribs.

He and Hawley didn't need the white-stamped pillowcases. They were stuffed on a back shelf in their Sag Harbor linen closet, numbering the many times Ben paid a call to PQ6, the dismal, marvelous place where he rejoined planet Earth.

Outside the sooty, red-bricked building, Ben put his envelope in the glove compartment of the silver stretch limo. He took the East River Drive back to Chase Manhattan Plaza, eating one of Dreesen's bagels as he adroitly steered the car through Fourth of July traffic.

35
Messages

They stood in a circle in the green carpeted conference room at Sally Singer Inc. staring at the open attaché case, the packets of 100-dollar bills neatly lined up.

There had been 50 of them, making $500,000, but Michael insisted on taking his share of the commission back in New York, $75,000 plus the listing fee, another $25,000 — 10 packets of one hundred $100 bills in all.

"I'm giving you a receipt. What's the difference if you give me the cash or issue a check? It's all on the record. Think about it," he argued.

Sally reluctantly agreed. It was his money. Only the mother in her didn't want him to have that kind of cash, fearing he'd be off to Atlantic City or the Metro Poker Club or someplace. Josephine Aquistapace spelled it out, counseling her after his first big deal, the Church Cemetery property.

"He's an adult. A-d-u-l-t. When you were Michael's age you had three children, a house, and a husband to take care of. You don't want to give him money because you want to save it for him. If that's the case, you shouldn't have given him this job in the first place. Real estate, *Marrone*," she cried, her hands as expressive as her strong featured face. "Real estate, with its high risks, big rewards, that whole commission syndrome. But if he earns it, that money is his. And what he does with it is his business not yours."

That Church Cemetery Property listing was special. Sally was one of a handful of brokers that had the listing. She was the only listing broker that wasn't a member of the parish.

Sally had befriended Father Donelly after Jean Bennet's funeral, eight years earlier, stopping into the rectory often, "as Catholic Jackie" she'd joke. There, in the small sitting room, with its comfortable, but shabby furnishings, she and the elderly theologian would discuss arguments for the existence of God, ontological, causal, and by design, compare Aristotle and Aquinas, and wonder at Spinoza's excommunication from the Jewish faith because of his notion of pantheism, *Deus Sive Natura.*

They disputed Pope Pius XII's lack of aggressive intervention for the Jews in World War Two. He, in his soft Irish brogue, invoking Augustine's separation of the City of Man from the City of God, she appealing to fundamental human decency, sins of omission, love, and mercy, citing Matthew 25:40: *Whatsoever you do to the least of my brethren, that you do unto me.* Off the record, the elderly priest conceded it may have been over the root of all evil, money, guiding the church more than St. Augustine, the fear of collapse should their enormous wealth be confiscated by the Nazis. Sally liked him even more for that concession. They had other common grounds; both were believers, both were waiting, he for the second coming, she for the first.

Once Sally Singer Inc. got the unexpected listing, Michael brought it to the president of the Jewish Center, Lester Wolff, the accountant who sued a lot. Its congregation had been fruitful and multiplied in the 15 years since Michael's non-bar mitzvah. One had to prepare for their passing away. A deal was made.

Before that, when Michael disappeared, she went to Father Donelly for comfort. When Michael returned, she sought out the elderly priest for guidance. "Let God play God, not you, Sally Singer" he said. As to her fears about Michael's earnings, he agreed with Josephine, but in different words. "Pray my child. Trust in the Lord. Give the man his money."

She did, less what he owed her for the tennis club loan. So today, as well, she let Michael disappear with his earned $100,000 which left $400,000 facing them, neatly stacked, as they gathered around the conference table in the green carpeted room.

"I'm not leaving until I count it," Andy said. "We should have done it in New York."

"I want to put it in the safe, Andy. We can't keep Jim up," Sally yawned, finding it hard to keep her eyes open. "If it's short, there's nothing we can do anyway."

"I'm counting," he insisted.

"There's four of us," said Jim Foster. "Why don't we each take ten stacks, pray there's a hundred in every bundle and count it. Is that okay?"

As rain fell in the parking lot, $400,000 in cash was tallied by eight hands in the storefront office, Ben whistling *Happy Talk* throughout. It went into the large Mosler safe behind Sally's desk to be banked on Tuesday. That taken care of, the group disbanded.

Ben left first, his PQ6 pillow case secure in the glove compartment, $500 for the day's work in his pocket plus the money that went to Transhampton. He never wanted to get a real estate license, so Sally could not, by law, give him fees as "commissions." He drove down the turnpike to the little place he shared with Hawley Bennet off Division Street in Sag Harbor.

Reading the message his mother, Cora, left for him, Jim Foster phoned the station, his tired but professional voice echoing the day's reports: *a dozen accidents, roads flooding, toilets overflowing,*

*power outages, parking lot scuffles, renters about missing keys, no
water.*

Sally and Andy checked their pink slipped messages. Sally
noticed that Michael's were marked received. He must have called
in, she thought, ruffling through them. He had calls from Lester
Wolff, Charles Hawley, Hiram Hawley, Jess Kingsley, Fred Unger,
Adam Slavka — she stopped there. Andy was watching too carefully.

Charles Hawley was finally on speaking terms, thanks to, of all
people, her mother. But Hiram Hawley? Why was a Southampton
Hawley calling? Why was Lester Wolff, who'd never cared for the
Singers, so tight with Michael lately?

Sally sighed. She knew why. The sharks looking for deals.
Michael was hot. There was a message from Doug Slavka, as well,
addressed to both of them. For Sally, *he wouldn't be up after all this
summer, she could let his room Ha! Ha!* For Michael, *please call.*

She flipped through her own calls. Mrs. Aquistapace, Your
mother. Others, too. They could wait. She dialed Josephine.

"It closed. I was tough. We brought home the bacon. I may
vomit. Block out some time in October for you and Vince to go to
The Palm with me to celebrate," was the message she left on the
Aquistapace machine. Then she called Florida. Her mother wasn't
home.

Sally locked up after 10:30. "C'mon give us a kiss," she said
to Andy, trying to sound like Marlene Dietrich in *Witness for the
Prosecution.* "There's no point in having a sour puss. You made
such wonderful money today."

"I worked for it," he said defensively. "You made it, too. Your
office has a quarter of a million on top of it."

"How long am I going to be punished for something I never

did? Even murderers get a sentence, Andy." She tried once more to be funny. "Isn't there a statute of limitations?"

"Yeah, yeah," he said, turning his back and walking to his dark blue thunderbird parked near the A&P. He said good night, but didn't turn around.

Seated in the large yellow Checker Taxi, the Sally Singer hallmark, Joe's old cab that she'd had rebuilt, the car her tony customers thought such a kick, Sally watched him disappear before pulling away. It occurred to her that two positives could make a negative

Yeah, yeah.

Neither Sally nor Andy noticed the two men in the shadows of the recessed, neon-lit doorway of Cut-Rite Liquors, the store next to Sally Singer Inc. Real Estate.

36
Calls in the Night

Sally reached the Dayton Lane house exhausted and gloomy. The phone rang. She grabbed the receiver.

"When's the last time you made love?" asked a male voice softly.

It was unexpected. Sally didn't answer. She wanted to hear him say it again.

"Say, lady, when's the last time you made love?"

"I think you know the answer to that."

"Are you sleeping alone tonight?"

"As a matter of fact, I'm not."

"Anyone I know?"

"The guy who lives up the street." She smiled, her first real smile all day.

"I heard they had to deal with one tough broad today."

"News travels fast."

"I told you there were no secrets in a small town."

"You told me you were going away."

"I was. It's not every day a guy's old camping and hunting grounds are sold."

"To foreigners? People from away? Is that what's on your small-town mind?"

"You are mean and tough."

"Can you handle mean and tough, tonight?" she sighed.

"You city gals will never learn." It was his turn to give a quiet laugh.

"I'm so glad you're here. I've got to shower, get rid of that awful closing, scrub the real estate lady away. I'll leave the door open."

"No doors open, Sally. *You really will never learn*," said Jack Bennet. "I'll use my key."

37
Night Visitors

"**I**'ll get it," Andy Singer told his wife, Emily, when he heard the knock at the door. They lived in a rental property on Deep Six Drive in the heart of Springs.

Two men were outside, headlights of their parked car glaring into the house.

"I thought I told you guys to stay away from me. What the fuck are you doing at my house?"

They had tracked him down once before, on the day of his wedding at Ashawagh Hall. (The Springs schoolhouse from days gone by was now a community center.) It was there the ceremony and reception took place.

After Town Justice Foster MacMullin married them that October day 10 months earlier, Andy grabbed Michael. "Do you know what happened to me this morning, you dumb fuck?"

"I have no idea. But that language can't be necessary, Andy."

"They thought I was you. It didn't help that I had your ID in my wallet when I showed them my driver's license."

Michael had given him the identification to use with his wedding gift to them, a three-day stay in Atlantic City for which Michael was comped.

"That must have been unpleasant," Michael said, smiling. "You shouldn't carry other people's papers, I guess. Did they say what they wanted?"

"Yeah, you, asshole," said Andy poking Michael with his finger. "The money you owe them."

His new brother-in-law, Jim Foster pulled him aside, before the poke became a fist.

"There's a warrant out for your brother," he said.

"Which one?" asked Andy. Had Ben finally lifted something useful, something valuable?

"Michael. He gave a bad check that was sent to the Sheriff's office. I think they should—"

That's when they heard the strange grunts and a crash. Both of them turned around. They saw Junior Hawley (Em and Jim's half-brother, Charles Hawley Jr.) collapsed on the floor, clutching his neck, his face already blue.

Next to him was Joe Singer. His father — how would *he* know about hard bread — had stood there while Junior was eating a croissant. (It crossed Andy's mind that his father may have given it to him. But it was Andy who'd insisted on croissants at his wedding, the newest thing in East Hampton since bagels.) Jim and his dad, Plumb Foster, together with Hawley Bennet tried to do the Heimlich Maneuver, but couldn't get Junior into position. Charles Hawley's retarded son had not matured well as he got older, his body turning to severe obesity. Andy and Michael tried unsuccessfully to lift Junior, but he was too heavy to move, lying there on his back, kicking his legs, jerking his body like some over the hill burlesque queen.

It seemed like hours, but it was only seven minutes later when the Springs Volunteer Ambulance Squad got there, with oxygen and a doctor from Southampton Hospital on the radio. Oh, they worked on him all right, huffing and pounding and jolting, but Junior was gone way before they arrived, the soft, moistened croissant, tasted but unchewed, clogging the trachea, enveloping his wind pipe.

Junior's Mom, Cora Foster, fainted. Charles Hawley looked like he was going to punch out Joe, saying, "I should have done this that first day I met you, you goddamn sunnavabitch."

He broke down in tears as Jack Bennet came between them. Most of the guests were in shock, standing around, most of them related one way or another. Grandma Bea holding Cora Foster in her arms, was mumbling something about God's justice and punishment for the lack of Singer bar mitzvahs. In any case, his mother-in-law revived long enough to scream, "not our God, maybe yours." Em had burst into tears.

Of course, there was no honeymoon, so he never needed the phony identification in the first place. Some family wedding! But what could he expect from his family?

Between Freddy the Finger and Jim Foster's tip-off, his older brother disappeared the next day. In the end, all of that landed Michael, the fugitive, this great job in his mother's office.

The car's bright lights were bothering Andy's eyes. "Will you shut them the fuck off?"

"Where's your brother?"

"Those lights are going to scare my wife."

The Finger gestured with his hand and the goon walked over and put them on dim. "Now, where's your brother?" he repeated

"I'm not my brother's keeper."

"Answers like that'll only get you in trouble. I don't want to point this finger at you. It's your brother I'm looking for."

Two dogs, Bonac black labs Andy'd found abandoned, were at his side.

"Yeah, well, even if I knew, and I don't, I told you last year I wouldn't tell you people anything. Not after what happened to that guy from Amagansett."

"Hey—"

"Look, I'm not accusing you of anything, but you're wasting your time. Your money's probably floating on some crap table or riding on some horse."

Andy looked around. He'd never heard the other guy, the one with the 50 pound neck, speak. Last year on his wedding day, when Freddy'd first found him, the same goon just stood there staring, like tonight.

"If that fucking guy doesn't stop looking at me, he'll get in trouble. You don't intimidate me, Mister."

"Stop staring at the kid," Freddy ordered, pointing at the burly man. "Hey, we're not here for you. But I don't want to lose my temper. Your brother owes us money. He said he was going to pay this weekend, that there was a big deal happening."

"That's not my business."

Andy understood now Michael's urgency about the deal closing.

"We came early in case other creditors got here first, to protect our interests. I stuck my neck out for your brother by not turning him in."

"What does that mean, not turning him in?"

"You don't want to know."

Andy shot a look at the guy he called the goon. His eyelids were drooping slightly over his eyes.

"Michael didn't come home with us tonight. Said he'd be back Tuesday. That's all I know. Ask my mother. She's his boss."

"Yeah, well your mother's kinda busy right now."

For the first time both men laughed.

"Who is it, Andy?" asked Emily Foster Singer, looking ready to pop a new Foster-Singer any minute. Like all the Fosters, Em had red hair and freckles.

"Just some guys on business, honey, I'll be right in."

"Why are you making them stand at the door? It's so wet out, the mosquitoes—"

"Just let him know we're looking for him," Finger said, under his breath with his finger pointed, obviously meaning business. "We have to go. Sorry to bother you and the missus," he added for all to hear. Then he whispered, with some respect, while making gestures with his hands. "That since the wedding? You're some fast worker, kid. *May your child be a —*"

"Don't fucking finish that sentence," Andy said, shutting the door before Finger could say *masculine one.*

As they slid the Eldorado out of the driveway, a police car pulled over.

"I'm glad you gentlemen decided to leave. I can't keep you out of town. It's a free country. But, I don't want to see you around my sister's house again," said Sergeant Jim Foster, waiting for them to make their turn off Deep Six onto Old Stone Highway. He followed the black Cadillac to Town Line Road, out of East Hampton.

38
Calling Hands

"I call and raise four," said Joe Singer, sitting at the poker table July Fourth evening, with a lock, 6-4-1-2-3, in his hand. It was seven card high-low stud. He'd had the sure half-pot winner in the first five cards, but made the offbeat raise on the sixth card, which gave him a pair of aces showing. If he could scare the high out, he could take the whole pot. It was a gentle raise for a five-and ten game.

"Who do you think you're fooling not taking the full bet, Joe," said Liz, who knew numbers and investments, knew poker was a money management game, but had little feel for playing the players. Table stakes would have been her strength, not bet limit and raise limit poker like they played. "I hear your hotshot son made a killing Friday."

"Which son?" asked Joe, watching the other players react to their seventh card, dealt down.

Those reactions, the lighting of a cigarette, suddenly slumping or sitting erect, pulling on an earlobe, could tell a lot about their hands. They called them *tells* for that reason.

"Which son is the hotshot, hotshot?" replied Liz. Though still too thin and bony, there was a softer bearing to Liz. The lean and hungry look was gone.

"They all did very well, I understand," said Joe, not looking at his hand until the bet came to him. "Sally's doing all right."

"But Michael was the brains behind this deal," said Nancy. "It certainly wasn't Sally. What does she talk to her customers about? People falling off roofs, space, time, chaos, order?"

Joe knew he could rattle Nancy. That was why she wasn't a good poker player. She could be reached. And she would have a few drinks during the game. You never played serious poker if you were tired, hungry, angry or under the influence.

"Why do people say made a killing? What's wrong with making a living?" asked another, a player named Beverly. An attorney from New York who specialized in real estate and matrimonial matters, Bev drank soda water while the others had the hard stuff. She had an annoying foot-tapping habit the other players complained about when they would lose a pot. She said nothing, her tongue pushing out the sides of her cheek.

It was a seven-handed game, not one of Joe's, not one that Joe cut. It was known as the lesbian game, since all the women were successful, affluent lesbians. Some went or had gone both ways. Yet here, in the presence of their preference they were comfortable, competitive and happy, even when they argued. Like any other regular poker game among people who knew each other a long time, there was a lot of baggage. It would look like Alice was down on Lillian for raising, always making too much of two pair, "costing all of us a ton," she'd scream, but there was a lot more than that going on. That downside of familiarity gave Joe an additional edge. Shrill voices, quarrels, accusations, denials, it was as much an encounter group as a card game. Old punchlines, too.

They were all Jewish. They were all of an age, either side of 50, where in places less liberal than East Hampton they had felt forced to hide their gender preference. At least once a night, one of them would say, "but kikes are never dikes," bringing the same kind of uncontrolled laughter as when they'd heard it for the first time, from the same Irish girls sitting in the lunch room at the same city college.

One room in Nancy's large, traditional Amagansett house was set aside for poker. The octagonal, felt-covered table was always up, arranged that way for Joe. It had a plywood cover which they used sometimes with a spread. Sometimes they left it as is, when there were going to be a lot of games that week. A hanging Tiffany lamp illuminated the table's center, on a rheostat so it could be adjusted. Everything was an antique in the house, with provenances as boring as Sally's mind games. Liz would furnish no other way. Asset appreciation was her way of thinking. People were stupid who didn't buy that way, she'd say.

"Suppose they don't have the money," Joe had said the first time.

"Then they'll not only be poor," said Liz, "but they'll be taste-less, too."

He hated that attitude, would have liked to rap Liz in the mouth. But otherwise there was a treaty between them and a mutual re-spect for money.

The antique ladder-back chairs with thatched rattan seats were not too comfortable, but they were treated with respect by the woman players. Two drinks made sitting easier to bear. The men used the leather cushioned bridge chairs. Men weren't as careful.

There was always an elaborate buffet in the kitchen, ordered from Dean & Deluca's for the women — and made clear that it was — and from Bucket's local deli for the men. Tonight, the spread of paté, sturgeon, Nova Scotia, hickory-smoked turkey, rare roast beef with pasta salads, assorted breads, and finger pastries was well received. There would always be too much. In the men's games, there were platters of sandwiches, cole slaw, and potato salad, or large Italian style heros reminiscent of Uncle Milty's Colossal Tornadoes.

It was the last hand of the night. Joe made a full raise when the bet came to him, slowly checking his cards, as if that last card had made his hand. Maybe they'd think he filled or straightened and was betting the high. He couldn't fool Beverly, the foot-tapping attorney, who called high with two pair into open aces.

"That was a risky call," Joe said with a smile, as they were splitting the money between them. He made a mental note that the next time she would pay dearly for such an aggressive call. "Didn't you think I at least had aces up?"

"If you had aces up I would have lost," Beverly said, her no-nonsense tongue pushing the side of her cheek. "But you didn't and I didn't."

She was the last player to leave. It was 2:30 a.m. None of the women who worked in New York had to report in the Tuesday after the Fourth. They were now positioned in life, successful enough — an attorney, two psychoanalysts, an editor, a journalist — where they could return from the Hamptons at their convenience, Tuesday night or Wednesday morning.

They played for cash, making it convenient to understate one's losses, exaggerate winnings, and more important to Joe, making it difficult to know how anyone else did other than one's self. That charade kept the game going. It kept the fish from feeling foolish, publicly. Still, Joe wasn't a regular. He only filled in to make the game when they were short. Though he knew how to keep losers coming back for more, lots of respect and $4 bets in a five-and-ten game, he also knew these women were no fools. No one knew for certain how anyone else did, but a battery of phone calls among the women the next day usually yielded a pretty accurate tally. That was part of the game's pleasure. A two-day event. The playing, then the bullshit, bitching, and dishing afterward.

Careful not to count his winnings in front of the women, Joe went upstairs, leaving Nancy and Liz to clean up and to decide the night's *menu*. He left it up to them. It worked better for him. Women were never the issue with Joe. His freedom, his independence, getting by, getting laid, not worrying about paying bills, not having to solve other people's problems were what mattered. There was everything he needed at Nancy's.

When they all settled in, more than a decade ago, Nancy made it clear that Liz was as important to her as he was, and that he was free to have his own women whenever she was in Liz Cycle, as she called it. The key was discretion.

"People mind their business in this town, because everybody knows everybody else's," she'd warned him. "But we can't stick it in their faces, nor can we be too exotic."

Joe made it clear that he had no interest in fucking both of them, no interest in watching them, no interest in being in bed with more than one woman at a time. He'd seen all that stuff before he married.

"You're tamer than I thought," said Nancy.

"Less needy," said Joe.

He looked at Nancy's books on the night table, remembering Sally's financial aid volumes. Thumbing through them did as much for him as all that fellowship and grant information. The four Eros editions, he had been told a thousand times they were collectors' items, erotica not porn, had no sexual appeal for him at all. Shit like Faye Emerson on why we love Jack Kennedy, some guy's Florentine sex life during the Renaissance, love in the Bible and

Shakespeare — who the fuck did this guy Ginsberg think he was kidding. Playing cards and the cigar boxes were okay, and the Monroe collection, but that only because he liked Marilyn Monroe, not because they gave him a hard-on. Nancy had another one, too, The Sex Book, men and women's privates, a sex dictionary for those who needed it. That didn't do anything for him, either. As aggressive as she'd been with him, she was less than open about sex in the bedroom. Erotica not porn! Hah! No doubt she loved it, but Joe figured it was as much about conquest and power as anything else for Nancy. He let her play her little games. She was imaginative and had great hands.

The stuff Liz had, slick magazines showing everybody doing everything from licking clits to sucking dicks, that action was more straightforward. But Joe didn't need it. He couldn't explain why, but he was a natural for needy pussy. It always came his way.

Liz walked into the room before he and Nancy went to bed. "I left a call for Michael on Friday. From what Adam told me about the deal, he's got a real nose for prime real estate and for structuring. I'm going to ask him—"

"You had too much to drink. We can't do any real estate deals in East Hampton," cut in the Supervisor as the Planning Board Chairperson was explaining.

" . . . if an out of town deal ever comes around," Liz continued sharply, "undervalued, but prime, to let me know. You, too, of course. Unless you think I'm too stupid to understand the constraints our positions place on us."

"You'll have to stay wide awake with Michael," laughed Joe. "That's a full-time job."

"I can count," she said tersely. "And Adam and Max are pit bulls. My pit bulls," added Liz, shutting the door as she left the room.

Michael was in action, Joe thought with a smile, big action, but Joe couldn't pay attention to that for long. Nancy, naked and oiled, had placed herself on top of him, sliding herself slowly up and down, up and down, cylinder and piston, slow motion controlled, for now, up and down, up and down. She held his wrists, commanded him not to move. Not yet, not yet, not yet . . . .

39
People and Places

Michael decided to go to Florida from Coram, after all. All things considered, it was the smarter move. He could pocket the listing he'd gotten from Wolff until he returned to East Hampton, buy some time without getting his mother or brother mad at him. It was Tuesday evening. There was an office ruling that all listings must be shared as soon as they came in. He wasn't at the office, therefore, it didn't come in. Technically. What could anyone do? Some things, Michael laughed, were not meant to be shared.

When he spoke to Adam Slavka, Adam said he and his father wanted to go out with him on Thursday. Well, he'd call tomorrow to say he couldn't make it till Friday. Let them salivate. He knew he had a winner. He had to get into the game . . . things to do, places to go, people to see.

In any case, he thought on take-off, making sure his seat belt was secure, he'd made a good decision about this past weekend. It was worth it. He got the listing, had been creative with it, and, he kind of liked the rest, too, though it wasn't the driving force. He'd covered all bases as well, leaving a message on the office machine that Cora Foster wouldn't pick up until morning.

It worked out exactly the way Michael thought it would.

"The message was simply that he'd see you at the end of the week, that he went south from Coram," Cora Foster explained to Sally the next day, for the second time. "That's all he said."

"What's in Coram? I couldn't find Coram if you put a gun to my head." Sally knew New York and she knew the Hamptons. Everything in between, the rest of Suffolk County, all of Nassau, was what you had to get through to travel from one place to the other.

"What's in Coram? Michael said *he* was in Coram," said Andy. "If you want to believe that. He's probably holed up in some casino, figuring a way to get home. Or get lost if the money you gave him is gone."

"The money he earned," Sally corrected. No matter where she was in the office, Andy would appear when he was there, missing nothing. Josephine told her it was a middle child trait.

"Those two men were in again, Sally, asking for Michael," reported Cora.

"Couldn't someone else take care of them?"

"They only wanted Michael."

"Ain't loyalty great?" Andy gave a sarcastic laugh. "I think those guys do the taking care of people. I'm out of here. I want to show Emily the new Unger estate. Mrs. Unger's there, in residence now. With her nurse. She hasn't been well at all. Her heart." Andy announced the news with some importance, an insider, finally, with insider information.

Sally pictured the 12 acres on the ocean. It was out of Gatsby, the stables, pools and tennis courts, a new gardener's cottage standing guard at the front of the long driveway protecting the 10,000-square-foot mansion a half mile further down on the dunes.

"Should Emily be doing that now?" Sally asked. "She looks about to pop. There's still some construction debris on site near the cottage."

"I can take care of my wife," he said, walking out the door. "I thought we had this discussion when I brought home the dogs."

"I love dogs, too, Andy. It's Em's pregnancy that makes me concerned."

"She doesn't look it, Sally, but Emily's built like a brood mare," intervened Cora. "Takes after them Fosters, red hair and all."

"If you say so," Sally said, watching as Andy disappeared.

"Oh, yes! Both Ungers, the brothers, called for Michael."

"What did they want?"

"They're in. Have him call. That was the message"

"What does that mean, they're in?" said Sally, wondering if that was why Andy was really going over to the Ungers' mansion. "Like in a deal or in at home?"

"Hard to tell," said Cora pleasantly.

Sally sighed. "What did you tell them?"

"Tell who?" asked Cora. "The Ungers?"

"The men who were here, who asked for Michael."

"That he was out of town," Cora said. "Only that."

Looking at her watch, Sally saw it was 11:30. "I'll be at O'Mally's for lunch with Josephine . . . in case Michael calls," Sally said, casually, too casually. She had an uneasy feeling something was going on.

O'Mally's, nestled in a mews off Main Street, was a good place for a quick lunch during the summer season. There were no luncheonettes in the Village since Eddie's and the Marmador closed. If you went to O'Mally's early, you'd find mostly year-round people.

In the muted lighting, Sally could see Josephine seated in the back near the stone fireplace.

She prepared herself, feeling the attention when she entered, the looks of recognition, respect and, yes, envy. She could hear the murmurs, the whispers, *Hi Sally, that's Sally Singer the real estate lady, that's the one that makes the big deals, that's the one that has the best office in town, nice packaging, too.* Sally knew men still found her attractive, was aware she made heads turn whether they knew she was *the* Sally Singer or not. Faded jeans hugging her compact, high-legged body, a peach tank top revealing firm, rounded breasts, aviator sunglasses over a renewed tan, she felt good about looking good. Jacqueline Bisset was probably a stretch, but close enough. She threw her shoulders back, standing straighter, keeping her eyes on her destination,

Sally had worked hard for all of this, worked at things she didn't care about, giving up things that mattered dearly. But she won, won the respect and admiration in this town that, 15 years earlier, asked her and her three sons to leave, in this town where her children once were on free lunches, and where her family was talked about as the *poor* Jews as opposed to the other kind. She'd conquered the local families, any small town provincialism, too. Wasn't she in with the Fosters and MacMullins through Andy? Didn't she have a connection, no matter how exotic, with the Hawleys and the Bennets through Ben? She didn't have to count Jack. He was there, on her side, from the beginning.

There was satisfaction from the stir she was causing, especially since she knew there was a buzz about the deal that closed Friday. That was a Singer deal and a Singer effort. She led the Singer team. As she edged her way through the crowded restaurant, her eye caught Liz and Nancy with that Maidstone brat Dunny Slykes dining off to the side. You either hated Dunny or liked him; no one loved him. Sally put herself in the like column, reluctantly. He did have something! Liz was trying to get her attention. Even Dunny gave a hand salute. Sally pushed on.

She thought of that day at Gosman's when she swore she'd come back and come back right. She had and she did. She was a presence in this town. And that was an achievement no matter how little she knew the tough real estate dame she'd become, no matter how far she was from the life of the mind that she loved. She had won . . . something.

Sally took a deep breath before seating herself.

It smelled like a perennial barbecue, O'Mally's pub, but it felt like New York, not East Hampton. The framed snapshots of local athletes were the only reminder you weren't back on Third Avenue. There were exposed brown rafters, a menu on a blackboard, Heineken bottles displayed behind the polished dark wood bar, ring photos of Dempsey, Marciano, Zale and Graziano. Directly over their table was a picture of the East Hampton High Football Conference Champions, with wide receiver Andy Singer staring down, helmet in hand.

"Some entrance," said Josephine Aquistapace.

"Yes, well, we're both a long way from our housecleaning days, aren't we?"

"You! You had to. You'd never have lasted on the job, leaving notes to my customers with hints on keeping the house in order. Marrone! You surely weren't going to make it that way."

Sally laughed. "I can't get away from him," she said, pointing at the picture of Andy. "He's like Big Brother . . . in the office . . . here. Oh, well, one I can't find, one I can't get away from, and the third wasn't always all there in the first place."

She was breaking their time-out rule, a promise not to discuss business or children problems at these lunches. Time-outs may be punitive in nursery school; they were respites for grown-ups.

"I'm breaking the rule, too, Sally," Josephine said, as if reading her mind. "Is Michael working on something? Something big? There are whispers."

"Can't tell you. But he could be getting greedy. He's doing very well."

"It's not greed with that one. Did he go to Gamblers Anonymous? You know I spoke to him about it, let him know it was there."

"I don't know. I don't think so," Sally admitted, remembering the bad times last year when Michael returned from Vegas. "I don't think he sees himself as an addict."

"Yes, well, that's typical. The gambling dependency has the worst rate of denial."

"I hate when you talk that way with me. That professional way, the jargon."

"Yes, well, what about you and that *akrasia,* that moral weakness? Anyway, it's a mistake to think your Michael's greedy. Compulsive gamblers need money only to support their habit, not for acquisitions or security like the rest of us. I've told you that, and about enabling, too."

"You're doing more of it, that psycho-babble stuff."

"Yes, well, there may be more denial here than Michael's. In any case, my friend, there are whispers about some big deal he's doing. *Finito!*"

"So do we have a date for October at The Palm? You and Vince?" Sally veered to a safer place, first ordering her Vermont burger, rare, hold the lettuce.

Josephine ordered a salad. "It looks like Vince will have a show in New Hampshire, near Francestown, sometime before Christmas. He may be painting the end of foliage in October. We had a great weekend up there."

"A show! New Hampshire! Terrific! November then? Before Thanksgiving? "

"We could forget what we're celebrating by then, but who cares.

You have a new tan."

"It's a relief to be out of the office July Fourth weekend, no business, only bedlam. I was with Jack. He didn't leave town after all. We sailed and sunned."

"Did he bring up divorce again? Or is that a dead issue? You know you're really *pazza* about that divorce."

"Crazy or not, why should I legalize failure," Sally argued. "It won't make Jack and me closer. This way when people ask how long I've been married, I can say 26 years or whatever."

"Why would people ask? You don't wear a ring. What business is it of theirs?"

"Look, I'm the first direct line descendant in three generations that can say that, 26 years. I'm not getting a divorce and that's that. Maybe that's why Father Donelly likes me," she quipped. "So, what's the theme?"

Josephine rolled her eyes. "The theme of what?" she asked, moving her glass to make room for the salad.

"The theme of Vincent's—"

"Didn't you see me try to get your attention?" cut in Liz Slavka. "My God, Sally, you don't make it easy. Congratulations on the deal."

"Thank you. Thank you for the papers we needed, too. I sent you a note."

"Joe got quite a bundle for the medallion," Liz told her. "He was smart to hold on to it all these years. It was working for him."

"My burger's getting cold," Sally said.

"Yes, well, please have Michael give us a call. I've left several messages."

"Is this business?" Sally asked, a bite of bread in her mouth.

"Your burger's getting cold, my dear." Nodding at Josephine,

Liz walked away. Nancy was waiting near the bar as Councilman Dunny Slykes glad-handed the second tier of O'Mally lunch patrons, second-home owner summer-people, the meat of the Democrats' support.

"You weren't too good at that exchange, were you?" Josephine laughed.

"No, I guess I wasn't." Sally wiped her smile with the linen napkin.

"Still kind of fuzzy dealing with middle things, eh?" She pushed aside her plate with a grin. "Well, I told you, you wait so long that nothing less than murder's appropriate." Gesturing to the waitress for more coffee, she added, "Mountain landscapes."

"Hmmm?"

"The theme. The New Hampshire show. Mountain Landscapes."

"He has mountain landscapes after one weekend?" she asked, though she was thinking about Liz and Michael and the *something big* whispers Josephine mentioned.

"Only photos. He'll spend September there, at least the first two weeks in October to get the foliage, maybe more, if he's doing winter scenes, too. That's why I can't plan for dinner at The Palm. You know Vincent. The paint's always wet first day of his shows."

Sally was only half listening. Why would Liz want Michael to call? It bothered her.

After lunch, Sally phoned Jess Kingsley to see if Michael had returned his call. He told her Lester Wolff had taken care of all of that. He was handling the listing information. "That boy's a smart kid," he said.

What listing? Sally wondered. She learned that Hiram Hawley's call was in reference to the same matter. Not wanting to look like she didn't know what was going on in her own office she decided to

wait for Michael. If he was in Florida, she could call and find out.
Sally knew what was in Florida, besides her mother. Doug Slavka
was there. She decided to wait to see if Michael came in tomorrow
as he said he would on the message.

She'd take her salespeople out caravaning the new listings that
had come in over the weekend. A few brokers were in the office. It
was a good idea.

"We can't be lazy about this," she urged them. "We get the
jump. Anything good out there we tell our customers first. The only
things that distinguish one real estate firm from another are pro-
fessionalism, service and reputation. We've got all three. Remember, real estate is your ticket to financial independence," she lec-
tured, motivating them to pile into cars and buck traffic in the
uncomfortable, humid July heat.

As Sally was fighting her way out of the parking lot that Wednesday afternoon, Doug Slavka was asking Michael, "Is this better
than the Hamptons or not?"

They were strolling toward a broad stretch of white sand in
downtown Miami Beach. There was a flat-roofed hotel, shaped like
a sardine can, its freshly painted stucco a pastel green. Elderly
people sat on the verandah, like mannequins in a shop window,
motionless, looking out toward the water. The palm trees, bending
wantonly with any wind, were graceful and seductive in their per-
fidy. Crossing Collins Avenue to Ocean Drive, barely looking either way, they walked onto 14th Street Beach. The tropical air was
musky with the scent of coconuts, lush sweet-smelling flowers, warm
sea air and exotic fruits.

After all the years of waiting for his uncle's death, Doug Slavka
realized he had been more useful to him alive. Max had prevailed.
The inheritance was left to both brothers. There was no technicolor

future for Doug Slavka, Michael knew. A thoughtless gambler with expensive tastes and a need for flashy women, Doug could blow the money like a shot if he weren't careful. Girls were getting harder to impress. They were younger and more expensive each year, needed everything first class, from chartered planes to penthouse accommodations.

To keep costs down, Doug was leasing a small apartment on Meridian, another disappointment, the Uncle's lovely home on Normandy Isle sold to liquidate the estate. He invested in Treasuries for a livable income. And hated it. Doug didn't have to worry as long as he gave up his dreams, dreams on which he'd spent a lifetime. And his drugs. Giving up drugs in Miami, Michael thought, would be like giving up the sun.

"Nicer than the Hamptons, huh?" asked Doug, his face wearing a new, bitter expression.

"Yeah, in a way," said Michael, "less crowded, but it's safer up North. The greater Miami area has the highest crime statistics in the nation."

"Says who?"

"Newspapers, *New York Magazine,* I don't remember."

"New York papers, I bet." Doug took off his sweatshirt, tying its arms around his tanned neck. His stocky body was a little softer, more pudgy perhaps, but he had to be close to 50, Michael figured, as old as those Tropical Deco Hotels on Ocean Drive. South Beach. There were a lot of paint jobs going on, face lifts for this aged neighborhood they were trying to preserve by getting it on the National Registry. Doug's face could have used a lift, too. There was no trace of Redford anymore, just wrinkled, freckle-blotched tan with a sun-baked leathery texture.

"There are good deals down here. Futures. I know this place

will turn around. They can't let prime east coast oceanfront sink," Michael said, very professionally, glancing across the plain of sand to calm, turquoise ocean.

"There's some great looking girls, too," Doug replied, an unattractive smirk on his sun-dried face. "I make out like a rabbit. It just costs more to keep them happy."

"I may open an office on Washington Avenue," said Michael, staying on point.

"Can you spring for that kind of bread?" Doug looked surprised.

"Minimal space, a secretary . . . a phone."

Doug lit up, took a deep drag. Then, squeezing the tip, he put the joint back in the zippered pocket of his shorts. "You know you need a license to do real estate here."

"What kind of license do you need for that stuff? Shouldn't you be more discreet?"

"Yeah, discreet. What would you do about a license, hotshot?"

"It's just a thought. I have to finish things in East Hampton first. There's one sweet package, a Southampton deal, very creative, that needs all my attention. A home run."

"Southampton?"

"Yeah, a hamlet call Sagaponack. You've seen it. Those farms on the ocean side of the highway right before you hit East Hampton. Remember the Sagg Country Store and the Sagg Post Office in the same small storefront?"

"That flat stuff where you see the ocean from the highway? That's Southampton Town?"

"Stops at Town Line Road. There's a pond in there, too. Sagg Pond, more like a small lake. Ocean front, pond front, water views. A home run. Don't get any ideas though, Doug. It's a creative deal, but there's risk."

"Don't get stung by one of those suckers," Doug warned, skirting around the purple, blue Man-of-Wars stranded on the beach at low tide.

That warning got Michael's attention, until he saw the stranded jellyfish on the shoreline. "I can't sell any more pieces anyway. My mother wants in and I have no room," he gave a helpless, that's-the-breaks kind of shrug. "I can get a bigger piece than expected, at bottom price, because a partner is pulling out. Divorce complications. Have to raise some capital, that's why I'm going back so soon. Gotta take care of number one. The deal's too good to pass on."

"You do keep plugging. I admire that, Michael," Doug added. "Some say the Gulf Coast will be where it's at down here. Above the Keys. Like Naples."

"Maybe. But for quick turnarounds I'd always bet on the ocean."

"I think so, too. What's this Southampton deal that's so special, Michael?"

"Which one?"

"Don't give me that shit! It's the Doug you're talking to."

"The package I mentioned? Southampton?"

"The one your mother's after. I have no interest, but I'd like to see how you think."

"Look Doug. I'm telling you, don't get ideas. No matter how good these things are, there's always the risk. No risk, no reward. But listen, you've got your money placed safely in—"

"Treasuries, Michael. In Goddamn Treasuries."

"Okay, in Treasuries. They're not glamorous, but they provide a modest income. It's safe. Don't even think about anything else. That's the best advice I could give you."

"I thought we were friends, Michael. You wouldn't hold out on a friend."

"I'm glad we're friends. I know you won't mention it to my mother that we spoke about this. She's kind of sensitive."

"Look, kid, I know how sensitive your mother can get. I know your mother."

"I'm glad you understand. She's really after me. What can I do? I try to make a lot of money for the company." He shrugged the helpless shrug again. "I wish I could spend more time with you, but I have to visit my grandmother while I'm down here. Good news for her. My father's selling the medallion."

"The what?"

"The taxi medallion. It's worth 70 or 80 grand now. Some of that goes to her."

"Jeez, nice action for Joe. So Singer's doing okay. How'd he ever fall into that? I wouldn't be surprised if my former sister-in-law gave some advice. That dike's sharp that way."

"My father's smart enough," said Michael. "He made the killing by keeping the Medallion. letting it work for him. He has patience."

"Hey, no offense to your father, kid. Talk to me about the package. How big is your piece? What kind of numbers are you talking about?"

That night his grandmother took Michael to Miami International. Ben would pick him up at LaGuardia in the limo. Thursday morning he'd be at the office. As the plane smoothly left the runway, he could still hear Grandma Bea saying how proud she was of him and of course she'd keep it a secret.

40

Honesty . . . Before the Deal

Michael dropped the Sagaponack information into the new listing basket on Cora Foster's desk.

"Your mother's looking for you," Cora told him. "Did you catch her at home?"

"I stayed at the Ungers," he said. "I'll be back later this afternoon."

"Can you be reached? There's a lot of calls, including one from your Dad."

"I'm having lunch at O'Mally's," Michael said, looking at the message from his father. Using Cora's phone, he dialed the Ryner house. "Make it short. I'm pressed for time, Dad."

"Don't hold out on me, Michael. "

"Why would I want to do that?"

"You're not dealing with your mother."

Michael smiled. "I'll drop by later."

The Sagaponack listing from Wolff/Kingsley, who were handling the original Hiram Hawley piece, had been altered thanks to Michael's input. Sure, there was the same water table problem, but he was building a reputation on problem pieces. Under certain adverse conditions, lots of snow, very heavy rain, there was the ponding effect, bodies of water arose on the real estate making it more like a bayou than a farm field. But it was oceanfront, view and proximity. Maybe they could divert or preserve the worst of it.

That was Wolff and Kingsley's job.

His job was to sell the parcel before the Southampton Town Planning Board decided to copycat East Hampton's environmental zeal, before they upzoned the fragile piece from its current half acre and 1 acre zoning to 5 acre. Kingsley had been told environmental groups and some powerful property owners from away were pushing for this, only whispers, but enough to make Hiram Hawley nervous.

"Damn politicians will do anything they please with your property nowadays," Hiram Hawley complained to Michael over the phone. "Steal your lots by upzoning, devalue your land without so much as blinking an eye. Farmers, land rich, cash poor, that's our story. Damn newcomers want to steal that, too, one way or other. Upzone or subdivide. Wish we had the money to do it ourselves, but wishin' ain't doin'. A day late, a dollar short," he sighed. "Crop debts, high interest, need to survive. Everybody's getting rich off our backs. We get bones."

The farmer knew his real estate. If a map were filed today, Michael could see a four-to-one gross return. With future appreciation, who knew where you could go? Once you were whole on the investment, including soft costs and improvements, you could take your time.

Prime east coast oceanfront was at a premium. Where was your competition? Not over-built South Beach in Florida with its Tropical Deco hotels. And Florida didn't have New York, Washington D.C. and Boston, nearby. You could bank on a 200% return on investment, a great ground-floor deal. The zoning? The ponding? A risk, but a right risk. He had to act fast. Get backers to lend, promise them a high rate of interest on their money and a small piece of the action as the kicker, show prospects he was putting up his cash for confidence.

Taking the listing from the basket, Michael scrawled *almost at meeting of the minds* across it with his initials. All the listing information said was *see Michael S. for details*. That was enough to cause a fuss. His mother would probably get blamed for favoring him, for knowing about it all along, for doing something or not enough. She had a way of being the first to admit and the last to know that was not really healthy for her position.

"Tell my mother I'll catch up with her in the afternoon," he told Cora.

He drove to Springs on Accabonac in the office's burgundy Land Rover. He was going to Green River Cemetery to visit Junior Hawley's grave. Michael hadn't been able to do that when he first got back from Vegas, too much for him. He'd never seen anyone die before. It was hard to get that picture from Andy's wedding out of his head. Junior Hawley had trusted him, liked him, too. There was an attachment, probably the only real one he'd made in town. Now Michael came by regularly, talking with the man-child he had befriended, putting down flowers he'd taken from the other graves.

When he got to O'Mallys, Adam Slavka was there waiting for him.

"So what have you got for me?"

"Okay," he said. "Here's the home run."

Michael moved to the side away from the fireplace, away from Andy's demanding stare. No sense bullshitting the Slavkas. They were too smart for that. However, until Wolff told him everything was in place, he'd outline only part of the deal. All he was going to do later was make it better. Wearing tennis whites that looked whiter against his dark tan and jet black hair, Michael gave the impression of a tall Alain Delon.

"How's a subdivision in Sagaponack? A hot south-of-the-high-way area, Adam. All farms. Lots of open space. On the ocean."

"Approved?"

"Not yet, but we've got some leverage if we move fast. Old family involved."

"We have to sit through Southampton approvals? Is a deal conditioned on it?"

"Nope! There's the risk. That's why the deal's so attractive. Otherwise the price would be out of sight."

He was starting slowly, pro that he was, trying to hook Slavka who had more than his share of an attorney's suspicious nature. He would reveal the deal in bits and pieces.

"Look, Adam, it's ground floor. The seller's crunched. Two years of bad potatoes from the Golden Nematode pest and the punitive inheritance tax. For 25% cash down, he'll take a mortgage, interest only, five years."

"Yeah, assuming approval. Talk is cheap for a salesman like yourself."

Michael let him feel superior. It could only make him sloppy.

"He's taking back a note which is secured by the property, right?" Michael, if we sell lots, the value of his mortgage is diminished. There's less property behind the note . . . *unless* they take money out with each sale. We need release clauses so they'll take their money in pieces, " Adam said, with a show-offy look. He took a large bite of the burger, more then he could handle and had to wipe his face where the ketchup was dripping. "What about that?"

"There's ketchup on your nose," Michael pointed out. "I think if we give 50% cash down, non-refundable, we can get release clauses as favorable to us as they'll ever be."

"They don't have to hold the mortgage, you know. There's always financing. Your distressed person could get all cash right away, and for that, lower the asking price."

"I don't want to rob the guy," he sighed. Some people couldn't pay asking price no matter how good the return on investment looked.

"Where does it say someone has to make a huge profit? You should stick to tennis," Adam Slavka went on, gulping down his soda. "We're taking the risks. Try the cash deal out on him."

"The ketchup's on your shirt now. Above the man playing polo."

The tell. Like over-playing a hand in a poker game, Adam had said too much. Michael knew he had them. The return was a developer's dream. And Adam was going right where Michael wanted him. To the cash deal. With Michael's creative input, the changed deal *had* to be a cash deal.

"You understand, I can offer you and your Dad only a piece of this. I have other interest here. "

"You didn't say anything about partners. Is that what you're up to?"

" I can't give you the whole deal. We can worry about that later. I'd like to tie this property up." He paused as if looking for the waitress. "By the way, I may be able to arrange financing for some points on the deal. You can throw that in the pot."

No point telling Adam he'd be in for more than a few points, that he saw himself holding half the deal, more, with the points they'd throw him if he handled the financing. He would become the major player, the operator. The Ungers and Slavkas combined were the rest; let them work out their own percentages. He was feeling the rush, but his cool, boyish face revealed nothing.

"We'll have to see it, of course. I'll talk to my father. Probably this weekend." Abruptly, Adam pushed away the half-eaten fries and left the table.

When they see the Hawley property, then Michael would describe how big the package could be. Now watching Adam rush out, Michael had to laugh.

"What's so funny?" said Andy's voice. His brother was standing at the table, staring at him with the same hard stare that was in the team picture. He hadn't gotten away, after all. Michael laughed harder. "Share the joke, bub?"

"What are *you* doing here?

"I asked you what's the joke?"

"I'm the joke," Michael said, dabbing his mouth with a napkin. "I can't believe it. I got stuck with the check. And if you sit down, I'm going to get stuck with another one."

"Who are you kidding? Get stuck. You'll sign off for Sally Singer Inc. Like you do her checks. But that's not my business. Listen to me. I saw that piece of shit you call a listing. There's no fucking information. *See Michael S.* You're holding back. You're holding back on me."

"Why would I want to do that?" said Michael, using his stock non-answer.

"You held onto that listing. I was at the Ungers' yesterday. The mother said they were in something with you."

"Try again," said Michael. "That woman says nothing, but hello and good-bye."

"If you're doing deals with Unger, the commission split still stands."

"Listen to me, Andy. Unger was my listing. Whatever split you're talking about was for the Winston deal only. Do you think you own somebody for life? He *asked* me to bring him anything I could find, he said I was a spark plug and you were a loose cannon."

"I'm in on the commission because of the Unger split, shithead."

"Out of the kindness of my heart. You're going to be in because you're my brother. Remember that! Not because it's owed."

"I'm in because that's the deal, fuckface. I don't need your favors. Don't look away when I'm talking," snapped Andy.

Michael was looking over Andy's head.

"I said don't look away."

"Nice to see you," said the gravelly voice.

"I wish I could say the same," quipped Michael.

Andy turned. It was Freddy the Finger.

"I told you once before don't take nice for weak, Michael. It would be a serious mistake."

"How'd you know I was here?" said Michael, pulling out a chair for his bookmaker.

"The nice lady in your mother's office." He sat down, looking different in a suit and tie among all the vacationers. "Before you spend that bread you made, you've got to take care of other business. It's payday and you're late. I hope you have it, for your sake."

"You know I wouldn't stiff you. Here, it's ready for you. See?"

Andy watched as Michael took out a thick envelope.

"Not good enough," said the bookmaker, fingering quickly through the new bills. "I want it all. Paid in full. With the juice. You took when you won. You pay when you lose. You pay more when I wait. You know the number."

"I'm out of here," said Andy.

Michael sighed. Almost $60,000 gone. The juice was more than the loan. Time cost you. Shit! That was a setback. How would he get his part up?

"You're not interested in doing a real estate deal, are you?"

Finger gave him a look.

"I didn't think so." sighed Michael. "Sit down, have a burger. Let me at least tell you about it."

He had a long trek in a short time. What he hadn't said at all, hadn't divulged along with the creativity, was this deal had to close before Labor Day. Wolff gave him the exclusive listing for 30 days, as a kind of gift. After 30 days, Wolff/Kingsley would go elsewhere. Well, he smiled, beads of perspiration ponding on his forehead, life was a challenge. At least he was in action.

41
Principals and Principles

July had turned into August. Tomorrow was the Sagg/Hawley closing. Earlier that day when she was about to return a call to the lawyers from Georgetown, the ones who'd bought Hawley Bennet's beach house, Sally noticed the contract copies on Michael's desk. She stopped to look at them, never returning the call.

She thought about the contracts all evening. They were so complicated, so many groups involved, among the buyers and sellers. The Phoebus Group was one of the buyers. What Phoebus Group? A coincidence that the name belonged to the pitcher she hadn't bet on, yet won? The guy who stood in for Palmer? Michael's sense of humor to see if she'd solve the puzzle? It got her interested in a queasy stomach-dropping way. Old feelings. The amorphous shame tied to nothing, tied to everything, long-leased tenants that resided inside her. She could have brought the papers home to show Jack, but she didn't want to. She could call Lester Wolff, however, a casual night-before-the-closing call to see if things were in place. No loss of face there! After all, wouldn't a principal broker do that? A principled broker? The 10 O'clock News was going on; there was time. Jack was reading. Sally went into the kitchen.

"It better be in place," said Wolff. "Your son got the listing because of me, you know. Jess would have gone straight to you. A good head on his shoulders. That whole concoction was his idea, Sally, I brought him only the seed. A good head. *A Yiddishe kopf,* my mother would say."

Referencing Meyer Lansky, Arnie Rothstein, Nicky Arnstein, Ben Seigel and her father, Mike Lamb, grandma would say, *Yiddishe kopfs are sometimes a kopf vetig.* A headache!

"I get no *thank-you* on the other matter? I expected too much from you?" Wolff said, sounding hurt and as if he still wasn't crazy about her. "A good boy, Michael. Man I should say. Bar mitzvahed, finally. I didn't give him the listing for nothing. That Lubavitcher Group, the one you called with your idea to have a Jewish rite in a Christian Church. They left Brooklyn, came to Long Island, to Coram. I assume they're still strict enough for your orthodox sensibilities."

"Bar mitzvahed? Michael? Bar mitzvahed?" she echoed. "Yes, we're all happy. Orthodox is orthodox," she managed to say. "Goodnight, Lester."

Bar mitzvahed? Why? Why a secret? She called Doug. He was close to Michael. He'd seen him right after the Coram weekend. They talked often.

"Hey, I'm in this deal, Sally. No thanks to my gal Sal, by the way. Part of Michael's action. Part loan and part interest. You know Superboy and his back-end kickers."

"Michael's action?" She gasped.

"Come on now, Sally, you can't fool me. You're not in this home run for the brokerage fees. Did you think you could hide it from the Doug? My God, you're on the management committee! I insisted. Wish I could be there for the closing tomorrow. My lawyer will be."

"Management committee? Your lawyer? Max? Are you using Max?"

"That scumbag? You know better. I hold on to my grudges. Besides, he may be in there, too, with someone else. Michael's so mysterious. The man of mystery. I'm using the same attorney as your mother."

Sally shuddered, feeling an icy chill. "My mother," she echoed, hearing a death knell.

She called her mother.

"Isn't he wonderful? Reminds me so much of your father, Sally, the talented side, of course. The genius. He let me put the proceeds in from Joe's medallion sale up as a loan to him, 25% interest on the money. And then he gave me a small part of the deal, too. That's a grandson."

She called Joe. He was in, too. She hung up before he could tell her more.

Oh my God, Ben? Ben couldn't be involved. Hawley would have said something. Ben had so little, wanted so little. She called.

"Michael never approached us, Sally," said Hawley Bennet. "Ben would have told me. Was Michael supposed to?"

She gave a sigh of relief. Though he was with Hawley in a loving relationship, Sally saw protecting her *artistic* son as a lifetime commitment.

She hated to call Andy. But she had to see just how bad things were. She could hear Junior Singer crying in the background. When he was two weeks old, they'd finally named him Andy — against the Jewish tradition — and called him Junior in memory of Em's half brother. One way or another it worked. It was better than Charles Hawley Singer.

"He owed me part. Don't tell me no, Ma. Somehow he got the listing connection, but he still made the deal of the century," said Andy, both proudly and begrudgingly.

"You wouldn't happen to know where I could reach him?" she asked before hanging up.

She was dizzy. She felt stupid, careless. She didn't want Jack to know. But that's how Michael worked, secretly. That's how she let him work. Wasn't she the principal broker? Wasn't she responsible for everything that came out of her office? She went to her copy of the *Summary of New York State Real Property Law*, finding what she knew was there.

Demonstrated Untrustworthiness: Patterson v. Department of State; Berlow v. Lorenzo; Brabazon v. Cuomo. Broker's failure to represent the interest of his clients and his representation of both sides in a transaction; Broker's failure to disclose interest in property without knowledge of the seller; broker had a major interest to purchase the land and that broker did not disclose his true position to the listing owners. **Penalty: Revocation of License**

There were other references, too, felonious acts and the penalties for a broker involved.

There had been no disclosure to the seller. Not from her. The broker's family was involved. The Singer family. A grandmother, a son, and a loose husband she had lying around. That was illegal. Doug said her name was in the agreement somewhere. Who would believe she never knew? Savvy Sally Singer not knowing the score? East Hampton Empress of Real Estate?

Revocation of license! She wouldn't be able to work nor would any of her salespeople. Everything was on the line. Her business. Her reputation. Her economic security. Maybe her freedom. The ballooning realization made her reel. They'd sue. Everyone would sue. And she still didn't know what had happened.

What to do? The night before the closing. There was only one option. She had to call it off. Postpone it. Withdraw. Face it. Sally Singer Inc. would be out, of course. She'd lose the commission. That's if the deal closed. Suppose, just suppose, it didn't? What about the contract payments, if the deal fell through? They'd blame the broker. Everyone does. Lawsuits. Everything was in jeopardy! Without thinking, she grabbed a slice of bread.

Back in the bedroom, she posed a hypothetical to Jack. "What if . . . ." she spelled out the imaginary undisclosed broker involvement in a deal.

"Happens all the time with unscrupulous brokers. They pray the closing goes smoothly, take the chance. The seller better be getting market value, too. That's critical! If something goes sour and the seller files a complaint about the lack of disclosure, some broker will testify that the deal was not true market value, even if it is. Now it's more than demonstrated untrustworthiness. Collusion and fraud are charged, civil actions follow, criminal investigations not far behind."

"But the principal broker didn't know."

"No defense. The principal broker should know. You know that," he chided. "If the deal doesn't close and the buyers lose the contract fee, license revocation looks like a blessing at that point! Law suits proliferate. It's a rock and a hard place, once it starts rolling."

More lawsuits! Where would she get money to defend if she didn't close this deal? Most of hers went back into the business. She'd have to mortgage the house again. Was adjourning really an option?

"Do you think Dayton Lane is cursed?" she asked Jack Bennet in the darkened room, her voice small, childlike. "Your Jean? Charles' Junior? Michael? So many bad things."

"Sally, every street in town is Dayton Lane." He held her closer.

"How bad is it?"

She sobbed. He always understood. "Michael, other Singers, too, are in the Hawley deal," she whispered, tears streaming down her face. "I didn't know. I don't even know what the deal is."

She wasn't able to catch up with Michael recently. Always traveling. Appointments. In when she was out. Out when she was in. Things to do. People to see. Places to go.

"I must talk to him, but I can't. I have to call it off."

"Are you certain Michael didn't disclose to the sellers, Sally? He knows the rules."

"I never thought of that." She paused, then blurted. "I can't reach him to find out."

"Why's that?"

"Andy told me Michael's in Atlantic City."

42
Bet on the World

The phone rang at daybreak. She didn't want to wake up, didn't want to respond, but like a dentist's drill, the nerve-piercing jangle would go only deeper until its demands were answered.

"Hi, Ma, sorry to wake you, but we've got a big day."

"Michael?" He never identified himself with her, as if he were only one son. He was the only one who called so early when she was most vulnerable, he most in need.

"I assume you found the contract copies I left out for you."

She knew there was a laugh, though it was not audible. Like they were in some cat and mouse game and each time she found the mouse he'd planted, she won a round. He gave her a round.

"It's not funny, Michael." He toyed with her. She liked it.

"So what do you think?"

She was awake now. "Hold on, I'm going into the kitchen."

"Oh!" he exclaimed with a lilt. "Say hello to Jack for me."

Sally got up and pulled an old gray sweatshirt over her head. She was strangely chilled, though the August day promised hot and muggy, a leftover from July. She tiptoed into the other room, putting coffee on as she cradled the phone.

"Michael, thank God you called."

"What's up? You found the copies, right?"

"Did you disclose family interest in this deal to the seller?"

"The sellers," he corrected. "Do you understand what I did

here? There's been nothing before like it, Ma. Kingsley and Wolff said I was a genius."

"Did you disclose, Michael? You haven't answered me."

"Ma, that's small potatoes. The big picture. Life on the edge. I took a Hawley Sagaponack subdivision and turned it into a conglomerate, Ma. It's the biggest thing out here. Something Hiram Hawley said triggered it. He told me on the phone about farmers, land rich, cash poor, a day late, a dollar short, debts, high interest, need to survive. He talked about everybody's getting rich off their backs. I asked him if all his neighbors were in the same boat. When he said, yes, the Singer wheels were turning, the Singer/Lamb wheels. I was smart enough to call Wolff first. Something you would do."

"Michael, I don't know what you're talking about. Did you disclose the broker's interest to the seller?"

"Ma, Wolff loved it, he and Kingsley, as long as the farmers didn't get screwed. Ma, we're selling Sagaponack, the hamlet—"

"We're doing what?"

"We're selling Sagaponack, the whole hamlet on the Ocean side of the highway, 350 acres, Ma, 350 acres of prime oceanfront, view and proximity. With the current zoning, I put the yield at 500 prime to choice building lots: 450 at $70,000, 50 at $200,000. The raw land could demand $14,000,000. The farmers were willing to sell at 6; we've got it priced at 11 million, including brokerage. For my coming up with the deal, I got you the full 10 percent. That's unheard of, Ma. The return on investment, on sellout, I put at $41 mil at least. That's better than 200%," he paused for breath, it seemed. "Figure it out, Ma, do you have your calculator? Figure out your cut alone."

She poured some coffee into a mug, pulled the lone slice of

bread out of the toaster, took one bite and pushed it aside.

"Michael, I can't play with these numbers at 6:20 in the morning. I can't begin to understand what's happening. Are you here?"

"Ma, groups of farmers are selling to groups of developers and investors. Is that simple enough? Except the farmers' real estate all touch each other. I'm on my way."

"More groups? Michael, for the last time, did you disclose your interest, your father's, your brother's, your grandmother's, to the sellers?"

"You're missing the point, Ma. We're making history. Trust me, Ma. The Singers are making Hamptons history."

"How did my name get on these agreements? Doug said— "

"Oh, that was funny. The management committee. The Phoebus Group management committee. You'll like this. You're the tie-breaking vote. The only person everyone trusted, Ma. They wanted you on it, unanimously."

"They?" she whispered into the phone. "The disclosure, Michael?"

"Ma, the deal needed my attention first. The disclosure's being taken care of."

"The closing is today, Michael."

"That's what I mean, Ma. Few last things I need to get in place. Like the money."

"The money?"

"A deal like this is only a cash deal. No conditions, that's only fair. That worked for the sellers. Now we're a few dollars short, the Phoebus Group that is. Last minute, some jerk . . . anyway, I took a shot at something, but it didn't work. There's still a few resources I can tap. A few aces left. And I can get you in, free, Ma, no investment."

"Michael you're a genius, you're bar mitzvahed—"

"A good experience Ma. I threw them—"

"—and you're fired."

Sally hung up, put the dishes in the sink, the bread away. She hadn't talked about calling off the closing. Why didn't she tell Michael that? Why? She tossed the uneaten toast into the garbage.

Back in the bedroom, she returned the phone receiver to its hook. Why? She asked herself, climbing into bed, pulling the sheet and comforter over her head, the extra pillow held tightly in her arms. She wasn't going to call it off, she realized. She was going to take the gamble like the other unscrupulous brokers Jack had told her about. A million dollar brokerage? Was that her magic number? Had money become an end in itself? She recalled Grandma's warning, *When it comes between you and the world, Shifra, bet on the world.* A sure thing!

"I see you've worked things out," Sally could hear Jack say, in his dry, nonjudging way.

The phone rang again. She uncovered her head and grabbed the receiver.

"Don't you want to know the rest of the people in on the deal?" asked the voice she was supposed to always recognize. "Oh yeah, I may be a little late for the closing."

43
August Chaos

The small windowless conference room, its dark-planked floors tilting, was stuck in back of the Hamptons National Bank, a one-story shingled affair.

The weather had shifted as if the elements knew something big was about to happen. Though Labor Day was a week away, there was an autumn chill. Temperatures had lowered since the morning. A cold rain hammered the rooftop. A hurricane? A tornado? Something ominous.

People were cramped around the circular mahogany table in black leather-cushioned chairs, brass bolted to their frames. Some were sitting in jackets; others left windbreakers behind them on chairbacks. A ring of folding chairs encircled the black-leather ones, stuck here and there at random for those who came late.

Sally had been there for over two hours. Few chairs were left. Overflowing tin ashtrays, half-filled styrofoam coffee cups, spilled Creamora, torn blue and pink sweetener packets were strewn across the untidy table among half-open attaché cases, labeled folders and impatient tapping fingers. The damp, crowded room, smoke-filled, was charged with frazzled nerves. Wet clothing with tobacco combined for an unpleasant odor. There was the faint smell of alcohol though it was not yet noon.

Seated near Sally were Max and Adam Slavka and a foot-tapping woman lawyer named Beverly, decked out in a tweed no-nonsense suit. Her tongue kept pushing out the sides of her cheek. She was acting as nominee for two undisclosed partners. A mussed-up New York type lawyer, the kind that was always tougher than his clothes looked, was sitting next to her. He and the woman chatted, friendly like. The rumpled man was representing Joe Singer. She seemed to know Joe from a poker game.

A former playboy congressman, smooth and puffy, his chained pocket watch resting on his paunch, was there for Dunny Slykes and his Maidstone Group. Dunny was there, too.

Hiram Hawley of the Shinnecock Hawleys, who was black, a throwback to some 18th-century doings between Native Americans, freemen and settlers, was seated to their right, next to his Southampton attorney, who wore a vest. Then came the other farmers — there were five — all in uncomfortable tight-fitting suits, weathered and straw-haired with old-fashioned faces.

Ben Hawley was there representing Cora Foster, Councilman Angus MacMullin and Andy Singer. Andy, sitting next to him, had brought in his in-laws, the Fosters, who'd brought in their relations by marriage, the MacMullins.

"I deserve to be here, just like you do," Andy said at Sally's startled expression.

A tight-lipped, squinty-eyed man represented the Florida group, Doug Slavka and Beatrice Lamb. He had Slavka's power of attorney and Mrs. Lamb's, he said.

There was the closer from the title company with the sole telephone which she kept using, cracking gum nervously, writing steadily on a legal pad though the proceedings were delayed. Sally leaned over and glanced at the pad. It was a shopping list.

There were five bank attorneys to deliver the satisfaction pieces on the various farm mortgages each held, including the Hamptons

Bank attorney. He was sweating though dressed in short sleeves, tie loosened.

Fred Unger and FU2 were seated with their mother between them, the blue-caped nurse off in the corner with the ever-ready oxygen tank. There was a small Filipino named Fernandez with them. Sally thought she recognized him from the Winston closing.

Charles Hawley, Lester Wolff, and their attorney came next alongside an Albany type blue-suited fellow, there for Jess Kingsley. Kingsley had come and gone, saying sitting in a room with more than two lawyers made him nervous.

Sally announced repeatedly, each time a new person introduced himself, that she was there as broker, representing the sellers. Her voice was bravely strained, as if she were in the last stages of labor in a natural childbirth to which she wished she had never committed herself. The buyers threw remarks her way like, "Let's hope we all make money here," treating her as one of them, a collaborator, making her squirm and think only of disclosure, of *demonstrated untrustworthiness.*

There was a flurry in the room when a bearded gentleman with a yarmulke and other accessories entered, umbrella dripping, introducing himself as Rabbi Mintz.

"Are you sure you're in the right place?" asked the ex-congressman from the Maidstone Group.

"Is this the farm deal?" asked the Rabbi.

"Of course it is, Rabbi," said Wolff, who appeared to know the man, yet seemed as surprised as the others that he was there.

"Then I'm in the right place," said the Rabbi, reciting an unintelligible prayer before seating himself, after his long terminal, *Orrrmain.* "I represent Lubachai Ltd. part of the Phoebus Group."

He was also a real estate attorney and a CPA, Sally learned

from his card. It was hard to quarrel with that.

"I'm Sally Singer, broker. I represent the sellers."

"Mazel Tov, Mrs. Singer," said the Rabbi. "Better late than never," he added, obviously referring to Michael's coming of age.

"You mean we're partners?" asked the ex-congressman.

"I don't know about you, sir," said the Rabbi.

"Yes, well, welcome aboard," said the lawyer for the Maidstone Group, as Dunny Slykes got up to shake the Rabbi's hand, in a knee-jerk reaction for a potential vote.

Everyone was there but Michael Singer. Over two hours late, he'd called from La Guardia to say he was coming out by helicopter. People were glaring at Sally, accusing glares only large sums of money can generate. FU2 joined Beverly the nominee, tapping fingernails on the worn, but polished, hardwood table.

The room had the characteristic tension of a deal that had to close that day no matter what, of a deal where the buyers forfeited their contract payment if the deal went south. A deal that could be interrupted by a violent act of nature, the sudden, cold, teeming rain outside, a low pressure system in a high-pressure room.

Michael finally arrived, in his navy blue cashmere jacket, with Freddy the Finger and a dark, short, rounded man, who, despite his gray silk suit, couldn't help looking like he had a middle name in quotation marks. His face was expressionless. With them was a balding, bespectacled fellow who identified himself as an attorney.

"Hi, Ma," said Michael, bracketing Sally from the crowd, as if they were alone in the room. "It's a cliffhanger. But we made it."

Sally's heart lurched at the *we* and at seeing the expression on Michael's face. He was caught in the whirlwind of the action, a term Josephine used, whirlwind, whirlpool, quicksand, action supposed to provide momentary relief for some underlying, ever-present pain at the center of his being. He flashed a smile and the room lit up. He spoke and the room was recharged. Yet the wilting was there. Wilting. Vitality pushed to its opposite. The frayed joy of a German beer hall. Life on the edge.

"Now we can proceed with this closing," Wolff said, nervously.

"I hate this stalling," muttered Charles Hawley, who was part of the Kingsley/Wolff managing team. "Not how we do things."

"Not yet! I want to see the financing deal," demanded Max Slavka.

In a surprisingly strong voice, leaning through Unger and his mother, the bespectacled attorney who had come with the Finger outfit laid out the structure of the loan, throwing a hard-edged look at the shirt-sleeved bank rep, whose mouth had dropped open. He placed a bank check on the table.

"What're you lookin' at," Freddy the Finger challenged the bank rep. "The bread's on the table. Take it or leave it. You bank guys'd never do this. Not so quick and at the last minute. That service cost juice."

Max Slavka turned on Sally. "Is this the shit you and your son bring me after telling me the financing is in place? Everything's under control he said, last week. Everything's under control, he said, yesterday. The fees, points, rates, they make the State's usury laws look like charity. You must be crazy! There's no fucking deal here," he shouted at her. "Excuse me, Rabbi."

"What's happening?" cried Mrs. Unger.

"A typical Sally Singer closing," replied Max Slavka, in an unhinged voice. "But this time you've gone too far." He wagged a finger in Sally's face, as he pushed the *impossible* financing around the table.

The bespectacled lawyer pocketed the bank check.

Mrs. Unger started to groan.

Fred and Franklin arose, each taking their mother by an elbow.

"I remind you we are in *mixed* company," boomed farmer Hawley's vested attorney. He added, "If there's no closing today, you keep the farm, Hiram, and still walk out with a bundle. The same goes for the rest of you." He nodded at the farmers.

The Lubachai Ltd. Rabbi reached across the table, handing the vested attorney a card. He whispered a few words in his ear. There was a nod. That was followed by a handshake.

"Eh! Un vero casino!" said the quiet expressionless man in the gray silk suit. He motioned to his attorney with his head. The bespectacled lawyer gave the Lubachai Rabbi his card.

The Rabbi/CPA/counselor deliberated for a moment. There was no handshake, but eye contact firmed up some kind of deal.

"I'm familiar with these kind of shenanigans," observed the Maidstone lawyer, as if needing his presence to be known. "After all, I've been in Congress." Leaning into Sally's face, he added, "It's not our style to sue, madam, but this may be an exception."

Getting a whiff, Sally realized he was the source of the alcohol.

Max Slavka roared to the Ungers, "You're wasting your time here. I know you've wasted your money."

"They can't screw around with FU2," Franklin Unger thundered.

The Filipino's expression was unreadable.

"I'll have to contact my clients in Florida, immediately," boomed the tight-lipped, squinty-eyed man, referring to Doug Slavka and Beatrice Lamb. No one was listening. They all talked at once. He grabbed the closer's phone.

Where is my money? — What happened to my client's money? — The money, the money. — Where's the money? — Who's re-

sponsible? — default monies — lawsuits — fraud— collusion—
specific performance — words tumbled untidily in the discordant
room, cracking the air like rogue lightning in a storm.

Suddenly Andy Singer jumped up, crashing his chair to the
floor. He went toward Michael who was standing next to the bookmaker.

Like a flash, Freddy's hand went inside his jacket.

Sally screamed.

Mrs. Unger collapsed.

The lights went out.

Outside, the sudden Nor'easter darkened the sky and the first
howling wind blasted through. Beneath the deafening din, Sally
said to Michael, "How could you do this?"

"Do what?" he said, hearing her despite the clamor, as if a cord
united them.

"All of this," she gestured in the dark, as things moved quickly
from muddled to deranged.

"Look, I put all of this together. I just ran into some bad luck
with the money."

"The money? You played with these people's money?"

"I killed myself trying to make it work. And I did get the financing as I said I would."

"And me? Michael, how could you involve me like this? My
firm? All the work?"

"You forget very easily, Ma. I won the house for you. You'd
never be here if it wasn't for me. Anyway, things can still work out.
I just need some time."

He recounted how, running short himself, he'd borrowed from
people who thought they were investors, not lenders. Each time he
tried to replace the money in high-priced poker games, or Atlantic

City and on some horse named Sure Thing; well, she knew about his damned bad luck, one thing after another. He was even going to take a shot at her, but decided not to . . . .

Blah, blah, blah! Blah blah, blah! was all Sally could hear in the sound-swelled room, below the roaring racket, where everyone was talking at once. Blah, blah, blah and crashes of thunder.

"How much?" she asked.

"What?"

"How much?" she demanded.

"A few million . . . . "

"The buyers lost a *few* million?"

"That's because of South Beach Phoebus."

"Because of what?"

"There's Naples Gulf Coast Phoebus, too."

Sally gasped. "Am I on—"

"Yes, all of them. There's a lot of good deals around, Ma. This was the home run, to cover the others. But you know, time of the essence. The domino theory. You win some, you lose some. But the losses are spread around. People knew what they were doing. Here," he said, putting an envelope in her hand. "Is this what you were so worried about this morning?" he asked. "You're like Andy. You worry about the wrong things, zig when you should zag, zag when you should zig." She could imagine the remnant of an innocent smile under the exhausting defeat that lurked in his eyes. "Here, take it!"

"What is it?" Sally asked, holding the envelope in the dark.

"The disclosure statement. It's dated a week after I got the listing. It's signed and acknowledged by the sellers' representatives."

She was stunned. It wasn't the sellers from whom Michael was hiding his participation. It was from her. A wash of unthinkable betrayal darkened Sally's face more than any storm.

Lights returned to the noisy assemblage, the jammed room now a labyrinth of anarchy and deceit. Seeing the twisted faces, hearing the roared threats and counter threats, feeling the fears, the rage, somehow all directed at her, Sally understood the experience of chaos, finally, fully. It was incomprehensible. The room was a da Vinci convulsed. The Last Closing. No bread. No wine.

A paschal Sallylamb.

44
Messages

W hen she returned home, there were messages on the machine.

Josephine: What happened? The whole town's buzzing. Does this mean no dinner at the Palm?

Father Donelly: Perhaps we should have tea . . . soon.

Josephine: *Marrone!* 2nd message. Call me!

Doug: Don't think you can get away with this, Sally.

Joe: You're going to have problems, but you know I'm no fish. I wasn't in for much.

Hawley: Supper's in the oven. Ben and I will take you dancing this weekend. Mellowmouth? The Attic? Martells? Ben's voice interrupting: Try walking in circles, Mom. It helps me a lot.

Plumb Foster: Cora won't be coming in for a while. I'll be around to pick up her check.

Andy: I have my family to think of. That's all I want to say.

Doug: I won't be walked on, by you or your bastard son. (Hang-up): Bitch!

Doug: You sent him down here to steal my money.

Beatrice: Just like your father, Sallylamb. I'll try to help. I've asked Charles Hawley to come down to help untangle this mess. One less person to make you crazy. Can you send the piano? (She sounded animated, as if dealing with a recipe she knew full well.)

Jack: An untidy event, I understand. I'll be over later.

Kingsley: If it's any relief, it worked out for us, I'm told.

Liz: We've known each other too long, Sally. I'll do my best. The nominee, the woman attorney, represents Nancy and me. Who's representing you? She needs to know. By the way, I hope your favorite friend Doug isn't in for much, for your sake. You'll really find out—

The tape ran out.

45
April Fool's Day /1981

Muscular and safe-looking, the F.B.I. agent reminded Sally of a German Shepherd as he sniffed through the pile of handwritten letters. They were sitting in a small, windowless space on Newtown Lane, formerly a storage room, borrowed from her accountant in the interest of privacy.

"You say this man is your friend?"

"A friend? My God, he was like family."

Like family. Hah! Her thoughts turned to her family. Michael was detached, telling her nothing she needed to know, either too glib or too secretive. Andy barely spoke to her. Her mother hosted a festering Charles Hawley in Florida, playing the piano, running some undefined interference. What on earth was Charles Hawley, 16 years her mother's junior, doing in Florida? Did they talk about her? Like the old days?

She pretty much expected the rest. Crazy, insulting calls from Adam and Max Slavka, cold shoulders from the MacMullins and Fosters, Nancy Ryner's smirks, Liz's silence, Joe's *I warned you about Michael,* the anonymous threats from cranks, Franklin Unger's loud nastiness when he passed her on the street. Admittedly, the intensity, the invasiveness, the omni-present-piercing-all-barricades-anger took her aback. She was unprepared for its viciousness, but she never expected the letters from Doug, never.

Sure Liz warned about him, sure there were some glimpses of a dark side — but for Doug to turn against her? They traveled the world together. They reached out to each other, teenagers in a pool-room sport alienated from their parents. They were attracted. They played mixed doubles.

"At first, all he wanted was money," she explained to the agent. "There were a lot of letters, but I hoped they would stop."

"Without doing anything about the money?" he asked.

"Yes, well, I thought I was immune, inoculated by friendship," she answered.

"This is the last one? The letter you faxed to me?"

She nodded. "You see . . . uhh . . . he takes drugs . . . I'm not sure . . . . " She looked at the letter with him.

You can't stop me by leaving your phone off the hook. I won't stop until I get the money back from you. I'll see that you and your son are indicted and send letters to all the news-papers, to your whole town. I will come looking for you. My rage is so strong I feel it will burst. It never goes away. You think you can walk away from this nightmare? I will be on your back until the day you fucking die. You'll have to look over your shoulder all the time. I need money. Only death will come of this. My life has been ruined. Despair and die . . . .

"His life has been ruined?"

"That means he had to go to work," said Sally, her mind wandering to other matters.

She was meeting Jack and Josephine for lunch at O'Mally's. If they showed up. She thought they had sounded tentative, like they didn't want to be seen with her in public, a pariah in a small town. One of the local weeklies, *The Easthamptoner*, had called them both for the story it was writing. *The Easthamptoner* had called everybody, Sally, too, focusing on family. Her lawyer, $250-an-hour from upIsland, told her not to comment, adding only family and friends get close enough to hurt and mad enough to want to, as if that were a comfort. Why shouldn't Jack and Josephine want to distance themselves from her? She was trying to do it herself.

Lately she had taken to watching herself live, watching herself as in a screenplay, scene by scene. She hated the script, yet was its author, its star, both its antagonist and protagonist, its villain, its victim, its producer. Rarely did she feel like its director. Watching herself is the glue holding her together, particularly today talking about her childhood friend's death threats. What happens if she becomes unglued? The possibility terrifies her, the question refuses to go away, a noisy, relentless tenant residing in her brain, demanding her attention. The secret was to keep herself numb, anesthetize herself, so that she'd be able to act, but not to feel. Act! She had to fight this on her own. It was her problem. The cliché annoyed her. But it was. She had to get through this alone, not drag anyone else down. She felt contagious.

Had *The Easthamptoner* called the FBI, too? Had they called this agent who seemed more a prop than a person? "Mr. Noonan, uhhh . . . Agent Noonan . . . ."

"Just call me, Sam."

She heard that voice in her head, that noisy tenant muttering, "My God, dialogue from a B movie." Except this wasn't a movie. There was no other life to go home to at the end of the day.

"Sam . . . ." *Sam* is not comfortable to Sally. She wants to stand up and salute this prop/person, kneel down and kiss his ring, this person whose job it is to save people, to protect them. "Sam, uhhh . . . did the local paper . . . uhh . . . call you about all this?"

"It's not Bureau policy to discuss matters under investigation."

"I see," she said. That's how *The Easthamptoner* would read, *It's not Bureau policy* . . . .

"Now," he said, pencil and pad in hand. "Just give me the facts as best you can."

Facts. Facts explain nothing. How did this happen? What is it that happened? She knows the end, but not the beginning. Is barely familiar with the part in the middle. Sally witnesses her own testimony, hears her voice drone on.

"Okay," he says, finally, telling her she's finished. "For starters, contact the local police. Tell them the basics, that the F.B.I. is conducting an investigation. Give them my name. They'll know what precautions to take."

"I've contacted them," Sally whispers, so ashamed, her self-induced numbness wearing thin. "Do you think I need a gun, Sam?" It's unthinkable, but she fears her childhood friend.

"Guns can get you in trouble. You have to know how to use them," he says, his remarks sounding standard.

"Do you think I need a gun?" she persists.

He gives an aggressive sigh. "You'll need a permit, okay? And you might join a gun club."

"A gun club? Yes," she nods in agreement. It was not what she wanted to hear.

"Call if anything else happens," he says, handing her a card, standing up to leave.

The audience is over. She leaves, too.

Her head up high, preparing herself for the short walk to O'Mally's, Sally grits her teeth. Even if Josephine and Jack don't show, it's the right thing to do, be seen, she tells herself, don't hide. Yet, she knows there's a huddled self hiding inside her.

In O'Mally's, looking over the crowd, Sally could feel everyone beading down on her. How different the looks were from before. The disdain, the ill will and an odd sense of victory were tangible. That she could deal with. They didn't raise her children, pay her bills. It was the eyes that turned away, reflecting her shame, that were the hardest.

"Look Sally," Jack had reasoned, "anyone who knows you won't believe what they hear. Anyone who doesn't like you, you didn't have them in the first place. The ones on neither side? Those you can't control."

Easy for him to say. She took a deep breath, deciding if she'd gotten through the FBI she could get through anything. One step at a time, she tells herself, one step at a time.

"Hi, Sally," says a voice at the bar. She nods, without looking. Then there were hands waving. A wash of relief! It was Josephine and Jack, sitting in the back near the fireplace.

"How was it?" Jack asked, when she reached the table.

"A black and white movie. How do I join the gun club, Jack?"

"The gun club? Is that part of the Sally Singer hold-your-head-up-in-public plan?"

"You? The gun club?" exclaimed Josephine.

"Yup, the gun club. It's come to that."

"I thought about it, Sally. Richard the Third," Jack interjected.

"Richard the Third?" She wasn't following.

"Doug's last letter. The die and despair bit. He plagiarized. Anyone too lazy to invent his own death threats, well . . . ."

She gave a heavy sigh. Embarrassed, Sally looked away. "I need a gun permit, too. How do you get that?"

"In Riverhead," said Jack. "But you'll need three signatures, character references."

"Don't even think of me," said Josephine. "You with a gun? Holding everything in. Look at you! How much weight have you lost? You're going to implode."

"I'm not thrilled with the idea of a gun, either. It's dangerous, Sally," said Jack. "Though Doug's letters are off the wall." His voice changed to steely in a quiet kind of way.

"I'm not sure I'd want to be around you with a gun, either." Josephine told Jack Bennet.

"Riverhead you say? I'll be in Riverhead for the court appearance. I can kill two birds—"

"Don't throw that word around if you're thinking of a gun," Jack advised, his voice back to normal. "Won't a Bennet do?"

She paid some attention to his offer. "I can't bear for you to see me this way, Jack. I have to do it alone, to be alone, too. An only child syndrome." She added the last to soften her decision.

"Only child!" rebuffed Josephine. "Withdrawing like this is not the—"

"Sally Singer," called out the bartender. "Phone call."

"Gun club. I don't know which is worse, if she knows how to shoot or not," said Josephine when Sally went off to take the call. "She thinks everyone is against her."

"A little global, but close enough," said Jack.

"That was *The Easthamptoner*," Sally said when she returned, her face pale. "Something new. A last chance to comment. They asked about a criminal investigation."

May 21, 1981 *The
Easthamptoner* p.1

CHARGES STUN
REAL ESTATE WORLD

In a maze of complex lawsuits that have been piling up since a failed closing last summer, business associates and partners of East Hampton real estate developer Michael Singer are seeking over 20 million dollars in compensatory and punitive damages.

Court papers filed with the State Supreme Court in Riverhead by Unger Brothers Investment Bankers alleged that Mr. Singer diverted millions of dollars in investments for his own use. The matter has left a trail from Florida to New York.

His mother Sally Singer, owner of an East Hampton Real Estate firm, Sally Singer Inc., is also a named defendant in the Unger Brothers suit, as is her firm. Mrs. Singer, court papers reveal, is named on the management committees for many of the partnerships. Her firm acted as broker for Mr. Singer in transactions with Unger Brothers Investment Bankers and others when Mr. Singer was a salesman. Mr. Singer left his mother's firm late last year.

Mr. Singer's partners charge the large sums of money missing were used to support his gambling and vacation trips.

One partner, Max Slavka of New York and East Hampton, alleged Mr. Singer's mother may have a gambling problem as well. Mr. Slavka, an attorney who represented Mrs. Singer at the time she bought her present house, claims it was purchased from the proceeds of a bet 15 years ago. "They are a family of gamblers. Now they're doing it with other people's money," he said.

Money lost

A $1.1 million deposit made by one of Mr. Singer's partnerships last summer was lost when it defaulted on the contract for a large parcel of undeveloped land in Sagaponack. According to court papers, Mr. Singer allegedly brought numerous partners into the Sagaponack deal to raise the down payment.

Fred Unger, a principal in Unger Brothers Investment Bankers along with his brother Franklin, said Michael Singer had pocketed most of that money, and instead, attempted to borrow the needed cash at the last minute at usurious rates. Mr. Unger alleged that Unger Brothers Investment Bankers alone were defrauded of millions of dollars in monies it wired to several of Mr. Singer's business ventures. "He couldn't have done it without his mother's help, let alone her knowledge."

Attorneys for both Michael Singer and Mrs. Singer denied any wrongdoing and expressed confidence their clients would be cleared of all charges.

Partners of Mr. Singer in the intricate web of deals he made, are finding themselves as defendants in actions targeted at Mr. Singer. "It's been a nightmare for us, innocent people with unscrupulous partners," said attorney Adam Slavka of New York and East Hampton. "Michael and Sally Singer ripped everyone off." Together with his father, Max, Mr.

Slavka is a named defendant in the Ungers' complaint. They in turn are suing Michael Singer, Sally Singer and Sally Singer Inc. "Michael Singer and his mother are equally responsible for these fraudulent dealings, borrowing from Peter to pay Paul."

The Sagaponack property contract was bought by two of Mr. Singer's original partners, LubaChai Limited and Urbano Sanitation Inc., at a lower price because of the down payment monies forfeited when that deal failed to close. Neither LubaChai nor Urbano returned The Easthamptoner's calls.

A Family Affair

Disagreements over money reportedly have been a family affair for Mr. Singer and his mother. In the past year his brother Andrew Singer, also named in the Unger action, himself filed a counter suit against Michael Singer, Sally Singer, and Sally Singer Inc. "I hated doing it," said Andrew Singer, "but I had a responsibility to my family and my wife's family whom I brought into the deal."

Cora Foster (formerly Hawley, born MacMullin) of East Hampton, Andrew Singer's mother-in-law also filed suit against Sally Singer. Until last August Mrs. Foster worked for Sally Singer Inc. as office manager.

Joseph Singer, Mr. Singer's father was also involved in the Sagaponack transaction. "It didn't amount to much," said the elder Singer, reached at his residence in Amagansett. Mr. Singer has long been estranged from his wife. He has not taken any legal action.

Mrs. Singer and her firm, however, are suing Michael Singer to recover roughly $200,000 in unpaid loans and promissory notes that derived from monies "borrowed" while in the employ of Sally Singer Inc.

"Suing her son? A smoke

screen," said Max Slavka. "His mother stood to profit from his shenanigans. What's more she was on the management committee of every deal. We believe she violated her fiduciary responsibilities as broker to many clients. We urge them to join us in seeking remedies."

Another Slavka family member, reached in Miami Beach, is also involved. Douglas Slavka, allegedly a longtime friend of Sally Singer, and Max Slavka's brother, had this to say, "She's got my money. I was the last one in. And the kid got me. But she knew I was flush and she sent her son to steal from me. They're both crooks. And they picked the wrong guy to steal from."

Jack Bennet, a longtime Realtor and East Hampton native, said, "All of these partners, it seems to me, went into the deals with their eyes open." Mr. Bennet gave Mrs. Singer her first job in real estate. Her license suspended by the New York Dept. of State, the Sally Singer firm is operating on Mr. Bennet's license. The State's decision as to Sally Singer's real estate license will be rendered next week.

Careers affected

East Hampton Town Supervisor Nancy Ryner and her companion, Planning Board Chairman Liz Slavka, Town Councilmen Slykes and MacMullen, all Michael Singer partners, are defendants in Mr. Unger's action. Their participation was disclosed in the Sagaponack transaction when the deal failed to materialize. In addition, they are under investigation by the Town Board of Ethics for associating in a partnership arrangement with people who do business with the Town of East Hampton, namely the Unger Brothers.

Mr. Singer, only nine months ago, was reported missing in this paper, disappearing the day after his brother Andrew's wedding, in mired circumstances. Then a manager at a local tennis club where bounced checks and unpaid bills were the rule rather than the exception, Mr. Singer, as reported, turned up three weeks later in a Las Vegas hospital after a hotel fire where he escaped through a second-floor window. At the time his mother made his debts good.

In a related matter, Mrs. Singer is on record with Town Police as to death threats and harassing phone calls she has been receiving since the failed deals. There were rumors that Mrs. Singer called the FBI. When their regional office in Melville was reached by phone, The Easthamptoner was told, "It's not Bureau policy to discuss any matters under investigation."

"It was the strangest thing," said Michael Singer, when asked about this series of events. "I had a cash flow problem. So I went to people and asked them for money. They gave. I needed more. I asked. They gave more. It was like tapping into a money machine. You could say it got out of hand." Mr. Singer is represented by Paul Giorgi, a New York attorney.

"There is nothing civil about civil suits," said Sally Singer. She had no further comment on the advice of her attorney, Donald Loeb. Mrs. Singer has a third son, Benjamin Singer, who is not involved in these family deals nor in the family business.

According to sources, recent testimony submitted to the Suffolk County District Attorney's office has triggered an investigation of both Mr. Singer and his mother. The D.A.'s office had no comment.

—Brian R. Matthews

SINGER LAWSUITS MULTIPLY

The following are Singer related lawsuits filed in Suffolk County:

• Hamptons Jewish Center and Wolff vs. Sally Singer Inc.

[The Jewish Center cemetery grounds were purchased under Mr. Wolff's tenure as President through Sally Singer Inc. The Shinnecock Indians, appearing at a Planning Board meeting in full tribal dress, halted the map submitted by Mr. Wolff, saying the cemetery was sited on sacred Native American burial grounds. Hilda Unger is the sole person buried there.]

• Citizens for Ethical Gov't. vs. Town of East Hampton, Ryner, MacMullin, Slykes, Slavka

• Ryner, Slavka, MacMullin, Slykes vs. Sally Singer Inc. Sally Singer & Michael Singer

• Maidstone Capital vs. Sally Singer Inc., Michael Singer, Sally Singer

• LubaChai Ltd. vs. Lester Wolff [The Hasidic investment group claims Mr. Wolff involved them through a bar mitzvah ceremony for the then 26-year-old Michael Singer. Mr. Wolff said, "Sally Singer is a threat to the Jewish community."]

• Filipino Consortium vs. Sally Singer Inc. on Winston Estates Waterfront Moratorium

• Filipino Consortium vs. Unger Brothers Investment Banking

• Shinnecock Nation vs. Hamptons Jewish Center; Town /

East Hampton; Sally Singer Inc.

• Coalition for the Environment vs. LubaChai Ltd./Urbano Sanitation Inc.

• Barnes Landing Assoc. vs. Sally Singer Inc.

• The Estate of Hilda Unger vs. The Phoebus Group & Sally Singer Inc.

• Unger Brothers Investment Banking vs. LubaChai Ltd. and Urbano Sanitation Inc.

• Lester Wolff vs. Sally Singer Inc. and Sally Singer personally

• Lester Wolff vs. LubaChai Ltd. and Urbano Sanitation Inc.

• Lester Wolff vs. Michael Singer

• Lester Wolff vs. Sagg Farm Consortium

• Lester Wolff vs. The Shinnecock Nation and others

— *Easthamptoner,* p.14

LAWSUITS GO BATTY

The Easthamptoner learned of the existence of yet another legal action against the firm of Sally Singer Inc. by two Georgetown attorneys, arising from a Barnes Landing beach house sold to them by Sally Singer Inc. Apparently when the owners arrived at their property last summer, they found a maternity ward for local bats in the house.

"There was once a bat house on the property, not disclosed by the broker," the complaint charged. The bat house, according to court papers, may have been downed in a hurricane after the purchase.

Refusing to comment on ongoing litigation, Sally Singer said, "The synchronicity of these events is uncanny."

A local naturalist said, "The night-flying mammals are not easily evicted. They have a way of hanging on, you might say."

— *Easthamptoner* p.14

47

Suppose He Comes Back

"How'd you find me?" Sally asked.

"It's hard not to when you ride around town in that yellow taxi," Josephine whispered. "Are you okay?"

"What do you think," she said, tears streaming down her face.

"When I saw you parked in front of the church, I thought you were with Father Donelly. I went to the rectory first." She sat down in the front row pew next to Sally and handed her a tissue. "What are you doing in church?"

"Seeking sanctuary."

"Sanctuary? You? Here?"

"Did you ever hear of anyone seeking sanctuary in a synagogue? Besides there isn't any synagogue, just the Jewish Center and that place must be mined for Singers."

"I read that Wolff is on a rampage," Josephine said, giving a dry laugh. Both women held copies of *The Easthamptoner*. "I'm sorry about Andy, Sally. He's just trying to protect himself, but it must be killing you. You never told me."

"I was too ashamed. They're all angry, that family, the Fosters and the MacMullins. Cora's still sitting in a housedress, smoking camels and watching *General Hospital*. It seems she never told Plumb she was investing."

"Hey look, Sally. Cora Foster's not a child. She knew what she was doing. She worked in your office, for God's sake, lived through your problems with Michael."

"Jack says the same thing."

"Well, he's right. In any case, you have half the town looking up *synchronicity.*" She rolled her eyes. "Let's get out of here, get some coffee," Josephine suggested. Glancing at the other papers Sally held, *The New York Post*, *The Long Island Daily* and *Newsday*, she raised an eyebrow in silent question.

"Yes," said Sally, getting up slowly. "We're in there, too. But not as much detail. *The Post* Page Six and in *Newsday* a filler. The Hamptons are news, I suppose."

Josephine genuflected before walking up the aisle. "We could go to your house or mine, for that matter, whatever you want." she said at the back of the church.

"Look, Jo, it's important that I be seen in public, particularly today. I don't want anyone to think I'm going into hiding. Would you mind if we went to O'Mallys?"

"Of course not. Are you hungry? You look like you're in bread mode."

Sally sighed. "There's not enough bread in New York State to protect me from this."

"Well, you won't get the death penalty," Josephine joked, pointing to *The Post's* front page headline: GOVERNOR ASKS FOR LIFE WITHOUT PAROLE.

"I thought that's what we already had," Sally shot back. Leaving the safety of Mother of Mercy, she automatically dipped her hand in the holy water.

At O'Mally's they were seated up front near the bar, Sally's choice. It wasn't yet crowded, but Sally refused to look around. She was there to be seen, not to see.

"So where's Joe Singer in all of this?" Josephine asked. "It's his family, too."

"Joe's where he always is, in the background full of I-told-you-sos. I consider myself lucky he's not suing."

"You know, Sally, I read *The Easthamptoner* three times and I still don't understand what happened. Nobody will. On the other hand, the whole town knows *something* happened. What I heard that makes sense is Michael fell short of money, then walked into the closing with some shylock. Everyone lost their investment, and there were other deals that fell apart, too."

"Something like that, but I think it was *their* money he fell short of." She shook her head from side to side as she spoke. "There's good news, too," she added wryly. "They didn't revoke my real estate license. Nancy Ryner let me know. She has those Democrat connections"

"I suppose it's in her interest that you keep making money. She *is* suing, right?"

"Michael said she's suing because I stopped her promising political career with this scandal."

Sally ordered coffee and the soup of the day which turned out to be fish chowder.

"The same," said Josephine, handing the waitress back the two menus. "I thought you weren't talking to Michael."

"Yes, well . . . ." She let the words trail.

"I heard he was back in town."

"For the court appearance next week. He's staying with Ben." She paused, then said in a tone unmistakably somber. "I told Michael never to come to the house again."

"Never?"

"I have to protect myself. From my own son. From my kindred spirit." Her voice cracked.

"Are you okay? Are you going to be able to handle this, Sally?"

"I'm trying to stay together."

"Suppose he comes back like before? There's been a pattern, you know."

Sally stopped toying with the steaming bowl of fish chowder. She leaned back against the black leather banquette, hesitated, as if searching for the answer.

"Yes, well, I'll probably kill him," she said.

48

Appearances

A clap of thunder awakened her at dawn. Listening to rain pellets spray the roof, Sally felt good, clean and good, but there was a sense her feelings, like some emotional stock market, needed correction. In that carefree neutral zone between sleep and awake, she tried to remember. Then her eye caught the calendar with its large red circle around a date.

Yes! It was that day in June, *the day,* her first court appearance. In Riverhead. They'd all be there. The suers and the sued. The sewers. After that, the fingerprinting for the gun permit. Two birds with one stone. She allowed the recollections and their attendant feelings to flood over her, a sea of despair and anxiety. Filled with appropriate gloom, Sally wondered, again, how she'd gotten into this mess.

Had it started with *Guys and Dolls?* Or earlier? Was gambling, as well as autism, in the genes? Was everything wrong from the beginning, her faulty premises yielding rotten conclusions in life as in logic? Did she think too much? And yet not enough? What ever happened to *Brigadoon?* She gave a sigh, shaking her head to stop the noisy voices tenanted there.

Dragging herself out of bed, Sally was careful not to disturb Jack. The patch of dark blonde hair on his frownless forehead made him look younger, a dab of Tom Sawyer. He seemed to know her better than she knew him. It was always a surprise to Sally that they were together. She would go alone today, she told him last night. Jack put up little resistance.

Tying her sneakers, she reached for her old sweats and a cotton shirt thrown over a nearby chair. In the kitchen she switched on WLNG and jogged to the music. Building up a sweat, dancing and jogging, she recovered some feeling of well-being. An ounce of well-being in 117 pounds of turbulence. Joe Ritter, the early morning news announcer, said it would rain all day. She had to get ready.

Before leaving, Sally grabbed the envelopes of bills she'd paid last night. Unable to sleep, Sally was up until one in the morning writing checks, tossing out the unopened junk mail — mail order houses, magazine solicitations, politicians' newsletters using franking privileges and a green-lined envelope from a mortgage outfit, probably an application, she judged from the thickness. Green for money, she guessed. Thank God, she was through with that expense, thanks to the Winston closing last year. Lord, she thought back, was it only a year ago?

Passing Jack's house on Dayton Lane, Sally recalled the woman so cursed with a noxious dependency who once lived in that house. What were Jean Bennet's secret pains? Sally never got to know her well enough to find out. She flipped the visor down. Glancing at the vanity mirror, she saw the clasp of her pearl necklace had moved. Pulling it around, she made the adjustment.

At the last moment, Sally had decided to show respect for the court, discarding jeans and a workshirt. She threw on a bra and her sleeveless, black linen sheath. Pearl earrings replaced the plain silver posts she ordinarily wore; black sandals supplanted the sneakers.

It was a 35 minute ride to Riverhead, Suffolk's County seat. The county offices and courts sat in the memory of a lovely rural

town in eastern Long Island at the head of the Peconic River on
Peconic Bay. The town was the land nexus between the North and
South Forks of eastern Long Island. Known historically for its pro-
duce, Riverhead had few farms left in 1981. In their place were
welfare motels, honky-tonk commercial areas, parking lots and
shuttered stores. The locus of litigation and prosecution, lawyers'
offices mushroomed in bunches, too many in too little space.

Sally parked behind the Suffolk County Supreme Court building, a dismal concrete edifice, blackened and gray, a scummy shrine
to a lost abstraction. The yellow taxicab seemed oddly at home,
somehow belonging in these environs where things askew expected
to be righted. Sally waited, doors locked, as a wraith of a man,
rain-drenched, unshaven and toothless, drinking from a brown paper
bag clutched at the neck, wound his way through the field of cars.
She shivered despite the warm muggy air. The nonaddicted must
never judge the addicted, she thought, beginning to cry.

"This won't do. I have to pull myself together, be the tough real
estate lady," Sally said aloud, taking a deep breath, wiping tears
away with her hand. "Can't come unglued or I might as well walk
in and write a blank check to these bastards. We're here to find
justice," she cheered herself on, not knowing how she'd misplaced
it or why the *we*.

Scanning the crowded car-filled lot, her thoughts went to the
packed parking lots in summer East Hampton. The June season
was upon them. But Riverhead was not East Hampton. These fender-
to-fender cars sought relief and revenge, not recreation. She gave a
sigh. Riverhead, the county seat, was indeed an appropriate re-
ceptacle for the county's backside. She exited the car, slamming
the door shut and raced toward the Supreme Court building.

Inside Judge Warren Whitlock's chambers were three makeshift rows of folding chairs, not enough to seat everyone, she guessed. The small room fell short of its grandiose name. It was dank, poorly lit, mustard-colored paint peeling from its walls. Steam heat, like an unnatural geyser, was hissing from the radiators, impervious to the temperature, as if the room had dirty secrets not cleanly flushed. She could have worn her jeans.

Standing in the back of the room, near Michael, was Sally's attorney, Donald Loeb, Esq., the most expensive lawyer in the county at $250 per hour. Barely nodding, she took a seat up front to avoid seeing her adversaries. There were no friends here. Except Michael. Hah!

She was footing Michael's expenses, too. Loeb said it was in her interest that he have the best defense, telling her if Michael went down it was more likely she would. He made sense.

Loeb instructed her, as well, as to the defendant's edge: justice deferred was justice denied. That's why this first appearance had taken so long since last November's chaos closing. He did all things the legal system allows for delay, as did other attorneys for defendants named in the Unger suit. He made motions, appeared, adjourned, conferred, deposed, interposed, counter-claimed, made more motions, motions devoid of movement — his meter running all the time.

Now she was responding to the judge, bald and black-robed, who for some reason had selected to address her among all those cramped in the room. Was it because she was the only woman, save Beverly, the no-nonsense lawyer in a sensible black suit? Was it the front row?

Her voice was a hoarse whisper. "I'm Sally Singer."

"Speak up!" the judge demanded.

"Sally Singer," she croaked, her throat closing.

"What?"

"Sally Singer," she mouthed, soundlessly. So much for toughness. She was choking, terrified that she was coming apart, feeling the room with its cracked tributary walls closing in on her. "I'm, uhh, I'm uhh—"

"She's Sally Singer, your honor, president of Sally Singer Inc. Real Estate in East Hampton, a defendant in this action," Michael said, his voice firm and clear.

$250-an-hour immediately sprang up. "I'm Donald Loeb, Your Honor. I'm defending Sally Singer Inc. and Sally Singer, individually."

Judge Whitlock looked at Michael. "Are you representing this woman, too?"

"No, sir."

"What?" snapped Whitlock.

"No, Your Honor, I'm not representing—"

"Who are you?"

"I'm Michael Singer, your honor, a defendant."

"Yes," he muttered in recognition, fingering through papers in front of him. "The son. In my court, Mr. Singer, you will not speak until you're spoken to, not for your mother or for anyone else. Do you understand?"

"Yes sir, Your Honor."

"Until my clerk can untangle this holy mess and until I can understand the complaints and counter-complaints, this case is adjourned for, uhh . . . let's make it 90 days. God willing, I'll reach my retirement before I have to deal with this can of worms." With that, the judge abruptly left through a side door.

Sally was stunned. The appearance was over. Nothing happened. It was as named, only an *appearance.* Her mind wandered. Appearances and reality! Stick that in with chaos and order, time and space, mind and body. Is what we see what really is? Can we ever know what really is? Kant didn't think so. She shrugged, wondering if these problems were genuine or were they created by the very philosophers who then tried to solve them? Good for business? Maybe what you see is what you get; clearly what you do is, at least Grandma thought so.

She rose from the uncomfortable folding chair carefully, making sure her posture was straight and proud, appearing unafraid, confident and tough. Michael was at her side as she was about to leave the room.

"You forgot your purse, Ma," he said, handing over the tan leather sling-on. "By the way, I went to one of those meetings. In Patchogue — yeah, I know you were conceived in Patchogue. It was boring. A polyester crowd. Wanted me to go to the track with them! Everyone there was being blackmailed, had to come, they said, or their wives would throw them out." He smiled and gave a wink. "Put it this way, you're not going to find Roone —"

Lightbulbs flashed in their faces in the hallway, capturing Michael's smile, the tail of his wink, capturing his closeness to her. *The Southampton Press, The Easthamptoner, The Long Island Daily, Newsday* . . . .

"They've empaneled a grand jury," whispered a breathless Loeb, catching up to her, hands waving, trying to shield her from the press. "On Michael. They haven't decided about you."

"They?"

"The D.A.'s office."

With her face pallid and her posture going limp — so much for appearances — Sally bolted, ran down the hall, down the staircase through the parking lot to the safety of the yellow taxi. Leaning on the steering wheel, gasping for breath, she heard something stir in the back of the cab. When she looked through the rear-view mirror, she gasped.

The rain soaked, brown-bagged drunk she'd seen earlier had taken refuge in her car. Their eyes met. Now she screamed. He leaped from his shelter, scared and incoherent, but not before urinating in the back of her car. Anchored in her seat, hearing echoes of her shrieks resonate in her skull, Sally wondered if there were anything else left to make her crazy? She was coming unglued.

Taking deep breaths, cementing her thoughts to focus on agenda, she rolled down the window to fight the urine/cheap alcohol odor. It occurred to her if she'd had a gun a few moments ago she might have shot the besotted intruder. Yet, he'd done nothing more than seek cover and relieve himself. Well, maybe the nonaddicted should not judge the addicted, but they had to protect themselves from them. She pulled away from the parking space, driving toward Riverhead Main Street to complete her day's mission.

So why couldn't she deal with Michael? She did judge him, swinging back and forth like a pendulum between defense and accusation, torn between his betrayal, her anger and vestigial remnants of a profound love. Josephine was right, of course. There was a pattern between them.

Michael. A grand jury. How grand? Would they indict her son? How could she not be on his side? He was blood, more than blood, a kindred spirit. How responsible was she? Everybody has a little Michael in them. Everybody has larceny, easy money, a tendency to fool around with truth. Yet, how could he have drawn her into all of this with his lies and his con, ruining her name, her business, threatening her financial independence, betraying her enduring trust? What about her freedom? *They haven't decided about you,*

Loeb said.

Sally pulled over sharply near a phone booth and called Jess Kingsley. He'd find out what was going on in the DA's office. Then, getting wetter as the rain continued its assault, she took the *Hamptons'* beach towels from the taxi's trunk, soaked them in puddles of rainwater curbside and scrubbed the inside of the car as best she could, removing the brown paper bag with its empty bottle.

She found the Pistol Licensing Division in a trailer next to the Suffolk County Correctional Facility. Sally found that combination almost amusing. Both lay in a desolate five-square-block area resembling a construction site. The four-story flat-roofed prison looked like a concrete cage. Tall chain-link fences encircled the perimeter; behind them were coils of razor wire, six feet high. Passing a guard house, Sally parked between the jail and the office.

There, on a cement ramp leading to a side entrance, a group of people were queued up, waiting. Several young black girls, one white woman with two small children, a few older black men, fewer middle-aged white men, stood together in the rain. Sally looked at their faces. They were lifeless, except for the teenage girls.

"I'm wait'n for ya fucker, ya heah me?" a black girl, entertaining the others, was shouting toward an upstairs window. "You get what ahm sayin' mothafuckah? Ah'll be wait'n fa yewww. Ah can't get rid a ya, what ahm gonna do to yewww, what yer gonna doota me, ya heah what I'm sayin'? Mah black ass is wait'n. Yer in mah fuckin' head." The other girls were laughing and chanting, "Yo, mothafucka," an echo, a responsorial psalm, a foul prayer in the baptismal rain.

The ashen sky flickered in the distance. Thunder rumbled. The expressionless white woman, her two small children listless and subdued, leaned against the ramp rail. Her umbrella kept turning inside out as the wind gusted over the concrete meadow. These people, Sally realized, were connections for those inside. They were visitors.

She shuddered. An uncertain glimpse flashed before her. Déjà vu? Prescience? She didn't know. Would she ever be locked up in there? Would Michael? Would she be waiting on the ramp with these people who knew too well about how the world worked when things went wrong? Or would she be inside?

Someone touched her arm firmly. She gave a cry of alarm.

"Come on, Sally, let's get out of here."

It was Jack.

He led her away, waving on Ben who was sitting in a Transhampton limo, the black railroad cap he'd once lifted perched on his head. She caught a glimpse of Andy, too, wondering how she could have missed him in the judge's chambers. Of course, he had to be there. Sally sighed, one more transgression he could chalk up on his injustice slate.

"Loeb doesn't think the case is much, Sally," Jack was saying. "Are you listening? He said it was a bunch of civil litigants trying to win a suit off a criminal decision with the taxpayers' money. Loeb said Michael's attorney was going to make that argument and move to dismiss. I drove up with Ben and Andy, Sally. I was at the court house. I talked to Loeb."

"How long?" she asked, feeling numb, experiencing the drugged, childlike trance one had after serious surgery. "How long did you talk to him?"

"Maybe $65 worth," he whispered, holding her close to him, stroking her head.

49
Reality

Though it was after 10, Sally was not yet dressed. Barefooted, she went outside and picked up *The Long Island Daily* from the lawn, leaving *The Easthamptoner* in the mailbox.

She brushed away the perspiration on her forehead. It was so hot, had been for days. Though August, the weather this week was like the worst kind of July, springtime in Kenya, Josephine had joked, rushing up to New Hampshire. In East Hampton, the spell continued. Smoky chalk skies, broken occasionally by a smear of white-hot sun.

Dressed only in a long summer T-shirt, Sally strolled back to the house, not caring if the neighbors saw her. She shut the front door to keep out the heat. Shades were drawn on all the windows, a defense against the sun. The house looked like twilight.

Wiping her brow on the white cotton T-shirt, she walked slowly to the kitchen sink and turned on the cold water. She let it run over her blue-veined wrists. Something her father taught her once, saying it cooled the blood traveling through your body. Sally didn't know if that was true. She could never tell with her father. She put her head underneath the tap and lingered there till the water was numbing. Shutting it off, Sally let her wet hair drip onto her shirt and the floor. Only a few minutes later, the soggy shirt clinging to her, Sally could taste the salty sweat dripping down her face. She sat down in the kitchen to read *The Daily*, page by page, slowly.

Bad news would come soon enough, but it had to be less painful than the more detailed *Easthamptoner*. When she reached page seven, she stopped.

GAMBLERS UNITE IN 600G MORTGAGE FRAUD

Seven men who authorities said met through Gamblers Anonymous were charged yesterday with fraudulently obtaining $600,000 in mortgages to pay off gambling debts and bet on horses.

The defendants were members of a Gamblers Anonymous Chapter in Patchogue and include disbarred lawyer, Jerome Levy, a former Suffolk County Assistant District Attorney, Patrick Venadio and five others. As members of their organization they were required to transfer their assets to their spouses.

According to the District Attorney's office, they would take out mortgages in their wives' names and come to the closing with forged documents giving them power of attorney or indicating that the deeds had been transferred to them. In two cases, however, unencumbered Hamptons properties were picked at random, using fraudulent instruments and fake identification provided by one of the seven men who had a copying business at the New York Stock Exchange. The former attorney, disbarred for misuse of escrow funds, helped draft the papers and notarized the fake signatures.

"They were desperate for money," the D.A. spokesman went on. "They went together to Aqueduct Race Track and bet on horses." None of those charged have prior criminal records.

The injured have filed civil suits to have the phony mortgages on their homes discharged. The group may have acquired as many as 17 bogus mortgages. Charges against the men include various counts of grand larceny, fraud, conspiracy, possession of a forged instrument and making a sworn false statement.

The District Attorney's office was tipped to the scheme by one of the group of supposedly recovering gamblers in return for immunity. Reliable sources say the tipster is under indictment on a separate matter.

See FRAUD on p 23

She turned to page 23 to continue. But there it was, on p 23 buried in the fillers, what she had been looking for in the first place.

HAMPTON DEVELOPER INDICTED

An East Hampton developer was indicted for third degree grand larceny, passing a bad check from a partnership account in the amount of $30,000 as partial payment for a business loan from an investor to close a teetering deal.

According to the District Attorney's Office, the charge stemmed from a complaint by Douglas Slavka, a Florida resident, against his former partner Michael Singer of East Hampton. Mr. Slavka attempted to cash the check twice. It bounced both times, the spokesman said.

Mr. Slavka said, "I was promised 25% on the loan. The deal didn't close; I got no interest on my money; the principal was never returned. Singer pocketed my money, plain and simple."

There were other undisclosed complaints made by Mr. Slavka, but the DA's office claimed they fell into the purview of civil actions, not crimes against the State.

The grand jury, convened in June, disbanded after handing down the indictment, dispelling published rumors that other family members were involved in wrongdoing along with Mr. Singer.

Making an unusual arrangement with the District Attorney, Mr. Singer's attorney, Paul Giorgi, said he would deliver Mr. Singer for arraignment some time next week, rather than surrender him immediately. "I'm convinced my client will be cleared," he said.

There was the continuation of the other article — FRAUD — looking up at her, but Sally, turned back to page seven. She carefully re-read the GAMBLER'S piece again. Then, the paper in her lap, a concrete block hardened inside her chest. Staring blankly, she let the paper slide to the floor. She was in jeopardy: 2+2 always equaled 4. Feeling as if she were suffocating, Sally knew what she had to make herself do.

50
Appearances and Reality

When she called Gamblers Anonymous, Sally learned there was only one "room" in Patchogue. It had to be the same group Michael joked about. Patchogue! Nagging at her was the second piece of junk mail from the mortgage company — the same green-lined envelope not as thick this time. She'd tossed it last week. Unopened. Unworried.

Sally called the County Clerk's office. "Is my house encumbered?" she asked the clerk whose name Jess Kingsley had given her. She recited the tax map numbers, the filed deed index for reference. She knew the answer before they told her and hated that she was always right.

She called Ben's house.

"I bet you're looking for the fugitive," Hawley said lightly, as always trying to make her feel good. "I imagine everyone else is, after reading today's *Easthamptoner.* I'm on my way out, Sally. Here's Ben."

"Mom! I told Michael you'd surely call after *The Easthamptoner* story, that you'd be worried. He's just back from Atlantic Ci—"

"Put him on," she demanded, her voice trembling with rage.

"Hi, Ma," said the smooth, lilting voice she loved. "I'm surprised you called."

"I read *The Daily*" declared Sally, steely-voiced, driven by a rumbling force erupting inside her. "I'm coming over."

She slammed down the receiver. Throwing a windbreaker over her slept-in cotton T-shirt despite the August heat, she blindly grabbed the shotgun from her closet, the gun Jack gave her after the permit episode. ("This way if you do hit something, Sally, it's unlikely to get up.") Once outside, still barefoot, she ran back into the house for shells.

"She sounded angry, Michael," Ben said, reminded of that long-ago day at Nancy Ryner's studio. "Really angry."

"It'll be okay," said Michael. "You know Ma." He went into the bedroom.

Ben called Andy. "I think you should come over. Right away. Mom's mad. She's coming here to get Michael. It doesn't feel right."

Ben and Hawley's Sag Harbor house was right off Route 114 on Division Street. Like other Sag Harbor row houses, it was a small Victorian, theirs painted a pastel green. Hawley had done the interior stark white, including the shiny polyurethaned floors. Sparsely furnished, using color, his less-is-more style, it had ceiling-to-floor mirror panels on either side of the front door.

"Where's Michael?" Sally said, slamming the front door shut.

"Mom! What are you doing with that gun?" asked Ben, obviously alarmed.

"That's some outfit for hunting," Michael said, as he came into the room. "That thing you're carrying looks like a cannon, Ma," he quipped. "What's the problem?"

"What's the problem?" Sally screamed, knowing she was out of control, unglued, but no longer caring. "What's the goddamn problem? You ruined my business, took those years of work, work for you and your brothers — God knows I hate real estate — and just threw them in the garbage. You stole my reputation in a town that lives on reputations. You used my good name like some $2 whore.

You lied. You stole money. And now you'd steal the home I live in? The roof over my head? How could you mortgage my house, Michael? You know I have no money. I paid for both our lawyers. Like a fool. You stole my past and want my future, too. Where do you stop? Why is your affliction everybody's? You don't get better. And you kill everyone else. There's no fucking immunity from you . . . " She stopped, breathless, starting to reel from the heat of her anger and from the heat of the small room.

"You're getting upset for nothing, Ma. I got the money. You can sue for discharge of a phony instrument. It's a civil suit, but you'll win it. That mortgage is no good. A no brainer. We beat the system, Ma. You got the house. I got the bread."

"We beat the syst—"

"Hey, if you want the truth, part of the house is mine, anyhow. I won it for you. You wouldn't have it if it wasn't for me. But forget that. I just told you we beat the system." He gave an uncertain smile. "Hey, don't do that," he shouted at her, going for the door. The shotgun was pointed at him.

"Mom!" Ben yelled. "Don't!"

The moment was bracketed, for one instant taken out of time and space. In that vacuum, Sally had a glimpse of herself in the mirror next to the doorway, half-dressed, hair wild, shoeless, feet grassy green from the damp lawns, a screaming banshee, holding a shotgun, looking like the third act of Lucia, standing with these grown men—

Men! That's what she saw in the mirror. A reflection of men. Men as strangers. Not kids!

Not children! Sons perhaps, but men!

The recognition stopped her. She came back to herself. What on earth was she thinking about with the shotgun? They'd be after her with a net.

The room was pin-drop still. The men were looking at her. Waiting.

"Give me that gun, Ma," said Michael, standing in front of the door.

She hesitated, then angrily shoved the unloaded weapon through the air at him. Michael dodged. It hit Andy, grazing his shoulder, as he rushed in, saying, "Did I get here in time?"

"What the hell is the matter with you, Andy? What are you doing here?" Sally snapped. "Always intercepting someone else's blows. Well, now you have one more promise I broke. Chalk it! I didn't kill him."

"I called Andy, Mom. I was scared. I still am."

"It's okay. But for God's sake, Ben, don't start walking in circles. Wait till I'm gone!"

"An Italian movie scene," said Andy, looking as if he were about to approach.

"Back off! All of you," Sally told the men in the room. "Don't push me. Don't anybody call, either. Don't come by. I need to be alone tonight. Maybe for a while."

Sally scanned the room once more, to make sure she was seeing men and not three small and vulnerable black-haired boys, with peaked faces, whom she had adored and for whom she had tried to do her best. She picked up her shotgun and left. Driving home to Dayton Lane, her mind was still shocked by the images in the mirror, an appearance that showed more truth than reality.

51
Habits

Once back home in her dusky house, Sally put the gun in the umbrella stand, then locked the doors. She didn't expect anyone.

Jack was in New York for several days with his editor going over the his genealogy manuscript. There was a suggestion he pursue Kent, to see what kind of people came over from England. Nobody had done that before.

It was hotter than ever.

She showered, washing the green stains from her feet. Wrapping herself in a large towel, she went to the VCR in her bedroom. She did not want to think anymore. She was exhausted from seeing things as they are. Looking over her collection, Sally selected *The Godfather* and slipped into bed. The hours passed. Eyes glued on the small screen, she was hypnotized as she watched Michael Corleone get his recognition as the new *Don,* redeeming his family's honor. *Michaels, the world was full of Michaels, Lamb, Singer, Corleone.* On that note, she fell asleep to the hum of the rewinding tape.

Mike Lamb returned home with a job, clean-shaven, dressed to kill in a dark blue suit, bearing gifts for Beatrice, for Grandma, and for 6-year-old Sallylamb a birthday gift of $5. The scene changed. No more dark blue suit, no more shaven victory, only unpressed trousers, white-ribbed sleeveless undershirts, his dark stubby beard of defeat. He would sit, hunched over the small

Emerson radio, listening to ball games, while her mother was at
work. The 6-year-old waited with dread for the walking out, her
father to go for the papers in his undershirt and pants — and not
come back. Then it was the following morning, a Sunday; her father and her mother were home. Saved, she was standing outside
her apartment building, her friends in church. The man who owned
the corner newsstand called her over. He asked her to deliver a
note to her father. The thick, syrupy dread returned. Fearful of
ugly scenes between Beatrice and Mike, fearful of the walking out,
fearful of more shame, she opened the envelope in the lobby.

> Dear Mr. Lamb,
>   Four weeks ago you asked me to lend
> you five dollars, which I did, and which
> you promptly returned. Two weeks ago you
> again asked to borrow five dollars, which
> I gave you, and which you promised to
> repay the next day, which you failed to do.
> I would like the money returned immediately.
>   Today.
>   Sam Kaplan

The Sallychild knew her father couldn't pay the debt. She could
tell by the way he sent her to get him a few cigarettes at a time from
the luncheonette around the corner. She didn't want her father to
read the note and do nothing. She didn't want him to beg for the
money from her mother. But Mr. Kaplan was waiting. How could
she go back out? The child didn't want the scary scenes. Didn't
want her parents humiliated. The shame, the shame, the shame.
She went upstairs and took the $5 birthday money from her drawer,
put it in the envelope, bringing it down to the corner newsman.

Mike walked out anyway a few days later.

Sally awoke, tears cascading down her face. This dream was different. Not a dream, but a memory, a long forgotten memory. It had happened. She gave a convulsive shudder. A Michael borrowed. A Sally paid. Michaels got in trouble, Sallys bailed them out. The safety net that did no one any good.

It was all too much. Getting up, Sally checked the clock. It was after five. Pulling up the shades and opening the windows, she felt a cooler breeze. The spell was lifting. She called Father Donelly.

She had to talk to someone, someone she could trust and not feel ashamed.

52
A Full Deck

Sally arrived at Mother of Mercy during the Liturgy of the Word as the congregation was reciting the Alleluia: "But, Jesus answered, scripture says, man cannot live on bread alone, but needs every word that God speaks."

After the gospel reading, Father Donelly began his homily. Though white-haired and slightly bent with age, his voice was strong and clear, seasoned with a faint Irish lilt.

"Though we find the bread alone quotation in Matthew, Jesus is referring to a statement 1,300 years earlier in the Hebrew Scriptures, Deuteronomy: '. . . man doth not live by bread alone, but by everything that proceedeth out of the mouth of the Lord doth man live'."

"What is meant by those words? By the simple assertion 'man doth not live by bread alone' that is meant to sustain us through life, through this vale of tears? As the material body seeks comfort through food — bread, the staff of life — so the human soul requires the words of God, the staff of our spiritual existence. Aristotle, the great pagan philosopher, claimed it is man's very nature that requires nourishment for his rational self. In Christian terms, as set forth by Saint Thomas Aquinas, it is man's soul, his spiritual self, that survives by the words of God . . . ."

The service was short, a weekday Mass. People had to go to work.

"I enjoyed your sermon, Father. It was as if you were talking to me. I have a unique relationship with bread," she said wryly, "the kind that you butter." They were walking on the paved path to the shingled rectory next door. "I didn't mean to be late, but my lawyer called as I was about to leave. I was making some serious decisions."

Sally went into the parlor, a shabby but spotless room, comfortably furnished in brownish hues. It was clear that many members of the parish had contributed to the room's decor. There was a standing lamp with a large brown shade that didn't fit, a leather settee with an upholstered hassock, a frayed captain's chair, two lamps from different sets on end tables with nothing in common. Yellow nylon curtains, grown pale from too many washings, adorned the windows, hanging past the sill.

On the wall next to a wooden crucifix there was a sepia photograph of Mother Teresa and another of a skull-capped priest who may have been the archbishop of the diocese. It wasn't the Pope; he was hanging in the waiting room. The room's scent was musty with faint aromas of many boiled meals and worn upholstery. The elderly priest brought in a tray of tea and chocolate cookies, setting it down on a faded ivory doily.

"The parishioners were buzzing. Despite exhortations on the sin of gossip, the church is a regular beehive, Sally. Are they after poor Michael?" he asked, pouring tea from a china pitcher, taking a cookie for himself.

"Poor Michael?" She told him about the gamblers' group. "He has a trail of victims from here to Texas."

"It's a curse he has, Sally. You mustn't judge him. Protect yourself, but don't judge him. He told you he wasn't trying to harm you. Beat the system he said? Only one way I know to do that. With the help of God." He offered her the cookie tray, taking another for himself. "So the lawyer called you, did he?"

"He wanted me to pay for Michael's criminal defense, too. I've been picking up the civil suits for both of us."

"What's happening with those? There were so many?" He took another cookie. "These are my downfall, Sally. Don't think the parishioners don't know it, supplying me all the time."

"The Hasidic group and the bookmaker types are selling the contract to the original partners, some of them, I understand. The deal's not as great, now, with the Southampton Planning Board paying some attention. It's still worthwhile. The nuisance suits? Who knows?"

"And did you agree to pay for Michael's defense?"

"Father, God forgive me, my own son, I refused." She tried, unsuccessfully, to hold back the tears. "I told the lawyer my business was gone; I wasn't kidding myself. But, either way, I decided no more safety net. It's not easy, not to help a son." She told Father about the dredged-up memory of her father. "I refused to put up bail, too." She accepted a tissue to wipe her eyes.

"Sally, you can't heal Michael. You've bailed him out all these years. It hasn't worked so far, has it? Allow him his life. That life isn't yours. Allow him to experience the consequences of his behavior. That's his only chance, my child. We bear our own crosses," he sighed. "Sons and mothers, mothers and sons. The lesson of Eve. The lesson of Mary." He offered her more tea, taking another cookie.

Sally took one, too. "What happened to my beautiful *Brigadoon*, Father?" she asked mournfully, thinking of her once perfect picture of a safe place protected by time from most bad things in life.

"Don't you know? *Brigadoon* is in you, Sally. Nowhere else."

They talked some more, Sally telling all the great plans and hopes she once had, thinking they would grow in this small town. "Only the town grew," she quipped.

The rectory bell rang. Sally got up to leave.

"And how is your mother?" the priest asked, as they stood at the door before he showed her out.

"My mother?"

"A lovely woman. I saw her at Andy's wedding," he explained. "How is she coping with Michael?"

"She's with Charles Hawley, believe it or not. In Europe. A honeymoon without a wedding, she called it. Michael's too painful. Old memories she lived through. My father was a gambler, too, you see."

"I see," he murmured. "Don't judge her either, Sally. Trust in God. I'll pray for Michael." With that he blessed her.

Walking home, Sally thought about Father Donelly, his many kindnesses to her, his compassion for Michael, so sensitive to what he called problems of the afflicted, never judging. He was an East Hampton gift she wouldn't have had on Manhattan's Upper West Side. More at peace with herself, she began to jog, her long-legged strides quickly turning into a run.

In her mind, she looked back once more. With that insane love mothers have for their sons no matter what, she wished things better for Michael. She mourned for the precocious, kindred spirit, the little boy, long gone, who could make her laugh. And Andy, her angry offspring, wanting only a normal family! He was never going to have that, Sally smiled. But he'd endure, a survivor, like herself. And dear Ben would always be safe. He'd made peace with his world, wherever that was. She quickened her pace.

Breathless on Dayton Lane, approaching her house, she saw

the broad sheets of *The Easthamptoner* pinned to her door. Sally cooled down with some trepidation. Reaching the door, she read, *you said not to call, Andy,* scrawled along the top of the paper, opened to the letters page, an arrow in red singling one out.

Exceptional qualities.

Dear Editor:

A colleague of mine — a regular visitor to your celebrated resort — subscribes to your weekly paper. I have read with interest the ongoing trials of one Sally Singer, whom your pages seem to be treating rather poorly.

A Sally Singer who moved to East Hampton attended my class on Social and Ethical Ideas at City University during the fall semester 1965-66. I am happy to testify that she is a lady of exceptional qualities, a sharp, well-trained intellect, and an unswerving passion for getting to the bottom of a subject.

She would have made a devoted, sympathetic and inspiring teacher. Her honesty as well as her rigorous mind would have an admirable effect on anyone she worked with, as well. I had no hesitation, years ago, in recommending her for any post in which a very acute mind, warm heart, genuine enthusiasm for ideas, and comprehension of them are regarded as an asset.

Mrs. Singer was invited to Oxford back then, but changed her plans. More's the pity.

> Yours sincerely,
> Abraham Paris
> All Souls College, Oxford

Sally was astonished. After all these years! The person Paris described was a stranger to her, but she was moved as much by Andy's personal delivery as by the professor's kind words. Andy the bearer of something good . . . for her? It left her reeling.

Sitting down on the front step, Sally read the letter again . . . and again . . . and again.

When Jack returned that night, ready to comfort her, Sally handed him the letter.

"Whew!" he marveled. "You don't get many of these."

"I called him, Jack, I called Paris at Oxford."

Jack studied her, his eyebrows raised.

"With the little money I have left, I'm going to Oxford. Aristotle and moral weakness are still there to be examined. Pack your bags and come with me, Jack, or stay a while, help Andy take over the business — on his name, not mine. But either way, Sally Singer's leaving town."

Epilogue

The Suffolk County Correctional Farm was off a four-lane highway in Yaphank, once the center of neo-nazi activities before World War II. Like most of Suffolk County, the land was flat and unexceptional. Yet the farm was exceptional to many because it offered the soft time for its tenants, lawbreakers all, but unworthy of prison. Michael Singer spent three nights in the less generous County Jail in Riverhead before being sentenced to serve 11 months as a guest of the State. His face left some of its innocence in Riverhead before his arrival in Yaphank.

Father Donelly in Roman collar was waiting patiently in the large visitors room when Michael came through the wooden door accompanied by a guard, an East Hampton Foster, who gave a friendly nod.

They shook hands, the priest and the young, dark-haired man. Michael Singer's hands were soft, unthreatening, with tapered fingers, the kind that could never hold onto money.

"I heard from your mother, just this morning," the priest said. Michael Singer said nothing.

"She's going to stay another term. They've asked her to teach."

"I know. She writes to me, too, Father."

"I'm told that Doug Slavka person was given another official warning, you know, to stop harassing. He's in Connecticut, now, living with his brother and nephew."

"I reunited his family," Michael said, giving a small smile. "Do

I get any time off for that?"

"Is it trying for you here, my son?"

"Not really, Father. No worries. Everything's free, you know." The smile turned into a grin.

"Your brothers are doing fine."

"They come to visit. So did Jack before he left. And Mrs. Aquistapace. I can't complain, Father. I'm glad the farmers have their money, too. I see the new owners have their headaches with the Southampton Planning Board. I read that in *The Southampton Press.*"

"You must have a lot of time to think."

"I do," Michael said, not smiling. "I do. Where do I go when I get out of here? I think about that a lot."

"Trust in God, my son." He handed over a bag of bagels and chocolate cookies. "The sweets are from my parishioners, tempting gifts they bring to me." He got up to leave. "Till the next time, Michael, my boy."

Back at the rectory, later that afternoon, the white-haired priest climbed the stairs to his bedroom. Opening the bottom drawer of a tall, mahogany chest, he took out an old wooden cigar box, GARCIA, barely legible, printed across its top. Sitting down on the white chenille bedspread, Father Donelly went through those worldly things priests are allowed to keep.

Brown with age, ink faded, was the long-ago check Beatrice Lamb sent him to repay a loan for bus fare and a taxi to visit a man in prison and show him his child. *Budna.* He'd always remember *Budna.*

Shutting the box of memories, Father Donelly wondered when he would tell Michael Singer he was the spitting image of his grandfather.

FROM AWAY

In Memory of
Joseph "The Colonel" Crenshaw

October 1, 1937 — June 9, 1997

About the Author

Few Writers have the firsthand knowledge of the *real* Hamptons scene Lona Rubenstein possesses. A Hamptons' survivor, Ms. Rubenstein, while raising three children in East Hampton, sold cookies, cleaned houses, took in laundry, tutored students, served as an elected official, cooked for Andrew Stein, was tipped by Sidney Zion for making breakfast, established her own real estate agency and was hired by Lauren Bacall, appeared with Peter Jennings and has been a valued political consultant to Hamptons' politicians and politicos throughout New York State.

A Carnegie Scholar, a Woodrow Wilson Alternate Scholar and Department Fellow, Ms. Rubenstein received her B.A. and M.A. in Philosophy from CCNY and continued her doctoral studies at the City University of New York. Her work has appeared in *The New York Times, The Miami Herald, The East Hampton Star* and other publications.

In FROM AWAY, her first novel, Ms. Rubenstein explores the trials of a struggling Manhattan family trying desperately to make a life in The Hamptons, despite a dangerous current of addictive gambling that runs through three generations. The author has had some firsthand experience: She is a top-notch poker player and practices often at Foxwoods Casino.